A Hunter and His Legion

Book III in the Ongoing
Praetorian Series

Edward Crichton

Copyright 2013

Acknowledgments

Normally, this is where I thank all the people who I thanked in the acknowledgments sections of my first two *Praetorian* books, but they're all too busy to read my work now. Instead, I'll thank my sister Amanda (who did read it) and Teresa, my new editor who emailed me out of the blue and kindly offered her services… which I sorely needed. Thanks!

Books by Edward Crichton

The Praetorian Series
The Last Roman (Book I)
To Crown a Caesar (Book II)
A Hunter and His Legion (Book III)

Starfarer
Rendezvous with Destiny

Table of Contents

How the F#!% We Got Here
In Haiku
By: Johnathon Archibald Santino III

It was World War Three,
The year 2021,
And the end seemed close.

Russians and Chinese,
Americans and assholes,
Fighting each other.

The war was pointless,
But then I joined a new crew.
Ended up in Rome.

I joined a new team.
Badass Special Forces, all
And Hunter came too.

Sent to Syria.
Our mission: Kill terrorists.
But we screwed it up.

Time travel exists.
How do I know, you may ask?
I'm in Ancient Rome.

That's right, ANCIENT ROME!
Met all kinds of cool people,
Oh, yeah… *ANCIENT ROME!!*

We met the Caesars.
Caligula was awesome.
Claudius, a dick.

And Agrippina.
Damn, she's a hot piece of ass,
But a total B.

Claudius rebelled.
Caligula reclaimed throne.
History was changed.

Caligula dead.
Agrippina was made queen.
Wasn't my first choice…

So she exiled us,
And for years, we were homeless,
Wandering Europe.

Guy named Vespasian.
Hunter said he's the right guy,
So we went to work.

Failed to capture her.
Big fight in Byzantium.
Broke Caesarea.

I'm struggling here.
Haiku can kiss my big ass.
Really… fuck Haiku.

So let's wrap this up.
Agrippina kicked our butt,
Again. Yeah… *again.*

But then others came.
New time travelers arrived,
and saved our asses.

They helped us escape.
We went East to Damascus,
To hide and lay low.

I told you I could,
I just knew I could Haiku.
So F U, Hunter

fin

Part One

I
Revelations

Outskirts of Damascus, Syria
October, 42 A.D.

While indistinguishable from each other in terms of function, held within my hands were two objects vastly different in design. In my right was paper, the kind akin to what I remembered as printer paper from the nineties, perforated edges and all, while my left hand held a medium for writing that was heavier, stiffer, and far larger. It was a piece of papyrus rolled into a cylinder and then flattened, but yet to be opened. And in each document was information, but while I had no desire to actually read them, I knew I owed it to both authors to try, especially Him.

Him.

I wasn't sure if I was ready to think about Him just yet.

I let my hands fall into my lap, the weight of my arms heavy upon my legs, just as my shoulders felt around my chest, and my mind within my head. I looked up and out, surveying the small oasis where we'd made camp, located a few miles east of the ancient Middle Eastern city of Damascus. The scrub brush desert land around us was vast and desolate, the small blip that was Damascus notwithstanding – a perfect place to hide. An oasis may have been an obvious place to lay low, but the desert was immense. With luck, we'd evaded our pursuers long ago, giving us time to regroup and come to grips with our current situation, which again was something I'd rather delay thinking about for as long as I could.

The oasis was small, no bigger than a basketball court if adjusted properly. A few stray palm trees dotted its perimeter, lending a certain amount of shade to the area, but bushes and scrubs were the dominate flora in the area, as was the small lake, no bigger than a pond really.

With the sun setting on the horizon before me, the spot was quite beautiful, tainted only by the thoughts that raced through my mind and the pain that emanated from my side whenever I twisted or pulled in the wrong direction. But pain I was trained to deal with, and my mind could be placated when I concentrated hard enough, yet nothing could remove the foul existence of the two documents held firmly within my hands.

I looked at them again.

In that moment, instead of debating which to read, I tried to discern how such unassuming objects could feel so heavy in my hands. Paper and papyrus. Fifty pound dumbbells they were not, yet they felt even heavier, so much so that I had trouble lifting them from my knees to hold at eye level again.

But I did.

As I looked at them, I knew the object in my left hand could wait. The papyrus. The information contained there was likely more important, but the only thing that could truly soothe my curiosity and frustration was held in my right hand.

I gave the papyrus one last long look before leaning to my left and placing it within the bag that rested comfortably next to the rock I was perched on. A second bag just to the side of it caught my eye, but despite wandering fingers that inched in that direction, I fought off the urge to grab for it. With a clenched fist, I straightened carefully to avoid further discomfort in my side. I tried to relax my upper body but winced at even that slight gesture, and took a moment to lift my shirt and prod the thick bandage that covered my entire left flank, from nipple to shoulder blade. Its former whiteness was now a pale red around its edges, but a darker streak ran right through its center.

I suppressed a gag reflex from the sight of it, and turned to look out over the water at nothing in particular, carefully repositioning my shirt over my midsection at the same time. But after a few moments of quiet introspection, I again returned my attention to the paper held before me. Six in total, each page contained two columns of information. On the right side of each page were photographs of a tattered and ancient piece of paper with a barely legible but familiar scrawl written upon it, and on the left was a transcription of these photographs – or so I was told.

I separated the first page from the rest and turned it over a few times and back again, inspecting its quality. It didn't appear digitally rendered and enhanced, as I would have expected of such a thing from my own home, but more as if someone had simply taken both the original document and the transcription, placed them on a copy machine, and ran them off onto a single piece of paper together.

Considering what I already knew about where the paper came from, I couldn't say I was surprised.

I placed the sheet back with its siblings and stared at them again without reading, preparing myself as I had done every night for the past few days. On each of those nights, I'd sit upon the very rock I sat upon now, and would look out over the small body of water, unable to read that which I had already written once before...

In another lifetime.

In an entirely different life completely.

Written by another me.

The Other Me.

I'd kept a journal for about the past six months of my life, something those of us in the military liked to call after action reports: a self-reflection of prior missions and an outlet for arranging thoughts. I'd written nine entries and my friends had provided two others, but somehow, someway, a twelfth entry existed within my hand.

They'd told me I'd written it.

But I hadn't written it. Not me. Not exactly. It had been *another* me.

An alternate me.

The Other Me.

The one that hadn't made it. A me that had died, initiating a chain of events that led this very document to reside within a cargo container for two thousand years before it was finally found, and then brought back to *me*, the actual me, the me right now. It had spent two thousand years rotting away in the desert only to travel back in time to the day it had been created – just three days ago.

I squinted at the top page, but a sudden dimming of light delayed my inevitable reading of it.

I looked up again, noticing that the sun had just kissed the horizon, and that dusk was upon us. At first I considered myself saved from the task before me, but then fate, as it always seemed to do, intervened.

"Here, Jacob."

The voice was close, only a foot or so behind me, and I marveled at either the interloper's stealth or my own distractedness. Either way, I didn't bother to turn, as I already knew who it was by the sound of her voice alone. But even if I hadn't, I knew there was only one female in our group who would risk approaching me in a time like this.

Preceding her was a bright green glow, the radiant light produced from a simple glow stick used by millions of raving teenagers back home. She held it out by my shoulder and I accepted it with my free hand, nodding in thanks for the gift. I clipped it to the collar of my shirt, letting it dangle in front of my chest, and I suddenly had plenty of light to read by.

"Thanks," I told her.

"No you're not," she countered, but there was humor in her voice.

I smirked to no one but myself. "No, I guess I'm not."

"Nobody's forcing you to read it," she said as she placed her hands on my shoulders and kneaded them gently. "Even Archer said it might not be a good idea."

An annoyed breath escaped my lips as I sneered at the name. "I know, but I have to read it. I… just have to. I have to know what happened to the Other Me."

She took her hands off my shoulders and I heard her take a step back. I waited for her usual monologue of encouragements and reassurances that usually followed such comments, ones that also usually fell on deaf ears, but they didn't come. I continued to wait, but the silence lingered, and I felt sad. Maybe she'd finally given up on me after all.

Or maybe she was simply trying to see if I'd grown up a little.

"I may be here for a while," I said, deciding a continued silence wouldn't help either of us. I turned my head so that she could see the side of my face, and smiled for her benefit. I could just barely see her tall form at the edge of my vision, but I managed to catch her nod.

"Try not to be too long," she said as her voice moved away. "There's something I want to show you."

Wondering what could possibly exist in this godforsaken world that was worth showing me, I completed my turn so that I could look at her, but she was already walking away. As she strutted away, my eyes were drawn downward to her backside, clad in the last of her black, tight fitting running shorts. But what really drew my eyes to her was the way in which she walked – lifting her hips high with every step in an exaggerated catwalk.

Just before she was out of sight, she turned her head to look at me, and while her face was concealed in shadow, too dark to make out her expression, my imagination filled in the rest. I turned back to the document eagerly, and like a kid who knew he had to eat his broccoli before he could have his ice cream, I settled my nerves and decided to read. When Helena was in that kind of mood, I'd be an idiot if I didn't shovel that broccoli down my throat as quickly as possible and get back to her.

So I read.

Mission Entry #12
Jacob Hunter
Syria, October 42 A.D.

I'm done.

It's finished. I've kept myself alive for months for reasons I no longer remember. I've been dying for months, buried alive in a supply container, left with nothing more than the clothes I wore the day we were captured, a glow stick, my journal, and the orb.

The orb. It works. I can work it. Every few hours, I've used it, and gone back. Hour after hour. Day after day. For months? Years? Gave me time to think. To think. To ponder. To remember how they all died. To relive each death over and over.

The memories, the pain, the anger.

They took us an hour after we survived Agrippina's trap. SHE took us.

Wounded. Pained. Slowed. Hurt. No ammo. No chance.

They took us.

Killd my friends. Tried to break me. Made me watch. Them die, one by one, over the course of weeks... months? I can't remember. Crucified them. Tortured them. Made them suffer. Made them die. Agrippina. Made me use the orb. Watched over and over.

They'd saved Santino and Helena for last.

Helena… I… She… Gone 4 good this time. Gone. They…

"Never thought you'd actually come around to reading that thing."

I jumped, the voice so abrupt and my mind so enraptured that I hadn't heard it coming. I tumbled from my rock and fell in a heap beside it, but somehow managed to hang on to the papers in my hand. I just barely avoided slipping into the cool water, and a spike of pain erupted out from my side and I was forced to clench my teeth to help bear the pain.

I let myself lay there for a few seconds, trying to slow my racing heart and stave off embarrassment and pain alike. While the latter diminished slowly, the former lingered, and I almost didn't want to return to my feet at all. But a hand was lowered before my eyes, almost helpfully, surprising considering the source. I looked up to see a man with a bare upper body that was encased by a harness of combat webbing meant to carry gear. His entire physique was immensely strong, hard, and solid, with a series of weed like veins stringing their way along his outstretched arm. Atop his body was a chiseled face, not one I was entirely used to anymore, with blue eyes and topped with blond hair cut like an overgrown crew cut.

I looked at him suspiciously but brought myself to grip his dangling forearm, allowing him to pull me to my feet, surprised at how genuine the gesture seemed. Once upright, I ignored the man who'd helped me up, and dusted off my pants and shirt as I returned to my rock. He sighed as I reseated myself and held the pages out before me with my left hand, and wrapping my right around my body so that I could hold my wound. With no intention of speaking to my new guest, I prepared myself to pick up where I left off.

"How far in are you?"

I froze again and my eyes shot to the sky in silent annoyance. I let the papers fell between my knees as I glanced at my guest, who now stood beside me eating noodles from a steaming Styrofoam cup.

I took a deep breath and decided to play nice. "Almost done with the first page."

"Skip the second and third pages, Hunter," the man said, his voice hard, as he twirled his eating utensil at me. "For all our sakes."

I looked at him with chilly eyes as I inspected his face, which was illuminated by the light of his own glow stick attached to the right shoulder harness of his gear webbing. He was in full combat gear sans a shirt – at least what could be passed off as "full combat gear" by these newcomers, as their kit seemed no more advanced in terms of design and quality than what grunts had used back in WWII where I came from.

"Why?" I asked, not even trying to hide my frustration.

The man slurped another fork full of noodles into his mouth and chewed patiently as he gazed at me. He swallowed and wiped his mouth with the back of his hand and pointed his fork at me. "You've always been high strung, Hunter. The past six months especially. We could all read it in your journal. You let things get to you. And I know what's in those next two pages. Listen to me when I tell you: do not read them. The Other You rambled, and it isn't pretty."

I nearly lost it at that point, no longer in the mood to hear what *anyone* thought about *anything*, especially when it concerned me, and I certainly didn't care about *his* opinion.

"How could you possibly know anything about me?" I asked, looking out over the water. "I don't know anything about you! From where I come from, you're dead! You've been dead for half a decade as far as I'm concerned, in fact." I paused and leaned away from him. "You don't know a thing about me."

He shrugged. "Believe what you want, Hunter, but you seem exactly how I remember, even if you are from some… alternate timeline, or whatever, and not the actual Hunter I knew. I can't explain it and neither can anyone I've talked to, but that doesn't meant I don't know *you*. I do. Just try and convince me otherwise."

I didn't even bother. We both knew I couldn't.

"See?" He asked. "Exactly as I remembered. Now explain that."

"You know I can't. Net yet, anyway."

"That's fine, Hunter. Take your time. It looks like we're going to be here for a while."

"Great…" I muttered.

He ignored me and decided to put his hand on my shoulder. I felt my head instinctively snap toward it, my mouth ready to bit off a finger or two, but I didn't. I just sat there with the pages between my legs, looking at his hand.

"I know we've had our differences in the past," the man said as he squeezed my shoulder, "but the Hunter I knew made his peace with me, and so did Artie. I just wish you and I could do the same, so let me start by saying again: do not read the next two pages."

He finished with that and left as abruptly as he'd arrived.

I turned to watch him walk away, his back a wall of muscle as his figure was slowly obscured by the invasion of night. I watched him go with a frown, feeling little comfort at his words. The only reason I'd decided to read the Other Me's twelfth mission entry in the first place was because I'd hoped to learn where he'd screwed up and what he'd done so wrong that ended with Archer, Artie and the rest of them showing up here. I'd also hoped to find answers as to why and how they were such different but eerily similar versions of the people I remembered, but it wasn't exactly something I *wanted* to do. I'd always been too curious for my own good, or at least that's what people kept telling me, and my present circumstances hadn't changed that.

After Archer and Artie had told me that they'd found my skeleton in a cargo container with nothing but the orb and my journal in some warped, alternate version of the year 2021, I'd known almost immediately that I had to read it. But I had been terrified of what I'd learn, and still was, and now that I'd gotten my first taste of it, I was glad for Archer's warning.

Despite how convoluted the Other Me had started, I'd been drawn to his words, entranced by his broken story. If not for Archer's intervention, I would have read right through to the end without pause, only realizing what I'd done once it was too late, because I already knew how it was going to end. I already knew the evidence that the Other Me had gone insane would be quite evident in his words.

I knew this because I could already feel it happening in myself.

It started six months ago when I tortured one of the most beautiful women in antiquity.

It had continued when I saw a friend's head blown to pieces.

It was furthered when I'd witnessed another friend's stepson crushed beneath a slab of concrete.

Or, finally, when I'd watched the woman I loved die for a second time, a memory only exacerbated by the fact that she'd been carrying our unborn child.

Then again, maybe none of that should matter, because through the grace of God, science, and/or magic... whatever... the man with the shattered head had recovered. The crushed man had regained his lower half. And the woman I loved had been raised from the dead, and our baby preserved. But while they'd all come back, the pain I felt at the memories lingered, building and growing and becoming harder to handle as the days rolled on.

Archer was right.

I could do without the gory details and soliloquies I was sure the Other Me was bound to add. I was prone to them myself, and if what I'd just read was true, and if he'd repeatedly operated the orb, reliving the same moments over and over, thinking and thinking, trapped in a voluntary *Groundhog Day* scenario with nowhere to go and no one to interact with for what may have been years...

Well, I didn't want to think about it.

Without another thought, I pulled up the pages again, peeled off the top three and placed them behind the rest. I angled my head down and read.

believe it's come to this. We were ready. Prepared. So prepared. Shoulda listened to Helena. Should always listened to Helena. Never again. But never more. Dead.

Must find way to fix. Had two weeks to think.

How to fix this.

I've thought of something.

My name is Jacob Hunter. I was born in Greenwood, Indiana.

August, 199...

At 6, family moved to Columbus.

Dartmouth U.
History an Classical Studies.
Became Navy SEAL
Find my sister. Diana Hunter. Should be a astronaut.
I don't know how the orbs work. Not really. Been using mine. Feels good to use. Been using mine for months but have no idea how. It just work. But the first time I connected with a Roman. Marcus Varus. Hes dead, but we connected.
I think. I thnk Diana and I can connect. Just like Varus and me. I... I dont know. Maybe she can help me. Help me somehow. Brng some light. So dark.
I need help.
I...

"How's the ending?"

I didn't jump at this latest voice, because it was far more recognizable than the last and I was used to it popping up when it was least expected – or wanted. I glanced up, only two pages left, and searched for the unwanted voice. I looked to my left but found nothing, and to my right, but also nothing. I hadn't thought the voice had come from behind me, but maybe it had.

"Over here."

This time it clearly came from my left and I looked at the small shrub that sat there. A shadow moved and grew taller, revealing the shape of a man. I sighed and stacked the pages against my knee and tapped them there to realign them. Neat and orderly, I held them up to cover my face.

"This really isn't a good time," I said.

The man in black strode closer, clad in his combat fatigues and gear, complete with face concealing balaclava. Acting as our quick reaction force should our Listening Post/Observation Post call in a bogie, he could react instantly while the rest of us geared up. It was standard operating procedure these days, and one we took very seriously.

The man in black shrugged. "Just curious."

"Do you want to know what happened? Really want to know??" I asked, anger rising in my voice.

"Well, yeah," he answered.

I flipped through the pages in my hand, tearing free the skipped few, and flung them at him. He caught them in midair, but no more than ten seconds passed before the pages were held out before me again.

"Never mind," he said. "I don't want to know."

I nodded and retrieved the pages, placing them back in their proper places. The man took a step back, just beyond the glow from my light source, but I could still see him cross his arms as we contemplated each other in companionable silence.

I probably shouldn't have snapped at him earlier, but my mind was growing ever more difficult to reign in these days. My eyes reflexively peeked toward the bag at my feet, but I looked away just as quickly.

"So..." my companion started, never one for awkward silences or missed opportunities to annoy me, "...about that sister of..."

"Don't even think about it."

"What? All I wanted to know is whether brown is her natural hair color or not."

"This conversation is over."

He chuckled. "Keep telling yourself that, buddy."

"She's *off* limits," I said flatly. "God knows how many STDs you've picked up since we've been here."

He laughed out loud this time. "You wish. I'm clean. Trust me."

"Not. Happening."

"Lighten up, Hunter. I'm just busting your balls."

"*Please*... for the love of everything sacred... leave my balls out of this conversation," I pleaded.

He snorted and I couldn't help but smile as well. In that moment, I hardly cared about Artie's innocence or keeping her away from this smiling buffoon, because all I felt was that old tingle of happiness at the banter and idiotic levity he never failed to offer.

Which was why I kept this particular idiot around.

Because I loved the guy.

Platonically, of course.

"Just get out of here," I told him with a wave of my hand. "I'll let you know what happens later, but I wouldn't expect a fairy tale ending if I were you."

He held his hands out in front of him. "I've read enough. Don't bother. Just remember that this didn't happen to you. It happened to *him*."

I nodded, knowing the truth behind Santino's words, and like always, was thankful for his random bursts of clarity and insight that were so unbecoming his normal character. I glanced at the closest friend I'll ever have and watched as he melted into the shadows while I remained, keeping my ass firmly planted on the dry, hard, uncomfortable rock.

And read.

...need help.

I'm terrified. Made so many mistakes. Every one led us... me... here. There's nothing to do. No more tricks. No more friends. No mre magical blue balls. Nothing. Nothing left. Just me and this box. My grave.

Air is thin. I can feel it. Could use orb, but Im done. Finished. Ready to die. Ready to join my love, my life, my... everything.

Helena.

I regrt. Much. Most everything. All my fault. Would never b in Rome. Only no regret is helena. But i killed her. Kill her baby. keeled them both. my Son. my grl. WIL nevEr kno.she wuld have be great mom. uch A woman. the prfct womn.

sory. Head feals lite. Gting dark.

rgrets. Regret what I did 2 timeline. i know it brokem. nothing is will besame. I feal it in m bons. Evrything is gainst me, an theres nothing i do. not thing.wouldt no wht do if ere ws

my falt.

Falt.

i...

I...

sory. Trying to focus...

im ramblng.

I dont kno wht to do.

HELP

I stopped.

The Other Me continued on for a few more paragraphs after that, but I didn't see the point of continuing. He had clearly lost his grip on reality long before his final words, and I was certain the orb had led him down the dark path we all suspected it could, and that it had plagued his mind, taking him on a quick trip toward insanity. He had been just as insane as Caligula in the original timeline and Claudius in the last.

I'd read enough.

My heart was pounding against my chest as I thought about it all, a rhythmic thumping that seemed to beat faster by the second. I placed a hand there to steady it, and felt the drum of my beating heart begin to slow, but the pain in my head continued to linger. The Other Me's journal had more of an effect on me than I'd first suspected it would. It wasn't so much from the content but from the fear of what had happened to him, and how I knew it could happen to me as well.

I pinched my nose and bit back the emotion swelling in my chest.

The man who had written those words *had been* me. He'd been a me that, for all intents and purposes, had sacrificed himself so that I... *me*... could live. Without his journal reaching my sister in the future of his timeline, there never would have been an opportunity for them to come back into mine and save our asses. Without Archer's intervention, we would have been dead, just as dead as he was because he hadn't had their assistance. Instead, we'd created yet another timeline, one where we'd all escaped Agrippina's trap in the villa because Archer and his troops had arrived.

Just like when my friends and I had shown up two thousand years in the past, and had created a timeline that ended with us dead a few days ago, when they showed up, their presence had changed the timeline as well. We were now in yet *another* timeline. Whether their presence would affect more positive change in the long run was still up for debate, but since it had at least resulted in the continuation of our lives past a few days ago, I was okay with it for now.

I lowered my hand from my face and pushed off my rock, still clutching the six pieces of paper. I let my attention linger on the horizon, the shimmering water reflecting the moon's image just below my focus, and found my mind wandering. I closed my eyes and breathed deeply before opening them and glancing down at my hand, realization setting in.

I was alive.

All of us were alive.

This arrogant, self-centered, pessimistic, wimpy, know-it-all Other Me had died so that I could live. Had it been a heroic death? No. In fact it pained me that his death was more of the opposite. It had been a whimpering death, one where he had died alone and unable to help himself, all while he fought a losing battle for control of his sanity. But that no longer seemed to matter anymore. The Other Me had died and I had lived. Whether he knew it or not, his mistakes were not so horrible after all because I would learn from them. I wouldn't make the same mistakes twice. Not when I had a second chance.

I edged closer to the water and tore the six pages in half, then again, and again, until I was no longer able to continue halving it. I lost much of the document as I voraciously tore what remained to pieces, but when I was finished, I threw the rest into the lake like a relative releasing the ashes of a family member into the ocean. I watched as they scattered across the water, floating off into obscurity before dissolving into nothing.

I stood there thoughtfully, watching them go, when a soft sound emanated from behind me. Unconcerned by what sounded like someone coughing politely into his fist to garner someone's attention, the only thing that concerned me was the identity of my latest visitor. I turned to see the outline of a small man standing a polite distance away, loitering near my old rock. He wore his night ops combat pants and a t-shirt that I assumed was white. Attached to his shoulders was a backpack that seemed comically large for his slight frame.

At the moment, he seemed embarrassed, almost bashful, but I knew better. Most of the time he was just as big of an ass as

Santino, only this one knew how to read his audience and act appropriately when necessary.

"Sorry, mate," he said in his Welsh accent. "I didn't mean to intrude."

I walked toward my rock and rubbed my palms against my pants, ensuring any last remnants of the Other Me's documents no longer remained.

"Don't sweat it," I said. "You're not the first person to show up tonight unannounced, but I'll at least give you extra credit for politeness."

The figure shrugged. "You seemed pretty distracted. Considering the few days, I didn't want to interrupt. I saw what you were reading and figured you had a lot to think about."

I smiled. "You the team's psychiatrist now too?"

"No," he said as he shrugged off his large bag. "I'll leave that bullocks to the Frenchy, but I'm still your doctor. Now sit down and remove your shirt."

I complied with his order and once again sat upon my rock, but found that removing my shirt wasn't so easy a task anymore because of my wound, so our friendly medic had to help.

"Thanks," I said as he finally pulled it over my head. "I'm having mobility issues with the arm."

"Expected," he said as he pulled out a small head lamp from his bag and secured it over his forehead. He flicked the light on and examined my side before beginning the procedure of unwrapping the gauze from around my chest. "Your entire left flank was carved up pretty good, mate. You'll be jammy if you gain full mobility at all, and it'll certainly take a few months before you're a hundred percent."

"Wonderful," I said with a wince as he removed the pad attached to my side with a sticky, wet sound. "I think I've had just about enough purple hearts for one career. Time to cash in my pension and get the fuck out."

"Not bloody likely," he said as he completely removed the blood soaked pad.

I didn't want to look, but my curiosity, like it always did, got the better of me, and I very nearly threw up at the sight and smell of it.

"Aye," the medic said, "pretty nasty piece of business there, and you've managed to pop a few of the stiches as well... great. Give me a minute to sew you back up."

I nodded and gritted my teeth in preparation. I felt a syringe plunge its way into the area, the morphine taking its sweet time before finally working its magic, but when the area felt numb, I risked another look, again immediately wishing I hadn't.

The laceration was at least seven inches long, and despite the stiches, the wound was flayed open in places where they had popped, and the dark red wound gaped like a ravenous maw ready to devour anything that came near it. I was almost worried my surgeon would lose a finger or two to its voracious appetite, but my fears were quelled when he stitched me up in seconds, his deft movements dancing with practiced ease.

When he was finished, he carefully set his tools on an already laid out piece of cloth and removed another large gauze pad. He placed it carefully over the wound and used some tape to hold it place. Removing a large roll of gauze from his bag he got to work wrapping me up.

"Thanks," I grunted as he pulled the wrap tight.

"Not a problem, Hunter. Just try not to pop the stitches this time or it will never heal."

"Agreed. I'm sick of your bedside manner anyway."

He chuckled and tied off the dressing, giving it a final inspection before nodding to himself. He then dug around in his bag and removed a cleaning rag and a bottle of disinfectant, which he used to sanitize his tools while I worked my shirt back on. Even with my arm refusing to cooperate fully, putting it on was easier than removing it, and by the time my companion was finished, I'd just about secured it around my waist.

The medic stood and shouldered his medical bag over one shoulder and turned to leave without another word. I twisted at the waist, immediately regretting it, and called out after him.

"Wait."

The small, former member of Britain's Special Air Service turned to appraise me with his large, round eyes that tugged just slightly at the corners. "Need something more for the pain?"

I shook my head. "I'm good on that actually. It's just that I was, um… just wondering what you thought about everything." I shrugged. "About… where to go from here."

He didn't answer immediately, and it would have been nice to see his face in that moment, but his own glowstick was attached to his pack behind him, not in front. I waited patiently, swinging my legs around so I could more comfortably wait for his answer.

"I'm not sure, Hunter," he said after not too long, pointing toward the bag at my feet before continuing. "But even though we got what we came for, we don't have a direction. I know you've spent a lot more time thinking about everything than I have, but it seems to me that the orb is the most important problem we have right now. You may feel like you have an obligation to 'fix the timeline,' but what good is all that if we never get home? We'll never even know if it's fixed or not. I don't know about you, but I think it's time we learned as much as we can about those things before we use one again."

I nodded and looked toward the ground, an old movie quote coming to mind at his words.

"If the wine is sour," I whispered, mostly to myself, "throw it out."

"The wine, Hunter?" He asked.

"Hmm?" I asked in return, barely hearing him. "Oh, never mind, it's just a quote from an old movie."

I didn't bother to explain, realizing I was better tasked with focusing on my friend's point instead. All this time I had been too preoccupied with the notion that I had to save the world from itself, that I was somehow the hero in this story because I'd caused everything to go wrong to begin with. I'd worried about Agrippina and what she could do with the power of the orb – what she could do simply with the entire Roman army at her command – but she shouldn't have been my priority. History shouldn't have been my priority. Debating theoretical time travel mechanics shouldn't have been my priority.

The orb should have been my priority.

It *always* should have been.

If the plan was shit, we needed a new one.

Wang was absolutely right. This whole story revolved around the orb. It was our MacGuffin, the reason for everything that's happened to us, and I should have known better than to ignore it. I knew what it did and I knew how it worked to some degree, and I knew to leave it well enough alone unless I really needed it, but I didn't have *all* the answers. Not by a long shot. But that information had to be out there.

The answers I had always sought had to be out there somewhere.

"Thanks, Wang," I said. "I think you're right. And I think I have an idea of where to start."

"Cheers," he said as he turned and moved back into the camp.

I watched him go until he was completely concealed in shadow, and glanced down at the little bit of gear I'd brought with me to my rock. I had two bags, one being my typical go-bag containing a few soldiery essentials like my Sig P220 pistol, a flashlight, a multitool, extra socks, and the like. This one I picked up and shouldered on my good side. Once secure, I leaned down again to grab the second bag, but my hand stopped mere inches from where it lay. A great longing overwhelmed me to reach down and take it, a familiar sensation in recent days. My hand moved of its own volition, but with a tremendous effort of will, I clenched my fist and felt it shake as I struggled against the draw, but as the seconds passed, the yearning settled, and I was able to pull my hand away.

I stood, breathing heavily, staring down at the menace at my feet wrapped inconspicuously within a primitive burlap bag. The thirst I'd felt earlier seemed to have dissipated completely now, and I took a painful step back before forcing myself to take another, no longer feeling influenced. I didn't know why such a feeling came and went like it did, and I didn't know why I felt so drawn to the orb in some moments but not nearly so in others. However, I also suspected that when the orb was ready to send us home, I would need to interact with it more regularly, but until that time came, I knew it was best to just leave it alone.

Especially now that we had two of them.

Besides, Helena would already be mad at me for taking them to begin with.

For a reason I no longer remembered.

I left the bag where it rested on the ground and took a step back, followed by another more confident one. Despite all the things I didn't know about the orbs, both mine and the one Artie had brought with her after we'd connected days ago, the one thing I did know was that they couldn't move on their own. At least, none of us had ever seen such a phenomenon yet.

Feeling more at ease, I turned fully and made my way through the camp.

A half dozen or so tents had been set up only two days ago, half that looked familiar, the other half not so much. Even after five years of constant use, our tents still looked sharp and stylish when compared to the others that wouldn't have been out of place in a movie about the Korean War. I shook my head as I passed by them, still unclear of the details surrounding Archer and his comrades, but was far more patient about such surprises than most other stuff.

I passed by a pair of the newcomers who were seated around one of their tents, a small fire blazing just outside. Santino was there as well, still geared up as our QRF, talking with Cuyler and Stryker.

Gunnery Sergeant Alex Cuyler was the new squad's sniper, equipped with a rifle that looked a lot like an old M-14, a damn fine precision rifle back home that had been at the height of its popularity decades ago. Cuyler himself was maybe the oldest of the new bunch, of medium height, and slim, and had a shaved head with a full, red beard, a look he'd reportedly crafted for himself days ago, just prior to embarking on this mission. It seemed an odd styling choice for a Gunnery Sergeant, but I wasn't about to question what exactly it meant to hold that rank in their alternate military.

Warrant Officer TJ Stryker, by contrast, was a burly younger fellow with a barrel chest and large arms, although of similar height. He didn't look made for distance running, but if he could sprint, I wouldn't want to be a bad guy running away from him. He had close cropped dark hair and gentle features with thick eyebrows, so at least he didn't come off quite as imposing as his build suggested. They both seemed like nice guys during the few times I'd spoken to them, and they were certainly respectful, as Marines generally were, but since Cuyler was a sniper just like me, I figured I already shared some kind of bond with him.

As for what the trio was speaking about, I only had one clue.

Stryker had produced a sleek but wicked looking steel crossbow, and had it displayed out before him. Santino, who preferred close quarters combat with a knife, still appreciated any weapon's lethality, and reached out to grip it expertly in both hands. He looked it over and nodded approvingly, and held it up to look down its sights. He aimed it off in no particular direction, but then I heard, rather than saw, a metal arrow streak through the sky. I cringed in preparation for it embedding itself in my eye, which would have been just my luck right now, but it never came, and I opened my eyes just in time to hear the arrow ricochet off of a rock before I heard the painful scream of someone in our camp.

My first thoughts were of Helena and Artie, because the cries were clearly from a woman, but the pitch didn't seem quite right for either of them.

To my right, I saw a petite woman emerge from a tent, hopping on one leg while her hands clutched the other. I couldn't quite make out her face, but I assumed it was Staff Sergeant Georgia Brewster, who had been part of the U.S. Army before joining Archer's team. Shorter than even Wang, she had a fair complexion and pleasant, if plain, features, with light colored hair that fell to her shoulders.

The woman came bounding out of her tent so quickly I was certain she would fall over herself, but amazingly, she kept her balance. As she hobbled closer, I could see Santino's arrow implanted in her calf. She raised a fist in his direction, but the first words out of her mouth weren't directed toward my friend.

"Stryker! Get back here and get your toy before I shove it up your fucking ass!"

I smiled unwittingly, thinking of how many times I'd uttered a similar line at my old pal. I glanced at the trio of men, and saw Santino toss Stryker's crossbow into the air and take off into the night. Stryker, so caught up in catching his weapon, barely even noticed Santino's escape, and he desperately looked to find the man who was to blame as Brewster hobbled toward him. Cuyler, meanwhile, took that moment as a sign to leave as well, leaving Stryker alone to deal with the irate woman, but luckily for him, Brewster tripped and fell just as she passed by me. I lashed out with a hand and managed to grab the woman before she hit the dirt, but when I looked up for help, Stryker had vanished just as easily as Santino had earlier.

I looked back at the downed woman.

"Medic!" I called out, but without shouting.

Wang popped his head out from his tent, and I saw it fall against his chest in annoyance before he dipped back in to retrieve his bag. He trotted over seconds later and knelt beside Brewster, but then another woman fell to her knees beside him.

Technical Sergeant Patricia Martin was in the Air Force, and while I didn't remember what the outfit was called in her military, it had sounded a lot like the Pararescuemen, who were combat troops that were doctors almost as much as they were warriors. Their motto was, "That Others May Live," a slogan they took very seriously as they risked their lives to drop in behind enemy lines to rescue downed military personal who were too wounded to help themselves. They were a valorous bunch, and were just as well trained as my SEALs, only they were practically M.D.s as well.

As for Patricia Martin, she was tall and relatively good-looking, with brown hair not unlike my own, only cut even shorter and more haphazardly. She also had a tattoo of a blazing, red sun on her left cheek, something that wouldn't have been allowed back where I came from. The tattoo and close cropped hair gave her an intimidating vibe, which seemed odd since she was a medic.

Days ago, when Archer, Artie, and the others had traveled back in time and joined us here in Ancient Rome, I'd originally thought Artie the only girl in the bunch. I had been dazed and woozy from the pain, medication, and my own episode with time travel, so I hadn't even noticed Martin and Brewster being women until hours later when they'd removed their face masks and let their hair down – well, at least Brewster had let her hair down.

I'd been surprised to see such a high ratio of women to men in what was apparently a Special Forces unit, but when I'd later asked Archer about it, he'd nonchalantly made it clear that women had been serving as equally as the men in their armed forces for many decades. His comment made me think of Israel, and how women in that country had fought alongside the men for many years before the idea even entered into the minds of other militaries.

Wang looked at Martin's arrival in surprise, not used to another medic around to help patch us up, but the two quickly got to work treating the wound and it was nice not to see friction between the two healers.

I stood and moved away from the downed Brewster before I found myself in the way. I knew when I wasn't needed most of the time, and this incident was clearly something beyond my professional pedigree. I turned my head and noticed our pair of Romans, Gaius and Marcus, standing just outside their tent – this one clearly of the local variety – observing the medical procedure beside me. I sent them a wave and they returned it before the pair moved off to join Vincent, Titus, Archer, and Cuyler around the camp's central fire.

I watched them go for half a moment before setting off again toward my intended destination. I noticed with an amused smirk that since I'd left my rock, I'd managed to stumble across every single member of our little contingent, both new and old, with the exception of four individuals: the camp's remaining three ladies and Bordeaux.

The latter was situated on a small hill with clear sightlines all around the camp. It was a good location for our concealed Listening Post/Observation Post, or LP/OP, and Bordeaux could call in a threat from two miles out if he had to. With Santino's UAV for aerial reconnaissance I was confident we were quite secure, although after Madrina's not-so-proficient handling of it a few days ago, it wasn't nearly as reliable as it once was.

That left the three women.

Madrina, Bordeaux's German wife, was still recovering from a bout of unconsciousness suffered on the day we'd failed in our mission against Agrippina. She'd been little more than an ordinary house *frau* months ago, and hadn't nearly been prepared for the shit we'd put her through. She'd been lucky, and while Bordeaux had rarely left her side since, I suspected the big fella could still use the time alone after what had happened.

And then there were two.

As I grew closer to my tent, I couldn't help but overhear the faint giggles of two women laughing hysterically at something I was sure no one with a Y chromosome could ever find even remotely humorous. I stopped and did everything I could to build up some courage for what was to come. Taking a deep breath, I pushed into the tent.

Their conversation ended when I stepped through to loom in the entranceway, and both turned to regard me with smiles on their faces, heaving for air. The woman to my right was clearly the more attractive of the two, but I had to admit that I was slightly biased. The other woman, after all, was my sister, and while she had a cute smile with round cheeks and long, fine brown hair, I could never bring myself to admit that she was attractive.

Not that that it mattered, because the other woman was more than simply beautiful. She was gorgeous. Radiant. Ethereal. I could have come up with a slew of other descriptors, but I didn't need to, because she was the love of my life and the mother of my unborn child. I smiled as I looked at her, remembering just how lovely her face was when she wore a happy expression, one she didn't wear very often anymore.

Her jet black hair, when she stood, flowed like a waterfall past her waist and framed a face with sharp but lovely features upon chestnut skin, but it was her large, vibrant eyes that everyone always noticed first. A bright, glowing green, they were so intense they often seemed capable of piercing right through solid objects.

"Am I interrupting something, ladies?" I asked casually, hoping I was.

The two women glanced at each other and snickered. Both were dressed for bed in loose shirts and shorts, and had I not known any better, I could have almost imagined the two as young preteens throwing a slumber party.

Helena looked at me happily with her green eyes and reached a hand in my direction. I gripped it and let her pull me to the floor beside her.

"Oh, not much, Jacob," she said, turning back to her new friend. "Artie was just telling me a story about how you found a naughty video once when you were children, but you were too embarrassed to watch it and told your mom."

I shot a glance at Diana "Artie" Hunter – my little sister. "I was, eight! And you were like six and a half!"

She ignored me and leaned in closer to Helena. "See what I meant about the 'like' stuff? He's got the worst poker face."

Helena clapped her hands and rolled onto her side in laughter, finding something – I wasn't sure what – extraordinarily funny. I watched her, but couldn't help but feel amused as well, finding myself mildly surprised as I'd never seen her like this before. While we'd found time for happiness in the past, rarely did I see her cut loose with such raw emotion like this, and even if it was at *my* expense, I was happy to see it. There'd been too little opportunity for laughter in our lives, and if anyone could use it, it was Helena.

"Oh... I've..." Helena managed around bursts of laughter, "...noticed that,"

I scowled at them both, but turned to Artie. "What else have you told her?"

She shrugged mischievously and didn't answer.

I turned to Helena who was still on her side. "Don't listen to anything she says, Helena. She's been waging a smear campaign against my good name since high school."

"There's a reason for..." Artie started, but I cut her off with a raised finger and a very nasty look. She smiled at me smugly and flicked her eyebrows, and I knew it was only a matter of time since I couldn't chaperone these two forever.

"Just get out, Artie," I ordered. "I want to have sex with my girlfriend."

"Eww!" She said, recoiling in disgust before smacking my arm. "That's disgusting, Jacob. I don't need to hear that."

"What?" I asked. "How do you think I got her pregnant? First..."

"Just stop!" She nearly yelled, before looking at Helena who had finally calmed down. "How did you put up with him all this time? I mean... I had to. I'm his sister. But you? You had a choice."

Helena smiled at her from the floor, but the wink she offered was directed toward me. "Well, the sex really is quite..."

"Stop!" Artie said again, cupping her hands over her ears as she made her way toward the exit. "I can take a hint."

I smiled again.

This Artie might not have been my Artie, but she was obviously still my sister.

"Same time tomorrow night?" Helena asked hopefully.

Artie glanced behind her as she reached the tent's exit and smirked. "Definitely. I've got a great spin the bottle story about Jacob and another bo…"

"Out!" I said, my finger pointing toward the exit.

Her smile grew before she crawled away, taking the time to zip the tent closed behind her. I lifted a hand to my head and shook it, realizing just how much dirt my sister really had on me.

Luckily, Helena proved a quick distraction, taking my hand in her own so that she could pull me to the floor beside her. I let her, lowering myself so that I lay behind her on my uninjured side and scoot myself in close. I tried to wrap my weakened arm as carefully as I could around her, but I couldn't quite extend it around her abdomen, so I simply left it lying atop her hip. My right arm, however, was beneath her head and wrapped around her chest, gripping her left arm tightly. I held her against me snugly, taking a joyous moment to inhale the smell of her hair.

It was comforting and relaxing, but as it sometimes did, her long hair tickled my nose so much that I had to pull away to keep myself from sneezing all over her. I felt her body bobbing slightly in well humored giggles at my sensitive nose.

"What?" I asked, already knowing what.

"It's just that I've always loved how romantic you are," she said, kidding around, although she had a point. Romance was something I wished I was better at, but considering our current life circumstances, I could never find the energy or will to try.

But I tried now as I caressed the soft skin of her leg gently with my hand, while Helena shifted contentedly in my arms, enjoying the touch. She hummed pleasingly to herself, so I shifted my hand lower on her leg, but then I touched a patch of slightly rougher skin and everything stopped. Even Helena's excitement ceased as quickly as flipping a switch.

I touched the scar on her leg gingerly, as if pressing against it too hard would somehow make it worse. I traced my finger along the length of it, moving my finger from the outside of her leg upwards along her hamstring. My finger stopped just below Helena's backside, and I heard a sharp intake of breath from her as my fingers brushed against a more sensitive area. The scar was long and thick, and an obvious blemish upon her otherwise flawless leg, but it wasn't necessarily the sight of it that disturbed me.

I lowered my other hand from around her chest and lifted her shirt, peeking down to notice another pair of scars along her abdomen and lower back that mirrored each other but were no taller than a wallet. With a slow breath, I lowered her shirt and gently removed my arm from beneath her head. She didn't try to stop me as I pulled away from her and carefully maneuvered myself into a sitting position so that I could hang my right arm over my raised knee. I sat there, contemplative, before Helena leaned up as well and wrapped an arm around me.

She didn't say anything, nor did she ever have to. She knew what to do. She rested her cheek against my arm and waited patiently, but something was different this time and she seemed to know it.

She pulled away and rested her chin atop my shoulder. "You're not upset?"

I wasn't actually. Nor, was I really all that sad. I was barely even introspective, just... contemplative.

I nodded.

"Feel any responsibility?" She asked.

I shook my head, but with slightly less confidence.

"That's good," she whispered. "I think that's progress."

"Maybe," I said just as quietly, feeling better already.

Helena lifted her chin and kissed my shoulder, scooted away from me, and started searching for something, but couldn't seem to locate what she was looking for.

Finally, she turned to me. "Where are the orbs?"

My eyes looked away guiltily. "Uh... I left them by the rock."

"Jacob..."

"I'm sorry!" I said defensively. "I couldn't help myself. You know what they do."

She nodded as she stood, all too aware.

"Well, that's it then," she said. "You're *done* with them."

I watched her walk past me. "Where are you..."

"I'm going to have Jeanne destroy one and I'm going to hide the other!" She snapped at me, but not angrily. "I don't know if they're making you worse or what they're doing to you exactly, but I'm not going to let you grow addicted to them, and we certainly don't need *two* of them." I rose as well, but she pushed me back down and pointed at me. "You stay here. I'll be back."

I winced at a spike of pain in my side, but it wasn't too bad, and looked at Helena as she looked at me. There was nothing to indicate she was angry at me in her eyes, just horribly, horribly concerned. She turned and left the tent, her long shirt that reached halfway to her knees billowing at the movement.

When she was gone, I looked at my feet.

Even without the orbs, I still felt constantly overwhelmed by just about everything. There was more on my mind than ever before, including Agrippina's continued existence, the orbs themselves, Archer's unexpected arrival with his troops, the drastic changes to Roman history, and so much more. Often, responsibility for Helena's numerous injuries weighed on my mind just as heavily, but it seemed like I was beginning to lose that one. She'd never blamed me to begin with, and after five years, letting go of at least that responsibility felt good.

I thought about all this is as I scooted to the back of the tent, and slowly lowered myself onto my back. I stretched my legs to work the kinks out, and rested there peacefully for a few minutes until an explosion off in the distance jolted me upright again.

Like the last time we'd destroyed an orb, I wasted a moment of thought wondering if something would happen to us, but like last time, nothing did. Slowly, as my heart rate steadied, I lowered myself to the ground and raised my right arm to drape it across my forehead. I was quite comfortable in that position and felt myself growing sleepy.

Helena returned sometime later, but I wasn't sure how long she'd been gone. I'd just about drifted into sleep during that time, but it was the noise from the tent's zipper being closed that roused me awake, and I lifted my head and peeked through droopy eyelids to see Helena standing before me, gazing down at me. She stood with her hands on her hips and looked at me without betraying her emotions, so I lowered my head back to my pillow of bunched up clothing.

"Find a good place to hide it?" I asked.

"Find a good place to hide what, Jacob?" She asked.

I lifted my head again. "The o…"

"A good place to hide... *what*, Jacob?" She asked insistently.

I smiled. "Never mind then."

She smiled back and I found myself staring at her as she stood there in her loose shirt that looked more like an exceptionally short dress, the scar on her leg barely even noticeable now. She cocked her head coyly at my inspection and placed her hands on her thighs, and slid them up past her hips to rest along her waist.

"See something you like, Lieutenant?" She asked.

My grin widened. "Maybe."

She raised her chin and looked at me with smoldering eyes, and reached under her shirt with both hands before slowly lowering them, her shorts coming down with them. She kicked her shorts in my direction but I managed to dodge them. She took a step forward and lowered herself to the ground, positioning herself over me so that she could lean down and kiss me while I reached up to comb a hand through her hair.

She pulled away and kissed my nose before gazing softly at me.

"Feel better?" She asked.

"You always did know how to cheer me up," I answered. "Even if it's doing something as simple as taking my mind off of a time traveling blue ball that also has the power to warp people's minds and turn them into raving..."

She interrupted me by lowering herself beside me on my good side and moving her hand to unbuckle my belt. She looked at me as she worked, her eyes filled with annoyance, but she didn't stop what she was doing.

I lowered my head back against my pillow and smiled. "Never mind. I'll just shut up now. Keep doing what you're doing."

II
Paradoxes

Outskirts of Damascus, Syria,
October, 42 A.D.

I woke the next morning as happy as I'd felt in a long time.

The last time Helena and I had shared such intimacy *without* the world crashing down around us in one form or another had been that one wonderful night in Byzantium when we'd settled our differences and I'd given her an apology gift in the form of a necklace. Helena liked to think that had been the moment when we'd conceived our child as well, but she wasn't quite sure. We'd had a few other opportunities to succeed at such a thing since then, but Helena, unlike me, had a bit of a romantic streak in her.

I stretched out my arms around my head and extended my right arm to pull Helena in close, but all it met was air. I opened my eyes and noticed she was gone, and tried to think of where she could possibly be, but then I remembered she had LP/OP duty from six to one today. I glanced at my watch and noticed with wide eyes that it was almost noon. I bolted upright as quickly as my damaged flank would allow me and got dressed.

I found my favorite pair of smiley faced boxer shorts first and gave them a quick sniff. They smelled fine enough, so I slipped them on before retrieving my mulitcam patterned combat fatigues and stepped into those as well. Lastly, I clipped on my web belt that held my pistol's thigh holster and secured that around my leg. Deciding I didn't really need a shirt, and since I couldn't immediately see one anyway, I retrieved my pistol, slipped it into place, and stepped out into the late morning sun.

It was a hot morning, and the sun glared brilliantly from high above. I held out an arm to shield my eyes as I allowed them to grow accustomed to its intensity, and reached into a pants pocket in the hope that I'd left my glacier style sunglasses, complete with side shields, there. As luck would have it, I had, and I slipped them on and surveyed the camp. Most everyone seemed out and about and doing something, although Santino was missing, probably still asleep after his late night/early morning QRF duty, and Bordeaux and Madrina were missing as well. I noticed Helena off to my right, a few dozen meters away from our horseshoe shaped camp, situated atop a small hill. She had a pair of binoculars fixed to her eyes as she glassed the horizon, her DSR-1 sniper rifle lying across her body in her lap.

She seemed focused so I didn't bother her, and made my way to the center of the camp and its central fire. Arrayed around it were Vincent, Titus, Patricia Martin, TJ Stryker, Gaius, Marcus, Archer, and Artie. Georgia Brewster, who was rarely seen in Stryker's company, was laying out on a blanket near her tent, Alex Cuyler was on QRF duty, and Wang was off to the side, cleaning his medical equipment.

My stomach grumbled as I inspected our camp, so I made my way toward the fire in the hope of finding food. I took a seat next to Vincent and he patted my shoulder warmly in greeting with his remaining hand. His left arm from the elbow down had been lost during the Battle for Rome over four years ago, but he'd never lamented its loss nor acted like he deserved sympathy. He'd simply adapted and grown accustomed to his limited mobility and moved on.

I nodded in greeting and offered his stepson a nod as well.

"How's the leg, Titus?" I asked him.

He looked down at his right leg and placed his hand upon the large cast that encased it.

"I feel it healing, Jacob Hunter," he replied and I ground my teeth at his continued use of my first and last name. "And Wang says he will remove the cast in perhaps a month."

I looked at the young man's cast and smiled at its appearance. Just like in junior high, it had a number of drawings and messages scrawled all over it. Artie had been the first to contribute, and I thought back to yesterday morning as she'd leaned in and wrote a quick get well message, signing it with her nickname and little "X's" and "O's" like any teenager would do. When she was finished, she'd noticed my curious inspection of her display and asked me, "What? They didn't do this in your timeline?"

I'd shaken my head in surprise at the comment, not really paying attention to her words, but the meaning behind them instead. Obviously, school children had done exactly the same thing in my timeline, just another reminder that while our timelines were obviously very, very different, there were still peculiar similarities that didn't make sense. I had no idea how the course of history could diverge so clearly, but still leave it almost exactly the same and completely different all at the same time.

I'd ignored Artie's question at the time, playing it off by taking her pen and leaving my own contribution to Titus' cast, and over the course of the day, everyone else had added their own sentiments as well. Helena had colored her lips with some local lip coloring she'd picked up at one point and left a kiss below her message, while Santino had cheerfully drawn the one thing every young boy loved to draw on another boy's stuff: male genitalia – for whatever reason.

I sighed as I noticed the drawing, remembering the time back in high school when a friend had drawn one on my backpack without me knowing, causing me to receive a demerit because *obviously* I'd draw the thing myself on my own backpack for every single teacher to see…

I'd gotten him back though.

Santino's smut notwithstanding, the gesture had helped break the ice between the two teams and offered some lightheartedness before the reality of our situation set in. While the bonding experience had left Titus' cast covered in color and words, the sight of it brought back that original curiosity and misunderstanding concerning our two timelines, and how we'd apparently fucked it up, as Archer had so eloquently stated upon our first meeting.

I glanced up at Artie now, a question on my tongue, when I felt something hard poke against my arm. I looked over and noticed Marcus prodding me with a plate containing steaming pieces of meat, and finally noticed the animal skewered upon a spit that must have been recently taken off the fire.

I reached out and took it, picking up a piece of meat with my fingers to inspect it.

"What mystery meat is it this time?" I asked the Roman.

"Antelope," he reported. "Helena killed it this morning."

I glanced at her, seeing that she dutifully sat with the binoculars still fixed to her eyes, and smiled.

"Sounds good to me," I answered, having no problem with the less than normal meal. I popped the stringy but juicy morsel into my mouth and started chewing. I swallowed and felt my stomach immediately settle, and I sighed contentedly as Vincent passed me a small loaf of bread. I tossed another piece of meat into my mouth and savored its warm, flavorful texture before swallowing it down.

"Feel better, Hunter?" Archer asked mockingly.

I turned and offered him a momentary look before turning away, doing my best to appear unfazed by his tone. I leaned my head back and closed my eyes as I tore off a piece of bread with my teeth, and chewed.

"Indubitably, my dear Watson," I replied with a smile. When I noticed Stryker and Martin trade questioning glances, I decided to return my attention back to Archer. "What? They don't have Sherlock Holmes in your timeline?"

The man stared at me angrily.

"Apparently not," I said with the flick of my eyebrows.

"*Obviously* not," Archer clarified. "I told you before that you fucked things up! We're wasting time here. We need to start figuring out where things went wrong and how we can fix them."

"Have patience," Vincent said, punching his open hand in a downward motion. "Time, believe it or not, is on our side now."

I gave Vincent's shoulder a pat in appreciation before speaking. "If only it were as easy as you think, Paul. I've been trying to figure this shit out for years. A few conversations over breakfast isn't going to help you."

"No, but it's a good place to start," he countered. "My team and I volunteered for this mission knowing it might be a one way trip, knowing that we may be here for a *very* long time, *knowing* that fixing the timeline may mean we'll be unable to return to our home at all, but that doesn't mean I'm willing to simply waste my time while you get your shit together because you can't get a handle on your emotions!"

I shot to my feet and he joined me, and I got ready to throw my metal plate at his face, but Artie also stood and placed herself directly between us.

"Stop it!" She ordered with upraised arms. "Bickering isn't going to get us anywhere."

She had a point, but my anger wasn't diminishing at her words. I felt my arm starting to raise the plate on its own, but Vincent lifted his hand to push it down, enticing me to sit as well.

"Take a seat, Lieutenant Hunter," he ordered.

My anger subsided at his words, and I slowly sat with a nod of thanks to the older man, but I wasn't placated completely. I could never trust Archer, not after what he'd done to Artie, and warning bells were going off in my mind not to start now. There was something off about him, something that suggested he was keeping things from me, only I didn't know what.

Archer sat as well, but Artie remained standing. She stared down at Archer intently, but he refused to meet her eyes, so she turned back to me.

"Archer isn't wrong, Jacob," she said. "We did come here for a reason. We need to talk and get our stories straight. All we really know about what happened here was recorded in your journal, but that wasn't much to go on."

I shrugged noncommittally. "Fine. I'm all ears then."

She rolled her eyes. "It can wait until tonight after everyone's settled down. Besides, I think Helena and John will want to be a part of the conversation as well."

I blinked at the name *John*, realizing a few seconds later that she'd meant Santino.

Great…

"Fine," I said. "What did you have in mind then?"

She glanced around as she tried to think, before her eyes caught something off to her right. "What's that city over there again?"

"Damascus," I answered.

Everyone present craned their heads to look, seeing the small city of Damascus a few miles away at the bottom of a shallow mountain. The city was very old, with clearly Roman influences, but it wasn't large, and I knew that it had been completely rebuilt a number of times before the 21st century rolled around.

At least it had in my timeline.

To my right I heard Stryker and Martin mutter obscenities under their breath, and Artie looked almost shocked at the name as she continued to hold her hand out in the city's direction.

"What?" I asked.

Archer leaned in and spoke. "Damascus is the capital of one of the most powerful caliphate empires in the Middle East. Just last year they were responsible for the destruction of Paris."

I blinked at his words, understanding every single one of them but not the context in which they were said. I glanced at Vincent and he looked back at me, his eyes indicating he was just as surprised as I was.

"I concur that it's time to talk then," Vincent said, and I found myself agreeing wholeheartedly.

After a few moments, Artie finally regained her composure. "I think we could all use a break from this camp anyway. I, for one, am not used to so much camping, and I'd like to explore a little, even if it's... *that* place. I think a group of us should head down there this evening so that we can talk. How's that sound?"

I glanced off toward Damascus again and sighed. The only reason we'd decided to camp so far away was because we were worried about being discovered by Agrippina's Praetorian ninjas, but we'd been off their radar for days, so in all likelihood, the ninjas either hadn't even come to Damascus or had already inspected it and left.

We could take the chance.

I turned back to her and nodded.

***

Later that evening, Helena and I walked arm in arm through the city of Damascus. The team had trickled into the city over the past hour, trying to keep our entrance subtle and unnoticed, and the two of us were the last to enter. Using Santino's UAV, we'd mapped out the city's layout two nights ago and had determined a location that would suit our purposes: a wide, open public park with eating areas scattered around its perimeter. It was a familiar atmosphere for anyone regardless of culture or time period, and we'd decided it was the best meeting place in town.

As we passed into the city proper, Helena moved to place her cheek against my shoulder, and we took the opportunity to simply stroll and drink in the sights. Having left our rifles and machines of war back at the camp, we tried to enjoy ourselves. Cuyler had the city covered with his sniper rifle and a few of us still carried pistols as well, so barring the city coming under siege by a Roman legion, we felt fairly safe.

Much like the city of Caesarea had been before it had been destroyed months ago, Damascus was a beautiful city, shaded in tans, whites, beiges, browns, and with green plants as vibrant as Helena's eyes. I'd never been to modern day Damascus, although the last place I'd visited in the modern world had in fact been in Syria, but I already knew this city probably looked nothing like its modern equivalent.

Narrow streets with cobblestone pathways connected towering adobe buildings where patios jutted out into the streets and hanging gardens cascaded everywhere. Green plants with yellow, red, and orange flowers littered the city in a beautiful mosaic of color and opulence. Greek and Roman influences were evident in the architecture and fountains that sparkled in the bright sunlight, and combined with the chattering of locals and the selling of goods, the city seemed almost utopian.

These people probably had no idea the province of Judea was being razed to the ground not all that far away, but I tried to not let myself think about that. Instead, I glanced down at Helena as she clung to my arm and waited for her to look up and meet my eye. When she did, I gave her a smile, which she returned sweetly before resting her head back in its original position as we continued on our way.

By the time we arrived at the large park area, the rest of our party were already there, and had situated themselves around a fountain with a few stone benches. Those who couldn't fit on the benches sat on the lip of the fountain or sat on the ground nearby. Someone had even thought to bring some wine, cheese, and fruit to munch on – a nice touch for our charade. Vincent, Wang, Santino, Artie, Archer, Stryker, and Brewster sat in a tight cluster and even Bordeaux had managed to haul his massive frame away from his wife to join us. I looked at the excessively large Frenchman, noting his sandy brown hair and sharp features that seemed almost different now. As a warrior, he was as ferocious as they came, but was no more volatile than a kitten when at peace, a gentle giant really, but there was anguish in his face now, an expression I recognized in myself quite often these days.

Bordeaux avoided my inspection as Helena and I found a place to sit, so I shifted my attention to Vincent, whose own weathered face seemed like it always had, if not just a smidge older. He had to be in his mid fifties by now, but that didn't mean he was any less capable than the rest of us. Helena sat next to him, but as I took my seat next to her, I was distracted by Artie explaining something to Santino across from us.

"So, an alternative known as the magnetoplasmadynamics thruster allows for denser plasma by forgoing the Hall current in favor of a current that is mostly aligned with the electric field, and far less prone to..."

I shook my head at whatever scientific mumbo jumbo she was trying to describe. I was a pretty smart guy, and knew a bit of rudimentary science and basic engineering, but my knowledge was insignificant in comparison. Back home, when the two of us would get into conversations about the stuff, she often had to settle for describing her work as "*Star Wars* stuff."

I wondered if this current Artie's work had been nearly as advanced, or if *Star Wars* even existed there for her to reference.

As for Santino, he had his chin in his hand and was staring at her intently, hanging onto every single word she uttered, but his eyes told me better. They were glazed and distant, and I knew he hadn't really heard a single word she'd said. He was probably fantasizing about a knife wielding vanilla smoothie with big boobs.

He was just that kind of guy.

I settled onto the lip of the fountain and gave the soft cushion someone had left there an approving sigh. I reached for one of three bottles of wine on the ground before me, and Helena accepted a pair of goblets from Stryker's helpful hands. She held them out before me and I poured us helpful servings of the viscous liquid, but looked at me like I was an idiot, and I quickly remembered that she was pregnant. I shrugged and downed half her glass before handing it to her. While alcohol wasn't great for unborn babies, water in the ancient world was probably far more toxic, and the girl had to drink something.

She shook her head at me and turned away.

I utilized her distraction to study Archer, and tried to make sense of not just the man, but his very presence. I'd hated him well before I'd ended up in Ancient Rome, even if the two of us had begun our acquaintanceship as friends. He too had been a SEAL officer, and I'd almost considered him a brother then, especially after he'd started dating my sister. Their relationship had even built to the point where he'd considered proposing, but then he'd cheated on her and broke her heart, and that fairy tale had crashed to a halt.

I'd never forgiven him for that.

And neither had my Artie, since he'd died in North Korea on a mission not long before I'd ended up in Ancient Rome, but this Artie had, just another interesting, temporal deviation.

And now we had to work together, trapped in a magical realm of treachery, despair, anger, literal insanity, and murder. If there was one positive note I could take from Artie's newfound friendship with Santino, it would be that he could stand up to Archer. A few days ago, I'd gotten the feeling that Archer still felt something for my sister, and I just hoped his attitude didn't elicit a stupid reaction from Santino that would force my friend to do something equally stupid. They were both extraordinarily dangerous men, and I wouldn't want to have to step into the middle of a scuffle between them – even for my sister's sake.

I sighed and took another sip of my wine, Helena's body resting comfortably alongside my own, her touch a subtle reassurance. Besides Artie's love life, what made my mind whirl more than anything else was the fact that Archer, Artie, and their team were literally walking paradoxes.

A simple contradiction of basic logic.

Five years ago, I traveled two thousand years into the past and had, apparently, changed things. Caligula and Claudius were dead years before their time. Thousands of humans were dead who shouldn't be, and hundreds of lives were saved that otherwise would have ended. The course of human events had changed. That fact was clearly evident in Archer and his team. Their gear was outdated by over seventy years, although in the grand scheme of two thousand years, that made even less sense than if nothing had changed at all. If they were going to be different, why weren't they still wearing plate armor and running around with swords? Why instead was their gear different, but still all too familiar?

What I couldn't understand was why Archer and Artie, whom I knew very well in my original timeline, were almost exactly as I remembered them in this new one. The only major difference being that Archer had been MIA in my timeline and assumed dead, when in this new timeline he was still alive. How could the grand scope of world history be so different, yet both these people were just as I remembered them? Apparently, the Jacob they'd known had even fallen out of the same treehouse I had, breaking his leg just as I had. Did that mean his college girlfriend as a freshman had been just as bitchy as mine had been?

Why were some things so different, but others so similar?

It didn't make any sense.

We'd learned within minutes of meeting Archer that Helena was a major in this new timeline and that her father was a US Senator, as opposed to a newly commissioned lieutenant and her father a member of the German elite. Archer had also spoken of a North Atlantic Federation, whatever that was, and of the Ottoman Empire still existing. Another revelation was that both his team and ours had been sent to Syria by the President, not the Pope, and on a completely different mission that had ended with the same result: time travel.

They hadn't yet elaborated on the lives of Wang, Bordeaux, or Vincent, but something told me their parallel lives would be equally odd but still strangely similar as Helena's was.

All these contradictions simply did not add up when combined with the fact that everything about my childhood with Artie from this new timeline – Artie 2.0, for lack of a better term – synced up almost perfectly. Our mother had bought me a puppy for my tenth birthday, although in this new timeline I hadn't named him Argos in reference to Odysseus' dog, but Rex instead. How fucking original. Other similarities included my dad and I still not getting along, I'd never once had a cavity, I went to the same schools, and my first sexual encounter was still with little Suzie Lu from across the street when we were sixteen.

How this Artie had known about that last point, I didn't know, but I decided I didn't want to know anyway.

But there were other minor differences as well. The kid who'd beaten me up in seventh grade was named Jason in this new timeline, instead of Billy. My college girlfriend's name had not been Shannon – no word on her level of bitchiness, however – and my roommate freshman year at Dartmouth had been named Dan instead of Casey, but from what Artie 2.0 had said, was basically the same guy. There were other small differences as well, but interestingly, nothing specific about the Jacob from her timeline had changed either. Artie said I seemed like pretty much the same Jacob Hunter she'd grown up with.

I'd tried asking other questions concerning the world they'd left, but even Artie had been pretty tight lipped. Cuyler had seemed interested to learn of sports called Football and Basketball, and had indicated that the only sport played in the United States was Baseball, if only to keep troop morale up and little else, but I'd learnt little else from them.

Later that first night after they'd arrived, Helena had let me in on a few secrets she'd discovered on her own. Apparently, the idea of a sports bra was non-existent to Georgia Brewster and Patricia Martin, and they'd been extremely impressed with Helena's wide array of under garments. I'd had no idea how a conversation about underwear even got started amongst women, but I had been less interested in the content of the conversation as I had in the context. In terms of world history, sports bras were a very recent invention, and it was still another interesting difference.

My musings were interrupted when Santino's chin slipped off his hand and his palm slapped loudly against his pants, silencing all conversations around me. All that was left were the sounds of rustling leaves, the chirping of birds, and the passing of people in the park around us. I half expected Santino to cover his embarrassment by starting things off, but it was Artie who spoke up first.

I groaned, remembering she wasn't one for awkward silences either.

"I suppose it's time for answers then, isn't it?" She asked simply.

"You invited us here for exactly that," I shot back.

She placed her hands in her lap before continuing. "Well, where should I start?"

"How about at the beginning," I said.

She gave me a stern look and moved her arms to cross them against her chest. "Why don't *you* start at the beginning? It begins with you after all. Fill in what your journal missed."

I opened my mouth to raise my voice at her, but Helena stepped on my toes and answered far more politely for me.

"Our story begins with our mission to capture a biological arms dealer and scientist named Mushin Abdullah," she answered, giving me an angry, sidelong look. "He was a terrorist who worked for the Russians before going rogue and attacking the Vatican and Jerusalem. When intelligence networks finally pinpointed his position in Syria, we were tasked with retrieving or eliminating him."

Helena didn't pause in her explanation, but I noticed Artie exchange a worried look with Archer, while Stryker and Brewster shared a rare glance. Anything that got those two to trade almost compassionate expressions had to be something important.

"There, we found a blue orb that transported us to Ancient Rome," she continued, simply enough. "There's no sense trying to explain it, because I have no idea how it works, and since you're here, you already know about as much as we do."

Artie smiled at her new gal pal and gestured for her to continue. Helena nodded and glanced at Santino, Bordeaux, and Wang in turn, waving a hand at them.

"Feel free to jump in whenever you want, guys," she said.

Bordeaux nodded politely but Wang beamed at her, saying, "You don't need any help from us, Helena. Just don't forget Hunter's more embarrassing moments."

Helena returned his smile and patted my hand while I scowled at the Brit. He hadn't been that bad during our first year in Ancient Rome, but his recent time with Santino had made him a relentless jokester. They were a regular comic duo, and with the addition of Gaius and Marcus, who had devilish senses of humor themselves, and the impressionable young Titus, whom they'd already taken under their wings, that entire quintet was starting to get on my nerves.

Helena turned to Vincent. "Sir?"

The older man offered her a half smile. "You're doing fine."

She nodded at the reassurance.

"Okay then," she said, taking a small breath before explaining in detail the past five years of our lives. She explained our dealings with Caligula, Claudius, and the Roman general Galba, and later the Battle for Rome. She then went on to describe Agrippina in the colorful way only Helena could, as well as detailing our time on the run when she, Santino, and I had taken the mantel of *Vani*, acting as Sheriffs of the Roman Empire.

She finished by describing the team's reunion a few months ago, our dealings in Caesarea that initiated a Jewish-Roman civil war, and our introduction with Vespasian – currently the man in charge of said war. Finally, she described the battle that had gotten us all killed a few days ago, that is, before I went back in time and saved the day.

Each of the new arrivals sat quietly, processing Helena's tale, and it was Artie who spoke up first, and nodded her head at me. "You went back in time again just before we arrived here, didn't you?"

I nodded. "Sure did. It was completely by accident but it was enough to save our asses."

She slowly leaned back and looked off into the distance. It was a response I was used to in her. Whenever Artie was exposed to new information worth pondering, she would simply close up into her own little world and think, only to snap out of it when she was ready, or by an outside force akin to a tornado.

The rest of Archer's party continued their silence.

"Have any of you studied ancient history?" Vincent asked. "Does anything of Helena's tale sound familiar to you?"

Again, no one responded until Archer finally turned to Brewster and gestured to her with a "come on" gesture.

"History lessons haven't exactly been a priority for any of us," he answered. "We've been too busy fighting a losing war for decades, but the closest thing we have is Brewster here."

All eyes turned to the tiny woman as she shrugged, still digging around in her bag.

"I was an Art History major," she clarified. "Never finished though."

I chuckled. "So tell me, Art History Major, what can art tell us that will make sense of anything?"

"Actually," she said, finally pulling something large and square from her bag, "not much. Luckily, we brought this."

She finished by tossing the object – what looked like a book – at me, which landed with a loud thump on the ground by my feet. I peered down at it, noticing its front cover was emblazoned with an image of the globe on it, with a series of different pictures from what looked like multiple time periods scattered around it, although none seemed familiar.

Still… it was all too familiar at the same time.

Even though I could read the cover, and knew exactly what it was, I still felt the need to ask, "What the hell is this?"

She smirked. "It's a high school social studies textbook. One of the better ones, I'm told."

I looked from the book and back to her. "You have got to be kidding me."

Brewster shrugged again, but Archer cut off any response from her.

"Feel free to flip through it at your leisure, Hunter, but not now," he said. "World history isn't the priority here. Determining where the break in our timelines occurred is."

His tone was paternalistic and dismissive, and I felt my anger growing. Since the moment Archer had arrived, his demeanor had been authoritative and commanding, as though anything we had to say was of little use to him. He seemed to think his arrival meant we were now all under his command, and that we no longer had any purpose but to help him and his timeline only.

An attitude like that wasn't going to get him very far with me.

"Why don't you tell us what your present is like," Vincent suggested. "and please, just for clarifications sake, did you leave from the year 2021?"

Whether it was because of Vincent's age or calm attitude, Archer's tone grew more respectful. "Correct," he answered, "but as you can already tell from our gear alone, your 2021 and my 2021 are considerably different."

"But why, Archer?" I asked, already paging through the history book, beginning at the end, and flipping to the beginning, nothing jumping out at me. But when I reached the title for the very first chapter my heart nearly skipped a beat.

It was labeled: *The Dark Ages.*

I looked up at Archer in disbelief. "Have you ever even heard of the Roman Empire?"

He glanced at his teammates again, shifting in his seat before answering.

"Yes," he said easily, "but what we know of it is very limited, and most of what we do know begins with its fall, which is why that book begins where it does."

"But we had a dark age as well," I said, frantically flipping pages. "So much history, knowledge, and technology were lost, and Europe went to shit for centuries, but much of it was preserved by outside forces and the Renaissance also saw a lot of information retained. Where did your timeline go wrong?"

I continued leafing through the book, occasionally glancing at Vincent, whose knowledge of history outshone even my own. Unfortunately, he didn't seem any more helpful than Brewster's history book was at the moment.

Archer shrugged. "We don't know, Hunter. That's why we're here. We need to fix whatever event it was that you screwed up."

I glanced up from the book slowly. "Is your world really that bad?"

"I suppose it depends on who you ask," Archer replied, "but from where *you* come from, Hunter, and where the rest of us come from, it is. Very bad."

"You mentioned the Ottoman Empire earlier in the present tense," Vincent interjected. "Can you explain?"

"The Ottoman Empire is just one of many Islamic empires throughout Eurasia," he replied. "They control Anatolia, some of the Middle East and their Eastern European holdings. Then there is the Moorish Caliphate who controls Africa as far south as the Congo, Spain, and Italy. Finally the Kingdom of Sauds control most of the Middle East through western Asia. There are a number of smaller nation-states that comprise the hegemony, but those are the big hitters. The only thing that has kept them from wiping out America and Great Britain is that they don't always get along."

"When did these Muslim empires begin their invasions of Europe?" Vincent asked.

Archer shrugged. "None of us are historians, remember? If you want details, read the book, but if I had to guess, I'd say some time in the fourteenth, fifteenth, or sixteenth centuries, I really don't know."

I whistled through my teeth but I still couldn't buy it completely.

Not yet.

"I guess all of this makes sense," I said. "Even with a dominant Islamic force throughout Europe, Africa, and the Middle East, America still would have been discovered by Spain by an Italian explorer, England would have later colonized it, we would have later gained our independence, and I still would have been born in Midwestern Indiana to parents whose grandparents had called Central Europe home."

"Right, Hunter," Archer said.

"Wrong!!" I shouted, clapping my hands at him, causing Vincent and Helena around me to jump. "Don't you realize what you're saying?! You're telling me that even though Europe went through an extended dark age, didn't enter a time of medievalism, so no knights and conflict with Islam over Jerusalem, Islamic containment in the Middle East, no rediscovery of Roman and Greek knowledge, probably no invention of firearms until much later, and yet you're still going to sit there and tell me that, 'in 1492, Columbus sailed the ocean blue,' and everything else managed to fall into place perfectly? Tell me, was Washington even the first president and did Lincoln free the slaves?"

Archer cleared his throat. "Everything you've just said is true, Hunter. 1492, 1776, 1812, 1865... Are these dates important in your history as well?"

I looked at the ground and pounded a fist on my thigh. I could not understand what was happening. None of this made any sense. I closed my eyes and tried to think, but Archer wouldn't let me.

"Well?" He demanded. "Are they?"

"Yes, yes," I said, leaning back and wrapping my arm around Helena's waist, more for my own piece of mind than anything else. I looked back at Archer. "Okay, smart guy. Say I buy all this. What do you plan to do about it?"

"Fix it," he said, his voice even.

I pulled my arm from Helena and shook my fist at him. "Just like that then? Just... fix the universe? Without even knowing where to start? Good luck with that, buddy, I'm sure you'll do a..."

"Stop it, Jacob!" Artie exclaimed, having apparently pulled herself out of her stupor. "This isn't all about you, you know. We've lived our entire lives in a world at war, as did our parents. Don't ignore what he's saying just because you can't imagine how horrible our lives were."

Her scolding took me by surprise, and left an empty feeling inside my stomach.

"I guess I'm sorry, Diana," I said meekly. "It's just that it's been nearly impossible for us here. It's been hard for me to even remember life outside of this place."

"You'd better believe…" Archer started, but Artie cut him off.

"Shut up, Paul," Artie said, shooting him a look. "You read Jacob's journal too. You know what they've all been through. You don't have an excuse for making an ass out of yourself either."

Archer looked at her angrily, but then turned away under her scrutinizing gaze. I almost smiled at Artie, but then remembered that I wasn't completely innocent in all this either. Silence befell our group again, but there was still a lot to talk about.

"I think it's time we shift topics," I said.

"To what?" Archer snapped.

"The orb," I answered, "and how it can get us home. Because I don't know about you guys, but every time I've used it, something different has happened, and I don't come out of it any more enlightened."

Every head immediately turned toward Artie as she sat there, completely oblivious to our attention, still fuming over my interchange with Archer. After a few seconds, Santino poked her in the arm, and she snapped her head around.

"What?" She asked.

"We need to discuss the orb," Archer said before I could.

"Why are you looking at me, then?" She asked. "Jacob's had way more experience with it than I have."

I stepped in before Archer could take control of the conversation again.

"You're the closest thing to a scientist we have, Artie, and you have a higher I.Q. than Santino and Wang put together," I said, receiving asinine smiles from them both. "And like you said a few days ago, I'd just go off explaining it with movie refer…"

"Shh!" Santino interrupted with a finger over his lips.

"Oh come on, John, you know I didn't mean anything by…"

"*Shh!*" Santino repeated more insistently this time.

Defense mechanisms kicked in at Santino's insistence, as they did in everyone else who knew him. The only time Santino was ever really worth listening to was when he sensed something was wrong, and I could tell he wasn't goofing around right now.

I scanned the courtyard but found nothing amiss, while Helena reached for her bag and what I assumed was a pistol hidden within. I swore under my breath for not bringing my own but felt assured by the fact that enough of us had, but there didn't really seem anything wrong in the vicinity to justify Santino's sudden plea for silence. I looked at him sitting opposite me in our circle, noticing that he seemed as alert as ever despite my lack of understanding. He rose to his feet with great caution and stared unblinkingly over my right shoulder, at an area of the park that was nothing more than an open field filled with dirt, some scrub grass, and a scattering of trees. There was nothing there, and I started to wonder if Santino was getting paranoid in his old age.

Much like I was.

"What's wrong?" Archer asked, and for once I didn't have a problem with his question.

In response, Santino snapped up his left hand and held it in a halting gesture. He had his pointer finger extended toward the sky but then slowly lowered it so that he was tracking it right to left. I kept my eyes on his finger, waiting for more information.

"There!" Santino yelled, lowering his left hand and drawing his pistol with his right in one smooth motion. The gun lifted so effortlessly that even my trained eye had trouble keeping up with what was happening. I tore my eyes away from Santino and finally saw what had spooked him. A few dozen meters away were Agrippina's ninjas, wrapped in their dark clothing and armed with swords, knives, bows, and arrows.

I dropped to a knee, giving Helena a clear line of fire in their direction and keeping my ears away from her gun. Taking cover, I saw Wang, Stryker, and Archer go for their weapons at about the same time as Santino and Helena started firing. Artie dove to the ground and crawled toward my position, and I wrapped an arm around her protectively and kept her body as close to the ground as possible.

"Stay down!" I yelled at her and she nodded vigorously.

I lifted my head and saw ninjas nocking arrows to bows and releasing them in our direction. I pushed Artie closer to the fountain for cover and pressed myself against it as well, relying on my friends to handle the situation.

Helena dropped beside me and continued firing.

As I kept myself out of the way, I felt a pain in the back of my head like an intense headache pounding away at my skull. My first thought was that I'd been hit by arrow, but that didn't make much sense. Instead of thinking about it, I squeezed my eyes and cringed at the pain, raising a hand to my temple in the hopes that it would somehow help, but it didn't. The pain inexplicably increased and stars burst into my vision as the back of my head impacted the marble fountain when I fell to the ground.

I barely took notice of the arrows falling around us by the dozen.

I hadn't heard the screams from someone hit by one just yet, but my head hurt so badly that I wasn't sure such a sound would even register. It seemed ready to explode at the slightest touch, but then someone tugged at my sleeve and yelled for me to crawl away, but I could barely comprehend the spoken words let alone comply with them. All I could do was fight off the pain in my skull and hope that it went away on its own.

I turned to Helena who was in the process of reloading her pistol, her head directed toward me, her mouth moving to form unheard words. I shook my head and turned toward the rest of my team, noticing they'd taken up defensive positions behind trees or beneath benches, but in the next second, all I saw was blood.

Like an image flickering to life from a faulty movie projector, the entire scene before me suddenly became clear. One of my friends was already dead. The body I saw was Wang's, his chest perforated with a half dozen arrows and another through one of his eyes. He sat against a tree almost casually, but his head hung lifelessly to the side, his pistol useless in his hands. Seconds after realization set in, my attention was diverted to Vincent, who took an arrow to the stomach. It hit with such force that it went clean through, not a life threatening injury, but it dropped the older man to a knee and out into the open.

Time seemed to move in slow motion now, as it often did in combat, but never quite like this. I felt myself trudging through reality at a pace that would have made a snail seem swift, and as time continued to unfold around me, more of my friends started going down. Santino took an arrow to the knee, Stryker to the arm, and Brewster right in the chest. I couldn't believe what was happening, so I closed my eyes and forced time to pick up again, willed it to accelerate and go back to normal.

I was rewarded with another sensation, however, when the pain in my head seemed to just disappear, and when I opened my eyes, everything had changed again.

Wang was gone, as was Santino, Vincent, and Stryker. Artie was no longer next to me but over by Archer and Helena, who was also no longer by my side. Dazed, confused, and suddenly exhausted, I struggled to my feet, and continued my inspection of the area. The scene was pristine and there was no blood, like nothing had happened at all, and I started wondering how long I had been sitting there with my eyes closed.

A moment later, Helena noticed me rising to my feet and rushed over. She grabbed me by the arms and helped me sit on the lip of the fountain again.

"Jacob... Christ, are you all right?"

"I, uh..." I started saying as I tried to think, "...I'm fine. But what about Wang and...?"

"What about me, mate?"

I craned my neck to look behind me and saw the man who had been dead just seconds ago standing in a very non-dead like position, looking as healthy as ever. My eyes narrowed and I looked at Wang in a state of utter shock before turning back to Helena, who looked very concerned.

"What happened?" I asked.

"I was just going to ask you the same thing, Jacob," she said, shifting her head from side to side gently, studying me. "You passed out."

"I did?"

"Yes, you did. Just when Santino spotted the scout."

"I did?" I asked again, unable to accept such a story.

"Sure did, buddy," I heard Santino say. I turned again and saw him approaching from behind Wang, perfectly fine and without a mark on him. He and Stryker were carrying a body between them. "But don't worry, sweetheart, I kept you safe."

I would have sneered at him if I wasn't so confused.

I turned back to Helena. "What happened?"

She didn't seem eager to answer, but she did anyway. "Santino spotted one of Agrippina's ninjas who must have been a scout for his *Octetus*. Cuyler took him out before any of us could react, but the rest of his group wasn't far away, and everyone else went after them."

"Two got away, the squirmy bastards," Wang said as he took a seat beside me.

"But not this guy," Santino said as he dropped the body unceremoniously to the ground. The man coughed as he hit, and Santino kicked him in the side to keep him down. "You were just *too* slow, weren't you, guy?"

"Cuyler's on the runners," Stryker reported. "And Gaius and Marcus are covering the perimeter, but one could slip out of the city if they're lucky."

I nodded distractedly and looked at my hands, but Helena reached up and took them in her own. She lowered her voice. "What happened, Jacob? I've never seen you just pass out before."

I shook my head. "I don't know... I really don't."

I hadn't lied to her, not exactly. I *didn't* know what happened to me, but I wasn't exactly keen on sharing what I'd experienced. Everyone thought I was already on edge, and some may already suspect I was going insane, so now wasn't the time to provide them with further evidence to support the argument.

I tried to shrug off my confusion for Helena's benefit and to maintain my authority. I noticed the body of Agrippina's ninja on the ground out of the corner of my eye and pointed at him.

"He talk yet?" I asked.

"Not yet," Wang answered as he retrieved a scalpel from his small trauma kit.

Santino grinned at the sight of it and kicked the man on the ground again, and I was only mostly sure the two were just putting on a show for their attacker's benefit. But when Santino's kick struck the man's body, there was no reaction. Stryker kicked him harder, but the result was the same. The two traded glances before Santino knelt down and rolled him over but pulled back almost instantly.

"Fuck!" He yelled as he jumped away, doing everything he could to avoid a spray of arterial blood gushing from the man's neck. The downed ninja must have had his hand clamped over the self-inflicted wound until the moment Santino rolled him over, and the blood had just come streaming out. I wasn't sure when the man had died, but he'd clearly killed himself to avoid interrogation.

Santino looked irritably at Wang. "I thought you searched him!"

"I thought *you* searched him," Wang shot back.

Both men glared at each other before turning on Stryker jointly, who held out his hands innocently. "Hey, I just got here. I don't even know who the hell this guy is."

Wang and Santino bobbed their heads in reluctant agreement and turned back to me, so I turned to Helena, not sure what we should do.

"I think it's time we leave," she said coldly, and I didn't think anyone would disagree with her.

***

An hour later, we were all back at camp.

Cuyler hadn't reported anyone tailing us as we returned, but we'd all mutually agreed that we had over-stayed our welcome here and that it was time to push on. There was only one place any of us could think to go, and that was back to Caesarea where we could report in to Vespasian.

Once we arrived, Helena and I immediately went to work collapsing our tent and preparing our gear for immediate deployment. The atmosphere around the camp was energetic and chaotic as over a dozen people scurried around to make their preparations for egress. The sun had recently set, and without fires for illumination, most everyone performed their tasks in the dark. Some utilized flashlights occasionally, and I'd even used my night vision goggles as I packed our tent away into its pouch, but the darkness only served to slow the entire process. Even so, Helena and I were among the first to finish, having performed this particular ritual a hundred million times over the years together.

We then shifted our attention to our gear, but we always kept most of it packed up for rapid deployment anyway, so we were ready to go. We took our packed tent and all our spare gear to one of our large carriages and loaded everything carefully. All of our horses were nearby, but since we didn't have spare ones for the newcomers, we had to pack the carriages tighter than normal to leave room for them to ride along.

I passed a small box to Helena who stood in the cart, and watched as she tied it down. It was the last of our gear, so Helena moved to jump down from the cart. I stopped her, and placed my hands on her hips so that I could carefully lower her to the ground myself, something I was happy I could even do with my wounded side. Once she was back on the ground she smiled at me and flicked some hair out of her eyes.

"Thanks, Jacob," she said and moved in to hug me.

I let her, and wrapped my good arm around her tightly. She clung to me with powerful arms of her own, her head pressing hard against my shoulder.

"Are you sure you don't want to talk about what happened earlier?" She asked, her voice slightly muffled against me.

I made no move to pull away. "I don't know what happened. I really don't." I lied, but what else could I do? I didn't need her worrying about me anymore than she already did. "I feel fine now, honest. I was just lightheaded, I guess. I didn't really eat much today."

She didn't move or say anything, and it was obvious she wasn't convinced, but she knew better than to press me. Then again, after everything we'd been through, I wondered if she *should* press me, but neither one of us mentioned it as we embraced in the moonlight, a position I could hold forever if only life would let me.

Helena shifted against me and I felt a sudden stiffness in my pants. Helena noticed it too and looked at me wryly, but the source wasn't me. Curious, I pulled away from her and reached into a cargo pocket to discover Varus' note that I'd left there last night. The long roll of papyrus that had been flattened was about the length of my forearm, but I'd folded it in half again last night for safe keeping in my pocket.

Helena and I looked at it for a few heartbeats before she pulled away and patted my chest.

"Go," she said. "Read it."

"I'm not sure I want to, Helena," I whispered.

"I know you aren't," she said, her voice soothing and reassuring, "and nobody blames you for that, least of all me. But we both know the only person he would have wanted to read it, is you."

"You think I owe him that much?" I asked.

"I don't think you owe him anything, Jacob," she said. "I think you owe it to yourself. You'll never be at peace over his death unless you read it."

I took in a long breath through my nose at the thought, and then let it out as I looked into Helena's eyes. They appeared sad and worried, as they often did these days, but they were also supportive. They were always supportive. No matter what I did or how close to the brink I came, Helena would always be there to pull me back.

Always.

I pushed her away gently and walked toward my favorite spot in the camp. I passed by Santino and Wang who were bickering about the proper way to fold their tent, as well as Gaius and Marcus who sat patiently, having already packed up their gear well before even Helena and I had. I looked to my left and saw Bordeaux happily holding his wife's hand as they carried a few bags to their carriage. Madrina seemed unsteady on her feet, but it was the first time I'd seen her walking since her time spent unconscious.

Bordeaux caught my eye as I passed but he immediately looked away. A heartbeat later, he glanced back and held his attention longer this time, but betrayed nothing before having to avert his eyes again as Helena approached to offer a hand.

The big guy hadn't been very happy after I'd ordered him to reset his bomb that had destroyed Agrippina's villa a few days ago. With the knowledge I'd gained after going back in time, shortening the bomb's fuse had been the only way to forestall Agrippina's murderous rampage and save everyone's life. The only problem was that Madrina had come snooping around after we'd been captured, not knowing what had happened, and had been knocked unconscious by the bomb's blast. It had taken her a long time to recover, and Bordeaux had been of a mind to kill me once we'd all had the time to catch our breath, but once he'd learned that what I'd done had saved his life, as well as Madrina's, he'd understood to some degree. He must have still felt bad for attacking me, but I wasn't about to force an apology on him. He was upset at himself, and I knew what that felt like enough to know that I'd want to be left alone as well.

A short walk later, I found myself back on my old rock, the one I'd perched myself on last night to read the Other Me's journal. I stared at it as I walked around it, preparing myself for what was to come. It was too bad the rock wasn't capable of offering any helpful advice or input. It was just a rock. A large, sturdy one, sure, as rocks should be, but a rock nonetheless. I wondered what had gone through the mind of the rock that had held Odysseus in his opening moments in *The Odyssey*, where he had spent every free moment he had perched there, staring out at the sea, crying for his lost kingdom and his wife, Penelope.

That man had been a true wreck. He'd spent decades away from Penelope, fighting wars, battling monsters, watching his entire crew be killed or devoured in one grotesque way or another. It had been a miracle that he hadn't caved completely – that or Homer's clever wit – so I tried to remember that even though I'd gone through a lot, he'd gone through far worse.

And at least I still had Helena.

I let out a long sigh as I mounted my companion rock, and retrieved Varus' note. I unfolded it so that it resembled its original, rolled appearance but paused when I noticed the small seal that kept it closed. It didn't have a fancy symbol or signet punched into the red wax, just a red depression, completely puritan in style. The only thing that assured me it had come from Varus was the handwriting which I immediately recognized as his always calligraphic print.

I smiled at the lettering, thinking about Varus and how proper and fastidious he'd always been in his presentation and in his work. A quiet scholar who'd never asked anything of anyone, he'd been a brilliant linguist, a knowledgeable historian, a dedicated friend to Caligula – an odd relationship lost to history – a good husband, a proud father, and my pal.

It was unfortunate then that besides his wife, I wasn't sure anyone else knew these things. Even Helena and all the rest had barely really known him – Hell, I'd barely even known him. I hadn't seen him or spoken with him in years, but we had been close in the short time we'd known each other, sharing a connection that neither one of us had ever really understood until much later. I'd always suspected he'd been some long lost ancestor of mine, which was why the two of us had been able to connect through the orb, a theory that had later been confirmed by Artie and her arrival here.

I still wondered if there was more to how the orb worked than just that, but with and another long breath to hopefully expel my continued confusion, I popped the seal that hid Varus' words from the world. Written there was a message that didn't nearly take up the entirety of the surface area available, written in stylish but clear Latin letters. Five years ago I would have driven myself to tears trying to translate this thing, but these days, I read Latin as easily as I did English. I was confident I could translate circles around all those old Latin professors of mine – the same ones who had once thought I'd never learn the difference between an ablative and a dative.

I supposed that was one of the few benefits of my time here: when I found my way home, I'd have quite the resume.

Not a bad thought actually.

I shook my head with a smirk, but cleared my mind and set my eyes to the page, ready to absorb whatever words of wisdom Varus had left to impart on me.

Jacob Hunter

Was it fate that brought us together, my friend?

Which odd twist from the hand of a divine was it that brought you into my life?

Sadly, I do not have the answers to these questions, but I do know that I am glad for it. Even as I write this, knowing what Agrippina may soon do to me, I am eternally grateful to have known you, and to have had the opportunity to research this great mystery you have brought into my life.

The orb.

I kept nothing from you on that fateful night aboard Agrippina's barge, for I had not yet divined its secrets. Please do not think that I kept from you what I am about to tell you here, for that is not the case. Much has happened in the months since then. More than I'll ever truly come to understand.

Agrippina did not expect you on that night, try as she might have to convince you otherwise. She may have known then – as I finally do now – what the orb does, but she has never been able to wield its power. She is a cunning and shrewd woman, and had been lying in wait for you since the moment you left Rome on the tragic day of Caligula's death. She later confided in me that she had been purposefully placing herself throughout the empire over the years to draw you out. That's all she had ever done, but she succeeded on that night. Do not let her words intimidate you. Do not let her suggestions sway your judgment.

And for the sake of the gods, Hunter, do not think with anything other than your mind when you are with her. Her nature is her greatest asset, and it is an alluring one. Do not let your thoughts stray around her.

But the orb.

The orb is the key. And I know now what it does only through a mere fluke. An accident. I have once heard how most great discoveries are done so only through such tricks of... yes, fate.

After what happened aboard the barge, Agrippina urged greater haste with my research and even allowed me access to the orb. After all those years, finally, I was able to study it in person. As I am certain you already have inklings as to what it does, I feel safe in my assumption that as you read these words, you will not be surprised at what I learned in those wonderful few months.

The orb is a time manipulation device.

You are from the future!

Or course!

It all makes such sense now. How could I have been so blind? It is so obvious. So obvious. I was quite angry at myself for some time once I had discovered the truth.

I tested it with a number of people in Agrippina's retinue, but not once did it operate between two different individuals as it had you and I. However, through a single accidental encounter later, I was able to replicate the results we shared and duplicated the orb, but I will not describe that event here.

But regardless, once I had the orb, I pleaded for Agrippina to allow me leave to visit the library at Alexandria to further my research. After much convincing, she relented.

That was two months ago as far as she knows, yet, from my perspective over two years have passed.

Can you imagine it?

Can you?

The amount of knowledge I gained in those two months... those two years... is simply incredible. I could not take anything with me during those temporal trips, nothing except my mind and my memories. I learned so much in that time, however, compiling data and decoding lost histories. The man I worked with at the library could not understand how my knowledge grew as it did.

I was not bored in that time. Nor did I age and I never felt any ill effects from such prolonged use. It was simply amazing. My mind grew but my body stayed healthy. What leaps in knowledge I could have gained had the orb not been taken from me!

But I get ahead of myself.

Once I had gained as much research as I felt I needed, I recorded my findings. This took several weeks, and often I would use the orb to ensure I had everything in order. My research assistant was Flavius Rumella, a scholar employed with the library. He and I worked together to make sense of it all, and... Jacob, what we learned was astounding. I dare not speak of it here for fear that this document may fall into the wrong hands, and I feel I should begin to close as well before I utter too much in my excitement.

Go to Britannia, Jacob Hunter

But first, go to Alexandria.

Find Rumella at the great library.

Tell him who you are. He is expecting you. If something happens to me, he is your only hope of discovering the answers you need. I know you have no wish to remain here and I wish nothing more than for you and Helena to find some semblance of happiness together, but this cannot happen here. You must go home. And if helping you is the last thing I do on this despicable world, then at least I can rest eternally assured that I did something to be proud of.

If we never meet again, and you find your way home, take care of yourself, Jacob. Take care of the woman you love. Everything you do, you must do for her and for the both of you together. Nothing else matters.

I am sorry our time together was so short, as I am certain that had we more time, we could have solved the orb's mysteries long ago. It is a great regret of mine. I have always felt that the two of us had a connection. Some form of bond that made us the sum parts of some greater whole. I cannot explain it, even now, but it makes me sad to know that we never had more time to learn more of each other.

Good luck, my friend. Go to Alexandria. Hopefully you never have to read this, but if you do, well, you'll know what to do. Tell my son how proud his father is of him, and please… trust in yourself, Jacob. Trust your friends. Do not fall prey to Agrippina and her manipulations. Everything you do from here until the end rests on your ability to trust.

I know you will do me proud.

Your friend,
Marcus Varus

My eyelids drooped heavily over my eyes as I read. Tears were forming there, although I hadn't yet found the courage to let them fall, but as the note ended, I decided there was no longer a point in holding them back. There was no one to impress, and even if I wasn't all alone, it would do Marcus Varus no justice to contain them. I let them go and felt two droplets splash against the roll of papyrus, one after another.

I felt my lower lip quiver as my tears turned to sobs, but I pulled it together. I bit my wayward lip and tightened my resolve. I couldn't believe how deep Varus' words stung. It was less the words but the depth to his message. He had written that letter to me and me alone, had tasked me with a mission of monumental importance, and had asked me to tell his son that even though his father was now dead, that he still loved him very much and that he was proud.

How was I supposed to do that without telling the kid I had basically killed his father?

That it was my actions that had resulted in his death?

It was Agrippina who had been directly responsible for his murder, that I knew, but only because it seemed her sole purpose in this world was to hurt me. I was convinced of that. I had put Varus in that horrible position, and without my presence here, he would still be alive.

I felt a hand come out of nowhere and place itself on my shoulder. I jerked at the touch and looked up, expecting Helena's comforting presence beside me, but it was Artie who had risked approaching me instead. She looked down at me with consoling eyes, but I could only look at her accusingly, as if all this was her fault too. I barely even recognized her in that moment, but could think of nothing else to do but place my head in my hands, and let the document that Varus had so valiantly risked writing sop up the tears that streaked down my cheeks.

I felt Artie's arm wrap around my back and she pulled me in close. I let her, trying to remember that none of this was her fault either. Not at all, because it was all *my* fault. No one else's. She wrapped her other arm around me and drew me in so that my head rested against her shoulder, and whispered soothing words that I barely understood.

"It's all right, Jacob," she whispered. "We'll fix all of this. All of it."

It was difficult to believe her.

I wasn't sure if I could fix anything anymore.

Or if it was even worth fixing.

III
Generals

Caesarea, Judea
October, 42 A.D.

Later that night, we finished packing and set out for Caesarea a few hours before midnight. I opted to ride with Helena atop our carriage, since the idea of being alone upon my horse during the cold bleakness of night was far from appealing.

Thanks to Artie, who had successfully contained my emotions earlier as I'd sat on my rock, I'd managed to avoid prying eyes and judgmental looks from my friends as they continued their preparations. Santino and Vincent had already been perched atop their horses, while Stryker and Martin had their gear and most of their supply containers loaded onto my carriage, and had themselves plopped upon it. Most of the others had been just about finished as well, so when Artie left me atop my wagon with a squeeze of my knee, we were ready to go.

With the exception of Helena, Madrina, Titus, and myself, every member of my team rode their horses to act as scouts, flankers, or rearguard, while the only new member atop a horse was my sister. Quite the little equestrian in her youth, even in this new timeline, Artie was an expert horse rider and could ride circles around Santino, who was still by far our worst rider.

Once on the road, Helena remained mostly silent as I recalled the details of Varus' note.

She hadn't asked to read it and I hadn't offered it to her either, neither one of us thinking it was appropriate since Varus had addressed it specifically to me. She'd been most interested in Varus' proclamation that we go to Britain, but had also voiced concern over going to Caesarea first.

We suspected Agrippina had gone north to Anatolia so that she and her Praetorians could deal with the Parthian threat, but her ninjas were still out there. Gaius and Marcus, former members of Agrippina's Sacred Band – and two of her ninjas as well – had confirmed that while we had thinned their ranks considerably in recent months, had warned that she had a large supply of recruits to call on.

Helena was far from a coward and she would never back down from a fight, but she had grown taciturn in recent weeks, often voicing her dissent about putting us directly at risk, especially when it concerned Agrippina. She wanted nothing more than to strangle Agrippina to death, but also seemed more aware than the rest of us how adept she had become at besting us. Helena knew we had to take risks if we were to get home, but she didn't have to like it, especially not when she had our baby to think about, something I couldn't blame her for either. But the idea of heading to peaceful Alexandria to perform a low risk/high value mission for once appealed to her. She wasn't exactly excited about me ensconced in a library with tons of information to absorb and then regurgitate back to her, but she knew she had to pick her battles. Better to be bored to death rather than stabbed, as she, unfortunately, well knew.

We spent the next three days in transit heading southwest, relying on help from the random people we encountered for more precise directions. A half dozen pointed fingers later, we found ourselves atop a small mountain with a grand view of Caesarea, still miles away, but sadly no better in appearance than when we'd last seen it.

Even from this distance, we could see how its once pristine buildings had crumbled to nothing more than piles of rubble, and smoke plumes still wafted into the sky from innumerable fires set throughout the city. We could also just barely make out the various legion camps scattered around the city's perimeter, but with my binoculars, I could make out the shapes of soldiers running about in controlled chaos. And as if the sight wasn't bad enough, the stench of burnt garbage and decaying corpses was still strong, even as far away as we were.

Felix, my trusty black, Spanish stallion that I'd stolen from Agrippina all those years ago, grumbled beneath me.

I'd left Helena's side the day before yesterday, always feeling more protected atop Felix's strong back and sturdy legs, at least when I didn't need a shoulder to cry on as I certainly had that night. He made me feel powerful and gave me a commanding position high above any man on foot, but even horses had nerves, and like most animals, could sense things humans could not. The city before us was a haunting sight, and the ghosts of countless dead must have tickled the senses of my poor horse.

I reached down and scratched his mane, but turned to Archer.

"Set up camp here," I told him. "This shouldn't take very long."

He nodded and I led our away team toward the crumbling city.

Santino, Helena, Wang, Vincent, Artie, Gaius, and Marcus made up the team heading into the city, while the rest stayed behind with Archer in charge – for lack of a better option. We descended the low hill and made our way toward the legion camp we knew to be Vespasian's. It wasn't difficult to spot, right smack dab in the middle of a trench system that reached from shoreline to shoreline and around the city. Its appearance mimicked all the other legion forts I'd visited over the years, and would make for easy navigation once we breached its walls.

We made our way to the *porta principalis dextra*, where a legionnaire atop the gate's rampart stopped us, a half dozen of his comrades threatening us with their spear-like *pila* at the ready. Gaius, always our go to guy when dealing with legionnaires, maneuvered his horse to the front of our group and made our case for us. Luckily, he and Marcus were well known to this particular legion, so it wasn't long before the gates parted and we made our way inside.

As we led our horses through the camp, I was reminded of what death smelled like.

It had a rank and pungent odor that overwhelmed my senses and blurred my vision. I pitied these legionnaires for their chosen profession, especially since they were the only individuals I truly respected in this God forsaken land. Their dedication, professionalism, and martial prowess were arguably unmatched throughout all of history, so despite the dreaded atmosphere of the camp, in these men, I could at least find comfort and understanding. Gaius and Marcus were shining paradigms of this truth, and I found myself ironically at peace just now, surrounded by these thousands of automatons who knew little more than bloodshed and war.

But it was thoughts like those that reminded me how much this place in time and space affected me, reminding me of how much I hated it here and how much it had changed me for the worse. It reminded me that I had to do everything I could to protect Helena and my baby, as Varus had ordered me to do, and get all of us home.

Helena, always able to read my thoughts, tucked herself in close beside me after we'd dismounted and marched down the *via principalis* in the direction of the *praetorium*, any legion general's command tent. She glanced up at me, a bleak expression on her face, but quickly smothered it and placed her hand on the stock of the sawed-off shotgun she kept strapped to her thigh.

Archer and his men had never even heard of the ammo variant Helena's P90 utilized, so, drained of ammunition, she'd retired her trusty personal defense weapon and found our old shotgun, the one we had yet to fire in combat, and like in any good zombie flick, had sawed off the barrel and stalk, and had wrapped duct tape around its grip, creating a serviceable, quick draw blunderbuss of a weapon.

It didn't take us long to reach the *praetorium*, but my entourage and I were stopped by a pair of guards and were told to wait outside while they announced our arrival. Seconds later, a number of officers and administrators streamed out of the tent, shooting us looks of annoyance as they passed. We must have interrupted a meeting, although I had no idea why they appeared so irked.

Santino smiled and waved at them as they left.

One final man exited the tent before the legionnaire who had initially stopped us waved us in. I nodded in thanks and lead our procession in to meet with Vespasian.

His tent was sparse and orderly, as any good general's would be. It was furnished with a simple bed, a cabinet, a desk with three chairs, and was adorned with two spoils of war hanging from display stands: a five foot long longsword and a pair of twin bladed battleaxes, crisscrossed. As good a man as Vespasian was, he was still a Roman, proud of his endeavors and not beyond collecting trophies.

As for the man himself, he stood behind his desk, appearing as solid and impenetrable as a brick wall. Much like Santino in terms of height and build, Vespasian's visage was impressive. He had a square jaw with small lips, and his cheeks were hard and taught, completely unlike the busts of the man that existed in the 21st century where his face had softened and grown round with age and a career of administration.

Another man stood in the room as well. He was lean and tall, with dark curly hair and a full beard. His features were even more striking than Vespasian's, with a long pointy noise and small, predatory eyes, much like a hawk's. His face was all the more intimidating at the moment because of the menacing stare he was directing at me.

"You!" He shouted, his hand pointing threateningly. "How dare you present yourself before me!"

I almost smiled at his dramatic reaction. "It's nice to see you too, Herod."

***

"Bastard!" "King" Herod Agrippa shouted, taking a step toward me. "I should have you skinned alive before having the Romans crucify you!"

I knew his hollow threats of death were well intentioned and deserved, but I couldn't help but finally allow myself that small smile.

"Isn't it interesting," I whispered, leaning in toward Helena, "how many people have said things just like that to me before?"

She looked at me blankly. "I really don't think that's a good thing, Jacob."

I shrugged, turning back to Vespasian. "We need your help."

The burly Roman traded looks with Herod, who was still fuming as he probed his shoulder where Santino had stabbed him a few weeks ago. He had his arm in a sling, but didn't seem ill from infection. Gauging from the grimace on his face as he touched his arm, though, I could tell that the wound hadn't yet healed.

"Quick to the point," Vespasian remarked. "I should have expected as much, but why don't you introduce your friends first, Hunter?"

I started with Artie, but made no mention that she was my sister, nor that she had only just recently arrived. Vespasian gave her a curious look as he grasped her hand, maybe noticing she wasn't the military type or perhaps seeing the family resemblance, I didn't know. I then introduced Wang, who Vespasian greeted warmly, and then Vincent. Vespasian looked at the older man happily and shook his hand enthusiastically.

He already knew Gaius and Marcus, who saluted smartly as he passed, but when he stood before Helena, he reached down, gripped her hand, and kissed it in the same manner as he had the last time they'd met, my frustration at the gesture the same now as it was then.

"Can I marry him this time?" Helena whispered to me in English.

I ignored her and finished by introducing Santino, who looked around the tent distractedly, appearing as uninterested in life as he usually did.

Vespasian perked up at the name. "Ah, so you are the 'funny one' then."

Santino turned to me and smiled. "I've always liked that Galba."

I rolled my eyes. Santino was the only one of us our old Roman comrade, Galba, had seemed to like, but none of us had any idea why.

"I have something for you," Vespasian continued causally as he walked to his cabinet.

Only taking a few seconds to rummage through his gear, he brought out a long, thin object wrapped in a heavy cloth. He held it out for Santino, who looked at it stupidly before finally accepting the gift. Noticing his hesitancy, Vespasian beckoned for him to open it. Gingerly, and with a sidelong look at me, Santino gripped the cloth and peeled it open with excessive care.

I too leaned in for a better look, but all I saw was something metallic beneath the final fold. Santino, however, squinted at it with the first bit of interest he'd shown all day. The entire process was agonizingly slow, and either Santino was acting particularly stupid, which wasn't hard to imagine, or Vespasian's gift was somehow familiar to him.

Finally, unable to contain his curiosity any longer, Santino ripped open the cloth to reveal a long, fixed-blade knife. But not just any knife. *His* knife. The one he had lost all those years ago when we had tried to recover Agrippina's son, Nero. He'd thrown it at the then-villain of this story, Claudius, but it had been intercepted by one of his Praetorians instead. He'd lost it that day, something that had bothered him ever since, but it wasn't until just last year that we'd learned why.

I'd caught him one day staring longingly at the replacement knife Helena had bought for him years earlier. It was something he did occasionally when he had something on his mind, but I'd about had enough of his annoying sorrow over his lost knife at that point, so I'd confronted him about it. For someone who treated women like disposable paper cups, his attachment to the thing was disconcerting, and it was something Helena and I had been curious about for years.

His story had been surprisingly heartfelt.

I'd never known much about his childhood or his family, but he'd once told me about a younger half-brother who was still in high school back when we'd still resided stateside, which was about all I knew. If Santino even had a father, I wouldn't have known, but it turned out that his father had been quite real, and he'd been a good one at that. He'd been a welder, a salt of the earth blue collar man who'd worked hard to put food on his family's table every night, even if he hadn't always succeeded.

The man's only hobby had been the collection of knives. Everything from kitchen tools to ornate decorative ones, and even military grade hardware. His collection had been immense, but he'd never squandered his money at the expense of his family. It was his only vice, and one he acted upon responsibly, but it all ended when Santino was twelve years old and had discovered his father dead in his bedroom. Paramedics had later diagnosed it as a heart attack, something that happened to the best of people at the worst of times, and young Santino had lost something very special to him. The next day, a package came in the mail addressed to Santino's father, containing the very same knife Santino had carried until the day he'd lost it during our botched rescue attempt of young Nero. It was the last in his father's collection, and the only one he was allowed to keep when his mother had sold the rest to help pay for their move out of New York after she had remarried and given birth to Santino's half-brother.

As the story finished in my mind, I glanced at my friend, who stood dumbstruck by what he saw balancing in his palm. I couldn't remember the last time I'd seen Santino speechless, but he was now, like he was seeing his father again after all these years.

"H-how?" He finally stuttered. "Wh-where?"

Vespasian smiled. "It was sent to me during my time in Germany. It had a note on it saying to deliver it to 'the funny one,' but I had no idea what that meant at the time since Galba hadn't yet informed me of you people."

"Who sent it?" He asked.

"The note was simply signed: *Varus*."

Now Santino looked almost heartbroken. He dropped his hands to his lap and his jaw hung ajar. Every second Santino had spent around Varus, he had spent it pestering, annoying and bullying him. I wouldn't have blamed Varus one bit had he in fact *hated* Santino, but it had been a tremendous gesture to retrieve and send Santino's knife back to him, and while Santino knew Varus was dead, I wasn't sure if the reality of what that meant had truly sunk in until just now.

Slowly, Santino looked back up at Vespasian.

"Thanks," he said, his normally jovial disposition cast aside.

"You are welcome," Vespasian said. "We have sharpened it for you."

In response, Santino tossed his knife into the air and caught it in a reverse grip in preparation for a number of parlor tricks. He passed it from finger to finger before spinning it on a fingernail like a basketball, and then launched it into the air one last time, sheathing it as it fell. He'd removed his replacement blade mid toss, placing it in a bag once his old friend was secure.

His normal attitude returning, he threw a wink at Vespasian. "Thanks."

Vespasian nodded and turned back to me. "Now that formalities have been taken care of, let us return to business."

"I hope you mean the business of crucifying this man," Herod remarked dryly.

Vespasian offered the man a derisive look. "Herod, I am sorry about your shoulder, but leave it be, man. There are forces at work here that are far beyond you."

"Indeed?" Herod asked. "Please enlighten me."

"Sorry," I interrupted, "but you don't need to know."

"Do not speak to me, deceiver."

I rolled my eyes but ignored him.

"We need to go to Alexandria," I told Vespasian bluntly.

"Then go," Vespasian said, waving a hand. "You do not need my help to get there, and it is one of the few peaceful portions of this empire remaining. If you leave now you could be there within a week."

"Well..." I said, trailing off, "...Alexandria is only the first stop on a much longer journey, which is why we need your help."

"Is that so?" Vespasian asked. "And where will you go next?"

I worked my mouth, debating whether I should tell him or not, but then figured I should.

"Britain."

"And the help you desire?"

"The military kind."

Vespasian stood bemused but quiet, so I continued. "I need a few cohorts of legionnaires, an equal amount of auxilia, enough equipment for three times that size a force, and enough naval vessels to transport it all."

Vespasian snorted a sharp laugh. "Is that all?"

"What?!" Herod's face grew redder with each passing second. "You are not actually considering this, are you?"

"I'm not considering anything," Vespasian snapped. "Net yet."

I considered the stalwart Roman's words, not quite sure what he was thinking. My inability to read him had always unsettled me since our very first encounter, but I had to admit it was certainly a beneficial political tool. I tried to imagine his interactions with Agrippina, realizing that it must have been a bloodbath of wits.

"So, is that all?" Vespasian asked again. "I ask because you desire much, especially since you've returned to me without Agrippina, which we agreed you would do. And I would be most negligent were I not to mention that you have left this city, and this man here especially," he said indicating Herod, "in quite a state of disarray. And of course, we must not forget that it was your actions alone that have fractured this great empire into pieces."

I forced myself not to cringe. That very sentiment ran through my mind on a near hourly basis; I didn't need to start hearing it from him as well.

"What's happened?" I asked.

Vespasian didn't reply, but casually made his way back to his desk while Herod moved to stand behind the Roman, his good arm folded across his chest, clutching his injured one. I was still amazed at how familial these two were. Up until a few weeks ago, I, and every other historian for that matter, had no idea Herod and Vespasian had ever even met, let alone been buddies.

"It seems you are the catalyst for a great many things, Jacob Hunter," Vespasian said matter of factly. "I know little of what you consider 'history' from where you come from, but from what Galba told me, I assume Rome remained an empire for quite some time after the reign of Caligula, am I correct?"

"Yes, quite a while longer," I answered. "Centuries longer. Fourteen hundred years longer even some would argue," I finished, making the tired argument that Rome's true existence lasted till the end of the Byzantine Empire in 1453, an obscure fact only a sad few college students ever learned back home.

"Well," Vespasian said, "it seems we have quite the problem then."

"Please get to the point," Helena demanded, never one for historical digressions.

Vespasian smiled even though I suspected he had nothing to smile about.

"The vast empire of Rome has fractured," he said. "Rebellions have flared up all over the empire. The ceasefire with Germany has come to an end, resulting in Sarmatian aggression as well, Gaulic and Iberian nobles are growing restless in the west, the Parthians are ready to invade Anatolia in the east, and the Senate is completely divided on how to contain the situation, all the while their empress hasn't been present in Rome for over a year."

He paused, giving us time to let it all sink in.

I turned to Vincent. "Is all that possible?" I asked in English.

"Certainly possible," he answered after giving himself a moment to think, but he didn't seem willing to elaborate even if he could.

"Oh," Vespasian interrupted, "I believe I failed to include that Britain has rebelled against the legion I left there last year as well."

"Is that so…" I whispered, already seeing where this was going.

"It is," Vespasian said as he lurched to his feet, "so I have a proposition for you, Jacob Hunter. I give you everything you ask for and more, and in return… you reconquer Britain for me."

"Me?" I asked, truly stunned now.

"Not you alone, of course," Vespasian comforted as he sat on the edge of his desk with his arms crossed in front of him. "I have already sent a courier to Galba to make haste to Britain and await reinforcements. He is one of the most experienced military commanders I have available, and I believe he would be most happy to see you."

"I wouldn't bet on it," Santino said.

Vespasian ignored him. "I left only a single legion earlier this year under Legate Aulus Plautius' command when Agrippina ordered us to the German front," Vespasian elaborated. "I argued we needed at least another year to quell the countryside and leave no less than *three* legions to maintain control, but I was overruled."

"So how many are you sending with Galba?" I asked.

I tried to do the math in my head of how many legions were currently with Galba in Germany, Vespasian here, located in Britain, and scattered around the rest of the empire, but there were so many I couldn't nearly keep track of them all.

"Not a one," he answered

"Not a one, huh?" I repeated, growing suddenly frustrated. "What would you like me to do then? Win Britain over with my looks and charm alone?"

Vespasian smiled. "That will not be necessary, as I will be sending two legions with you instead: the *II Augusta* and the *XV Primigenia*. I believe you are familiar with the latter?"

"We worked with them five years ago when they were still training under Galba's tutelage," Vincent answered.

"Good, then you should be familiar with them. Furthermore, you will have one legion's worth of auxilia, the legion and its auxilia already present in Britain, and of course, you will have Galba."

"Oh good," Santino muttered.

I lifted a hand questioningly. "Wait, you're only giving me assets equivalent to what you wanted as a peace keeping force?"

"I have full faith in your abilities, Jacob Hunter. You can do things that ten legions cannot. Three legions should be enough."

I held Vespasian's eye for a second before I turned to my companions. Artie wore a blank expression, clearly not understanding a word we'd said. Wang looked interested, as did Vincent, while Helena looked worried and rubbed her belly distractedly. Santino, unsurprisingly, looked bored.

"What about Agrippina?" I asked, folding my arms to mirror Vespasian's posture.

"There is not much we can do about her for now, I'm afraid," Vespasian answered. "Word has reached me that she has taken her entire Praetorian force to deal with the Parthian threat, which I must lead as soon as I am done here, but, as fortune would have it," he said, clapping Herod on the shoulder, "Herod here has agreed to appeal to his forces to stand down, so I should be able to withdraw within the week."

"I would not have agreed to such terms had I known you would be working with *him*," Herod growled.

"Herod, for the love of the gods, will you shut up," Vespasian snapped, turning to glare at him. "This man did what he had to do. If you knew the full extent of his reasoning you would not be so quick to condemn. None of this, not even your arm, was personal."

"Wasn't personal!?" Herod shouted. "Thousands of Jews are dead, our peace with Rome in tatters, and people on both sides demand more blood, so how can you say this was not personal??"

I didn't want to frown, or show any kind of emotion, but I couldn't help it. Despite Vespasian's rationale, Herod was right. The killing of all those Jews and the deaths of all the Romans who had come to fight them was a tragedy that wouldn't have happened if not for my involvement, but I tried to think about the fact that I may have actually *saved* thousands of future lives. In all likelihood, the rebellion in Judea today had circumvented the rebellion that would have occurred twenty years from now, where even more Jews died in a much longer war.

I had to accept that justification. I had to.

"Herod," I said softly, and he finally lifted his eyes to meet my own, "please understand, there is more at stake here than you can possibly imagine. We used you, yes, and I'm sorry for that, but it was very necessary. Take comfort in the fact that should Vespasian wrest control from Agrippina, things will change for you and your people… for the better."

Herod stared at me with icy eyes, and I knew he would never trust me again. Something there indicated that if I ever saw him again, I'd better watch my back, but I only hoped he wouldn't get in the way now. There was too much at stake.

He held his predatory gaze on me before finally turning to Vespasian. "I am finished here."

He stomped out of the tent, but on his way out, made sure to bump against me with his good shoulder, muttering under his breath as he made his retreat. I felt a sharp pain in my side as he ricocheted off of me, and I winced and reached up to cover my wound with a hand as he stormed past

"Nice to see you too, buddy," Santino called out to his retreating backside. When Herod failed to respond as he finally disappeared, Santino turned back to me. "Don't people say goodbye anymore?"

I smirked at him as I rubbed my side, and turned back to Vespasian.

"He will be all right," he said. "He has a fiery temper, but a sound mind. We will soon have peace in the region, and I will be free to move on to more important matters."

I couldn't help but let out a small sigh of relief at that. "Good."

"Now, on to said more important matters," Vespasian said while moving to stand directly in front of me. "Tell me Jacob Hunter, would you consider a commission as legate of a legion?"

I blinked. "Me?? A general?"

"Why not? Were you not an officer in your country's navy once?"

"Well, yeah," I said feeling suddenly overwhelmed, "but I was of relatively low rank."

Vespasian chuckled. "I would not care if you had been but a simple foot soldier. You are our only option. I have been forced to reassign many legates in recent months and many tribunes have either fled back to Rome or are of worthless value. You will have a skeleton staff of officers, mostly administrative ones at that, but a full complement of centurions and I will also leave my own senior centurion with you. He goes by Fabius, and is a tough war master and not very sociable, but he is efficient and intelligent, and will serve you well."

"Well, uh..."

I tried to stall while I mulled over the possibility of actually becoming a member of the Roman legion. I'd once thought all the magic and childlike wonder I'd brought with me to Ancient Rome had died years ago, but I couldn't help but feel a small flutter of excitement at Vespasian's proposal. I turned to Helena who gave me a small smile, a look that said, *Come on, Jacob. You know this is something you've wanted since we got here.*

I nodded, and turned back to Vespasian. "So do I get some kind of ceremony?"

"No. As you are already technically a Roman citizen, there is little be needed done. I will have the official papers drawn up within the week before you set sail."

I frowned. "Rather anticlimactic, but fine. Anything else I should know?"

Vespasian squinted at me. "I wonder if I should ask why it is you wish to go to Britain at all, but I suspect it is for something beyond my understanding. Instead I will simply pray that the gods be with you as you begin your odyssey, and wish you luck upon your very first assignment as one of my generals."

"All right then," I said with a nod that must have seemed more confident than I felt. "Let's do it."

***

I still have vivid memories of packing for long trips as a kid.

My mom and dad would spend hours, sometimes a few days, gathering up all of our stuff before packing it away in the car. Clothes, toiletries, snacks, entertainment items, all that stuff. The whole process always seemed excessively involved and tedious to me as a kid, but those excursions were *nothing* compared to what I was preparing for now. Making matters even more difficult was that Caesarea was a disaster zone, and nearly devoid of any accessible supplies. The streets were strewn with rubble, decaying bodies, stray animals, and any semblance of civilization was all but gone. Residents were starting to rebuild, but there were only a few shops open that sold the things I now found myself in need of.

Without all the tribunes and magistrates normally associated with running a legion, I found myself quickly overwhelmed with all the administrative and logistical needs that came with running two of the damned things. Luckily, Brewster had volunteered her services to help oversee everything. Her family apparently owned an import/export business back home, and she'd spent her entire childhood dealing with procurement, trading, and business dealings.

She was a godsend, and oversaw the collection of everything from food to ensuring the Romans had appropriate attire for the coming wintry months in Britain, something I hadn't even thought about. She'd done a pretty good job so far, and since I had to basically finance this entire operation with the reward money Helena, Santino, and I had collected during our time as *Vani*, and since Vespasian had refused to pay me, I appreciated the fact that she was a shrewd businesswoman.

Despite her help, however, there was one item we needed that I couldn't let her handle. It was something I could barely bring myself to do, let alone ask someone else to do, because it was something I considered outright criminal: the purchasing of slaves to row our boats.

"Slaves?" I'd asked Vespasian a few days later after he had appropriated the vessels I needed, but without the needed hands.

"Of course. Who else are you going to have row your ships?"

"Hired hands of course," I said, the answer seeming obvious, not to mention historically relevant.

Vespasian shook his head. "You will not find anyone to do it. Not here. In normal circumstances rowers would be in fresh supply, but with so many displaced families and deceased locals, finding capable men will be near impossible. Slaves... however, are in abundant supply. Many have been with the legions since before Britain."

"Why can't we just use sails?" I asked, basically whining.

Vespasian shrugged. "Sails will get you where you want to go, but the Mediterranean is a very dangerous place. Many pirates still lurk in its waters even after Pompey did his best to exterminate them decades ago. You will need rowers to maneuver your ships should a time for battle arise."

I'd sighed, nodded, and moved on.

There was no getting around it. I had to purchase another human being – hundreds of them in fact, and it was a horrendous feeling. It made me feel evil. Even if the Romans didn't discriminate their slaves based on any physical or other attribute, it was still... *wrong*.

As I'd toured the slave pens, doing everything I could to keep myself from vomiting at the very fact that I was even there, I noted that most of the enslaved people were captured soldiers, but there were also many women, children, and families among them as well. Most of them were Jews, captured right here in Caesarea, but others were from all over, following Vespasian's legions as they traveled the empire, and it was with the families in mind that I did something no Roman would ever do when purchasing slaves: for every man I bought, I purchased a woman as well, and every preexisting family I could find.

The auction took place in the legion camp, and was much as I imagined slave dealerships in the old South during the time of American slavery. The location was muddy, dirty, grimy, and the stench of death was ever present in the air. Individuals were asked to stand on a platform wearing practically nothing, and were as groomed and clean as they could be. There they stood before potential buyers, and the auction would begin.

I was the only person in attendance.

It seemed slaves really weren't high on a Caesarean citizen's priority list these days.

My stomach churned when the first man was brought out for my inspection. I looked at him, measuring his physical fitness, and decided he'd be perfect. He was tall and broad in the shoulders, with long, curly red hair. I figured he was German. He stared at me coldly, and my stomach flipped over itself again as I turned to the dealer to announce my desire to buy him. Without anyone to bid against, I was given varying flat rates depending on the age and gender of the slave. The dealer signaled for the man to be taken to a holding area for pickup, and I did everything I could to not hate myself in that moment, again trying to justify it all by thinking that I was doing that man an enormous favor in the long run.

And so went one of the worst days of my life. I purchased hundreds of men and an equal number of women, passing over hundreds more. I made sure the dealer was aware that I wanted to keep families together, and he didn't seem to have any issue with that.

As a petite, young, blond woman stepped off the platform – the last to be purchased – I felt better about myself, having made sure that every woman, besides the ones who were already mothers, seemed young enough to bare children. Many were attractive as well, but there was no way I could bring myself to discriminate my purchases based on *that* qualifier, but finding ones able to start families seemed like the least I could do.

When she was out of sight, I paid the dealer for the damages, tipped him grudgingly by throwing a few pieces of silver at his feet, and tried to keep my mind on the future: when I would free them all the moment we landed on the shores of Britain, timeline altering ramifications be damned.

No other Roman slave holder would have done the same.

By the third day, I had my slaves and I had my ships, which were merchant vessels that Vespasian had ordered repurposed for military use. They were large, sturdy, quick, and wide enough to stand fifteen men abreast and fifty from bow to stern. Brewster began provisioning each ship as they became available, and by our seventh day in Caesarea, we were ready to go. Fully provisioned, manned, and loaded, we set forth into the sunset, ready to begin our next adventure.

As my flotilla pushed off into the calm waters of the Mediterranean, I stood at the stern railing of the ship I'd chosen as my command vessel, looking out over the water at the retreating city, wondering if I would ever see it again. It represented a dark place in my mind, a horrid reminder of my meddling in the past, and how I'd been responsible for so much death. Even with all my comforting thoughts of how it was better than the alternative, I couldn't help but feel extraordinarily sad.

I placed my elbows on the railing and held my hands against my cheeks, choosing to just lean there for a while as the city slowly grew smaller. I wasn't sure how long I'd been standing there when Helena walked up behind me and wrapped her arms around my waist, thankfully avoiding my wound that was finally healing properly. I was startled by her presence, but when she placed her head against my back, comfort returned.

"Vespasian's heading north," Helena reported, her sniper's eyes always sharp.

I looked up and noticed a thin line of Roman troops marching northwards along the coast. Barely the size of ants on the horizon, I saw what looked like a small contingent of horses, and wondered if Vespasian was there, hoping to God that he could pull the empire back together again if he was.

It was the only way I could ever really live with myself at the end of all this.

"Think we'll ever see him again?" Helena asked quietly.

"Probably," I replied, pushing off the railing and turning so that my back was to the water. I reached out and pulled Helena into my arms and held her tightly against my chest.

"Good," she said. "Because I still want to marry him."

I squeezed her tighter and pressed my cheek against her flowing, black hair, unable to bear letting go in that moment for fear that she'd disappear forever. Doing everything I could to keep such a horrible thought from my mind, I forced a smile and closed my eyes, wishing instead for this moment to last forever.

IV
Alexandria

The Mediterranean Sea
October, 42 A.D.

The seas were cool this time of year, even this far south, which was especially true once the sun went down. They were tranquil and placid, and on this particular night, the second since leaving Caesarea, there was no wind, so the slaves below were at their oars, methodically pulling the ship to the beat of a faint drum. As moments went, this one was as peaceful as they came, and out over the open water with no visible threats nearby, I allowed myself to close my eyes and do little more than enjoy the wind on my face.

I stood at the helm, my favorite olive drab fleece keeping me warm, while Santino stood nearby as well. As legate of the legion, I was not only its general, but also admiral of the fleet. I had free reign to do what I wanted, but the perks really were minimal. My ship was neither big nor fancy, and my personal state room was nothing more than a secluded corner below deck, separated from everyone else by a drawn curtain.

Admirals in the U.S. Navy back home were at least allowed pets with them.

Or was that just in the movies? It'd been so long, I couldn't really remember anymore.

I did get to name my first mate, however, which was kind of cool, and I picked Santino of course. He was competent enough, and his attitude made him good with the troops and sailors. He didn't have much of an official role, but his job was to make sure people were doing their jobs and to maintain morale. He also made sure the slaves – and I hated that word almost as much as the word 'fate' – were kept well fed, respected, and given some semblance of their humanity back. They wore no chains and their food was equal in portion and cleanliness to everyone else's. They'd been surprised by that, but I was trying to do everything I could to show them that their incarceration was only temporary, although I wasn't sure anything could convince them of my intention to free them once we reached Britain.

At least their doubt would make the surprise that much more fulfilling when I actually did.

But I would have to deal with that later, hoping simply that we arrived there in one piece. The voyage to Alexandria would only take about a week, and the weather had been calm so far, but I knew the trip to Britain would be another story. It would take at least a month to get there, and it was almost winter. If we overstayed our welcome in Alexandria, the last leg of our trip to the British Isle was going to be choppy, cold, and treacherous. While I may have been in the U.S. Navy and was therefore a 'sailor,' a seaman I most certainly was not, but at least we had a competent crew with us. In the meantime, Santino, Cuyler, Bordeaux, and I were taking time at the helm to hone the craft of basic seamanship.

"Hey, Jake, what's on your mind, buddy?" I heard Santino call over the faint sloshing noise of the ship cutting its way through the sea.

"That it's cold out here," I said, reopening my eyes. "Hurry up with that blankie already."

"It's not a blanket," he said with a pout, setting his needle and thread to his piece of cloth again.

I had no idea what he was doing exactly, only that he'd been sewing something onto a simple piece of black cloth about the size of child's bed sheet for the past two days now.

"Besides," he continued, "it's almost finished. Should be done tonight."

"Well, what is it then? Don't keep me waiting in suspense."

He smiled. "Nope. Gotta wait until tomorrow. I thought you snipers were supposed to be patient?"

I peered at him through the darkness, hoping to catch a glimpse of what he was doing, but there wasn't much to see. I gave up and turned back to my duties, readying myself for another hour at the helm before Cuyler took over, hoping he'd have a better chance of deducing whatever it was Santino was doing.

For all our sakes…

***

I rolled out of bed eight hours after Cuyler had relieved me, and I could see sunshine through the cracks in the hull and I knew it had to be around noon. With a great stretch of my arms, I yawned and smacked my lips, realizing I was very thirsty. I reached out and made for the wine jug that sat atop a cabinet next to my hammock, but while my hand encountered a hard object, it failed to find a grip on the carafe's handle. Squinting blurrily through one eye, I tried to zero in on my target, but was too slow to pull my hand away when I noticed that where my wine jug should have been, the blue orb now sat.

I should have flung it away or snapped my hand back immediately when recognition set in, but I did neither. I simply held my hand against its smooth, blue surface and looked at it, noticing that while it seemed inert, there was a faint warmth emanating from it, although I assumed such a phenomenon could have been caused by the sun.

I breathed out a quick breath, thankful I hadn't activated it.

While I'd snuck the orb out before, I'd always taken extra care not to make skin contact with it, which seemed like a reasonable precaution, but that didn't answer the mystery of why it was here now or how it had come to sit upon my nightstand in place of my much more desirable wine jug. Since I was fairly certain it couldn't move on its own, my first thought was that someone must have brought it here.

But who?

Did I have a mystery on my hands that would only serve to confound me at every turn?

Had it been Colonel Santino in the slave quarters with the Roman *gladius* who had committed the deed?

Or perhaps the orb really was an 80s B-Horror movie-type creature, stalking me.

I sighed as I pulled the orb off the shelf and into my lap. I really didn't have the time or the patience to steer this story into the mystery section and out of the action/adventure genre. I hadn't the mind for compiling alibis and questioning witnesses, and I certainly couldn't ask anyone I trusted to do it for me. The second they knew I had the orb again, they'd immediately assume I'd gone looking for it myself, and had concocted the mystery plot to simply throw them off my trail.

Agatha Christie's Detective Poirot would have seen right through such a thinly veiled guise in a matter of...

Wait, what was I thinking? I hadn't actually gone looking for the orb myself.

Had I?

I...

"Lieutenant Hunter?"

At the sound of the voice I scrambled to hide the orb. It was distant, still a few steps away, so I had maybe five seconds to think of something. I flung my head from side to side, searching for somewhere to hide it, but finally decided to simply sit on it, hoping the giant bulge under my butt wouldn't show that noticeably through the hammock.

With a second left, I composed myself and turned to my curtain-drawn entranceway, just in time to see Technical Sergeant Patricia Martin draw the curtain aside. Her short hair was disheveled and her eyes looked tired, as though she too had just awoken. I let out a breath of relief at the sight of her, knowing I couldn't have hidden the orb from Helena, but then I shook my head angrily, covering my fear.

"What did I tell you about the rank stuff, Patricia?" I asked. "We don't use it much around here anymore. We're all in this together. Call me Jacob, or Hunter if that's all you can manage."

She didn't look sheepish at her mistake, but simply nodded. "Sorry, Jacob. Old habits..."

"Die hard, I know," I supplied for her. "No big deal."

She cocked her head to the side. "I was going to say 'are hard to let die' but I like yours better. *Die hard*. Nice."

"Oh, my God..." I mumbled as I pinched my nose and shut my eyes, but I managed to recover from my annoyance quickly. "So what are you doing here?"

"Sorry," she said, back to business, "but your presence is required above deck."

I groaned. "Why? Did Santino or Wang set something on fire?"

"I... don't think so, but I really don't know. Santino asked me to get you. Quite rudely actually. I was still sleeping."

"Get used to it," I said, rolling my eyes. "Thanks, Pat. I'll be up in a second."

"Don't call me that," she said, her voice hard, but then she disappeared without further explanation.

I held my eyes on the spot she'd just vacated and shook my head again. Even more idiosyncrasies I had to figure out. Great. Just what I needed.

I pushed it from my mind as I pulled the orb out from under me and stared at it again. I still hadn't confirmed what it was that made it work in some instances but not in others, but I knew I wasn't going to figure it out now. I hopped out of my hammock and found my small Roman-style footlocker I'd recently pressed into service. I opened it up and spread out my little treasures, making space for the orb.

Helena wouldn't go snooping in here so it seemed like the best place to hide it.

Once the space was clear, I lowered my newest treasure into place gently, and with one last longing look at the orb, I placed a spare t-shirt over it, closed the locker's lid, and then immediately forgot why I'd pulled my footlocker out from beneath my cabinet to begin with.

***

After washing up, I found the stairs that led to the deck and started my ascent, banging my head on a low cross beam in the process. A burst of pain exploded from my forehead, and my body sent a hand to clutch it soothingly. My other hand went up to brace myself against the offending crossbeam, and I let myself just hang there for a while, my eyes squeezed painfully shut. When the initial shock wore off, I straightened and glared at the offending piece of wood, but grudgingly didn't try to get even with it, knowing I'd then have two body parts that hurt. With one last sneer in its direction, I finished my climb and emerged into a scene straight from the movies.

There were men climbing the beams and masts that held the ships sails, others were literally "swabbing the deck," while even others cleaned swords or practiced hand to hand combat. Although we left most of the legionnaires below deck to keep a low profile, we'd set up a rotation schedule that allowed each of them an hour of time in the fresh air every day. They enjoyed the looseness of time above deck, but there was always a centurion around that never let things get too unruly. In fact, one of my more junior centurions was currently running a static calisthenics drill with some of the legionnaires and Archer's troops, save for Patricia Martin who had arrived above deck only a minute before I had, and Alex Cuyler, who was asleep.

I turned my attention sternward toward a raised portion of the deck that held the ship's wheel. Helena was currently there, leaning against the railing, chatting with Santino, who looked considerably different than he had last night. I made my way toward them, throwing a visibly winded Archer a smirk which he returned with a glare.

The trip only took a few seconds, and I bounded up the steps to the second level two at a time, and finally got a good look at Santino as he turned to face me, causing me to pull up short on the last step and simply stare.

He was wearing a makeshift three point hat, had an eye patch over his left eye, wore a puffy shirt open to his waist, and also wore loose fitting linen pants tucked into his combat boots. He'd also grown out his beard again, and looked just like...

A fucking pirate.

"When the hell did you think this one up?" I asked him, finally taking the last step up to the stern deck.

"Oh," he said easily, "this scheme came to me years ago. I was just waiting for us to get a boat."

He took a step toward me with a fake limp, and I almost expected to see him with a peg leg, but luckily he hadn't gone so far as to ask Wang to surgically remove one of his legs just for the joke. Once he was beside me, he grabbed me by the shoulder and spun me around to face the forward mast.

"Check that out," he said.

I looked and found the black cloth he'd been working on last night, flapping violently in the afternoon breeze. Upon it was a white symbol ubiquitous amongst all early modern pirates.

A skull and crossbones.

The Jolly Rodger.

I smacked my forehead with the palm of my hand.

"Pretty gnarly, right?" He asked excitedly.

Helena was chuckling in the background and I forced myself to glance back at the flag again. It was childishly done, nowhere near what you saw in a movie, but the image was obvious.

I placed my hand on Santino's shoulder and looked at him. "You have serious issues, my friend."

He winked at me. "Oh, you ain't seen nothing yet."

He punctuated his announcement by drawing a curved sword from a scabbard at his waist, another costume ensemble he must have picked up from Middle Eastern Caesarea, and leapt down the half dozen stairs to the deck below, landing with his knees bent and his hands out in front of him like he was preparing to wrestle.

"Aargh, ye maties!" He growled at Archer and his breathless cohorts. "Ye scallywags ain't got yer sea legs yet! Avast!"

My eyes went wide as I watched him prance about the deck, yelling and cussing in his pirate accent.

Helena walked up to me and placed a hand on my shoulder. "He'll never change."

"Unfortunately, you're probably right," I replied. "I just hope the other kids don't make fun of him too much when we send him off to school someday."

She smiled. "Let's hope."

I turned to face her and took her left hand in my own. I gave her a smile and inspected her face, noticing that she looked a little tired, perhaps sick.

"Feeling all right?" I asked. "The sea making you queasy at all?"

"No worse than usual, which thankfully hasn't been that bad anyway," she said with a frown. "But if the water gets any rougher, that may change. My mother once told me that her pregnancy with me had been pretty easy, no real sickness to speak of, so luckily it seems that I'm in the same..." she paused and smirked at me, "boat as she was."

I had to smile. "Funny."

"I thought so, but I have to admit, this morning was a little rough."

"Sorry," I said. "I wish there was something I could do to help."

"Oh, you've already done enough as it is, Lieutenant Hunter," she said with a sly smile. "This is entirely *your* fault, after all."

"Mine?" I replied flippantly. "I'm completely innocent in all this."

"Uh-huh, sure you are. If you were so innocent, you wouldn't have done this to me without at least marrying me first."

Her tone was light hearted and playful, but it did sting a little. We'd never really talked about marriage, but it was something I knew we both really wanted. I only wish I knew how to go about doing it around here.

"Well," I said, "if that's really what you want, I did name Santino as my first mate."

She looked at me blankly, not understanding.

"You know," I continued, grabbing her arm and leading her toward the deck's inner railing so that she could look out at those below us. "As captain, technically I have the power to marry people at sea..." I paused for affect, "...and so does my first mate."

She stared at me with the same wide eyes I'd had when watching Santino frolic about the deck a minute ago, and we turned in unison to find him maneuvering a wooden plank out over the port railing.

He weighed it down with some ballast and demanded someone, "Walk the plank! Aaaaargh!"

Stryker immediately shoved Brewster toward him, and others gathered in on the fun by grabbing her arms and leading her toward the plank. She struggled and pleaded but Santino held his sword high and ordered her forward, and I only prayed he wasn't stupid enough to actually go through with it. In order to absolve myself of any responsibility should he do so, I turned back to Helena and folded my arms across my chest, and saw her already staring at me angrily.

"You can't marry people," Helena accused. "That's just one of your stupid movie things."

I cocked an eyebrow at her. "Are you sure?"

"No. Way," she said, poking my chest with a finger. "That isn't even remotely funny."

I laughed as I rubbed my struck chest. "It's a little funny."

"Not. Even. A little." She said with a series of small punches.

***

A few days later, and with thankfully all hands still aboard, the grand city of Alexandria came into view on the horizon. I stood at the helm, my sweaty hands gripping the wheel tightly, surprised at how excited I was. Every time I encountered something new in this lost place in time, I was surprised at how giddy I became. Despite my recent jaded disposition, discovering new locations or artifacts still enthralled me, and helped me focus by pushing the angry and moody portions of my mind away, locking them up and allowing me a fresh perspective. Of course, it didn't hurt that I was about to bear witness to not one, but two, of the greatest wonders of the ancient world that were lost two thousand years before I was born:

The Lighthouse and Library of Alexandria.

Both were long gone well before my time, the library damaged and then destroyed a number of times, and the lighthouse probably having just fallen away over the course of time. I wasn't exactly sure what had happened to it, but I knew tourists could book scuba dives near the port of Alexandria back in the future to see its ruins.

As for the library, if I remembered correctly, it was first put to the torch accidentally by Julius Caesar when fighting a battle there. It was speculated by some that he had actually destroyed the entire thing, but the subject was controversial, and I'd never put much stock in it, especially since Varus' note told me to go there now.

"Ten degrees to port," the Roman standing next to me ordered.

I glanced at him when his words broke me from my thoughts, nodded, and did as I was told.

The man didn't exactly use such precise terminology, but he knew what he was doing. He was short and bald, with a slight paunch running through his midsection. He was the merchant who owned the flotilla of boats we'd procured, but even though I had paid him handsomely for their use, he wasn't overly fond of being coopted by the military. He'd just sailed into Caesarea a few days after we had arrived ourselves, having had no idea that it had become a war zone.

And he hadn't been very happy.

"How's that?" I asked once my adjustment was completed.

"Better," he said approvingly, "but you are still sloppy. You have to pick a position on the horizon when approaching land and steer us toward it... not let your mind wander and crash us into very large rocks!!"

"I'll keep that in mind, Gnaeus."

He grunted an acknowledgment and went back to ignoring me.

I smiled. The man only tolerated me more than my friends because I was the one lining his pockets, but that didn't mean he was particularly friendly. He was only tolerant, which was fine with me. I didn't need any more friends on this trip. Things were getting crowded enough around here as it was.

"Hunter..." Gnaeus growled again, spurring me back into action.

I quickly shifted the wheel in response. "Sorry."

"Sorry will not keep us from smashing into very large rocks!"

"Enough with the *very large rocks* already, I said I was..."

"Anything the matter, boys?" Came the sweet voice of Helena from the steps.

We both straightened at her voice, and I glared at Gnaeus when it seemed like he was trying too hard to impress her, and he gave me a snobbish look in return.

"Everything's fine," I replied. "Isn't it, Gnaeus?"

"Of course," he replied.

Helena smiled at the Roman and put her hand on his shoulder. "I hope my dear Jacob hasn't been too much of a bother. He can be quite dense sometimes, believe me."

I tilted my head back and rolled my eyes, but kept my attention on our course.

"Can't you, dear?" She asked, moving to stand next to me and wrap an arm around me. She shot up on her toes and planted a small kiss on my cheek.

"Umm... sure," I answered.

Gnaeus grunted and looked away.

"Yes, well, he certainly can be," he said. "Now, if you will excuse me, I must prepare my things before we reach land." He paused mid-step. "Try not to crash us into the lighthouse, Hunter."

"Yes, sir!" I replied cheerily.

The cantankerous Roman merchant left, and Helena and I watched him go.

"You're welcome," she said.

I chuckled. "You won't be when I actually crash us into very large rocks."

"Oh please, you'll do fine. Just don't let me distract you."

"No more kisses then, if you please."

She smiled and kissed me anyway, but I managed to keep us on course.

Somehow.

***

For the next twenty minutes, I kept my attention locked on our destination and nothing else: a small dock near the southern edge of the city. It wasn't near the lighthouse, much to my dismay, but Gnaeus knew the dockhand and guaranteed us a safe place to keep the legionnaires aboard secret. Hopefully, we would only need to stay here a few days, but I had no way of guaranteeing that. If we stayed any longer than that, we'd have to devise some kind of schedule so they could get out and stretch their legs.

But one thing at a time.

For now, I had to make sure I parked this thing in a way that kept it from being smashed to pieces, but thankfully Gnaeus had returned not long after he'd left, and helped me maneuver us in, keeping his comments civil this time, probably because Helena was still around. He signaled to a man near the steps leading below deck, and a few seconds later I heard the rhythmic beating of the rowers' drum cease. They then pulled in their oars so that wind power could guide us the rest of the way in, while sailors collapsed a number of sails as well to slow us down. I bit my tongue as I made gentle course corrections, making sure I lined up our approach perfectly. Santino, meanwhile, stood at the bow of the deck with his right foot on the railing, guiding us in with his upraised sword – ever helpful.

"Careful…" Gnaeus whispered. "Careful…"

"Yeah, yeah," I mumbled as I pulled us in alongside the dock. "I'll show you careful…"

"Careful…"

But we were still going too fast. Unsure if it was my fault or not, I clung to the wheel in a death grip. A few seconds later, everyone aboard lurched forward as we crashed into the dock, and I watched as Santino was pitched over the railing and a few others on the upper deck fell to the main deck only a few feet below. I heard something crack loudly as we came to a stop and noticed Helena run forward to check on Santino.

Gnaeus was already glaring at me.

"Sounds expensive," I remarked.

He kept his gaze fixed on me for only a little longer before he tore his eyes away and stormed down the steps, shouting for someone to help him survey the damage. I looked for Helena and found her waving me over. I ran to meet her and followed her finger over the railing to the dock below. There I found Santino sprawled out on top of a smashed vendor stall, jumping fish scattered all around him.

"You okay?" I yelled down to him.

He moved his head slowly to look up at us.

"Yeah," he grunted. "Fish broke my fall."

He reached beneath him and pulled out a wiggling fish, and I let out a sigh of relief.

If he'd been hurt, I'd have never heard the end of it.

Helena patted my back.

"Ready?" She asked.

I looked at her. "Yep. Let's get this crazy train moving."

***

Thirty minutes later, every single temporally displaced member of our group was walking through the streets of Alexandria along with Gaius, Marcus, Madrina, and Titus, who hobbled along with Vincent's help. Much like Caesarea and Damascus, Alexandria had a very Middle Eastern vibe to it, only far more posh and upscale than their modern equivalents, and this city in particular was something special. Buildings were immaculate, dirt and dust were negligible, people walked to and fro at their leisure, and the city hustled and bustled like any twenty first century metropolitan city. The buildings were shaded in tans, browns, and whites while red brick and green shrubs littered the streets and walls in an impressive show of opulence.

"It's beautiful," Artie remarked from beside Helena.

"Eh," Santino uttered, walking at her other side, "seen one of these stupid cities, you've seen them all. I'm sure we'll be responsible for destroying it within the week, anyway."

I ground my teeth at the comment.

I knew he was just joking, but I wished he'd at least keep comments like that to himself.

"It is quite lovely," Archer said, but no one really cared what he had to say and stayed quiet, so he decided to continue. "But what exactly are we doing here again?"

"We've been over this," I replied. "This is where Varus wanted me to go. We're to meet a researcher that works at the Library of Alexandria and ask him about what Varus was working on before he was recalled to Rome. Then we go from there."

"What could we possibly hope to find in a library?" Archer demanded.

"I was wondering the same thing," Helena mumbled, still not thrilled with the idea of me in a library.

"How should I know?" I snapped. "But did Varus tell *you* to go somewhere else?"

Archer shook his head, not happy.

"Well there you go! We go to the fucking library then! If Varus left us some crumbs to follow, we should be able to figure something out."

"Ignore him, Jacob," Artie said, but then heaved a deep breath. "I only wish we spoke the local language, or any of these languages for that matter. I don't see how I can help."

"If we come across something technical, your expertise could come in handy."

"Then maybe I should stay on the ship?" She suggested. "It could be dangerous. We…"

"You'll be fine, Artie," I promised. "You have plenty of protection."

"Jacob, I've seen your scars," she said, but paused to look amongst the group as we walked. "I've seen all of your scars, and I know *you*, at least, didn't have them before you got here, and I assume they didn't either. This place is dangerous and I'm not a soldier."

"Just stick with Archer and his team. They don't understand the language either, but are still fully capable of defending you."

"Don't forget me," Santino said, sliding up beside Artie to loop his arm through her own. "Protecting beautiful women is a specialty of mine."

Artie patted his arm and rested her head against his shoulder momentarily as she smiled.

I frowned, but then thought of something.

"See Artie? You're well protected. You've even got your very own pirate bodyguard willing to lay down his life to save your own. Isn't that right, Mr. Pirate?"

Santino's look wasn't very confident, but he managed a nod.

Who the hell did he think he was fooling? It wasn't like I was going make this easy on him. It's what big brothers are for.

"So," I started again, "why don't we find some kind of lodging arrangements and rest up for a bit. Then some of us will go to the library while the rest of you do some sightseeing. How about that?"

"I suppose that will work," Artie agreed nervously.

"Great. Let's get to it then."

***

"What am I doing here, Hunter?" Archer asked impatiently, hours later.

"Providing backup," I replied carefully, not wanting to rile him up.

The truth was that I wanted to keep an eye on him, but it wasn't like I could just tell him that. The last thing I needed right now was to alienate him. I didn't want to risk open conflict between the two teams, but I still didn't trust him. I couldn't shake the feeling that he had some kind of ulterior motivations here, so the closer I kept my eye on him the better.

"And because I know you," I clarified. "At least, I knew a version of you, and I'm confident he, at least, could watch my back."

"I'm thrilled by your confidence," Archer said. "Your voice is just dripping with earnestness."

I grudgingly held back further comment, as his tone was no more supportive than my own, and I was reminded how careful I had to tread with him.

Luckily, the great Library of Alexandria was coming into view, and I couldn't be more excited. We were still a few hundred meters out, but I could see the complex of buildings in detail already. It was enormous, with a cream colored façade and large marble columns running along the length of maybe two dozen buildings that stretched out in a semicircle. Dozens of steps led up to the magnificent structure's central entrance and there were hundreds of scholarly looking men loitering about, deep in conversation.

It was as if Raphael's painting, *The School of Athens*, had come to life – only set in Alexandria.

Were these actual ancient philosophers or historians who'd come to Alexandria to study and cogitate on meaning of life stuff? Sure the likes of Aristotle and Plato were long gone, but acute thinkers still existed today, and besides Athens, I could think of no better place for learned men to gather. As we grew closer, I could see some men weren't simply talking, but were engaged in heated debate, and a part of me wanted nothing more than to jump right in and argue with one of these guys about whatever the topic of conversation was.

"Down, boy," Helena said from beside me, knowing what I was thinking.

I gave her a grin but reluctantly complied.

As my small retinue made its way up the exterior staircase, Helena covered her long, dark hair and her face with a shawl. This wasn't the Middle East that was so vigorously repressive of women from back home, but even these days, women weren't necessarily welcome in male dominated places either, so while Helena's veil wouldn't conceal her identity as a woman completely, it would at least discourage the men from staring.

Also along for the ride were Vincent and Wang – Vincent for his historical knowledge and Wang for his band aids, as we so often needed.

It took us nearly a full minute to make our way up the long, wide staircase and enter the building, and the interior did not fail to impress either. Like the nave of a great Romanesque cathedral, the library's main anteroom was as large as it was opulent, with a vaulted ceiling, hallways that led to other rooms, and exterior porticos that dotted its perimeter and led to other buildings. The circular interior of the large room we found ourselves in was lined with shelving ranges that created concentric rings that grew increasingly smaller as they reached the room's center, which was dominated by a large desk that I could see through a gap in the shelves. It was staffed by what I assumed were librarians, and I saw young pages hustling about with gathered documents and scrolls in their arms.

It was a sight that induced real excitement, even to my cynical self.

Having worked at a library back in college, I knew something about the inner workings of one, but seeing it on such scale here was breathtaking. So many documents. So many people. So much gathered knowledge in one place. But how many of these treasured artifacts were lost and forgotten by the time I was born? Maybe all of them. A simple fire could extinguish all this knowledge in the blink of the eye, something that I guess had actually happened.

What a shame.

I frowned, but was distracted by a tall, slender librarian approaching our position from the central desk.

"May I help you?" He asked, giving us an odd look. We were in local clothing, but it was impossible for us to ever really blend in with a crowd. We were just too weird.

"Yes," I answered easily. "We're looking for a Flavius Rumella. Is he in today?"

The man arched an eyebrow at us almost imperceptibly, and hesitated.

"He is... but may I ask what this is concerning?"

"I'm sorry, but I am not at liberty to say. A friend of mine was conducting some important research with him, and I've come to help."

"I see." His eyes narrowed and he looked about ready to turn around and leave us hanging, but then he waved for us to follow him. "Well, do come this way. He is in the Barbarian Mythology Research Wing, and has been there for quite some time. He refuses to leave and often sleeps there, and we are forced to bring him food for fear that he will die there and leave a smell. I am not too sure how keen he will be to receive guests."

"We'll take our chances."

The man hummed dismissively, and I glanced at Helena, whose bright green eyes suggested amusement. She jerked her head in his direction and we hurried to catch up.

Once we left the central atrium, the trip lasted a few minutes, with nothing but hundreds of thousands of scrolls and studious men intent on reading every single one lining every nook and cranny in the place, including the hallways. We continued through a second scroll laden hallway before entering another large circular atrium, although it wasn't nearly as big as the main one. I'd thought we'd arrived when the librarian continued his path around to the right and down yet another hallway before depositing us into a square room the size of a small gymnasium.

The librarian held out a hand and beckoned us in.

"The Barbarian Mythology Research Wing," he reported.

There must have been another ten thousand scrolls in this room.

"All of this is just for 'barbarian' mythology?" I asked.

The librarian smiled. "Oh no. Certainly not. This room merely contains the recorded information we possess on the mythologies of Rome's northern neighbors. Mostly Celtic, but some Germanic and Sarmatian as well. It is actually one of our smaller collections, but no less important I assure you. The other wing is comprised of mostly Egyptian lore, and we have entire buildings dedicated to Roman and Greek mythology nearby."

I turned to give him an amused look. "Shouldn't Roman mythology be in the barbarian wing too?"

He snapped his head up and sniffed derisively at me, turned on his heels, and stormed out of the room without another word.

"What was that about, Hunter?" Archer asked, watching him go.

I smiled. "The Greek word for "barbarian" really means little more than, 'those who don't speak Greek.' People in modern times obviously think of barbarians as something more...*barbaric* than just that, but Romans generally use the word with only its original meaning. I just find it funny how they always try to lump themselves in with the Greeks, even though they're a different culture completely, and while I'm sure most of the guys here speak Greek, your general Roman citizen certainly does not. It's funny."

Archer clearly didn't seem to understand what was so funny about it, but while Vincent looked humored by my comment, he shook his head at me.

"What?" I asked him.

"Jacob, you don't speak Greek either."

"Yeah... but... "I tried to think of a counter argument, "...well, at least I don't go around calling people barbarians."

He smiled and nodded humorously at my point as Helena grabbed my arm and pulled me along behind her.

"Christ, let's just find Rumella already!" She cried.

I chuckled and fell into step behind her, but it wasn't long before we stumbled upon the only occupant currently residing within the dusty and exceptionally musty room. There must have been mold lurking in this place as well because I suddenly felt my sinuses acting up. As for the man, he was hunched over a document, holding a candle to enhance the dim natural light that was leaking through an open window. He didn't even flinch at our arrival, so I cleared my throat to get his attention. He jumped at the noise and immediately looked annoyed.

"I told you, I am not finished yet! I don't have time to inventory the east wing of the Scipio Africanus collection. I am too busy for such nonsense."

The collection on Scipio Africanus alone required more than one wing?

Goodness.

"I'm sorry," I said. "I believe you have us confused with someone who actually works here. We're looking for Flavius Rumella and were directed here."

The man looked at us with a gaunt and lined face. His eyes were small and sat recessed deep within their sockets, and his expression looked tired and weak, but masked in a thick, gray beard. He was a small man as well, with boney arms.

"I am Flavius Rumella," he indicated. "Who are you?"

"We're friends of Marcus Va..."

"Jacob Hunter!?" He asked excitedly, shooting to his feet in a way that contradicted his age. "Is that you?"

"Well, yes, actually. It's nice to meet y…"

"Never mind that!" He yelled excitedly. "Do you have it? Do you have it?"

I glanced at Vincent and then Helena before back at Rumella. "Have what?"

"The orb of course! Remus' orb!"

I stood there in a state of shock. How could this tertiary, red-shirt character whom I'd just met know about such an integral plot detail?

"And what exactly do you know about that?" I asked suspiciously.

"Know?" He repeated. "Why, I know everything about it, Jacob Hunter. Everything!"

***

I paused cautiously.

Nope. Not buying it.

"If Varus told you of me," I started, "you should already know that I am not one for hyperbole, so you'd better start at the beginning."

"Of course!" The old historian cried. "But where are my manners, please sit down. Would you like refreshment?"

"We're fine," I said, taking a seat while the rest of my troupe settled in around me. I gestured in their direction. "These are my friends: Helena, Vincent, Archer, and Wang."

The old man blinked rapidly at the oddity of their names, and his jaw dropped at Helena as she removed the shawl from around her head. He quickly recovered and coughed into his hand.

"Charmed," he said with a weak bow in her direction. "You must forgive my reaction, miss, but there aren't many women who visit the great library."

"That's because your society is too busy repressing them and keeping them from growing brains of their own," Helena countered darkly.

"That is in fact not true," Rumella disputed without missing a beat. "In fact, any good historian would tell you that women have played an integral part in singlehandedly turning the tides of destinies and empires. Women have always been, in fact, exceptionally keen, and history is remembered as it is due in large part to their contribution. Take Livia, Augustus' wife. She..."

I had to smile at Helena as Rumella went on.

I wasn't sure if she'd been trying to legitimately scold the man, but he had deflected her comments quite easily, an impressive feat, since most men who encountered Helena's scorn usually came out of it flustered or confused.

I continued listening to Rumella speak of Livia, a topic I could listen to all day, but Helena glared at him angrily, and he quickly got the message and trailed off.

"Still..." Rumella said, clearing his throat, "...you do make a valid point that many women are not educated as well as they should be. A few may become learned individuals, some pursuing their studies even here, but there is a reason why they are discouraged from a life of scholarly pursuit; for it is the foolish man who does not fear the day when women are as evenly educated as they are, as women would certainly then no longer have a need for man, and the world would most likely be better for it."

He smiled at Helena and she smiled back, twisting her head around toward me and holding out a finger in his direction. "I think I like this guy."

"Yeah, I bet you do," I said, directing my attention back to Rumella as I lowered her hand to the table for her. "So, about the orb..."

"Yes, yes," he said quickly, finally taking his own seat, "I was just getting to that. It all started when young Varus came to the Great Library just five months ago. He spent an enormous amount of time here in this section reading everything he could, but the exciting work was not begun until two months later.

"Now, you must understand, this portion of the library does not receive much attention. There is not much scholarly work left to be done on barbarian mythologies, nor was there ever much to begin with, so it was to my great surprise that I found someone so willing to spend such an inordinate amount of time here."

"I see," I said. "So you just took it upon yourself to find out what Varus was working on?"

"There was nothing malicious about it, I assure you. I am simply a curious old fellow, and have become quite interested in oddities in my old age, and this room is filled with many."

"Had you already heard of Remus' orb before and suspected a connection?" Vincent asked quickly.

"Are you joking, sir? No one had heard of Remus' orb except Varus and anyone else you've told. It is an oddity to displace all oddities. The ultimate mystery. And it has overwhelmed my life ever since Varus invited me to help him in his research."

I cleared my throat. "Rumella, I think you should know that Varus is dead."

He stared at me blankly. "Truly?"

"Yes."

"Such a shame," he said as he shook his head. "Such a fine scholar. A man with his finger on the tip of a true discovery, not the nonsense the men outside endlessly debate. He was a brilliant man. I... I shall miss him."

"So will I," I said softly.

Helena took that moment to jump in, cutting the tension. "He died getting us the information we needed to find you."

"Then his death was not wasted," Rumella said triumphantly. "Now that you are here, Jacob Hunter, all will be revealed, and we will work on getting you and yours home."

"Don't bullshit me, Rumella," I said.

"I know not what the shit of bulls has to do with your predicament, but I assure you, I speak the truth."

"So let's get started then," I said.

Rumella sighed and glanced out the window where dusk had fallen. I hadn't even noticed, nor had I seen the staff members that must have surreptitiously swept through the room minutes ago, lighting the dozen or so candles here.

"The day is late, and I have not rested soundly for many weeks," Rumella indicated, "but now that you are here, I feel I can finally rest easy. Would it be impolite to ask that we reconvene in the morning?"

"We're actually in a bit of a hurry," I said. "Perhaps you can hit the key points tonight? For an hour maybe?"

"Yes, yes, of course," he replied wearily. "You must be excited to finally understand everything that has befallen you these past five years. Of course. But, where to begin?"

"Let's start with where the orb comes from," Vincent suggested. "Where could such an object originate?"

"Aha!" Rumella cried, his fatigue disappearing. "A most astute question. Perhaps the most important one as well. And in fact one you may be able to have answered by someone who has firsthand knowledge of it."

"But it's seven hundred years old," Vincent commented.

"Indeed. Of course I do not mean to imply the same person, but I do believe the group responsible for its existence still resides within the confines of the Roman Empire."

"Druids," I said. "In Britain."

"Yes," Rumella agreed, looking surprised, "but how did you know?"

"Druids we suspected for a while," I answered, "but Varus left me a note telling us to go to Britain."

"Foolish of him," Rumella commented. "Such information in the wrong hands could be catastrophic, but yes, you are correct. However the story is much deeper than that."

"How did you actually discover your information?" Helena interrupted. "These scrolls look like they've been here forever. People must have read them at some point."

Rumella turned to me, raising a hand in her direction. "She is not a historian, is she?"

I smiled. "No. She most certainly is not."

"Young lady," he said, looking back to Helena, "please do not take what I am about to say as an insult, but when it comes to research, one does not simply read. Analysis, cross-reference, speculation, assumption, guesses, interpretation, exploration, all of these things are needed to truly understand the meaning behind a story. Yes, each of these documents individually may have once been read, but to piece them together you need a point of reference, and the reference we needed was the orb. Without knowing of it first, it would be quite easy to overlook references to it, as they are few and with little description.

"It took Varus and I months to discover what we did, and some of our research had to be brought in from various Roman

History and Mythology buildings of the Great Library, as well as from other libraries entirely. We even sent men to Germany and Britain in an attempt to uncover more information, but most of those men have yet to return. So, please, you would do well to keep your comments to yourself, as it is not a process one can learn in a few hours' time."

Helena leaned back and crossed her arms, glowering, and I tried not to laugh.

"So where does the story begin?" I asked.

"Exactly where your friend here said it begins," he said gesturing to Vincent. "Seven hundred years ago, when a Druid associated with Romulus and Remus gave to them an orb of unimaginable and unexplainable power to conduct some form of ritual that would alter the course of history."

"What kind of ritual?" I asked.

"We never found specifics," Rumella answered as he gestured to Helena, "but we *speculated* it was a ritual meant to divine their destinies, and give them power over them. A way for them to go against the gods' divinations and the fates allotted to mere men."

I let out a breath dismissively. I'd never put much stock in the idea of magic, nor faith in the concept of fate or destinies, and I certainly didn't think gods – or even *God* for that matter – had that kind of control over me.

I liked the idea of free will.

"Now," Rumella continued, "what do you know of Druids?"

I shrugged. "Not much. Some consider them holy men or ever sorcerers, but in reality they were more like politicians, diplomats, tribal chiefs, and leaders of communities. That kind of thing."

"Ah yes. Indeed they are, but in the age of Romulus and Remus they were much, much more that that – at least according to legend. It is told that they had powers beyond those of mortal men, ones that could rival those of even Jupiter and his cronies. Manipulative powers that could alter the physical world as well as the unseen world."

"Unseen world?" Helena asked.

"Yes, that which cannot be perceived by man. Psychological. Elemental. Transmutation. Temporal.

"Excuse me, did you say temporal?" Wang asked, the first words he'd spoken yet. "As in manipulating time?"

"Yes. That was one of their rumored abilities."

He hummed, impressed, while I sat back, stunned that after five long years I was actually having a conversation with someone who may in fact be able to help us.

"So who exactly was this Druid?" I asked.

"Unfortunately his name is lost," Rumella answered with a frown, "but he was the last in what little recorded history we have to possess any power at all. He may have been the last of a dying breed, or perhaps the only Druid with any real power ever. I suspect we will never know."

"But why Romulus and Remus?" Vincent asked. "What made them so important?"

"This I also do not know," Rumella answered with a shrug. "Perhaps there is more to their divine birth than we care to acknowledge in this more modern age."

"I'm sorry to interrupt again," Helena said, "I really am, but I'm confused. If this Druid was so important, why exactly doesn't anyone know anything about him? Many people must have written about him."

Rumella smiled. "I shall take pity on you this time, young lady, for you are most beautiful and your questions at least suggest a curious mind."

Helena looked at him impatiently, but didn't interrupt.

"History lesson number one," Rumella stated with an upraised finger. "Who records history?"

Helena shrugged. "Those who write it down?"

"Excellent!" He threw his arms over his head and grinned from ear to ear at her answer. "In fact... probably the simplest but most apt answer I've ever heard! I shall have to remember it, but I am rambling, I apologize. History lesson number two: is the passage of time an influence on what is remembered?"

"I suppose," she said. "Things can be lost or forgotten over time."

"Yes, of course. That was an easy one. Now, to answer your question. Seven hundred years is a long time, and Romulus was in fact the man who ensured history was recorded after Remus' death. Perhaps he was jealous that the orb was Remus', as we assume it was from what little information remains, so he embarked on a campaign to strike the Druid's name, intentions, and existence from history, censoring any information of his otherworldly abilities as well. The end result is what all of us here know, which came from the few remaining references scattered across the thousands of documents that now reside within this room, which again is why I remind you that simply reading at random would do a scholar no good."

"What about the original document found with the orb?" I asked. "Were you ever able to translate more of it?"

"Try as he did, Varus was never able to fully do so, no," Rumella answered. "The language was too obscure, but the more he tried, the more it seemed a warning than anything. That much became clear."

"Oh, great," I muttered. "Now you tell me."

"Was there anything else to learn about the Druid or his time in Rome?" Vincent asked, his voice hopeful.

"Little of consequence. A few tidbits and factoids that I will eventually add in my planned treatise on the subject, but nothing that will help you."

I lifted my head in interest at that comment. "Plan on writing a book, are we?"

"Yes of course. The world needs to know."

I smiled. Indeed it did, but I couldn't exactly let that happen. It would be too big of a chink in history to get things back to the way they had been.

Great.

Now I had to play government censor as well.

"All right, fine," I said, frustration setting in over how little we were actually learning here. "So we can find more information in Britain then? Is that what you're getting at?"

"Well, yes, but we sent men there to retrieve just what you are looking for. None have returned."

"But that's where we need to go, right? Britain? But where exactly?"

"One moment," Rumella answered as he stood tiredly and moved to a shelf off to his right. He set aside scroll after scroll, rummaging for something in particular, when he finally found what he must have been looking for and held it up in success. He shuffled back to our table and laid it out, revealing what looked like a map. All of us leaned in and peered at it, but even I couldn't tell what it was.

Rumella sensed our hesitation. "It's a map of Britain."

I squinted, finally seeing said country come into focus. The "map" was about as detailed as a child's drawing of the island, but the island's general shape did seem properly displayed if one really looked.

"That's right insulting, mate," Wang muttered as he looked at it.

"Now," Rumella said, "most of Britain is uncharted or occupied by barbarians who do not properly explore and document landmarks, and certainly no location is known by the same name today as it was seven hundred years ago, but Varus and I did recover a number of hints as to where the Druids may have relocated."

"Go on," I encouraged.

"It's more of a riddle, really," Rumella said as he shook his head. "Perhaps a bedtime story for young Celts aspiring to become Druids. We never knew. We had to piece it together from a number of documents, but it was most fascinating, even if Varus and I could never understand it."

"Well?" I asked impatiently.

"A man with a grin faces west," Rumella recited from memory. "Atop his head sits a high crown, but upon the tip of his nose is where his treasure is stowed. It swims in the sea and threatens to leave, but never goes. It..."

"Wales!" Wang exclaimed, jumping to his feet.

I looked back at the map then back to him, confused. "How the hell did you get Wales from that?"

He reached out and pointed with a hand. "Look, Hunter! 'A man with a grin faces west' is Great Britain, *but*..." He trailed off, noticing everyone's confusion and took a moment to compile his thoughts before explaining.

"Look, here's the ear," he said, pointing at the small bump that jutted out of the eastern edge of the island, northeast of where London should be. He then moved his hand to cover the narrow bit of land that would be Northern England and Scotland. "This is the tall crown, and here's the lower jaw," he said, indicating where southeastern England would be. "And here's the upper lip and nose," he said, circling Wales excitedly. "And the mouth in the face is the Bristol Channel! It fits perfectly!"

"You are most astute, young man," Rumella said happily. "How did you see it so quickly?"

"That's where I'm from," Wang said, his voice rising. "It's my home!"

"Well," I said, unable to think of anything better, "if you say so, but Wales isn't exactly small. *Where* in Wales?"

Wang raised a hand to hold his chin, but didn't answer.

Helena pointed at northwestern Wales with a finger, which looked little more than a smooth curve on the primitive map. "The riddle said 'upon the tip of his nose is where his treasure is stowed' but if this is the tip, it could mean anywhere. It's just one big, open area."

"No, it's not," Wang said, his mind apparently piecing something together. "On this map, maybe, but on a modern map there'd be a... small... island there?"

Wang completely lost us as he thought out loud, his voice drifting. He didn't even seem to be in the room with us anymore as he gazed unblinkingly at the map. Archer noticed and waved a hand in front of his face, but still Wang looked distant, with something else in his eyes.

It almost looked like he was afraid of something.

I was about to ask him what was wrong when I noticed Vincent too looked spooked.

"What's wrong with you two?" I asked.

It was only then that the two of them snapped out of their reveries and took notice of the fact that the other had been just as distant as the other. They looked at each other curiously until Wang held out a hand and slowly counted his fingers down from three. When he no longer had any fingers held up, they spoke in unison:

"Anglesey."

Helena glanced between them. "What's that?"

I too had never heard of it, and was just as curious. Both Wang and Vincent looked startled again, but Vincent was able to bring himself around first and answer.

"Anglesey is an island off the northwest coast of Wales," he said, pointing at the map. "Today it's known as The Isle of Mona, and it's probably not on this map because a large mountain range almost completely obscures it from view from mainland Wales. It's... an interesting place."

I didn't bother trying to understand the odd tone in his voice, realizing that the Isle of Mona was definitely a place I'd heard of before, but my brain was having trouble remembering where.

"Ah, yes," Rumella commented. "I have heard of it. A place where..."

His voice trailed off and stopped completely when a look of shock and confusion crossed his face. His eyes turned and bored into mine, and I found myself feeling sadness before I had any idea why. The emotion lingered for only a half second, until Rumella dropped his chin to his chest and looked down, and we both discovered an arrow protruding from his left pectoral. His eyes went back to mine and he started to say more, but then he slumped to the table, dead.

"Ninja-thingy!" Wang shouted with an arm pointed toward one of the windows.

I followed his finger to see one of Agrippina's black clad... ninja-things... situated on the windowsill, a bow in his hand. Wang was already leaping over the table toward him, pulling a pistol from his bag in the process, and I wasn't very far behind him.

Helena rose to her feet as well, but I pushed her back down. "Stay here! We'll get him."

"I'm coming wi..."

"Stay here!" I shouted before turning to Archer. "You make sure she stays here. Head back to the group if we're not back in fifteen minutes."

The cocky former friend of mine nodded in deference to my order, probably guessing if something happened to Helena after I'd put him in charge of her, that I really would kill him.

Without another glance at her, I bounded after Wang, retrieving my bag and the pistol within. I jumped at the window, fully willing to fling myself through it when I finally noticed the precarious drop to the water below.

I pulled myself short and looked around, craning my head upwards as I heard Wang's shout, "Grab the rope!"

As he spoke, a rope fell from the sky and landed in my face. I grabbed at it, found my grip, and pulled myself hand over hand to the roof. I had to climb maybe twenty five feet before I pulled myself over a low ledge and onto a flat surface, panting at the endeavor and feeling pain in my side from my old wound.

I looked around, squinting into the night but couldn't see a thing. I checked my bag but remembered I'd left my NVGs behind. Instead I pulled out my radio, plugging the earpiece into my ear.

"Who's on overwatch?" I asked into the coms, directing my question to whoever was on duty as our lookout. Whoever it was, I knew he or she would be positioned in one of the tallest buildings in the city, with a complete 360 degree view.

"Cuyler here."

Good. The sniper.

I didn't waste any more time. "Where's Wang?"

"He's heading south-southeast of your position, about one hundred and fifty meters ahead of you."

I sent him a double click, assuring him I received his information, took a deep breath, and started running along the rooftop for yet another nocturnal, rooftop chase scene. I picked up speed and fought to catch up to Rumella's assassin.

Rumella.

Just another victim I was responsible for, and one who had just told us everything Agrippina needed to jump a step ahead of us.

"Update," I requested into the coms.

"Course correction: east. One hundred ten meters and closing."

At least I was learning something about Cuyler through all of this: he was damn efficient.

I shifted my direction slightly to the left and kept on running, jumping over small gaps in buildings, climbing a few walls, and once I'd left the library's immediate area and found myself in a residential neighborhood, dodged around and through laundry dangling from ropes strung between structures. After one particular jump, after almost missing the gap completely thanks to an annoyingly hung sheet, I landed roughly on my right ankle and rolled it over, but I fell into the roll, somersaulting myself back to my feet and avoiding more permanent injury. It would hurt, but it'd be fine.

My left side was another story.

"Break north," Cuyler calmly relayed to me. "Seventy five meters."

I did as I was told and pivoted to the right once again, finally noticing that I'd been running parallel with the waterway. Now, as I broke north, I was heading straight for it. As I ran, I felt something chitter against an adobe wall next to me, but I ignored it. A second later, I felt the wind along my right cheek breeze past me, but again I ignored it.

"Missile fire," Cuyler reported.

"Yeah, no shit," I sent back to him.

I zigzagged a bit to ensure whoever was taking potshots at me never found a clear shot, and I heard the clatter of a few more missed arrows around me, but none came as close as the first two. In a few more seconds I saw Wang ahead of me, hot on the heels of the assassin, the Mediterranean Sea only a dozen buildings away, and wondered where the assassin thought he was going.

As if on cue, I saw a medium sized ship sail in from the east, slowing as it approached our position inland, and I found the source of the arrow barrage. I aimed my pistol at one of the assassin's friends aboard the ship, and fired an entire magazine in his direction, but an enormous wall of fire suddenly ignited a few dozen meters in front of me. I skidded to a stop, throwing up a hand to shield my eyes from the blaze, and noticed that the fire was between Wang and the assassin as well, forcing my friend to pull up short before he careened into the flames. I looked west and saw a ninja with a torch, who summarily tossed it aside and ran.

The wall of fire spread, encompassing many buildings in both directions.

There was no way we could catch them now. All I could do was wonder if I'd just been responsible for the destruction of the great library by allowing this fire to happen, and I was so mesmerized by it that at first I didn't feel the sudden prick in my leg. It took me a few seconds, but I finally decided to look down and notice what had caused the bit of pain, only to discover an arrow protruding from my thigh. That's when it started to hurt, and when the blood started to spurt from it, and my instincts immediately suggested that the femoral must have been nicked. Realization sunk in and I fell to the roof, clutching my leg in pain and fear.

"Medic!" Cuyler shouted into the com, and Wang turned at the call and rushed in my direction. He arrived ten seconds later and immediately attended to my leg.

"Wang, it's my femoral!" I yelled, blinding pain seething through my body. I grabbed my friend's neck with a bloody hand and pulled him close. "God, there's so much blood!"

But Wang didn't seem nearly as concerned as I was.

"Hunter, what the bloody Christ are you talking about? You'll be fine. You were shot with an arrow not bludgeoned with a bloody battle axe. There's barely any blood at all."

I stared at him as my chest rose and fell heavily, near out of breath. When I looked back down, I found nothing like the disaster I'd just witnessed. He was right. Barely any blood at all. The arrow may have been lodged in my leg, but it went clean through muscle and little else. It still hurt, but not nearly as bad as it had seconds ago, and Wang's neck was also clear of any blood I may have left there from my hand.

"Just give me a second to patch you up," he said, but then looked at me. "But just so you know, I'm not telling Helena."

I glared at him and tried to steady my breath.

What was happening to me?

Just like the scene at the courtyard, both visions had seemed just as real as reality. I'd felt the overwhelming pain in my leg, had felt the blood splatter against my face, and had seen it smear Wang's neck, but now it was all gone. There was something going on here. Something going on in my head. But I wasn't even sure if the orb was at fault, since both episodes had occurred after Helena had already hidden it from me, and I hadn't seen it since.

What was happening to me?

I reached for the radio to distract myself. "Update?"

"They escaped," Cuyler reported. "I put down six archers targeting you from the boat, but the one who lit the fire only took one in the stomach. He may still be alive."

Efficient, professional, and deadly. Six kills in only a few minutes with the confusion of the fire was pretty impressive.

"Help me up," I ordered Wang, my sudden brush with death nearly forgotten. While the memory of the pain lingered, I no longer felt any effects from my phantom wound. It was nothing more than a memory now, as though it had happened twenty years ago.

Wang nodded and bent over to wrap his arm around my back before hauling me up. My leg was on fire, and I quickly found that walking to be painful, but with Wang's help, we hobbled around the extent of the fire, which was thankfully already burning itself out, and found the man who Cuyler had shot through the stomach. Wang let me go and rushed over to him, and gripped the downed man by the arm and flipped him over, pressing his knee into the man's wound.

"Where are they going, mate?" He asked the assassin calmly, adding the "mate" in English.

"I do not know," the assassin said in immense pain as he tried to push Wang's knee from his stomach.

Wang put on his tough guy face and shook the man by his shoulders. "How did you know we were here?"

The black clad figure slowly removed his face mask before answering, but then his muscles failed him and his head fell to the ground.

"Oi! Don't you go dying on me," Wang ordered. "How did you know we were here??"

The man came around briefly, offering a bloody smile, but then he collapsed again. Wang checked his pulse, but clearly didn't find one. He stood up and walked back to me.

"Well that was cheeky," he offered.

I looked at him, deadpanned. "Cheeky? *Really?*"

***

Once the fires burned themselves out with minimal damage to the area, Wang cased the scene for clues about our attackers. Unfortunately, they had been thorough, and had left nothing behind except their deceased comrade. After finding nothing of use on his body, Wang carried him to the low cliff overlooking the

Mediterranean Sea and summarily discarded the body into the water. He then retrieved the few shell casings left over from the discharge of my pistol, cleansing our involvement, and helped me back up and supported me as we hobbled our way to the hideout with the help of Cuyler guiding us in.

It was over a mile away, and it took us half an hour to reach it, but halfway there, I noticed something move above us. I glanced up to see a man rappelling from the building next door, dressed in the gray and black camouflage our new friends had brought with them. Upon touching down, he tugged on the rope and it fell along with its grappling hook. He wound it up as he made his way toward Wang and me.

"You all right?" Cuyler asked.

I shrugged. "Sure. What's another scar among so many?"

Cuyler didn't say anything, but I could tell from his eyes, even in the dim night sky, that he empathized. It spoke a thousand words, and I was surprised he had no other insight or unsolicited advice to offer me – as most of our group always seemed to have in abundance, welcome or not. Instead, he hooked himself beneath my other shoulder and helped Wang support my weight as we traveled the last half mile to our apartment.

And I found myself unable to *not* like the guy.

When we arrived, we found Helena leaning against the doorjamb, her arms crossed against her chest, not looking very happy. I wondered if she'd been listening in on the radio during our chase scene as the three of us passed by her and into the room, none of us having the guts to even look at her. She shut the door behind us and escorted us to the nearest table, at the far end of the room. After setting me down, Cuyler immediately got out of the way while Wang helped me remove my robes and take off my pants so he could inspect the arrow. I also took off my shirt to inspect my wounded side, which thankfully seemed fine.

I lifted my head and surveyed the room.

It was a pretty nice sized apartment with a number of connecting bedrooms from which the rest of my team now emerged, taking notice of our return, but I ignored them and focused on Wang. "How's it look?"

He replied by squeezing my thigh again, which didn't hurt nearly as much as I thought it would, but then he tugged slightly on the arrow, and that one hurt.

"Ouch," I said through clenched teeth.

"Hold still," Wang ordered as he removed what looked like a cigar cutter from his bag, a device that would slice the arrowhead from the shaft so that it could be pulled clean through.

With a quick cut, Wang severed the arrowhead and set the cutter down.

He looked at Helena. "Hold him still."

She complied silently, and moved to wrap her arms around me.

Wang then turned his attention to me. "Bite something, Jacob."

I looked around but had to settle with shoving my shirt in my mouth.

"Ready?" He asked.

I tried to nod but before I could complete the gesture, Wang pulled the arrow through my leg in one quick movement. It came out painfully and colored in red, but little blood came from the wound itself as Wang went to work cleaning and dressing it.

"So did you catch him?" Archer asked from his doorway.

I turned to glare at him, the throbbing pain in my leg fueling my anger, but when I opened my mouth to speak Wang answered for me, his eyes still on his work.

"Obviously not," Wang said. "He had a few chaps with him who were ready for us."

"We have to move fast now," I finally said. "It's only a matter of time before Agrippina learns where we're going, but we need to get there first. How are we provisioned, Brewster?"

The petite woman stood there unmoving for a moment as she stared at me, but then snapped out of her daze and ducked back into her room. When she returned, she held a notebook in her hand, already leafing through it, but she didn't look happy.

"We don't have nearly enough supplies to reach Britain," she said as she ran a finger across a page. "There was very little to purchase in Caesarea thanks to the siege, and I was told Alexandria would have ample food to purchase. I mean, we *could* leave tomorrow, but we'd be lacking certain... necessities."

"Like what?" I asked, jerking my leg as Wang did something to it that hurt.

"Wheat and salt," she answered immediately.

"Are you telling me," Stryker asked, leaning in his doorframe, "that there is absolutely no wheat or salt in this entire city for us to buy? How's that possible?"

"Of course not," Brewster snapped at him, clearly annoyed by such a question, "but shopping in the quantities we need on such short notice is not easy. I haven't even been able to contact local dealers yet, and most of what the city already has is owned by people who aren't in the market to resell it in bulk. We'll need to wait at least five days for new shipments to arrive that I can buy. Or so I was told. That was well within our original timeframe."

"We can't sail to Britain without ingredients needed to make *bread*," Helena advised wisely, knowing a legionnaire's basic campaign diet was sustained mostly on just that.

"Goddamn it," I mumbled, but I couldn't disagree. "Just see what you can do, Georgia. If you need to pay double to speed up the process, do it."

"But…"

"Just do it! We're not running a business here."

She looked solemn for just a moment before closing her notebook.

She nodded. "Got it."

"Everybody else should get some rest," Vincent chimed in from his own doorway, "but try to keep yourselves active. We're going to have a long trip ahead of us."

"You heard the man," Archer said with his arms crossed. "It's 2100 hours. Everyone should be up and ready for a morning workout by 0600."

"That's not how we operate, Archer," Helena said. "People keep their own schedules here when they're not on duty."

"Not under my watch, they don't."

"You're not even wearing a watch," Santino accused.

As he spoke, Artie poked her head out from his bedroom to place a hand on his forearm. He jumped at the touch, but got the message and didn't press the point, but I wasn't so easily calmed. Santino was driving me nuts with his incessant time spent with Artie, and I hadn't even known she'd been in there until just now.

"Hunter's out of commission," Archer countered, gesturing in my direction. "Until he can operate at one hundred percent, he shouldn't be the one giving the orders."

"You're right," Vincent said, stepping up behind him, "but as fortune would have it, I am already second in command."

Archer glanced down at his amputated arm.

"You? But you…"

"I what?" Vincent asked with steel in his voice, drilling his eyes into Archer's and making damn sure that he knew who was in charge.

Archer stared back at him, and to his credit, didn't immediately back down, but he was no match for Vincent. He held the older man's eye for a few more seconds before finally turning away and stalking into one of the corner bedrooms without another word or glance back.

"He's going to be trouble," Helena whispered in my ear.

I nodded as Vincent lived up to his command position.

"What are you all staring at?" He asked the gathered group. "Get back to work!"

Everyone jumped and drifted off at the same time to settle into chairs or couches scattered throughout the room, or to retreat back to their rooms, as Santino and Artie did, although they left the door open, much to my relief. I also noticed Bordeaux help his wife toward a small couch that sat directly in front of a fire we had going. He glanced at me briefly, but made no other gesture.

I was about to discuss the scene Archer had created when Wang suddenly smacked me on the thigh, just above the bandaged wound, which hurt a lot.

"And Bob's your uncle," he said. "Just try to let this one heal before you go and get yourself another."

I groaned, my leg feeling like it was on fire. "You *really* need to work on your bedside manner."

The small medic grinned and moved off to chat with Bordeaux and Madrina, leaving me alone with Helena.

"So should we just kill him now and get it over with?" Helena asked.

"Who, Wang? Totally."

"No Archer," she said, rolling her eyes. "Who else?"

"Well, you could have meant Santino as well. I could kill Santino right about now too…"

"Stop it," Helena scolded. "They kept the door open the entire time."

"Yeah, like that's any consolation."

"Jacob, grow up. They're both adults and are clearly interested…"

"*Not* discussing it!" I said rudely. "It's not that important anyway…"

Helena sighed. "I'm not sure it isn't so unimportant, Jacob…"

I ignored her. "What about Rumella?"

"We left him."

"But the librarian who saw us…"

"What were we supposed to do? Take the body to the authorities? You do remember there is a price on all of our heads, right?"

"I know, I know." I sighed, but refused to let Rumella's passing hurt me. "So what do you think? Do we head to Britain? Follow Rumella's lead on the Druids?"

"I think it's the only choice we have."

"Yeah… but Druids?"

"Jacob," she said, her tone suggesting she was preparing to lecture a small child. "If you would have told me five years ago that time travel existed, I would have thought you were insane. But now? Now, I'll believe anything until its proven impossible."

"Yeah…" I said. "I guess you're right."

"You don't sound so sure."

I didn't answer right away, trying to decide if I should come clean about my visions. I reached out to massage my bare leg just above my wound, but Helena noticed and reached out to stop the motion.

"Jacob, what's wrong?"

"I don't know," I replied. "I just got a bad feeling about all this."

"What kind of feeling?"

Concern was obvious in her voice.

"I just told you. A bad one. It doesn't feel right. Something feels… wrong."

"Something always feels wrong," she reminded me. "Since the moment we got here."

"I know that, Helena, but this time he's here with us." I said, placing my hand on Helena's stomach. "Or her. I couldn't live with myself if I let anything happen to either of you."

Helena placed her hand over my own and smiled at me.

It was so sincere and beautiful that I almost forgot everything that was happening.

Almost.

"You won't, Jacob. I know you won't. And…" she paused, "…well, if it makes you feel better, I promise I'll do what I can to stay out of harm's way. But only directly!" She clarified. "I'm still going with you and I'm still taking my sniper rifles with me. Both of them!"

I grinned and hugged her tight, giving her soft neck a gentle kiss.

"Thank you, Helena. That means a lot, and I know what that means to you too."

"It isn't easy for me, if that's what you mean," she said, squeezing my hand. "Five years ago I would have had no problem staying right here, but I can't do that now. You mean too much to me. Everybody does, but I understand your concern. I have more than myself to think about now, so I'll be careful."

"I know you will, Helena. Thank you."

She smiled and reached up to brush hair from my forehead. "See how nice it is to talk sometimes? I could get used to this."

"Yeah," I agreed, although my heart wasn't in the response. I was still keeping things from her, dark things, but I knew I was doing her a favor. I wasn't doing it for me this time, but for her. Her life was stressful enough, and I didn't need to make it worse, especially not when I had someone else I could turn to. Someone who'd been through a lot in his own life, and could see right through me as easily as Helena, but was for more understanding…

***

"Mind if I bother you, sir?"

Vincent looked up from the bed he sat on and turned to face the doorway where I was standing. When I'd come in, he had been tending to the cast around Titus' leg. The young man would be out of it for at least a few more weeks, but Wang was certain he'd eventually make a full recovery, and Vincent was taking care of him in the meantime, as any good stepfather would.

"Of course, Jacob. We were just preparing for us to part ways."

I shifted my look to Titus. "You're leaving us?"

"Only in the sense that I will be remaining here, Jacob Hunter," Titus answered. "It will be months before my leg is fully healed, and I do not wish to slow you in your journey."

I sighed deeply at the announcement. "Well, we'll miss you, Titus, but it's good that you know your limitations."

"I do," Titus said, "but at least I won't be alone. Madrina will remain as well. She has no wish to see combat again. Once I have healed, we will travel back to Judea and find my family, and then to Gaul. It's her home, and close to Britain, where we will await your return."

"Sounds like a good plan." I nodded and turned back to Vincent. "You're all right with this?"

"I am," he replied. "We put too much faith in them both before, but now that Archer and his reinforcements have arrived, I would rather not put either them at risk anymore. Neither would Jeanne. And it would be good for Brian Wilson and my wife to see Titus again."

I smiled, remembering how Vincent had named his son after his favorite member of The Beach boys, and turned back to Titus. "Consider yourself lucky. You've got a good dad there."

"He has done fairly well," Titus agreed with a smirk, and Vincent reached out to clip the young man on the chin with a light punch.

I smiled at the scene, but moved to clear the doorway. "Shall we?"

Vincent nodded and stood up. He made a quick stop to grab his pistol, and moved to join me.

"Where to?" He asked.

I pointed upward. "Let's get some air."

Our building was equipped with a tall tower, perfect for our LP/OP, and when Vincent and I climbed the stairs to the roof, we found Brewster and Stryker diligently manning their post, the perfect pairing since they'd never grow distracted by talking to each other. They were comically standing back to back, looking out in opposite directions.

"Take a break," I said to them both. "Give us fifteen minutes."

"Take thirty," Stryker answered.

Brewster said nothing, and neither said a word to one another as they moved to the steps, but when both of them tried to descend at the same time, a small shoving match broke out until Brewster squeezed through first. Stryker growled at her small victory but followed.

When they were out of earshot, Vincent whispered, "I wonder what their history is."

"Beats me," I replied. "I'm sure it's stupid."

Vincent moved to the low wall and stood beside it, pulling out his binoculars as he did. He brought them to his eyes and slowly scanned the horizon. "Rather jaded of you, no?"

I sighed and plopped Penelope's bipod on the low wall and sighted through her night vision scope. I glassed the city to delay immediately responding.

"I guess," I answered. "I just don't care, is all."

"Neither do I," Vincent admitted, "but that doesn't explain the attitude. What's wrong?"

I was happy he hadn't asked, "What's wrong *this* time?" That was generally the tact Santino took, and even Helena at times. It was the one thing I could always rely on Vincent for. He never judged me for the decisions I made or the way in which I dealt with the repercussions of those choices afterwards. He was simply there when I needed him to be, and he knew that when I needed to talk, it wasn't for some trivial thing. He was always ready to support, always there to listen, and never pushed his own thoughts and feelings on the conversation.

I continued my scan of the city, checking for anomalies, almost hoping to find something out there to distract us, but nothing seemed out of the ordinary.

"I've been having these… visions," I said carefully. "They started after Archer, Artie, and the rest showed up."

Vincent peeked at me behind his binoculars. "What kind of visions."

I closed my eyes as I remembered. "I guess they're more like hallucinations really. Gruesome ones. Extremely visceral, graphic, and all too real."

"What triggers them?"

"I'm not sure, honestly. The two times it happened, my visions were a reflection of reality, just skewed for the worse."

"Explain."

"The first vision was in Damascus. I saw... I saw all of us cut to shreds by arrow fire. I saw people die horrible deaths. But then it was all gone. Replaced by what really happened."

"I see," Vincent remarked quietly.

"The other time was just a few hours ago when I was shot. Instead of the minor wound I actually have, I thought my femoral was cut. There was a lot of blood and a lot of pain. A lot. But when Wang found me, the vision completely melted away."

"Hmm," Vincent muttered. "And you say these visions seem real? Like déjà vu or a dream?"

"Not even close. They are so much more that than. They *are* reality. I shouldn't even be calling them visions. I could feel the warmth of the blood on my hands, smell it in my nose, and see it spurt from my leg. It was real."

Vincent was silent. I tore my eye away from my scope to see him holding his binoculars against his chest, looking down at his knees.

"You all right, Vincent?" I asked.

"I'm fine, Jacob, but I won't mince words with you. I am worried that the orb may be affecting you. Remember our theories about its brain degenerative properties? What it may have done to Caligula and Claudius?"

"Of course I remember," I said, but without any scorn. He was just trying to make a point.

"Well, you've interacted with it more than anyone," he indicated. "Three times I believe. And unlike the Caesars, you have actually been able to operate it. Perhaps that's three times too many, and... and it's beginning to affect you."

"I've thought of that too," I admitted.

"It'll be okay, Jacob," Vincent assured. "Just keep it away from you. Maybe... just maybe, the Druids we're looking for can help."

I chuckled. "Hell, anything is possible at this point, but… *Druids*??"

"I agree," Vincent said, but he didn't seem amused, "but believe me when I say that you should not so immediately dismiss a Druidic presence that could help us. But I at least think it helps that you are aware of your ill effects. That simple awareness may allow you to overcome its long term negative effects. Just try to stay calm, and come to me whenever you see any more of these visions. I'll do what I can to help."

"Thanks, Vincent. I really didn't want to upset Helena with this, especially not now."

Vincent smiled and reached out to grip my shoulder with his hand. "We've journeyed a long road together, Jacob, and while you've sought my counsel before, never forget that you always have a friend in me. One who will always be there for you, ready to listen."

I returned the smile. "I know. It means a lot. Now let's go un-relieve Romeo and Juliet down there and get some sleep."

Part Two

V
Mediterranean

Western Mediterranean Sea
November, 42 A.D.

"Man your battle stations!" I shouted from the helm, steadying myself with the railing as the rough waters nearly threw me to the deck. "Prepare for immediate boarding!"

"Argh, captain!" Santino replied, nearly falling to the deck himself as he followed. "A blimey pickle you've blundered us into this time. Argh, argh, argh..."

I didn't even bother sparing a glance at him. A runner was just returning from below deck with Penelope and my go-bag filled with spare magazines. As soon as I caught his attention, he tossed me the rifle, then the bag. I waved in thanks as he returned to the main deck, and I slapped a fresh magazine into place and pulled back the cocking lever. I raised the rifle to my shoulder and peered through the scope, scanning the darkness with the optic's night vision activated. I glanced up at the sky briefly, noticing the thick clouds rolling by at a quick clip, and I feared our first storm of the expedition would soon join the fun.

Santino was right. This certainly was a blimey pickle.

The voyage had started so well, too.

Brewster had worked her magic, otherwise known as my money, and procured everything we'd needed within four days, although she'd practically bankrupted me doing it, which was fine. We'd loaded down the ships, secured our cargo, and waved goodbye to Alexandria, Titus, and Madrina three days later. It had been a hard goodbye for Vincent, and an even harder one for Bordeaux, but both knew it was for the best. Neither Titus nor Madrina really belonged in the field, and neither Vincent nor Bordeaux wanted to put them at further risk and had accepted their choices.

That was eleven days and about the entire width of Africa ago, making our current position just off the coast of modern day Algeria. It had been a restful voyage so far with only minor inclement weather, and it had given everyone the chance to relax and settle themselves after the tumultuous past few months. I'd spent the time doing everything I could to avoid instances that might incite a vision, convinced that even stubbing my toe could trigger one, and I'd been lucky so far.

The rest of my time was spent performing random ship's tasks, which included spending as much time with Helena, doing everything we could to enjoy ourselves. It wasn't easy, but below deck in our hammocks, we could almost pretend we were on a cruise. The food wasn't great, and Helena was having trouble keeping anything down as her pregnancy progressed and the tides picked up, but we made do. She was starting to show now as well, which was an amazing thing to witness as the days rolled on. And then there was the best part about her pregnancy: every night, she let me read to her stomach for about half an hour. In other times, she'd shut me up after about five minutes, but she was willing to allow it now.

With little reading material available, I read Brewster's high school text book to the kid. Helena would fall fast asleep minutes after I started, but I was captivated by the information night after night. I'd decided to start from the end and work my way backward in an attempt to better piece the puzzle together, and while I still hadn't found where the timelines had gone askew, I'd definitely learned more than I ever wanted to. I was only at the 19th Century, but it already seemed like I was reading an alternate history novel. There was just so much weirdness, one particular fun fact being that the light bulb hadn't been invented until 1932, and by a scientist in Egypt.

Enough said.

But after a relaxing week and a half, now we were here.

Staring down the business end of an ancient Mediterranean pirate fleet.

About one hundred years ago, Magnus Pompey, the man who would later cross swords with Julius Caesar, rose to power after clearing the pirate infested waters of the Mediterranean of the booty-seeking menace. He'd done a thorough job, and for the first time, the Mediterranean Sea was relatively safe. However, that was some time ago, and it wasn't long before pirates had slunk their way back into the area again.

As I squinted through my scope, I glassed the dark horizon as best I could, searching for the ships I had been told were coming. Lookouts from their perch high above had seen the outlines of at least a half dozen ships grouped tightly together out on the horizon, ones that had been following us for days. The shouts of the crew around me grew louder and I noticed my team setting up positions around the ship's perimeter. As the sounds of battle preparations increased, another rancorous sound rolled in from the West.

Thunder.

Just. Fucking. Epic.

A few seconds later, accompanied by a flash of lightning, came rain that poured down in sheets.

"Ships to port!" Came another yell.

I shifted myself around through the rain so that I looked to the left, and indeed saw two ships maybe a thousand meters away, but it was difficult to pinpoint because my line of sight was constantly bouncing up and down as the waves picked up.

It was going to make sniper work damned impossible.

I stormed away from the railing and headed for the helm, where shipmaster Gnaeus gripped the wheel in a vice grip.

"Why are they attacking us?" I yelled, the downpour turning torrential and making it difficult to be heard or even formulate words through the rain in my mouth.

He spun his head around to look at me. "This is a merchant ship! They think we're transporting cargo!"

It seemed so simple.

"So you're saying we could have avoided this by simply prancing our legionnaires around on deck more often?"

He spit water out of his mouth to speak, but was interrupted by a deafening thunder clap that preceded a lightning strike that touched down only a few hundred meters away. He turned from the blast and back to me. "Unless they were stupid! As you seem to be!"

"Contact starboard!"

This warning came from Helena as she sprinted past me to join Cuyler at the bow of the ship, where she carefully lowered herself to lay prone on the deck – favoring her left side – and propped her DSR1 sniper rifle on its bipod. Earlier, Cuyler had sawed off a few of the vertical railing supports that were scattered equidistantly around the perimeter of the ship, allowing them a wider field of fire. Gnaeus wouldn't be happy, but he was already less than happy about my own tactical decisions at the onset of the engagement.

I had been at the helm when the first call came down that we had contacts to port, and I had immediately maneuvered us starboard, away from land, hoping to lose them out over the open water. What I hadn't expected was that they were simply driving us toward their friends. I'd been a hard shooter back home in the Navy, not a naval seaman, and had even less of an idea about naval warfare in the ancient world. I'd maneuvered us straight into trap, and now our entire flotilla was surrounded. The other few ships in our convoy hung back but were no less trapped.

Now, we had no other choice but to drive our ship toward the larger pirate group to our starboard, hoping they concentrated on us, since we had the firepower the other ships did not.

"Gnaeus!" I called, swaying and lurching with the ship. "Break starboard! Head for the pirates!"

"Are you…"

"Argh, do it ye matey!" Santino yelled, taking the wheel in his hands and helping Gnaeus turn the ship.

I heard another loud boom from in front of us, and realized our snipers had already started shooting. I stumbled toward the bow with my hands shielding my eyes from the incoming rain, slid beside Helena, and placed a hand on her lower back, alerting her to my arrival.

"Hitting anything??" I yelled around the rain.

"No clue!" She yelled back. "But we must be hitting something! They don't seem happy!"

I smiled as I looked out over the roiling water, seeing nothing, but realizing that the superstitious pirates must have thought their dead to have been struck down by Jove himself.

Wang ran up to kneel on the other side of Helena, shielding his own face with a hand. "We don't exactly have the ammunition for 'no clue' kind of shooting, you know!"

"Shut up, Wang," I yelled. "Let her work!"

"Go back to playing doctor!" She yelled.

"I'll remember that the next time you get stabbed." He paused. "Again."

I winced at the comment, but Helena reached out and punched him in the ribs. He yelped and rose to his feet to join Bordeaux and Vincent near the starboard railing, while I heard a shot ring out from Cuyler to my left. Like the bow canons on a British man-of-war naval frigate in the eighteenth century, Helena and Cuyler continued to deliver punishing shots at the enemy in front of us.

But it wasn't enough. We needed a better plan. I looked back and scanned the deck, seeing for the first time as dozens of legionnaires in full combat gear assembled neatly into rows, using each other for balance, a centurion barking orders for them to stay in formation. I noticed Gaius and Marcus among them and left Helena to catch up to them.

"What's going on??" I yelled, listening to the rhythmic pelting of rain striking the metallic armor they wore.

Marcus tilted his head at me, causing his helmet to slip to the side. He lifted it back into position and ran a hand down his face, fruitlessly trying to wipe it dry.

"Is it not obvious, Hunter?" He yelled back at me.

I looked at the legionnaires that held formation beside me again, but then turned back to Marcus and looked at him with an impatient look. "*No!*"

"I thought you were a man of history, Hunter!" Gaius remarked. "You do know just how well our navies handle themselves, correct?"

Both he and Marcus smiled at me.

Of course I knew. I just hadn't realized it until now. Rome's navy had been the greatest of its day, but it wasn't because of any naval strategy or technologically advanced ship. In fact, their ships were just copies of those invented by other nations, but they were the best because they had adapted their acumen at land based warfare, and applied it to naval warfare. Their main naval tactic was to pull alongside an opposing ship, drop some kind of anchor to attach the two together, and board it. They would then let their unrivaled sword fighting do the rest.

Genius really.

I returned their smiles as realization set it, then craned my neck to look over their shoulders to study the enemy fleet formation. There were four ships dead ahead, two directly astern, and another two off to port. I didn't see what else we could do besides get close to the four in front of us, and shoot as many of them as we could before the Romans took care of the rest. Blood was bound to be spilt on both sides, but that was war, and I couldn't think of another option.

"Hunter!" The voice was loud, even over the roar of the storm. I looked to discover its source, but the weather kept me from locating it. I tried again but then gave up, turning back to look out over the water to await the coming battle.

"Hunter!" The voice yelled out again, but this time Archer came running through the gathered legionnaires in my direction. I reached out and gripped his shoulder as he came up to me, leaning in close so that we could better hear each other.

"What?"

"Why are you just standing here?" He yelled. "Let's take them out!"

"Unless you brought a few missiles with you, I have no idea how!"

He looked at me sourly. "What? I thought you were a SEAL!"

"Yeah, like five years ago! I don't know…"

"Come on!" He yelled, yanking my arm.

I stumbled after him as he led me to the stairs that led below deck. Legionnaires stood there, awaiting their turn up top should a comrade fall, and we had to push through them to reach the ship's interior. They slowed us down, but finally we made our way to the lower deck where the rain vanished and I could finally hear myself think again.

I stopped for a second to open my jaw and pop my ears, hoping to dislodge a bit of water that seemed to have gathered there. It remained stubborn until I tugged on my earlobe and pounded the opposite side of my head with my palm, and with one last shake, I felt clarity return.

I ran to catch up with Archer, finding him in our makeshift armory, which was a mess after the rocking ship had knocked down a number of boxes, some breaking open to spill their contents onto the deck. Archer was digging through one such overturned box, and I found myself growing concerned for his sanity.

"Archer, what are you…"

"Strip, Hunter."

"What?"

"Strip!" He said more emphatically, twisting at the waist to glare at me.

I really had no idea what he was up to, but I pulled my shirt over my head all the same.

"I really had no idea you were into me like this, Archer, but…"

"Just shut up, and hold this."

I'd just unbuckled my belt when Archer threw two small backpacks at me. I unzipped one of them and peeked inside to find a large explosive.

A powerful one.

My pants fell around my ankles. "Wait… you're not thinking about…"

Archer shot to his feet and pulled his own shirt off. "That's right, Hunter. We're going for a swim."

He kicked off his boots and pulled off his pants, and made his way top side in nothing but his compression shorts. I looked down at my smiley faced boxers and winced. I'd picked a bad day to wear them.

I ran to catch up.

"Archer, wait. I haven't been an active SEAL in over five years. I can't go swimming in a storm like this. And my side. I don't have full mobil…"

"Quit your whining," Archer said. "You can make it. Don't you want to save lives, or not?"

I stopped as Archer reached the first Romans blocking our way. I did want to save lives. Of course I did.

But like this?

"But I'm going to lose my favorite boxer shorts!"

"Not my problem," he yelled. "Let's go."

"I'm going to make it your problem…" I mumbled as I pushed through the Romans.

Off to my left, I caught sight of Artie as she was waving to catch my attention.

"What are you doing, Jacob?" She asked, glancing at my exposed lower half then up again.

"It's really best you didn't know," I called back.

"Tell me you're not going in the water!"

"Sorry, can't do that," I said, just before I was swept away by the sea of soldiers and toward the steps.

Once above deck, I noticed Archer speaking with Gaius and Marcus, who seconds later ran off. I made my way carefully toward him, noting that the waves seemed even worse now, but before I arrived, he was already running toward the port railing. I finally caught up with him a few seconds later, and reached out to grip the railing to steady me. Together, we looked out at the pair of ships that had maneuvered to sit just a hundred meters or so away while we'd been below deck.

"So this is your plan?" I yelled. "Just swim over there blind, plant a bomb, and then swim back?"

"There was a bit more to it than that, honestly," Archer commented, looking over his shoulder. I followed his gaze and saw Gaius and Marcus returning with huge rolls of rope coiled around their arms. Gaius handed an end to Archer, who immediately went to work tying it around his waist.

"Oh, this is much better," I commented as Marcus handed me my own rope. I grunted in frustration but took it, and tied it around my waist as well.

"Like your plans are ever much better, Hunter!" Archer yelled.

"Yeah," I said, "but my plans are shit, not insane!"

"Deal with it," Archer said before taking a seat on the railing and rolling backward off of it and into the water. I didn't even hear a splash. I turned and gave Marcus a hard look and pointed a finger at him.

"Do *not* tell Helena!"

He nodded vigorously as he held onto the other end of my rope, knowing better than to tell Helena anything at all. I gave him another frustrated look, but then leapt onto the railing and pushed off of it with a foot, diving far out into the water.

I hit like a knife slicing into a bowl of frozen yogurt, which was an apt analogy since the first sensation that hit me was the cold. It seemed freezing, but my mind knew it wasn't quite. The next sensation, one I was mostly prepared for, was the intensity of the tide and savagery of the currents. It was like swimming through an active ice cream maker. Every stroke I took was a strenuous endeavor, and after only a few dozen meters of swimming, fatigue had already set in.

But I kept swimming, working hard to keep Archer in sight ahead of me and my body near the surface. It was hard with the rolling waves, but I didn't want to go too low for fear of some sub-current whisking me off course. But this was what Navy SEALs were trained for. Sure, we took part in land battles and operations in every imaginable environment, and while other military units trained underwater as well, this is what *we did*. We logged more hours in the water than any other operator on the planet, and while I never thought I'd ever need to free swim in a storm like this one, that training was paying off now. Any lesser man would have been swept away, but my powerful lungs and well-honed swimming muscles, albeit underused ones, guided me straight and true.

Archer suddenly broke off to the right, but I kept going straight, pushing myself harder and harder when, finally, my hand smacked into the hull of my target ship. I was exhausted and out of breath, and forced myself to breach the water to find air. It was a struggle just to do that, and once above the water line, I found myself in a maelstrom of rain and waves and wind. It was a hellish environment and I could barely move, but I still had a job to do. With quick but methodic motions, I reached into my bag and removed the explosive. I held it in my left hand and reached back in to grab a tube of waterproof epoxy. I slathered it on haphazardly, threw the tube into the sea, and attached the explosive to the hull.

I was spent as I pressed it against the ship, but with a last burst of energy, I yanked on my rope, hoping Marcus felt the sudden tug. I grew lightheaded as I waited, struggling to breathe, but then I thought I felt myself being dragged through the water gently. A moment later, the rope around my waist seemed to tighten, and I was certain Marcus had received my message. Within minutes I was back at the ship and being pulled up from the water, two large, meaty hands picking me up and over the railing like he was reeling in a large trout.

I looked up and saw Bordeaux standing over me.

"You are the craziest man I have ever met, Hunter!" He exclaimed

I smiled and glanced to my left, seeing that Archer was just now being pulled from the ocean himself. He looked at me, panting for air as well, and nodded.

"Beat you!" I yelled, but then realized that the rain was starting to wear itself down, and that it was simply the pounding in my head from the swim that caused my diminished hearing ability. Archer smirked at me in good humor, and reached out a hand. Gaius placed something there, but then he extended Archer to me. I took it, recognized it, and then held it out for Bordeaux. "Care to do the honors, explosion boy?"

He smiled, took the detonator, and pressed the button. A pair of booms and fireballs went off behind me, and I turned my neck painfully to see one of the huge plumes of fire spread up into the rainy air, and the ship begin to capsize. The other did the same.

Bordeaux helped me off the railing, and I was thankful since I wasn't sure I could have done it on my own. The entire operation had taken no more than eight minutes, but I felt like I'd just run a marathon. I looked up at the large Frenchman and smacked his arm, his massive bicep as hard as a rock through his wet shirt.

"Does this mean we're friends again?" I asked.

"We never weren't, Jacob," He said, his voice apologetic as he dropped his head, "*Je suis désolé, mon ami.*"

"Nothing to apologize for, big guy. We all make mistakes."

He looked up but said nothing more, and I took his silence in stride and looked out over the deck. What I saw there was disheartening: a number of corpses lined along the starboard railing, some with blankets already covering their bodies. There were at least two dozen lying there, but as I looked up, I was at least comforted by the sight of the remaining pirate ships breaking off as the storm continued to calm.

"What happened?" I asked.

Bordeaux started to answer, but was interrupted by Helena leaping off the bow deck in our direction. She looked at me, clearly startled at what she was seeing.

"Jacob!" She yelled, rain sputtering from her lips, her hair matted flat. "What happened to you?" She looked down. "And what happened to your clothes??"

I looked at my lower half, finally taking notice of the fact that my fears had been confirmed, and that I'd lost my favorite boxer shorts. A low laugh escaped my lips, too tired to be embarrassed, while Bordeaux looked away sheepishly as he too realized my plight, and took a step backward before rushing below deck.

I watched him go but answered Helena's question by nodding my head toward the burning ships that were just now beginning to sink below the water line. She looked over my shoulder, but didn't seem to understand what I meant.

"What happened here?" I asked, trying to distract her before she actually figured it out.

She crossed her arms and shook her head, obviously confused.

"The pirates never came close enough for hand to hand combat," she said, not having to yell quite as loudly anymore, "but they pulled in close enough to throw spears at us, and hit a few legionnaires from what I've heard, but mostly members of the crew. It looked like they were about ready to board when suddenly they broke off." She gestured at the burning ships. "I suppose we have you to thank for that."

"It was Archer's idea," I clarified.

"Mmhmm," she hummed, before stepping aside as Bordeaux returned with a pair of pants. He held them out and I took them, embarrassment finally settling in.

One side of Helena's lips tugged upward, and she said, "Why don't you give us a minute, Bordeaux? Someone's got to help him put his clothes back on..."

The hulking Frenchman nodded awkwardly, and quickly stepping away, giving me the space I needed to get dressed. I stepped a leg into the pants and looked up at Helena.

"I'm sorry, Helena, but it all happened so fast. Archer and I were really the only two options. No one else..."

"It's all right, Jacob," she said, reaching out a hand and placing it on my chest. She leaned in and kissed me tenderly, and then pulled away with a small smile. "I understand. You probably saved a lot of lives."

I looked back at the bodies as I clasped the pants around my waist and zipped up the fly. "But not all of them."

"Hey," she said softly, placing her hand against my cheek, the rain no more than a drizzle now. "It wasn't your fault. You did more than enough, believe me."

She leaned in and kissed me again, and wrapped her arms around my neck. I put my left hand against her lower back and held her, but the comfort I felt at words was miniscule. She clung to me there for some time, until Santino wandered over and coughed into his hand. I looked at him and no longer saw the pirate persona that had been ever-present since the beginning of the trip, but instead saw my friend in a way I rarely saw him.

He looked just as tired and beaten down as the rest of us.

"Hey, John," I called tiredly.

He didn't say anything at first, content to simply stare at me blankly.

"There's something you should see," he finally said, waving a hand for me to follow.

I nodded and Helena was already pulling away. She gave me a small smile, and I returned it before taking her hand and leading her to follow Santino. We passed by the few dozen bodies on the deck, and I watched as those Romans who had lost friends, spend a few minutes presiding over their fallen comrades' corpses. Everywhere else, crewmen were scampering here and there, cleaning up blood, readying to make sail again, and surveying damage, but Santino ignored all this and continued his patrol, heading toward the stern. He climbed the steps slowly, using the railing to balance himself as he ascended to the bridge, while Helena and I followed, hand in hand, wondering what was wrong.

We reached the top and found our pair of teams gathered there in a circle, but I was too tired and there were too many people these days for me to perform a snap head count. Santino took an open spot in the circle while Helena and I shambled closer, and that's when I noticed the body on the ground. Helena stopped walking the second she noticed it, but I was transfixed by the sight of it, and against my better judgment, knew I had to see who it was. Vaguely aware of everyone's eyes on me as I drifted toward the body, I knelt beside it and gripped the blanket.

I let out a breath and carefully pulled it back.

Recognition set in immediately, and my lower lip started to quiver.

His eyes were open but lifeless, staring up into the night sky as rain continued to sprinkle onto his face, an old and tired one that I'd never seen look so frightened and concerned as it did right now, as though he'd seen death approaching. I squeezed my own eyes shut and lowered my head as the tears came, no longer sure I could continue looking at Vincent's lifeless corpse without losing it completely.

But then I lost it anyway.

I hated that tears came so easily to me now. It hadn't been so easy in my other life, not since my father had smacked and punched the tears from my system when I was just a kid. *Men don't cry*, or so he was always so fond of telling me, and the only time I could remember crying before arriving in Rome was at the news of my mother's death, and even then my tears had been light, and had dried quickly.

When I cried now, however, I *wept*, no longer caring what others thought or even being aware that they were nearby to judge. Even Homer's Greek heroes had openly wept, all the time in fact, from Achilles to Hector to Odysseus, and I was no different now. It was all I could do to keep myself from dying inside, all I could do to release my demons before they grew out of my control.

I felt myself leaning forward now, my head dipping toward Vincent's body so that my forehead could rest against his chest as I sobbed. My hand reached out and grabbed for his head, and around my tears, I wanted to do nothing more than to rip his hair out or beat his face to a pulp for leaving me like this. How many times had I gone to him for advice? Tell him of my issues? Seek his guidance in a time of need, knowing he'd never betray my confidence or lead me in the wrong direction? Like a priest he'd once pretended to be, Vincent had been such a consistent force for good in my life, one I could turn to at every impasse and seek everything a man without direction could need.

And even a degree of salvation as well, it had seemed.

He'd been the father I'd never had, and now, like with Varus, I would have to be the one to tell Titus and his infant son, Brian Wilson, that he was dead. That he would never again return to guide them, to teach them, to offer them the support they would need as they grew older.

All because of me.

"Jacob..."

The voice came from behind me, but it wasn't Helena's, and I was too distracted to recognize it. Nor did I want to. All I wanted was to stay by Vincent's side and let go of the pain within me, one tear at a time.

"Jacob... it's all right."

The voice was closer now, and I felt a hand land on my shoulder and rub it gently. It pulled me back, comfortingly, and I turned to pull whoever it was into a hug. I didn't even care if the hand belonged to Archer in that moment; all I cared about was the comfort he would give me.

Through blurry eyes, I looked at the man willing to risk interrupting my grief, half expecting it to be Bordeaux or Wang, both very supportive individuals in their own ways, but the man was neither large enough nor small enough to be either. I figured it to be Santino then, but when my eyes cleared, I discovered it was Santino either.

It was Vincent.

My tears dried up almost immediately and I recoiled from his touch, practically flinging myself to the side and away from him. I scrambled backward in a crab crawl, almost barreling my way into Archer and Brewster who stood on the other side of the gathered circle, staring at me with looks that would warrant the, "you look like you've seen a ghost," comment.

Because I had.

"It's all right, Jacob," Vincent said from where he knelt with his hand held in my direction. "It's all right to be upset. She didn't deserve this."

She?

Who?

My head jerked left and right, registering the faces around me. All of my original friends were there with Archer and Brewster standing on either side of me, and Cuyler was beside her, Stryker stood beside him.

It was then that Brewster knelt down and placed her hand on my back to keep me from scooting even further away, but she looked up desperately, not really knowing how to handle the situation. No one had any advice to offer her as they stood just as shocked and upset as I was – except those emotions were now clearly directed at my reaction, rather than the loss of their friend.

Finally, with my heart racing, I worked up the nerve to look at the body. I stood, Brewster standing with me and offering her support, but when I stepped forward she remained where she was. After another step, I looked down and discovered that the corpse below me was no longer Vincent, but Technical Sergeant Patricia Martin, her short, disheveled hair just a wet mop atop her head and the sun tattoo on her cheek somehow darker now.

The cause of death was obvious. There was a small, red circle in the center of her throat, either the entry or exit wound from an arrow. Perhaps Wang had been busy, or hadn't noticed and hadn't been there for her as he had been for so many of us over the years, and she must have bled out – a slow, lonely, terrifying death.

I looked up and saw Vincent's comforting eyes again, and he too seemed on the verge of tears, perhaps my own emotional outburst too much for him as well. In fact, the expression was shared by many. Tears streamed from Helena's eyes to intermingle with drops of rain that escaped her hair to pour down her cheeks, while Santino stood beside her, holding her with a consoling arm wrapped around her back, his own eyes looking just as dour.

But expressions all around were shifting now, turning to look just as confused as I felt. They didn't understand my initial, emotional outburst, how severe it had been, and how it had all just evaporated in an instant.

Nor did I, and it left me feeling empty.

I risked one last look at Martin, who was very obviously not Vincent.

My mouth quivered with unspoken words, but only a single thought continued to pervade my mind as I stood there:

What the hell was happening to me?

VI
Britannia

Oceanus Britannicus, the English Channel
December, 42 A.D.

"Land ahead!"

It was a simple announcement, but a great cheer rose up from the gathered individuals on deck at the sound of it nonetheless. We'd been at sea far too long, and people were beginning to get antsy. Once we'd turned north after passing Gibraltar, or the Pillars of Hercules as they were referred to today, the temperature had almost immediately started its downward plunge toward freezing, so everyone was very excited about the idea of huddling around a fire again, although my slaves were not quite as excited as everyone else.

Before we'd set out over a month ago, I'd told them to nominate one of their peers as a representative to approach me with issues. The Romans had balked at the concept, but they weren't in a position to argue, and when the representative came to me, it was often to remind me of my agreement to free them upon arrival, but no matter how many times I assured him I would uphold my end of the bargain, the man never believed me.

I guess I couldn't blame him.

There was just no way for him to know that their release was one of the things I was most excited for. The act of purchasing them still haunted me, and their eventual release was the only thing that could settle my emotional burden. Little excited me more than the idea of releasing them upon the Isle of Britannia, and seeing their faces as they came to realize they would be able to start a new life in a new world.

As for my team, they were holding up as well as could be expected.

No one had really been sure how to react after my episode with Patricia, least of all me. Everyone had just melted off into the night one by one, leaving me alone with Vincent, Santino, Helena, and Brewster, who had stood by me to the very end, having had no idea what to do with herself. She'd been the next one to leave, and then Vincent, who had looked at me in certain understanding as he'd disappeared from sight. He knew I'd had another vision, he just hadn't known what it was, and I hadn't had the heart to tell him.

Helena and Santino had then split apart, Helena to help me up and Santino to move the body of Patricia Martin to where the other bodies were being gathered. Neither had spoken to me, not even Helena as she led me below deck and helped me to bed. I'd slept for twelve hours that night, and it had been years since I'd last had so restful a sleep.

I'd awoken feeling immensely better, and ready to finish our sea voyage.

Interactions between team members had been awkward after that, but everyone, including myself, had slowly returned to normal. Martin's death had been hard on everyone, but since Archer's team had been thrown together only a month or so before they'd come to Rome, no one had been especially close with her. Her funeral at sea had been sad and heartfelt, but her body had been just one of many cast into the deep that day.

Today, only Santino still grieved, but nor for Martin, but because he had been forced to give up his pirate routine, and was now banned from ever uttering the sound "argh" or saying the word "scallywag" again. He'd packed up his eye patch and pulled down his Jolly Rodger yesterday, packing them away for what I hoped was forever. Everyone had gotten a kick out of watching him pull the thing down as slowly as he could, hoping to eke out every last bit of the joke as he could.

I smiled as the memory still amused me, but then grew impatient as a week seemed to have passed since the first announcement of land.

In that time a thin line on the horizon slowly began to take form, but it would still be another few hours before we reached our destination, although its sight was still comforting. I glanced to my left to inquire into Helena's thoughts on reaching land again, but I noticed she was no longer where I'd last seen her. I looked further to the left, and saw her leaning over the side of the railing. A smile tugged my lips again and I moved to join her.

I crept up beside her and crossed my arms atop the railing.

"Morning sickness?" I asked, looking down at her.

I heard her retch into the sea and I couldn't help but cringe and look away.

"I'm on a boat," she said, her head still over the railing. "It's not as simple as 'morning sickness.'"

I rubbed her back. "Don't worry. Only a few more hours and we'll be walking on solid ground again."

"Great," she said with another heave, prompting me to pull away from her. "Then I can do this wherever I please. Not just over the railing."

I wrinkled my nose. "You're not ser…"

"Oh, Jacob, just shut the hell…"

Another bout of sickness cut her off.

Her queasy stomach had only manifested itself a few weeks ago, but I was completely ignorant of how a woman's body worked during pregnancy, so I didn't know how normal this was. I'd thought pregnant women experienced this kind of thing early on and generally in the morning, but Helena was five months in and had seemed constantly sick since our encounter with the pirates.

I really hoped it was just the boat.

After a few minutes passed without another sound from Helena, I tentatively helped her to her feet. I held her by the arms and rubbed them to help warm her up. She smiled at the gesture, but didn't seem any less sick.

"Feel better?" I asked.

"Ask me again in five months," she responded, taking a deep breath and an exaggerated gulp. She shook her head. "I didn't expect to get so sick, especially since I'd avoided it earlier on."

"Is it normal to be sick so late?"

Helena laughed and smacked my arm. "My God, Jacob, you really don't know a thing about anything, do you? Every woman's pregnancy is going to be different. Although… my mother told me that difficult pregnancies tend to lead to girls rather than boys. It's just an old wives' tale, but… well, I can dream, right?"

I laughed. "Maybe you should start wishing for a boy as well."

She glared at me. "You'd better toughen up yourself, Hunter. If you think it's bad now, just wait till the end."

"I'll keep that in mind, but until then, think you can make it another few hours without losing your lunch?"

She looked out over the water and gulped again. "No promises."

***

Five hours later, with Gnaeus at the helm, we were just about ready to make landfall somewhere in southeastern England, interestingly, just east of modern day London. Traveling through the English Channel had been fairly smooth, and seagulls flew hazardously around the deck. One of our legionnaires had speared one in midair, and was already hard at work cleaning it in preparation for dinner. Supplies had been a bit limited these past few days, and the men were getting hungry. Stryker often poked fun at Brewster's logistical shortcomings, but the woman easily countered his jibes by indicating they'd all have starved to death by now had it not been for her.

That usually shut him up.

While no one had gone completely hungry, we were on two meals a day. We'd be fine once we connected with the legion garrison located at Camulodunum, modern day Colchester, where the Romans had established their capital, but our initial landing was bound to be chaotic. With crewmen, legionnaires, time travelers, and slaves all trying to get off the boat and return to land, it was sure to be a mess. At least the legionnaires were well disciplined, as nothing evoked unit cohesion like a hard ass centurion who made Marine Corp drill sergeants look like flower girls at a wedding.

"Ten minutes!" Gnaeus shouted over the sounds of the sea and excited crewmen.

I turned my head and saw Helena smiling at me, while Santino, Wang, and Stryker stood just beside her, leaning against the railing as well.

"What?" I asked.

"Nothing," she said as she looked away. "It's just that you look pretty happy right now, and it makes me feel the same."

"I do?"

She looked back. "You do. Keep it up."

***

"No!" I shouted. "This stuff goes here, and that stuff goes there! How hard is this?"

"Quite difficult," the random legionnaire reported, "when your friend's orders contradict your own."

He didn't stick around to clarify his report, and instead went back to unpacking his crate. I blew on my hands to warm them and then stuffed them in my pockets. It was too damn cold out here for this shit. I had over ten thousand legionnaires and half as many auxiliary troops milling about on the beach trying to get organized, yet I couldn't arrange our own pitiful amount of gear properly. Legionnaires were already hard at work digging trenches and building fortifications for our camp tonight, but here I was struggling to find our simple sleeping equipment.

I pulled my right hand from its pocket and immediately felt it grow cold as I pressed the push-to-talk button on my radio. "Santino, where the hell do you keep telling these guys to put our stuff?"

Santino was still onboard the ship, which had run aground and sat idle about forty meters from where I currently stood. I saw a small figure move over to the railing and look down at me.

"Where you told me," he said through the radio. "Weapons and gear near the sand dune, supplies and clothing on that clump of grass."

"No, I said the opposite!"

"Well maybe you should be more specific next time."

"More specific? How more specific do you need to me to be??"

There was a pause before he replied. "How more specific *can* you be?"

"Just make sure they get it right this time!" I ordered, very nearly losing my cool. "I have more important things to do."

"Like what?"

"Like running an army!"

"Oh, is that what you've been doing all this time? Could have fool…"

"Give it a rest, Santino," Helena's voice cut in over the coms. "Jacob's got a lot of things to do."

"I'm just trying to train him," Santino radioed. "Just wait until the little guy gets here. Then he's going to have *lots* of things to do."

"Well, in that case..." Helena said, but I didn't hear her through the coms, but from behind me instead. I turned around and saw her climbing the shallow hill, an amused expression on her face. She reached up and removed her ear piece, and didn't say anything else.

"In that case what?" Santino asked, but we both ignored him. "What?"

He continued asking as I took my ear piece out as well.

"See," Helena said as she walked up to me. "He's going to make a great uncle."

"Yeah, he's exactly the kind of uncle the kid will need," I said sarcastically. "Leave him alone with Wang and Santino for a few days and they'll warp his mind."

"Aw, you're being too hard on them. I think they'll be great uncles."

I looked at her in shock. "Who are you and what have you done with Helena?"

"Jacob, stop, you know they'd never do anything to hurt her."

"That's not exactly what I'm worried about."

"I know..." she paused. "But maybe the baby will need personalities like theirs around."

"You think we're going to be bad parents or something?" I asked, not really knowing how to take her comment.

"Of course not, but..."

"But what?" I asked, crossing my arms.

"It's just that we've been dealing with a lot, you and me. We aren't the same people we were all those years ago when we first met. We've changed, and it hasn't all been for the better."

"Helena, come on, we..."

"No, listen to me, Jacob. I'm not saying we will be bad parents or that we should hand her off to Bordeaux or Vincent to raise her without us, but I think she'll benefit from their influence. All of them, your sister's too."

I sighed and reached out to grip Helena's hands. "I suppose you're right. We're pretty messed up. I think me more than you…"

"Well obviously," she said with a laugh.

"Very funny."

"So are you ready to…"

"Movement in the woods!"

I looked beyond Helena to see dozens of legionnaires grab swords and shields as the warning was called out up and down the lines. Helena was already running toward our supply pile to pull her shotgun from a crate. She found Penelope as well and tossed it to me, but she caught me by surprise and I almost dropped her. I glared at Helena for her carelessness but she ignored me. Together we ran toward the front line of legionnaires setting up a perimeter around the makeshift camp.

It was getting dark, and I hadn't had time to grab my NVGs or attach my night vision scope to my rifle, so I couldn't see much as I peered into the woods. Bordeaux, Wang, and Brewster joined our position and fell beside Helena, their weapons raised as well.

"See anything?" Wang asked.

"Not yet," I replied.

To my left, a centurion crawled his way toward my position, knelt beside me, and looked off into the tree line. I immediately identified him as Vespasian's old first file centurion, Fabius.

"Legate," he said, referring to me, which was still weird since I hadn't had heard it much while onboard our ship. "Two of my scouts report a small band of men on horseback, maybe forty. They do not appear to be local barbarians, but my men were unable to identify them."

"Thank you, Fabius," I replied. I didn't know him very well yet since we'd been on separate ships during the voyage, but from the little time I'd spent with him, I'd learned to trust his instincts and rely on his advice. "Nothing two legions should be unable to handle, yes?"

"Indeed, Legate. They should be in range shortly."

"Good. Tell your men to act defensively only. I want to question them first."

"As you say, Legate."

I nodded and turned back toward the line patiently, but excitement rarely took its time around here. No more than a minute after I'd concluded my conversation with Fabius did I see a number of horses materialize out of the darkness. The troops laid low, not engaging immediately as Fabius had relayed to them, and I waited until the interlopers were well within missile range before I stood and took a step in their direction.

"Halt," I called out in Latin, not knowing if they would understand, "you have wandered into the camp of two Roman legions. If you wish to live, I would advise that you explain your presence here."

"Gods be damned!" The man yelled frightfully in a gruff voice. "Stand down, Hunter!"

I peered into the woods curiously, the voice familiar. "Identify yourself."

The voice didn't reply, but horses moved in my direction. Helena tapped my thigh and I glanced down to see her holding a flashlight. I grabbed it, flicked it on, took aim at the man who had spoken, and smiled as recognition set in. There was only one person I knew who could have so fat and ugly a face, but still have an exceptionally fit build and carry himself with such charisma.

"How did you know it was me?" I asked.

"Lower your torch," Servius Sulpicius Galba said, raising his hand to block the light. When I did, he lowered his hand and stared at me angrily. "I knew, because only you and your ilk bastardize Latin as horribly as you do, and only you, Hunter, could get me into a situation like this…"

***

"I will inform you promptly that I am not happy with my current appointment," Galba announced as we stood around my desk inside the *praetorium* that I now got to call my own – which was pretty sweet.

"Aw, and here I thought you missed us," Santino joked.

"What could I miss?" Galba grunted, turning a stern look in Santino's direction. "Your mere presence in my world has led to nothing but bloodshed and catastrophe, and dare I mention, has been detrimental to my career as well."

I rolled my eyes. Ever since we'd met Galba all those years ago, he'd shown nothing but distrust and resentment toward us. Yet, every time we'd sought his help, he came through for us and delivered on his promises – although he did so grudgingly and with excessive complaining.

"Galba," I said, "I already told you what happened to you in my timeline. Trust me; at the rate you're going, you'll end up better off."

"I do not need your help to achieve high station," he growled. "Nor do I need your help to be remembered."

I chuckled but let the man think as he did. He was an extremely proud and stubborn man, and there was no point trying to reason with someone like that. And yet, he was also a good man. He was a proficient and effective general, a loyal soldier, and a man we could count on to help us, even if he never knew why. I was glad he was here, despite his own misgivings about us.

"Just remember who's in command here, Galba," I told him bluntly. "Vespasian put me in charge."

"I remember quite well... Legate," Galba said with a nod in my direction. He clasped his hands behind his back and tipped what some would consider his chin at me. "I still find it difficult to believe that Vespasian has done what he has done, but even you are incapable of forging his seal, and I must believe these orders to be true. I shouldn't believe it, but I do. I must be growing stupid as I age."

"I'm glad you see it that way," I said with a nod of my own. "Now, what do you say we get down to business?"

"Fine," he said unhappily. "Allow me to discuss the military situation here in Britain first, and then we can decide on what to do with your little mission."

I did everything I could to keep the annoyance I felt off my face. Despite his shortcomings, I had to remember that Galba knew what he was doing. He had nothing but Rome's best interests at heart, interests that included the removal of Agrippina from power. That alone made him a rare ally, and while he'd never respect me, I knew he'd do everything I needed of him.

"Go on then," I ordered evenly, trying to remember my days as a leader of troops in another life. Patience was more than a virtue when dealing with recalcitrant subordinates, and I'd have to earn Galba's respect in the same way I had with the SEALS under my command a lifetime ago, the ones who had been combat veterans with many more years of experience than I once had.

"Very good," Galba said as he took a step closer to the table between us. Upon it was a rudimentary map of southern Britain, revealing only slightly more terrain than what Rome had already conquered. Central England, Wales, Scotland, and Ireland were nowhere to be seen.

Galba cleared his throat and delivered his report. "Earlier this year, four legions under command of Vespasian were finally able to subdue the populace of southeastern Britain prior to his redeployment to Germany. A number of tribes were offered the olive branch in peace, and many accepted, but most were put down through military force. The area was subdued, and Camulodunum became Aulus Plautius' seat of power, Agrippina's chosen governor in Britain."

I nodded. In my timeline, Aulus Plautius had been Vespasian's *superior* during the Invasion of Britain, not the other way around, except under Claudius instead of Agrippina, and was exactly who the emperor Claudius had named its governor once the invasion had concluded as well.

I was not surprised.

I held up a hand. "Whatever happened to Caratacus and..." I snapped my fingers and turned to Vincent, who stood beside Santino. "Who was the other guy?"

"Togodumnus," he answered immediately.

"Right, thanks. My Roman Invasion of Britain history is a little rusty."

Galba glared at me, clearly not amused. "Togodumnus was slain on the battlefield early in the invasion while Caratacus was later captured and sent to Rome for trial. It happened just before Vespasian and I were recalled to the German front. I have heard a rumor that he appealed to Agrippina for pity and forgiveness, regaling her with a magnificent speech to sway her opinion. However, he was unsuccessful, and Agrippina had him crucified."

My eyebrows arched in surprise and I turned to Vincent, who returned my look with a sad shake of his head. The only reason I even remembered Caratacus' name over Togodumnus' was because in the original timeline, Caratacus had given a similar speech, only to Claudius, who spared his life, freed him, and allowed him to live out the remainder of his days in Rome.

Although Caratacus shouldn't have been captured for another ten years.

Just another interesting parallel derailed because of my meddling.

"So who's raised up arms against Rome now?" I asked.

Galba shrugged. "It's unclear at this time. This land is rank with scattered tribes: Iceni, Atrebates, Cantiaci, Catuvellauni, amongst others, and I have not been kept fully up to date on the situation here since my time and attention has been, until recently, rather aptly focused on Germany."

I nodded absentmindedly as my eyes stared down at the map of Ancient Britain, my hand cupping my chin in thought. The map offered little help or insight, doing little more than act as a distraction as my eyes wandered toward where Wales should have been displayed. If the Isle of Mona was where I needed to go, that's really all I cared about. After everything we'd discovered in Alexandria, I was no longer interested in Roman politics, military strategy, or even the realignment of history.

I sighed, pushing such thoughts out of my mind, remembering that we still had other responsibilities. Vespasian had sent us here with a purpose, and I wasn't about to let down the one guy who was risking his life for us. We had to put down these rebellions so that Rome could establish its dominance here, allowing the English people in the coming centuries to develop a self-identity that aimed to emulate the Romans. If we didn't, there was no doubt in my mind that the Britain I remembered would cease to exist, and with it, even more bits of history.

I looked up with my eyes alone and looked at Galba. "Strategic recommendations?"

"I thought you were in command... Legate."

"I know when to defer to those with more experience, Galba. This is your area of expertise, not mine."

"Indeed," he replied, his voice suggesting he appreciated my confidence in him. "Well, we won't find any answers on this beach. I suggest we march your legions to Camulodunum and speak with Plautius. He's a good man and understands warfare well, and will appreciate reinforcements.

"Now, about this other duty you must embark on, please explain, and do not leave anything out that I may later deem important."

I sighed and took a seat at my desk, holding out a hand to indicate Galba should take a seat before me. Vincent moved to stand at my back while Santino stood off to the side of the tent with his arms crossed, but Galba didn't move.

"I don't need to remind you that what I'm about to say is extremely important and very confidential, correct?" I asked Galba.

"If it has to do with your orb, then yes, you need not remind me."

"Good," I answered before leaning back in my chair lazily. "Our mission here in Britain has nothing to do with fixing broken history or usurping heads of state. It has nothing to do with you, or the legions outside, or even anything to do with the Roman Empire. Instead, it has *everything* to do with the orb. It's a fact finding mission to track down people who may know something about its origin or how we can operate it properly."

Galba huffed and looked sidelong at Santino, then up at Vincent, before returning his attention back to me. "I do not even know where to begin, Hunter, but it would be a gesture of good faith if you would at least tell me where you were planning to go."

"The Isle of Mona."

"I have heard of such a place," he said, curiosity in his voice, and finally took his seat. A haven for vagabonds, criminals, and… ah… Druids. I understand then. Where is it?"

I leaned in and pointed at an empty part of the crude map. Galba glanced at my pointed finger and raised his eyebrows in surprise.

"Impossible!" He nearly shouted. "Even with both of your legions, such a trip would be suicidal. The territory between here and there is hostile, and I would not let you take even a single century of men with you. Your troops are needed with Plautius, defending Camulodunum and then counterattacking more local enemies come spring, not gallivanting across the country!"

I pulled my finger back and placed my hand in my lap. "I understand your concerns, Galba, but as you've already reminded me, you're not in command here. *I* am. And the Isle of Mona is where I have to go, so that is where I am going, whether you like it or not."

Galba stood so suddenly that his chair fell backward and crashed into the grass. He raised a finger and pointed it at me accusingly. "You've always been too arrogant for your own good, Hunter! I can't believe I just wasted seconds of my life listening to you lie about deferring to those with better judgment while you sit there now and countermand such logic."

"Sit down, Galba," I said impatiently, but he didn't listen. "I didn't say I was just going to take the legions with me and leave your precious ass undefended. I agreed with you that we need to reach Camulodunum and regroup with Plautius, where we'll be able to work out a spring campaign that will accommodate us both. I'm not in a hurry."

Galba glared at me and didn't speak, choosing instead to pick up his map and leave. I watched him go, oddly not caring that I'd just driven him up a wall.

Santino watched him go, and hooked a thumb at his retreating backside. "Again with these people not saying goodbye..."

Vincent walked around my desk and picked up the chair Galba had just overturned. "He's not someone you want to make an enemy of, Jacob. He's a competent general and a sound strategist, and he knows legions in a way that academics like you and I will never understand. We need his support."

"You think I don't know that, Vincent?" I asked. "I do, I just don't need him thinking that he has any actual sway over my decision making ability."

"Then why did you just lie to him?" Santino asked to my left. "Wait, did you just lie to him?

I looked up at him, frustration beginning to simmer in the pit of my stomach. "I didn't lie to him, John. All I want is for him to remember who's in command here."

I looked back to Vincent, who after a moment of thought, finished his movement and set the chair to stand on its legs. He gave it a look before straightening his posture and setting his eyes to look just above my head.

"With your permission, Legate, I'll take me leave."

I sighed and waved a hand at him. "Vincent, it's not like that. I'm..."

"With your permission, sir."

I felt my frustration with Galba turn into anger directed at Vincent, but before I let it, I lowered my hand to the table before flicking it to the side. Taking the hint, Vincent tipped his head, turned on his heels, and left my *praetorium*.

"I think I'll go too then," Santino said, but before I could ask him to stay, he rushed from the tent, leaving me alone.

I sat there in both verbal and mental silence for a few minutes, deciding there was no point in wasting my energy worrying about Santino, Galba, *or* Vincent. I found myself relaxing into my stiff chair and letting myself fall into a kind of mental daze, a state of mind that seemed to come so easily these days. My mind wandered, never able to lock onto anything specific or relevant, like a night trying to fall asleep when what seemed like every memory, song lyric, movie quote, life experience, or comment I'd ever experienced invaded and raced through my mind and refused to go away. I felt sweat bead on my forehead as I sat in my daze, but it was over in seconds and the distractions were gone.

When I opened my eyes and came out of my stupor, I found that I was no longer sitting behind my desk, but sprawled out on the grassy ground, my hands held out and placed on my footlocker. I looked at it, trying to divine its significance, but all I felt was a coldness that trickled down my spine as I realized my hands were completely numb.

I pulled them away and rolled onto my back so that I could stick them between my armpits, hoping to warm them. As feeling returned seconds later, I stood and made my way toward my bed, which I plopped onto without hesitation. I pulled the sheets up to my neck and tried to sleep – perturbed, spooked, and wishing Helena was there.

As though on command, I felt a slight breeze on my cheek, indicating someone had parted the tent's entrance flap. I opened my eyes on reflex alone, knowing only one person would dare enter the Legate's tent unannounced.

Helena crossed the small space between us in three long strides and carefully sat on the bed beside me. I shifted my body so that my head rested in her lap and stared at her growing baby bump, letting her brush my hair lightly with her hand. She looked down at me with a sweet expression and smiled.

"Feel all right?" She asked.

"Fine," I answered, hiding yet another lie. "You?"

"I feel okay," she answered. "I was just wondering what was keeping you. Your meeting ended an hour ago."

"It did?" I asked, looking away.

"It did. You must have fallen asleep."

"Yeah... I must have," I said to myself, wondering where that time had gone. I tried to think on it, but Helena's downtrodden expression diverted my attention. "What is it?"

Her mouth flickered and a supportive smile formed there, but it was slow to come. "I'm fine, Jacob, I promise. It's... it's just that the rowers are getting impatient about you coming through on your...."

"Christ..." I whispered, squeezing my eyes shut, feeling very angry at myself. "I completely forgot! God, I'm stupid! What the fu..."

"Calm down," Helena soothed, her voice concerned. "It's all right. Nobody's judging you for forgetting. You've had a lot of things to do today. You're not exactly a monster."

"I'm not?"

"Of course not!" She exclaimed. "What's wrong with you? The sla... rowers aren't even working, and we've even arranged for the men and women to mingle. They're content, just impatient."

I felt my frustration drift away at Helena's words.

"Quick thinking," I commented, forcing a small smile.

"Well, it was *my* idea," she quipped. "Now come on, General. Back to the trenches."

***

The next morning, my legions were marching toward Camulodunum.

At first light, the legions had begun the task of striking down their makeshift fort and packing all their belongings and gear for deployment. Their alacrity at completing such tasks never ceased to amaze me, and within hours, the entire contingent was lined up in marching order – legionaries, auxilia, cavalry, and time travelers all – although I'd been one of the last to ready myself for the march as I hadn't slept well the night before.

The act of freeing a thousand slaves hadn't been nearly as heartwarming as I'd thought it would be. I expected jubilant faces and dances of joy from those I had just freed from forced bondage, but instead, all I received were complaints, demands for work, advice on where to go, and threats on my life or certain body parts because I'd brought them here.

It all seemed like such a good idea two months ago in Judea. Had I not purchased them, they would have been sent to salt mines or forced to serve fruit while nude and painted gold to decadent Romans. I'd given them an opportunity to start over, in a land that was, for now, quite free of Roman influence. But this wasn't their home. Amazingly, a few of the slaves had been captured right here in Britain over a year ago and dragged all the way to Caesarea, but these I could count on a single hand. While they were happy to be home, Britain was a foreign land to the rest of them, as most had been prisoners of war brought to Judea from Germany by Vespasian's legions or recently captured in the Middle East.

In a cruel twist of irony, the only way to dissipate the irate group of former slaves had been to forcibly remove them at spear point and through the use of whips. I hadn't wanted it to happen, but they'd grown unruly and violent, and while in all probability most of them were happy or at least content with their current situation, the vociferous minority had ruined the moment for everyone, myself included. I'd watched reluctantly as the entire cadre of former slaves had been pushed past the tree line and into the wilderness, even the ones who would have thrown themselves at my feet and kissed my toes in thanks. It had been a horrendous sight, one I no longer wished to remember, but one I knew would stick with me for the rest of my days.

Only shipmaster Gnaeus had parted ways in good spirits, quite happy with all the money I'd sent his way. He and I had concluded our business dealings amicably later that night, although he hadn't had a single nice thing to say to me, and seemed quite eager to sail back to the Mediterranean and forget he'd ever known me.

Good riddance.

Helena had been supportive throughout the entire ordeal, but when we returned to our *praetorium*, I hadn't been in the mood for much of anything. I'd laid in bed for most of the night, not sleeping or even dozing, just lying there thinking and listening to Helena's rhythmic breathing, the kind that I knew indicated she was out cold and wouldn't be disturbed by a giant plodding through the middle of our tent.

Instead, I'd mulled over my recent bouts with what I was beginning to suspect was insanity – simple, good-old-fashioned, loony toon craziness. I'd always wondered if those deemed clinically unstable had felt themselves slipping into psychological oblivion, wondering if they could see it coming, knowing there was nothing they could do to stop it. I still didn't have an answer to that question, but I was fairly certain I could feel it in myself. Whether that meant they could as well, I couldn't be sure, but the one overlying factor in all of this was the orb.

I remember looking to my footlocker a number of times that night, but once my eyes fell upon it, I forgot exactly why it was I'd looked there at all, and I'd turn away again to stare at the ceiling.

According to Varus' note, he'd used the orb for quite some time, spending two years within the course of two months using the thing, and he hadn't seemed psychotic in the least in his letter. He had been sane, completely unlike the Other Me, and, interestingly, the jury was still out on Agrippina and whether she was affected as well. But as for me, I was beginning to suspect the worst, just as Agrippina herself seemed to have suggested back in her villa.

Was I going down the same dark path Caligula took?

Was I following in Claudius' exact footsteps?

I didn't know just yet, but if I was or if I wasn't, the legion marching beside me wouldn't benefit at all if I wasted all my effort trying to come to grips with my situation. They needed me for leadership and guidance, and although I wasn't certain exactly why, they'd latched onto me. The legionnaires from the *XV Primigenia* had heard stories over the past five years from those who had come before them, the same ones we'd fought with outside the walls of Rome. We were legends to these fresh legionnaires, and there were enough old timers still around who'd been quite familiar with us back then who continued to be in awe of us now. I, in particular, had developed even more of a reputation amongst them thanks to my relationship with Helena, something they'd all been quite jealous of.

And now I was back.

And now I was *leading* them.

I was their general.

To them, it was like being led by a god or something. Word had spread to the *II Augusta* as well, and even they too would stare slack jawed when I passed by, and while I didn't necessarily like how attached they'd become, I had to admit there was something gratifying in their appreciation.

Beneath me, Felix neighed in what seemed like annoyance and jerked his head lightly. I was so distracted by my thoughts that I almost fell off of him, but I managed to hang on. I glanced down and saw Felix shift his neck left and then right, as though he had heard every word of my meandering internal monologue and was trying to tell me that he didn't like it.

I smiled and patted his mane. "Don't be so upset, Felix. If I really am turning into Caligula, you probably stand to benefit the most out of it. Remember, he was the one who tried to appoint his horse as Consul."

Felix neighed again at the statement, almost like he was laughing at it now, only I didn't know if his laughter was directed at the joke or at me. I chose to ignore the idea that my horse was self-aware of his master's mental disposition and focused instead on the marching legionnaires beside and behind me.

Like everything a legion did, its marching order was methodical and practical. Cavalry scouts led the way and acted as flankers on either side of the marching column, while infantry surveyors and the pioneer corps that worked as engineers to clear obstacles or bridges followed. The officers' baggage train came next, then the main body of our cavalry, followed by myself, my fellow officers, and my friends. Behind us were the cargo trains that carried the legions' siege equipment, and behind that was the legion itself, which was easily the grandest spectacle to be seen as we made our trek toward Camulodunum. In all my years in Rome, I'd never seen a legion, let alone two, march its way toward a military objective, and I was very impressed.

Marching six abreast, they carried everything from their arms and armor to their rations and camp construction tools – earning their nickname of "mules." They were an impressive sight in their glittering *lorica segmentata* armor, freshly polished during the long voyage at sea. From our scouts to the camp followers behind the auxilia – which in turn marched behind the legions – our marching column may have spanned four miles. To an outside observer, it would have been a sight to behold, serving its intended purpose of telling the world: "Don't fuck with us."

And so far, no one had.

We hadn't landed far from Camulodunum, so we'd expected resistance from rebellious tribes almost immediately, but we hadn't seen much of anyone since leaving the beach. Even the landscape seemed as desolate as the local population. Open fields and rolling pastures were bordered by dense, deep forests that seemed quite spooky in their current state – their thick limbs now bare and dead-like as the winter months rolled in. The hills were also muddy and wet instead of green with grass, and an eternally overcast sky seemed to cloud us in a perpetual mist. I'd never been to England before, but it was very much as I imagined it would have been even in modern times. It all seemed very ancient, even in these *already* ancient times, and I was certain that once the snow came, the landscape would take on an even more mystical feel.

But it was also very peaceful, although the sounds of over twenty thousand individuals burst that serene bubble. These legions were going to war, and my friends and I would later continue on into the veritable unknown, passing into unfriendly territory without a guide or clear direction. Where we went once we reached the Isle of Mona was still anyone's guess, but I was certain it wouldn't be much of a vacation spot.

Hours rolled on as we marched and rode in silence, and I'd grown quite bored with myself, so at one point as the sun would have sat high in the sky were I able to see it, I finally turned to Vincent and asked him a question that had been on my mind since making landfall.

"If Camulodunum is Rome's provincial seat of power in Britain today, how come modern day Colchester isn't the capital instead of London?"

Helena, who rode to my left, burst out laughing, interrupting Vincent's response. We both turned to look at her, surprised at her sudden outburst. When her chuckles finally subsided, she asked, "You mean you don't know?"

I gave her a quizzical look. "Let's just say I forgot... but why the hell do you say it like that? Do *you* know?"

She gave me a smug grin. "I do actually."

This time it was my turn to laugh, and even Vincent displayed a rare smile. I turned to Helena and reseated myself on Felix's primitive make-shift saddle. It would have been a simple task of introducing the idea of stirrups to the Romans, but since such technology was centuries away from being invented, it seemed best just to deal with the situation and learn to ride without them.

I put on a display of making myself comfortable, settling in for a highly anticipated story.

"Oh, this I have to hear," I said.

She held up a hand. "Hold on. Let me enjoy this moment for a little while first."

I rolled my eyes and waited patiently. She watched me, but when it was clear I could wait all day, she let out a grumpy groan and began her story.

"In the year 60 or 61 A.D., I can't exactly remember which, the city of Camulodunum is sacked by rebelling Britons, and Rome's seat of governance shifts to modern day London... which I think is called... Londinium? Is that right?"

"It is," Vincent confirmed.

I stared at her with my mouth ajar. "How could you possibly know that?? You don't know anything about history."

She looked mildly offended. "I didn't know anything about *Roman* history, at least until I met you and your countless lectures."

"So how did you know that?" I asked.

"I took an elective at Oxford about women warriors throughout the ages, and the person who led the natives against Camulodunum was Boudicca. Know who she is?"

I rolled my eyes. "Of course I know who she is."

"Shoot," she said. "It would have been a good subject to lecture *you* on, and finally get a little payback."

"Why would that be payback?" I asked nonplussed. "Don't you have any idea what kind of a turn on that would be?"

It was her turn to roll her eyes at me. "Why exactly do I love you, again?"

"My cute butt?"

"Yeah, that or a lack of options, I guess."

"Ouch, Helena, ouch."

We grinned as we continued on our way, but then another question popped into my mind. I turned back to Vincent.

"Speaking of Boudicca, she should be an adult by now, right?"

He thought about it for a few seconds. "Late teenager, I'd say. Maybe eighteen or nineteen."

In the original timeline, Warrior-Queen Boudicca of the Iceni tribe had led a revolt almost fifteen years from now, but only after there was some semblance of peace in Southern Britain for maybe a decade, and after she and her daughters were horribly beaten and raped by Romans. Now, as a hormonal and idealistic teenager herself, and with a year of war in the books and more easily to come, I wondered what a younger Boudicca would do with her life.

***

"Form up the lines!" Shouted Galba from atop his horse beside me. "Cavalry to the flanks, slingers to the front. Auxilia on the right. Advancing formation!"

The orders were shouted at breakneck speed, almost too quickly for me to follow. Around us, however, centurions and runners were nodding their understanding of Galba's orders. The former went moving off and shouting their own more specific directions while the runners had taken off to find appropriate recipients of Galba's orders. I sat atop Felix and waited patiently while those who knew what they were doing did what they needed to do, and looked out over the city of Camulodunum and the fort constructed beside it that held the *Legio XX Valeria Victrix* along with its legate, Aulus Plautius.

It was dusk now, the sun just beginning to set off to my left, nightfall just a few brief minutes away. As the legions formed up around me into crisp battle lines and the enemy combatants swirled around the legion fort like water through a drain, I couldn't ask for a more stunning and epic set piece for the battle to come. The clouds had parted about an hour ago, and the moon was full and the coming night air cold and tiresome, offsetting the warmth and light coming from the countless torches held by legionaries and the brush fires scattered around the fort.

Felix once again fidgeted beneath me, and I couldn't help but feel a tinge of nervousness as well.

I let Galba and the professionals do what they needed to do without interference as I studied the battlefield before us, and watched as the unprofessional, but warrior-like Britons, ran amok as they battered against the fort, flung arrows and stone over its walls ineffectively, and circled in their chariots like vultures over a dying man in the desert.

While I'd seen chariots during the time Helena, Santino, and I had toured the empire, this was the first time I'd seen them actively used on the battlefield. The ones I'd seen in Gaul had been little more than relics owned by old war chieftain who'd fought the Romans decades ago, and had hung onto them for old time's sake. However, while the sight of hundreds of chariots circling the fort was an impressive one now, through the lens of academic study I'd cultivated over the years, I already knew why they were an impractical weapon of war against a professional army like a Roman legion.

Chariots were more than pimped out rides for wealthy barbarians, but tools of terror used to incite fear in those opposing them. Dramatic and intimidating, they carried armed men on a mobile platform drawn by a pair of large horses. That's scary. But like elephants, they were only useful in certain situations and easily ignored in other instances, especially now when it seemed as if these chariots were used for little more than rapid troop deployment and mobile artillery platforms, rather than bulldozers.

Through my binoculars I could see how a driver would make loops around the fort or go back forth along one particular wall while the warrior hurled spears. When the warrior depleted his ammunition, he'd hop off and run toward the wall, doing little more than bellow a war cry and thump his shield against his chest as the Romans waited patiently behind their fortifications. The charioteer might return later with fresh spears or just to pick up the warrior so they could continue their games.

Against fortified Romans, their siege strategy was a joke.

Perhaps the Britons had no understanding of siege war craft, although I had noted siege equipment off in the distance – onagers, catapults, and the like – but they were just now moving into position. In time, it was possible they'd do enough damage to knock down a few walls or entice the Romans to sally forth to counterattack, but now that we'd arrived, I didn't think it would do them much good.

I grimaced as I looked through my binoculars, realizing that the display before me was more like a Broadway musical version of a battle than an actual one. There weren't many bodies on the ground outside the fort, and I had to imagine there would be even fewer on the inside, and so far, little of consequence had happened. The Romans were waiting behind their walls and the Britons were riling themselves up on the outside for an assault. That was about it, but with our arrival, which had basically gone unnoticed by the Britons, things were about to heat up.

I turned to Galba. "So what's going to happen here?".

His eyes continued to study the battlefield before him, unflinching and analytical. "With all luck, hopefully very little. I will order the legion to march forward at a steady pace, conserving their energy while our Batavian and Germanic auxilia march on the right. However, as it often is when utilizing barbarian auxilia, they will be less calculated and reserved, and the sight of them alone should rattle the Britons into inaction, but the legion itself will most likely frighten them into retreat. Which I hope to be case here, as I desire no blood to be shed, because if they fight, we will route them. I count no more than four thousand men, more a mob than an army, and they will be dispersed as such."

"You don't want a fight?" I asked.

"Of course not, Hunter," he replied sternly, still without looking at me. "You yourself may be a glutton for blood and death, but I certainly am not. I have no desire to slaughter those who cannot possibly stand against the overwhelming might I so often bring against them. Everything I do is for Rome's protection and nothing more."

I pointed a finger at the Britons. "And invading Britain constitutes protecting Rome?"

With that question, Galba finally turned to face me. "Rome has many enemies, Hunter. That is a reality I cannot control. Were we to rest on our borders and do nothing, it would only be a matter of time before we were overrun."

Galba's prescience was impressive because he was totally right. Rome's stagnation and inevitable downfall was due in large part to their lack of expansion a few hundred years from now. Whether they even had the ability to expand wasn't the point. Their strategy then had been to do little more than hold the line, which in large part led, as Galba so astutely pointed out, to them being overrun.

But I didn't tell him that.

There was no need since Rome had to fall eventually.

Just not yet.

Instead, I nodded in silent agreement and returned my attention to the legion, which had just begun to march forward in a steady rhythm of choreographed footfalls. I watched them move forward for just a second before giving Felix a slight kick into his flanks to nudge him forward, but Galba stopped me with a word.

"Halt."

"Why?" I asked. "Leaders lead, Galba. From the front."

His eyes seemed to twinkle at my comment. "Unless you are Julius Caesar, which you most certainly are not, then a good leader stays in the rear where he can better direct his troops. He does not advance brashly into an awaiting horde."

"I'm pretty sure I'm better armed and equipped than Julius Caesar was. I'll be fine."

"There is no question that you are, Hunter, but what you lack is his charisma, zeal, luck, and… everything else that constitutes a real leader. You will stay here. You are the key to getting your people away from my empire, and while you dead will certainly solve the problem of *you*, it won't do anything for your friends."

His last words were dripping with condescension and anger, and I felt that bit of nervousness in my stomach turn into anger in my chest, but I did everything I could to suppress it. I was beginning to not like Galba one bit anymore, but I kept that resentment buried away in my chest for later use. I reminded myself that I needed Galba – for now – but such a fact was becoming harder and harder to remember.

I kept my mouth shut, but turned to my right where every single time traveler from Helena right next to me, to Artie at the far end, sat atop horses in a long line. The newcomers had finally been given mounts upon landing in Britain, and I'd been shocked to learn that they were all quite competent with them. Apparently, mounted warfare atop horses hadn't been very far removed in their timeline, and each of them was fully trained to ride into combat. It had only taken them a matter of minutes to acclimate themselves to a lack of stirrups, and the fact that they'd so quickly adjusted made me wonder if they'd even been invented yet in their timeline.

I hadn't asked because I didn't want to know, but I tried to look at it as a positive since they could all act as quick reaction forces to augment the legion far more efficiently than local cavalry.

I leaned forward so that I could look past Helena and caught both Vincent's and Archer's attention.

They too leaned forward.

"Take your men to the flanks and cover the legion and auxilia," I ordered them both. "Galba doesn't expect much of a battle so don't shoot anyone unless they directly threaten you. It's possible your gunfire will scare them more quickly than even the legion, but whatever you do, don't shoot first."

Vincent nodded, but Archer had more to say.

"Why not just kill them all, Hunter?" He asked. "Rome needs to conquer this territory anyway, so why not help them?"

I shot him a look that would have burned him to ashes had I possessed the ability to create fire from my eyes.

"I didn't come to Rome to conquer it, Archer!" I yelled. "If I'd wanted to, I could have, believe me! But that was never the point! Never the goal! How could you possible think that?? I wanted to affect as little change as possible, but *no*... we had to get involved, and then it fell on me to fix everything! But that doesn't mean..."

"But, Hunter..."

"Shut your fucking mouth, Archer!" I screamed, spittle flying from my lips. If not for Helena and Vincent between us, I wasn't sure I wouldn't have smashed his face in with the butt of my rifle. "Now do as I say! But leave Cuyler."

Helena and Vincent glanced nervously at each other, doing their best to remain inconspicuous but their presence barely even registered with me. My eyes were locked on Archer's, and his eyes burned back just as intensely, but he wasn't in a position to countermand my orders. I had two entire legions at my back, and I would turn them on him in an instant if I had too.

The tension lingered for what seemed like hours, before he finally turned away and ordered his men to the right flank. Vincent did the same with our group, directing them to the left, but when Helena kicked her horse into motion, I reached out and gripped the reins, stopping her horse.

"Where do you think you're going?" I asked, unable to keep the edge out of my voice, still upset from my argument with Archer.

She looked back at me angrily, her own voice unable to hide her anger. "Where do you think I..."

"You're going nowhere, Helena," I said, the scorn voluntarily there this time. As I spoke, Cuyler rode up with his sniper rifle slung over his back, his dark clothing making him all but invisible atop his white horse now that night had settled in.

I ignored Helena completely and turned to him. "Take Helena and follow behind the legion. Hang back and out of harm's way and provide sniper support, but just as I ordered Archer, don't shoot unless you need to and don't go anywhere *near* the fighting."

"Yes, sir," he replied with a salute, waiting for Helena to fall in with him. When I failed to release her reins, his normally stalwart expression grew uncomfortable before he urged his horse to trot away without her.

I turned back to Helena, and was too angry to be surprised at the fact that, for once, she wasn't looking back at me in the same way. Normally, she never put up with my shit, but in this instance she just looked terrified. Her attention was on my hand, the one that gripped her reins, and I too took notice of just how tightly I squeezed the rough cords, so much so that they were cutting into my palm and causing blood to drip to the ground. My heart beat against my chest like a jackhammer as I turned my eyes back to her uncompromisingly.

"Go with him," I ordered, "but don't you dare go near the fighting."

Normally, she may have smacked me or even punched me for talking to her like that, but not this time. All she could do now was hold her eyes on me as I let go of her bloody reins, letting them drop against her horse and paint her fur a dark crimson red. I didn't take my eyes off Helena's as she slowly reached down to take the reins in her hands and guide her horse toward where Cuyler waited.

And I didn't care.

I no longer even felt upset anymore, only caring about completing this battle as quickly as possible and moving on toward our true objective. When Helena met up with Cuyler, I turned away and returned my attention to the battlefield, realizing that we had already wasted more than enough time.

Out of the corner of my eye I noticed Galba looking at me.

"What?" I asked, not bothering to return the look.

"I know not what that conversation concerned, but I never expected you capable of directing such anger toward your woman, nor has it ever seemed possible for her to seem frightened of you either. What has happened to you, Hunter? The man in my tent months ago seemed desperate, but what I see in you now is something far worse."

I turned as menacing an expression on him as I could manage, and he flinched.

I was finished with people claiming I was a changed man, claiming that they could see how different I was than when I had last met them. Helena, Agrippina, Archer, Vespasian, Artie, Galba... who did they think they were?

The things I've seen...

The things I've done...

The world I've been forced to live in...

How can a man not change? How can a man remain the plucky, idealistic, jovial protagonist everyone can get behind and root for? That naïve shit was for people like Santino.

Galba's goddamned right I've changed.

It was well past time for me to find my center. To focus on more important things, even when others didn't understand. And most importantly, it was time to start doing what was necessary, no matter the cost. It was time I did whatever I needed to get home. My home. Not Artie 2.0's home, or any other bizarre variant. *My home!* Where my dog is named Argos not... fucking Rex.

What kind of asshole names his dog Rex?? Fuck you Rex! Fuck all of that!

And especially...

"... Fuck you, Galba."

***

The battle, and I use the term loosely, was over before it even began.

Like Galba had predicted, the sight of two legions, its accompanying auxilia and cavalry, and a dozen armed people with rifles were just too much for the besieging barbarians. Thirty minutes after we'd arrived, their entire attacking force dispersed in an unorganized mess. Everything about their attack had already indicated a lack of leadership, but their retreat had confirmed it. They'd scattered in a dozen different directions, not waiting around long enough to fall prey to a thrown spear or a rifle's bullet.

I'd asked Galba about their lack of leadership a few minutes after the "battle" had begun, and while he'd been reluctant to talk to me – for whatever reason – he'd responded grudgingly that it was certainly possible that the men attacking the legion had been little more than a group of sub-chieftains and their ilk. Were that the case, it was highly probable that this attack hadn't been sanctioned by whoever was still in control of the local tribes, or it had been little more than a probe of the legion's capabilities.

At least they'd been smart enough to flee. Even if they had been an organized, cohesive unit instead of the unruly mob that they were, their force would have been annihilated. While Galba had sent our cavalry to harry the retreating Britons as they made their way back into the wilderness, and I had no doubt there would be casualties as a result of such action, it was a necessary strategy to keep the enemy from double backing and hitting us while we prepared our defenses. Since the legion fort was already situated on good ground – away from the nearest tree line and close to a fresh water source – it was a simple enough matter for my legions to begin construction of their own camps alongside the original, giving them an outlet for the adrenaline they'd built up in preparation for the battle that hadn't happened.

I, on the other hand, had more pressing business.

With Galba, my time traveling companions, and two centuries of legionnaires from the *XV Primigenia*, I spurred Felix toward the gate that contained the *XX Valeria Victrix* and its legate, Aulus Plautius. Without a word, the gates parted, allowing us entrance through the *porta principalis sinistra*, the camp's left gate, and instant access to the *via principalis*, that would take us directly to the *praetorium* and its owner.

I rode through the gates at the vanguard of our procession with Galba behind me. Beside him was Vincent and Archer, but I was more surprised not to see Helena there as well. A quick glance behind me revealed that she was riding near the rear of our small group with Santino and Cuyler.

I was about to wave the three of them forward, when I was distracted by a roar from the camp's inhabitants. It startled me at first, but when I looked out at the gathered troops, instead of the horrific or frightening scene I expected, I was rewarded with the sight of the legionnaires yelling and screaming and waving in good cheer at our arrival. It seemed like a silly thing to do since little had occurred, but then I realized that many of them had no way of knowing how small the attacking force had really been. They may have expected a brutal, prolonged battle instead of the quick skirmish that had actually transpired.

Our arrival had kept them and their friends alive.

To them, it was something of a miracle.

I appreciated their cheers and good natured shouts, but then I realized that most of the adulation was being directed at me and me alone. Every eye I met was already looking at me and the mass of assembled troops did seem to gravitate around Felix. I was being swarmed from all directions, and I grew concerned that they would scare poor Felix, but he was a good horse, and he ignored them as they pressed closer, their hands groping upwards. I gripped a few arms as I passed, wishing those who I came into contact with good health or tidings.

A grin spread across my face at the adulation, and I found myself waving and flapping my arms up and down like an athlete trying to rile up a crowd. It worked, and the men cheered even louder. We were about a third of way to the *praetorium* when I let myself really bask in the glory and adoration I was receiving. Such appreciation was more than deserved after all I'd done in the past five years, and it was well past due. I was owed this like no one else knew, and I was ready to take it all in.

But the crowed began to disperse as we neared the *praetorium*, giving us more room to maneuver. By this point, I could see a short man with hard features standing outside the central tent that I knew to be the legate's quarters. Unlike the legionnaires around him, he did not seem particularly pleased to see me. Maybe it was a pride thing since we'd just bailed the guy out of a jam or perhaps my reputation preceded me.

Mere feet away, I pulled back on the reins gently and Felix slowed to a stop. Galba rode up beside me and stopped as well.

He saluted and initiated the greetings, as we'd decided on earlier. "Hail, Legate Plautius. You are well met."

The man nodded. "Well met, indeed, Legate Galba. I thank you for your intervention here," the man said in a tone that suggested he was hardly thankful for anything.

"Your thanks is unnecessary, Legate," Galba said with a low bow from his horse. "We were merely acting in the best interests of Rome."

Plautius nodded. "As do we all, my friend, but regardless, it is good to see you again. After what happened to Legate Hosidius Geta earlier this year, I feared a similar fate would befall you. Things are not the same as they once were…"

Galba nodded. "Exactly why we are here, Legate. Exactly…"

I cut Galba off with the clearing of my throat. We'd agreed he'd make the initial greeting and introductions, not hold a conversation with his old war buddy. Besides, I was technically his boss here, not the other way around.

Plautius clearly looked upset at the way I'd interrupted his friend, but held his decorum. "And you are, sir?"

"Legate Jacob Hunter," I replied. "Uhh… commander of the armies of the North, general of the Felix legions."

"What??" He asked, his voice rising. "Just who in Tartarus is Legate… Jay-Kob Hoon-tar?" The man demanded. "I have never even heard of such a name, let alone one holding the rank of legate.

Galba sighed loudly from beside me and Plautius turned to his old friend for clarification. The two met eyes and Galba shrugged wearily. "You don't have to like him Aulus," Galba clarified with a dismissive wave in my direction, "and believe me, you most likely will not, but he is a very important man and has important business that needs done here in Britain.

"We have much to discuss."

***

I was sick and tired of meetings around tables.

In fact, I hated them. Loathed them, really.

I'd had more discussions around tables here in Ancient Rome than I cared to remember, but my deep-seated hatred of such things began well before life in Rome. Most civilians never realized just how much of a Special Forces operator's time was spent planning an operation, which involved sitting in a conference room around a table, or in a small auditorium of some sort, watching, observing, discussing, and analyzing presentations detailing mission objectives and operating parameters. Often, thousand-slide Power Point presentations were created, many of them so intricate and information-heavy that they rivaled even the brightest seventh grader's presentation on how to make a compass using basic household items.

It was truly outstanding stuff.

No really, it was.

But I was done with them, and the truly glorious thing was that I'd never had the power to be done with them before.

But I did now.

If I had to sit through another meeting around a table with Vincent or Archer or Galba or Vespasian or Aulus Plautius or any other asinine Roman or other individual ever again, I was going to go nuts.

At least… more nuts that I was already going.

That's why we were already back on the road again having only spent one night in Plautius' legion camp, blazing our way through the hinterlands of Britain. I'd decided on our very first night in camp, that there was simply no way I could waste the next four months sitting on my hands before setting out to Anglesey, and even that one night seemed like too much wasted time already.

While Aulus Plautius had seemed a decent enough fellow, I had no need to bring him into my inner circle of friends or comrades. He seemed competent and humble in his position as legate of the sole legion left in Britain, and he came off as a good strategist and competent leader, but once Galba's introduction had been completed and he'd politely invited us into his *praetorium*, he'd gone all Roman on me, as they always did, and I no longer cared if I ever saw him again.

Vespasian's drafted orders to Aulus Plautius had been to allow me free rein to do as I wished in Britain, although the unwritten interpretation was that I'd help Plautius first. At least, that's how Plautius and Galba had understood my orders, but Vespasian knew I had no actual skill or experience waging mass warfare, so I never actually figured he wanted me to lead troops into battle personally. It seemed to me that he wanted me to deliver his troops to Britain safely, but then do whatever I needed to do as long as I had Rome's best interests at heart.

Granted, that was simply my interpretation of Vespasian's orders, but my two Roman companions had disagreed emphatically. Not only had Plautius disliked the fact that Vespasian's appointment had technically placed me above even *him* in the chain of command, but was also enraged that Vespasian had given me leave to pursue my own personal objectives at all. Plautius had no idea who I was and certainly had no reason to trust me, and even Galba's backing hadn't done much to ease his qualms. He'd been willing to accept my help and take my legions, but he hadn't been willing to divide that force so that I could do what I needed to do.

And he certainly hadn't been happy with my final decision to take off toward modern day Wales with three cohorts of the *XV Primigenia* as backup – a *reconnaissance unit in force*, I'd called it. Nor had he been happy with his old friend Galba when he'd, reluctantly, backed my decision. I hadn't asked him to, but either he must have empathized with our situation more than I'd thought, or else he felt he owed it to Vespasian.

Plautius hadn't understood in the slightest.

He'd ranted and raved about military strategy, tactical acumen, common sense, and the immoral nature of knowingly leading fifteen hundred men to their deaths, as I surely would do by marching them into the *Great British Unknown*, as he'd called it like it was a proper name.

The three of us had stood around a map of Britain as Plautius raged, which was exactly when I realized I would never again hold a meeting of such importance around a table, but it wasn't until Plautius had accused me of being a traitor – owing such suspicion to my odd accent, manner of clothing, and weaponry – that I'd punched him square in the jaw.

The strike may have hurt my hand more than it had his face, but damn had it felt good to put one of these Roman assholes in his place. I still didn't know why I'd snapped at the accusation of being a traitor, especially since I really didn't owe allegiance to anybody in this godforsaken time period, but laying him out had still felt like the right thing to do.

And Plautius had gone down hard.

I was a pretty big guy, especially when compared to most of these Romans, who were quite tiny in comparison. Obviously, each and every legionnaire was in impressive shape athletically, but I had two thousand years of evolution and modern strength training on my side, and had the mass and body strength to prove it, but I'd never considered myself a particularly intimidating person. I'd always considered my features too soft, almost boyish, but that had been five years ago. They'd hardened after my time as a Navy SEAL fighting in World War III, but the ensuing years in Ancient Rome had left me barely unrecognizable in the mirror anymore. Crow's feet tugged at my eyes, laugh lines that didn't seem so humorous pulled around my mouth, and my face seemed gaunter than ever before. While Helena never mentioned my changing complexion to me, I saw it almost every single day. Her own face may have remained just as lovely as ever, but over the past year especially, I'd watched my own grow hard and old and cold.

But even so, I still didn't consider myself particularly intimidating, but the look Aulus Plautius had on his face as he stared up at me from the ground seemed so terrified, that it scared me in return. What had a confident, competent Roman general seen in my face that had caused him to look at me in such fright?

I didn't know and I didn't want to know.

All I wanted was to go home.

Galba had helped Plautius to his feet, and Plautius hadn't been too proud to accept his help. He'd risen slowly, brushed himself off, and asked me to leave. I'd given the man a mock Roman salute, pounding my hand against my chest hard but then flinging an open hand with wiggling fingers at him lazily, before turning and leaving. Galba had caught up to me before I left and gripped my arm with an impressively powerful hand.

I looked down into his fat and ugly face and glowered at him. "What is it, Galba?"

The man stared up at me with his unusually hard eyes, no hint of concern present. Either he was too stubborn to be intimidated by me, or he just didn't care anymore.

"What are *my* orders, Legate Hunter?" He asked, his voice professional and without emotion.

I blinked in surprise, having forgotten that I hadn't yet decided what to do with him. I could have used him for my journey, his knowledge of the natives, general warfare, and diplomacy making him an invaluable tool, but I wasn't even taking half a legion with me into the wild. It seemed like a waste of resources to bring him along, as he and Plautius together against the Britons would be far more formidable than just one or the other alone.

"Stay with the legions, Galba," I ordered. "They'll need you more than I do."

Then another thought came to me as I stood there at the tent's threshold.

The journey to the Isle of Mona and beyond had the potential for being the most dangerous thing I'd ever done. Even without Agrippina's involvement for once, we were heading into uncharted territory where I suspected the natives were more likely to shoot first and ask question later, rather than the other way around. There was a good chance this was a one way trip; not a suicide mission per se, but one that had a number of possible endings attached to it, not all of them worth thinking about.

His hand was still gripping my bicep when I had this thought, and without thinking, I reached out to peel it off.

"Remember what I said back in your tent all those months ago?" I asked. "About your legacy in this world, or lack thereof really?"

His eyes widened at the question, and his expression seemed sad now rather than angry. "Such words are hard to forget."

"Forget I said them," I said, and his look turned confused. "Just forget I said anything, Galba. Make your own damned fate."

I walked away with those words, not really understanding why I'd said them, and Galba hadn't followed.

That was the last I'd seen of him before setting out.

After the entire ordeal in Plautius' *praetorium*, which had only lasted fifteen minutes from entrance to exit, I'd been depressed and furious at the same time. I marched directly out of Plautius' camp and trudged toward my own, which was still under construction, and went straight for my *praetorium*. I stormed my way inside and tore off my clothing, throwing everything but my boxer shorts into a corner.

It had been freezing that winter night in Britain, and my tent hadn't offered much insolation, but I'd barely felt even the slightest chill. Helena, seated at my desk and writing something, looked up at my entrance but didn't try to speak to me and I barely spared a look in her direction as well. It wasn't that I was too emotional to communicate with her; it was just that I didn't have a single thing I wanted to say.

Another thing I was sick and tired of were scenes in bed with Helena where we discussed her problems, our problems, or, especially, my problems. I wasn't going to go down that road anymore either. I was almost convinced that her weakness, caution, and recent unsupportive nature had been why we'd failed to accomplish anything at all since our operation aboard Agrippina's pleasure barge. I cared about her opinions, but I just didn't need them anymore.

She should consider herself lucky, really, since I hadn't found much to care about anymore as I'd climbed into bed. Not about the chill that crept through my bones or the impending march to the Isle of Mona. Not about Aulus Plautius or Galba. Not about the fate of Ancient Rome, my timeline, or Archer's skewed and freakish one. Nor even Agrippina, who I often thought about, wondering what she was up to. Honestly, I barely even cared about Helena anymore, especially not when she'd stared at my back as I tried to grow comfortable in my bed. I hadn't needed eyes in the back of my head to feel her discomfort or know she was looking at me, because I could actually *feel* those green eyes of hers on me.

And I'd felt a lot of things recently, most of it *not* good, but there was something subtle dangling in the deep recesses of my mind. Something elusive, meandering, but undoubtedly present. I couldn't quite understand what it was yet, but it was enticing. Alluring. It was a powerful feeling, one that could lead me to do great things if I could just find some way to harness it.

I'd thought of little else that night, our final night in the comforts of Roman civilization, and while it had been hours before I'd finally fallen asleep, I had been quite content to think and ponder on the potential of that great power I may one day wield. Even after Helena had slid into bed behind me, the warmth of her body close but not against me, I'd thought of nothing else. It had only been because of severe exhaustion and mental decay that I'd finally drifted off to sleep well into the morning, but I'd been quite content with my last thought:

That I would soon have all the power in the universe needed to fix it.

VII
Wilderness

Central Britannia
December, 42 A.D.

"This sucks."

"Yep."

"No, really; this really, really sucks."

"Yeah, I got it."

"I mean, this sucks so much that I think I'm beginning to hate you."

"Join the club, John."

There was a pause this time.

"It's really fucking cold out here, Hunter."

"I've noticed."

Another pause.

"For Christ's sakes," Santino pleaded, "at least pretend like I'm annoying you. Not only does this suck and not only is it colder than a polar bear's asshole out here, but I'm also bored out of my mind. Help me out here!"

I glanced over at Santino as he strode beside me, pulling his horse along behind him just as I did. "Sorry, buddy."

"Buddy?" He asked mockingly. "Buddy? Well, I *suppose* that's progress. I wasn't even sure you cared anymore."

I sighed, but was interrupted from answering when one of Felix's legs sunk deep into a small puddle of mud, forcing me to coax him out of it. He was certainly a good horse, but he was still an animal, and the thought of being stuck in mud terrified him. It terrified me as well, having been one of a billion kids who had cried when Artax from *The Never Ending Story* had died from exactly the same issue. Luckily, this story wasn't nearly as bleak as that one, at least not yet, so I managed to get him under control and pulled him free.

Such occurrences had been normal over the past week since leaving Camulodunum. The ground wasn't quite frozen yet, although it was getting close, and treacheries along the underdeveloped roadways we'd been traversing were numerous. To even call them roads at all was a grand overstatement, and the

Romans in my reconnaissance force had grumbled often about the lack of efficient and sturdy Roman roads in the area, and I couldn't blame them. We were slopping our way through Britain right now, and it was slowing us down more than I wanted.

To make matters worse, as Santino had just complained about, it was damn cold outside, but apparently not cold enough to freeze the ground beneath us. It was like Mother Nature was playing a silly joke on us, but it was bound to get colder as we progressed deeper into the winter months and into Britain itself, so the ground would eventually freeze and our progress would accelerate —at least until the inevitable heavy blankets of snow arrived. Unfortunately, until then we had little choice but to march through the worst combination of weather conditions I'd ever encountered.

Felix and I quickly caught up to Santino once I'd calmed him down with a bribe in the form of a nearly frozen carrot. Both Santino and his horse were covered in mud, and both seemed exhausted. It was late in the day on this seventh day of our estimated two and a half week journey, and all four of us were due for a break. Santino and I were currently on picket duty for the marching recon force, while other groups were responsible for our flanks and rearguard, but we had the worst duty, as we were the ones responsible for discovering the most suitable terrain for the rest of our force to travel upon, so we were in turn the ones who blundered into the worst of it.

When I finally caught up, I glanced at Santino and shrugged apologetically.

"I've had a lot on my mind lately."

He looked at me quizzically before shaking his head and turning back to the direction we were marching. "You *always* have something on your mind. Always... and why the hell do I have to keep reminding you of that?? That's not a fucking good excuse anymore!"

"Sorry?"

"That's better," he said with a sigh. "God damn, Hunter, you're going to drive me into an early grave at the rate you're going. And I can't believe you and Helena used complain about *me* all the time."

I couldn't help but smirk. "Do you blame us?"

"Of course not," he said proudly, "but I've always been the way I am. That's my excuse. You don't have one."

"Ah, right," I said, chuckling. It seemed like only Santino could talk to me these days and not get my blood boiling. He never minced words around me, and I appreciated that. He said what was on his mind – just in his own unique way – and it didn't hurt that he rarely let life get him down. He was an eternal source of childish optimism, something we could all use more of.

I glanced down at Santino's hands, and noticed him tinkering with our UAV. He had his horse's reins looped through his elbow, but in his right hand he held our small unmanned aerial device, little more than a sleek block with three little helicopter blades that stuck out from it, forming a triangle. And in his left hand was a multi-tool. While our UAV was a durable little device, even though solar power kept it working, it had been on the fritz ever since our time in Damascus.

"Still not working right?" I asked.

"Yeah," Santino said as he turned it over in his hand, using the screw driver tool to pry at something near one of the helicopter blades. "I think it's finished. This one rotor blade just won't spin properly anymore, and I don't have any more replacement blades to fix it with. I don't think it'll ever maintain a stable flight level again, and is more likely to crash into your face than fly properly."

"There's nothing you can do?"

"I've been MacGyvering this thing for years, Jacob. It's an intricate piece of military hardware, one that hasn't been properly serviced in over half a decade. I've done what I can, but I think it's time we dig it a grave."

I nodded, feeling a slight pang of regret at the loss of our little guardian angel. It had served us so well over the years, allowing us to pinpoint enemy troop movement or scout out areas before we even entered the area. The thing was practically invisible in the modern world, but to these ancient denizens, even if they saw it, they wouldn't even know what it was, let alone how to bring it down.

But without it, we'd never have the ability to perform advanced reconnaissance or monitor our perimeter again. Other technical assets had already been lost to us, such as our snake cam, a number of our computers, a few wrist mounted interactive displays, and our IR optics among many others. But at least we still had our radios. All the advanced tech and sci-fi toys in the future could never really replace a good, old-fashioned radio. It was the most reliable piece of electronic gear we had, a testament made real by how they still worked while most of everything else had gone to shit, and was a device even Archer and his men utilized. Their durability was reassuring, but the continued loss of our technological edge only served to amplify my anxiety.

At least we had ammo again thanks to Archer's arrival. It had been a miracle that their ammo was even compatible with our own, but despite different brand names and appearances, Archer's ammunition worked just as well as our original stuff. Divided between us all, we didn't have nearly as much as we'd brought with us initially, but at least we all had loaded magazines with some ammo to spare. All except for Helena's P90, of course, which still rested comfortably in forced, early retirement. But unlike our ammo situation, the loss of Santino's UAV was a reminder that once our modern tricks and fancy tools were depleted, we'd be no better equipped than a standard Roman legionnaire. Once we were reduced to nothing more than a sword and shield, we were as good as useless against Agrippina's Praetorians or her ninjas.

A frightening thought.

"Just see what you can do," I ordered Santino.

"Yeah, yeah," he said as he went back to work.

I nodded and returned my attention to the path before us.

Dusk was not long off, and it was about time to send out a few centurions to locate a suitable location for our legion camp. The nice thing about Britain was that there was plenty of open ground, well-forested areas, and rivers. The same thing could have been said about anywhere in Europe around the turn of the most recent millennium, but it was still nice. It gave my scouts plenty of options to pick from, and they had done a good job establishing defensible locations every night this week, and I only expected the streak to continue.

I twisted at my waist to see the legionnaires of my three cohorts marching in unison behind me, their kit looking large and uncomfortable upon their backs, and signaled for the nearest centurion to rally his fellows in search of a fortifiable area. He saluted and went off to complete his orders.

The rest of us continued on our way.

Despite the cold, the mud, the random flakes of snow, and the walking instead of riding, the trip was relatively pleasant, at least in the sense that we hadn't yet been attacked by locals who'd spotted half of a Roman legion marching into their territory, but our presence hadn't gone completely unnoticed. Our flankers had spotted interlopers pacing our formation as we continued westward since day one. Even the Romans, well versed in marching orders in foreign territories, weren't completely certain what our guests were up to, but it didn't take Julius Caesar to determine that their intentions were probably not good.

The fact that we'd been unable to determine how large a force it was only made matters worse. My scouts could only breach the fog of war surrounding my contingent so far, meaning they could only recon what they could see, and what they could see was restricted to how far they were willing to venture from the protection of our main force. The distance wasn't by any means negligible – they were professionals who knew what they were doing – but they couldn't see the whole island of Britain. Had Santino's UAV been operable, we would have been able to scout miles around our perimeter, penetrating deeper into the fog of war well beyond what the local Britons would expect out of us, but unless Santino fixed it, we would never have that blanket of security again.

Hence my growing apprehension.

But we didn't have a choice in the matter. If Santino could fix his UAV, great, but until he did, we had to make do with what we had. I was determined to press on no matter what, and nobody seemed willing to turn back anymore either. We were too close.

Minutes passed as we continued our march, and a half hour later, a runner worked his way through the mud in my direction, Santino still fiddling with his poor UAV beside me. Like when his beloved knife had once been lost to him, I wasn't sure he was ready to accept the death of yet another of his old friends.

The runner, in full legionary armor sans his marching kit, came to a stop a respectable distance from me and saluted. He didn't seem even remotely winded.

"Legate, we have located a suitable location for camp two miles away. You're *praetorium* is already under construction. If you will follow me, please."

I nodded and signaled to the cohorts behind me that we were about to deviate from our current path. I received no response from any of them, but I hadn't expected one. I turned back to the runner who had already veered off to the right, and followed, Santino beside me. We entered into a lightly wooded area, a path that disrupted the precise marching formation of the cohorts behind me, but the runner and the centurions who had picked our camping location knew what they were doing.

As I suspected, we were only within the wooded area for a few minutes before we emerged into a large clearing many acres in size. Off in the distance and down a low hill, I could see a narrow strait of water that barely qualified as a river. It ran east to west, and beyond it was another clearing followed by a dense forest that continued for miles.

Perfect.

***

Hours later, I sat hunched over my desk, writing down my thoughts about our campaign.

Since Julius Caesar had recorded his memoirs while in the field, warring against all manner of barbarian tribes, I figured I should too. The sounds of Romans completing the camp's construction were all around me, threatening to lead me toward distraction, but I'd grown used to them in recent weeks and found them almost soothing now. Besides, I was dedicated to turning this whole story into a book series one day, and I needed the practice since I'd nearly failed out of my creative writing class back in college. In fact, I'd dropped the class at the last possible second, which ended up working out quite well since it had given me the time I'd needed to focus on my history classes.

Then again, the only reason I was even in fucking Ancient Rome is because I was a Navy SEAL with a college degree in ancient history. If not for my inability to write coherent sentences with any kind of snap or pizazz, I might not even be here! It would be some other poor asshole instead. Although, since the chances of him sharing the same connection I had with Varus seemed extremely low, maybe nobody would be here at all. If not for that stupid creative writing class, no one would probably be here. We'd all be back home, living our stupid, meaningless…

"Calm down, Jacob," Helena said from our bed. "You're going to snap your pen in half."

I shot a look at her, but took notice of my journal page out of the corner of my eye. My latest sentence had started out well enough, but then had transitioned into a series of zigzagging lines of gibberish that ended with the page being torn because I'd been pressing too hard.

Angrily, I flung my pen at the desk and watched as it skipped off it to land on the ground. I swore and shoved myself away from the desk, and stalked my way around it, bent over, and retrieved the pen. I gave it another long, angry look before hurling it through the tent's entry flap and out into the legion camp.

I stared after it for a long while before Helena let out a long breath from behind me. "That make you feel better?"

I ignored her and stomped my way to retrieve the pen again, since it was my last, knowing I wasn't about to start using ink and a stylus if I could avoid it. I walked out into the blistering cold night air, searched for my pen in the thin layer of snow that had accumulated in the last hour, found it, and picked it up. I glared at it again after straightening, but movement to my left drew my attention away. Standing there were Wang, Santino, and Stryker, holding steaming cups of something in their hands, on their way back from doing… something – I didn't care what. They looked at the way I held my pen and then shook their heads in unison at me and walked away.

I watched them go, a part of me wishing I could catch up with them and have some fun. But there was something about being in command that kept me from doing it, as did my writing responsibilities. I couldn't just hang out with the guys anymore, and it didn't help that Stryker had replaced Titus as the third member of the Three Stooges over there.

I guess he was the group's Shemp now, and I only felt more and more left out because of it.

I sighed and returned to my tent, taking a second to glance at Helena on the bed as I shook the light coating of snow from my shoulders. She was leaning back on a series of pillows, reading through Brewster's social studies text book that was propped up on her growing belly. I smiled at her, unable to help it even though my mind told me I shouldn't even bother.

She noticed my attention and peeked over the book at me. "What?"

"*Now* you grow interested in history?"

She tilted the book down so that it rested against her knees. "It's pretty... interesting, isn't it?" She said, finally closing the book. "It's almost like reading a historical horror story, only everything is wrong."

I frowned. "Tell me about it..."

Indeed that textbook really was something of a horror story. Everything contained within it was a demented bastardization of everything I knew about history. Everywhere I turned there were references to Islamic nations and empires that spanned continents, only to implode or explode into fragments of itself, but then pull themselves back together again into extremely dominant global factions. In my history, Islam burst onto the scene after Muhammad learned to read and write and drafted the Koran. Islamic armies then went on a tear throughout the Middle East, Africa, and into Europe, but they were slowly beaten back by western forces, and while entities like the Ottoman Empire had been the Mediterranean's true dominant force for nearly a thousand years, once World War I had ended, they too lost their influence, allowing the Middle East to finally slide into the chaotic mess that it had been when I'd last seen it.

It was almost easy to feel sorry for the nations that made up the Middle East, since their empires hadn't really been that different from any western European one, only they'd followed Allah instead of God... who was really just the same damn guy anyway. Their contribution to science and technology throughout the Middle Ages and beyond was something few remembered, and even much of what was lost during the Dark Ages had actually been recovered by Islamic scholars as well.

But in Archer's history books, Islamic countries in the Middle East were the equivalent of nations like Great Britain, America, France, Australia, Germany, China, and many other world powers, while Europe and Asia had become little more than recalcitrant nation-states that warred amongst themselves and rarely got their shit together long enough to prosper, again, much like the Middle East I remembered. Only America and Great Britain to a degree seemed immune to the perils of Europe and other formerly prosperous nations, something I still could not wrap my head around. It was crystal clear from Brewster's textbook that the vast majority of modern American history had played out almost exactly to how I remembered it, allowing America 2.0 to turn out very similarly to the America I'd once been a citizen of.

Somehow.

Someway.

"You should really read it from the beginning, Jacob," Helena suggested, interrupting my thoughts. "There's some very odd stuff in here. You know I'm not an expert, but even I find some of it... odd."

"Like what?" I asked, curious for the first time in days about something she was going to say.

She returned the book to her lap but looked over it so that she could still see me. "Don't get too excited, Jacob, it's just that there are things recorded here that don't seem to make any sense. Even to me."

I moved closer and sat on the edge of the bed, my curiosity perfunctorily piqued. Helena shifted positions carefully around her growing belly and scooted closer, opening the book in her lap. She flipped to the beginning, a few pages into the section entitled, *The Dark Ages.*

"In what way?" I asked

She worked her jaw left and right before answering. "Well, take the very beginning for instance. It discusses the Greeks and the Romans briefly, indicating that Greece was a proto-nation that eventually evolved into the Italian based Roman Empire..."

"God, I love the way you say '*proto*-nation'," I said.

"Down boy," Helena said, although the humor in her voice was lost before she'd finished her quip. "But then it goes on to say that much of their history was lost early on in the first millennium when, 'a great upheaval overturned the once powerful Roman Empire that had become so successful because of its ability to maintain control over their client states, which in turn caused its downfall when this control floundered...'"

"Boy," I said, "I could have written this stuff."

"Maybe you did," Helena suggested, turning her head to look up at me.

I wasn't even remotely amused. "That's not funny."

She smirked. "It's a little funny."

I gently twisted her head back toward the book with a hand. "Just keep reading before I start calling you Santino."

"Well, that's really all there is," Helena said. "The book then discusses how much of the information known about Rome and Greece was rediscovered when certain Islamic nations were undergoing their own kind of renaissance, but that most of it has been kept from the west."

My mind churned. I hadn't read any of this yet, so it was all new information to me. It seemed interesting that these powerful Islamic empires would have such knowledge of Greece and Rome, but western European nations would not.

I reached out and took the book from Helena, which she relinquished happily, and flipped through a few pages before landing on a map. It looked a lot like a map of the Roman Empire in its latter days, when Rome had split its seat of power in half, allowing emperors of equal power to sit in both Rome and Byzantium, which was then renamed Constantinople. I squinted at the map, noticing again how everything from Western Europe through Italy appeared Red while everything from the Balkans through Iran appeared blue. Nothing seemed out of the ordinary until I realized that the blue in the east did not represent what would soon be known as the Byzantine Empire, but indicated Islamic influence instead. Not only that, but the map's legend also indicated that the Red wasn't Rome either, but simply *unconquered* territory.

It was dated 721 A.D.

"Holy shit," I whispered.

"What?" Helena asked.

"Holy shit!" Was all I could say, only much louder this time.

"What??" Helena demanded again, just as loud.

I didn't answer, but ran instead toward tent's exit.

"*What??*" Helena yelled.

At the tent's threshold, I turned to her, more excited than I'd been in a long time.

"The fucking Byzantines, Helena!" I exclaimed. "No Rome, no Byzantines, no defense against Islam, Islam spreads like a wild fire! It's so simple!"

"What?" Helena asked again, although now she just seemed confused. "Wait, where are you going?"

I didn't have time to respond directly. Instead, I bolted from the tent, yelling, "*Vincent!*"

***

"The Byzantines," Vincent said, quite impressed, his arm crossed against his chest. "Well, that was easier than I thought it would be."

"I know!" I exclaimed. "It's all so simple. Thank God Helena reads books like a normal person or I'd still be trying to figure it out."

Vincent nodded quietly, his mind probably processing this information as easily as my own had.

"Will one of you explain to me what a Byzantine is," Archer demanded.

I'd asked him join Vincent and me outside Vincent's tent as well, since he needed to know this more than anyone.

"The Byzantine Empire was the eastern continuation of the Roman Empire," Vincent explained. "Its seat of power resided in Constantinople, or Byzantium, as it's currently named. For many years, Constantinople and Rome shared power equally, but then Rome fell into chaos after hordes from the east invaded Europe, while the Byzantines prospered. Their history is impressive and extensive, but what is important about them for the sake of this conversation is that they were also a buffer zone between Europe and the Middle East. They kept the powers of Islam out of Western Europe for almost a thousand years, never letting them grow too powerful until the fall of Constantinople in 1453 when the Ottoman Empire sacked the city."

I nodded. That was a fairly succinct summarization for a culture and empire that had been almost as influential in the Mediterranean area as Rome had been. Not only had they been an important military barrier, but a preserver of so much Roman and Greek history and knowledge, that without them, it all may have been lost. For instance, the only reason I had the pleasure of reading *The Odyssey* at all was because just prior to its fall in 1453, the few surviving Greek copies were moved out of Constantinople to the west.

That, at least, explained why I hadn't named my dog Argos in Artie 2.0's timeline. It was completely possible that in her timeline, *The Odyssey* was completely unheard of in many western countries, and young Jacob 2.0 had never even read it. I wondered if there might have been a little kid named Muhammad running around Egypt playing catch with his dog Argos in that timeline.

Crazy.

I turned to Archer. "Ever heard of something called Civil Law?"

Archer shrugged. "It's a legal system."

"Yeah, sure, but who uses it?"

"Mostly Islamic countries," Archer answered. "As well as in their former colonies in South America and Africa."

I waved a hand in his direction knowingly. "There you go. I guess instead of Justinian preserving all that stuff, the Muslims found it... although, I'm surprised they don't use a type of religious law."

"It's a hybrid," Archer clarified, "but it's grown more secular over the last century."

"Really?" I asked. "Interesting..."

"Just get to the point, Hunter!" Archer demanded.

"Yeah, yeah," I said dismissively, too interested in the implications of all this alternate history to really give a shit about Archer anymore. "Well... I guess we now know why there's no mention of the Byzantine Empire in Archer's timeline."

"We do?" He asked.

"We do," Vincent answered for me. "You see, in order for the Byzantine Empire not to exist, the Roman Empire must not have existed long enough for the split to occur. Sometime between today and the early fourth century when Constantine moved the seat of power from Rome to Constantinople, the Roman Empire must have floundered."

"Yeah," I agreed, "but I don't think we'll need to wait nearly that long..."

Vincent nodded, his mind coming to the same conclusion: that because of the events that were happening now – that is, the fracturing of the Roman Empire under Agrippina's rule – Rome was about to fall, and no one would be around to pick up the pieces.

"I knew this was *your* fault, Hunter!" Archer yelled, his eyes ablaze. "My world went completely to shit because you had to stick your nose where you shouldn't have! My world is suffering because of *you*. Because of *you*…"

That's when I punched him hard in the stomach, knocking the wind from him along with his fucking words. He doubled over, and I reached out to grab him by the shoulders to pull him into my knee that was already being thrust into his chest. He would have fallen on his own then had I let him, but I decided to slam my fist into the back of his neck for good measure as well.

He went down hard, and I leapt on top of him to continue my assault, but Vincent body checked me off of him before I could. The two of us tumbled in different directions, but I scrambled to my feet far quicker than the older man, yet still he moved to intercept me again. I was operating in a fury now, and I didn't care who stood in my way, so when Vincent attempted to block me from attacking Archer again, I hurled a fist into his jaw as hard as I could.

He slammed into the ground, and my hand exploded in pain.

I took a moment to shrug it off, keeping my eyes on Archer, who remained on his stomach, panting and cringing through the pain. Vincent, too, was immobile, but at least on his knees, holding his chin.

Once the pain in my hand subsided a second later, I leapt for Archer.

I never even got close, because I was tackled again, only by someone far more agile than Vincent this time. Wang was already grappling with me as we hit the ground, and the little Asian-Brit, whom I outweighed considerably, wrapped me up in a submission move from behind so easily that I didn't have a chance against him. The little bastard had always been stronger than he looked, but more so, he simply knew how to fight with the best of them, and I couldn't do anything to free myself from his grip.

"Calm down, Hunter," he yelled as I thrashed against him. "Don't make me put you out, mate!"

My struggles subsided although the anger still coursed through me, but even with all that negative emotion fueling me, I knew Wang could render me unconscious just as easily as he could count to three. I grew calmer but still Wang held on until he was absolutely certain I wouldn't fight back.

"Well?" He demanded once I went completely still.

"I'm done," I answered, and he let me go.

I scrambled to my feet and immediately moved toward Archer again, only to be stopped by Wang's powerful grip. "I'll embarrass you again if I have to, Hunter," he said.

I tore my arm away but didn't move from where I stood. Instead, I glared at Archer as he slowly rolled up into a sitting position. To my right, Vincent had found his way to his feet, and while he looked at me sternly, he didn't seem outright angry. I ignored him and turned back to Archer, pointing at him accusingly.

"Don't think for a second that you know anything about me," I told him, reiterating the same thoughts I'd given him months ago outside of Damascus. "Haven't you realized how much I already hate myself for doing exactly what you said? I know this is all my fault! I've known for *five* goddamned years! You know nothing about me because even if you did, I'm not the same guy you knew at all! Don't you understand that?? I hate myself, Archer! I *hate* myself!"

I stopped yelling as those final words left my lips and the anger subsided as realization finally rang true. Those were the words I'd been trying to conjure up to describe how I felt for months now, and they were the truest words I'd heard in years.

I hated myself.

In every sense of the word.

With that realization came panic, a panic induced by the understanding that a person could actually hate himself, and that such a person was me. I looked up, horrified at my sudden awareness, and found that more of my friends had gathered around me. Helena stood there too, looking just as shocked as I was, her hand covering her mouth, a sight that broke my heart even further.

So I left without further comment.

I walked back to my *praetorium* slowly and alone, where I could hide from it all, hoping beyond hope that Helena knew better than to join me tonight. I couldn't face her. Not now. I needed to be alone with nothing but the thoughts that seemed to come so clearly to me in my bed that was always positioned just beside my treasure filled footlocker.

***

The next morning we were back on the road.

Helena hadn't come home last night, and I hadn't spoken to another person since my incident with Archer. I'd been a mess as I'd stumbled into my *praetorium* but felt almost immediately better the moment I'd landed in bed. I'd snuggled up with my blankets and thought of a million ways Archer was wrong, how he was an asshole, and how the fate of his world was about to join my list of things I couldn't care less about.

Besides, my world was no better off than his really.

It had been World War III, without an end in sight. Who cared if western powers had, for the most part, beaten back Islam? There were still the Asian, African, Russian, and South American powers to deal with. It was all a giant cluster fuck, with no one, not even the Pope, having a moral high ground to stand on. I simply could no longer bring myself to care that Archer's timeline was so different anymore. So what if the Muslims had won and had beaten back Europe? Who cares? Let them have their moment. God knows the Middle East had suffered enough. Besides, Archer was still alive in his timeline and it wasn't like Artie 2.0 was really my sister. Not really.

Perhaps it was best just to let their timeline burn…

These were the thoughts that had accompanied me to sleep that night, and I'd been surprised at how refreshed and rejuvenated I'd felt come morning. I had been energized and ready to go, outpacing even the normally spry Romans at breaking down our camp. I'd heard a few grumbles amongst them about the pace I was setting, which was fast, long, and without remorse considering the horrible marching conditions we found ourselves in, but they could grumble all they wanted. This was my army and they were as loyal to me as Romans could be to a general, perhaps even more so than the vehemently loyal soldiers under Julius Caesar who had practically followed him to hell and back.

Either they'd come around in short order or my centurions would make them.

All of this had left a lot for me to think about as the day wore on, and although I was still full of energy, I was happy that the day was already over and that it was time to call for camp again. I hadn't yet apologized to Vincent, or to Archer, but it was only Vincent who deserved one.

I exited my *praetorium*, and immediately encountered the construction of our newest security precaution. At the onset of our journey, Cuyler had suggested that the Romans build a scaffolding about thirty feet high that could act as our LP/OP. Such an outpost was meant to be concealed, but within the confines of a fortified position, it worked all the same. The centurions hadn't quite seen the point of such a structure until we'd provided a few with our binoculars. That had been more than enough to have them assign two engineers to design and construct the platform immediately.

It was almost complete, and Gunnery Sergeant Cuyler was patiently waiting beside it. He noticed my arrival but didn't seem particularly pleased to see me. I suppose I couldn't blame him, since I'd just laid out his commanding officer last night, but he still managed a nod in greeting as I passed by.

I didn't bother returning it, and continued on my way.

Everyone else was pitching in with the camp's construction, even Archer and his troops. While they'd already been in Ancient Rome for a few months now, the culture shock of living and working with a campaigning legion had been intense during their few days since Camulodunum. This had been the first time they'd participated in a legion march, which was a grueling and tiring affair, but still Archer's people had thrown their weight into the construction effort every night, and despite the legionnaires' professionalism, they appreciated the help.

I found Vincent a short distance from my *praetorium* in the small area near the camp's corner which my team called home. He was busy stepping on a stake to anchor his tent to the hard ground that had finally frozen over. I walked up behind him but didn't interrupt his work, and it was only when he turned around that he noticed me.

We stood there regarding each other evenly, when finally he slapped his hand against his thigh sympathetically. "It's all right, Jacob. Archer stepped over the line, and we all make mistakes."

I nodded. "I suppose we do."

But that's all I said, and Vincent waited patiently while I simply grew impatient.

A moment later, he finally asked, "Is there something you came to talk to me about? Have you seen any more of your visions?"

"I haven't, actually," I reported, which was true. "I just wanted to remind you that we have a status briefing in ten minutes."

"Oh," Vincent said like he was surprised. "Yes, I remember, but is… was there anything else?"

"Not a thing," I replied as I spun on my heel and headed back to my *praetorium*.

"We are about to enter Ordovices territory," my most senior centurion, Minicius, reported.

I'd left my first file, Fabius, with Galba, figuring he'd do more good with the legion's main body than with our reconnaissance force, but in turn, Fabius had recommended Minicius for my task. Minicius was an easy going fellow, but he had a cruel streak in him that I'd come to appreciate when it came to keeping the legionnaires in line.

"Rome has not yet had much contact with them," he continued, "but reports indicate that they are an extremely bellicose tribe, one that will not sway easily to Roman rule. Prior to Caratacus' removal to Rome and in an act of good faith, he indicated to Legate Plautius that he had made numerous attempts to bring their chieftains under his chain of command to aid in his campaigns against Rome, but that he had failed. It seemed that they were worried about expending their forces in an unsuccessful campaign against us, leaving their territory undefended. It seems their foresight has become our disadvantage."

Vincent pointed to modern day Wales on my map. "But their lack of contact with legions may also indicate they may not immediately move against us militarily. They don't yet hold a grudge against Rome."

Minicius nodded. "Quite true, but it is never wise to expect such things."

Vincent huffed a laugh as he returned the nod.

"Either way," I broke in, upset at myself for continuing to host these meetings after my time with Plautius, "since the Ordovices haven't yet had cause to worry about Roman legions marching on their territory, chances are they're at least not expecting us."

"This I can confirm with confidence," Minicius said. "Plautius' officers supplied me with copies of every intelligence report gathered on the tribes of Britain since our forces were redirected to the German front earlier this year. Much of the eastern region is in open conflict with Rome, but the western region is docile. As fortune would have it, and as you predict Legate Hunter, I expect that any Ordovices force will be quite surprised at our arrival, and unprepared to attack."

I sniffed sharply. "Well, at least that's *something*."

Minicius tilted his head down in silent agreement.

"What about the Britons that have been shadowing us since Camulodunum?" Vincent asked. "I expected them to break off days ago, but they're still with us."

"They are a concern," the centurion agreed. "I have sent advanced scouts to gather intelligence beyond what our normal forces can reconnoiter, but I have ordered them to be cautious. Alone and cut off from reinforcements is not a place to squander resources, especially if there is no guarantee that their efforts will garner results."

"What have they found?" Vincent asked.

"Little," Minicius answered. "They have only been able to tally a count of six dozen combatants, but this is absolutely no indication of their true numbers. This country is vast, and it would be a simple enough task for them to conceal their actual numbers from us."

"Any idea who they are?" I asked.

"I suspect them to be members of either the Iceni or Catuvellauni tribes. Perhaps both. They have been the most belligerent tribes we have yet encountered in Britain, and they harbor the most resentment toward Rome. Furthermore, they can field sizable forces on the field of battle."

"Makes sense to me," I said, turning to Vincent with a sigh. "We could really use the UAV here. Probably more than ever."

"I would agree," he said, "but even back home, we knew better than to rely on technology."

"Still, we…"

I was cut off by a commotion outside my *praetorium*. Minicius, Vincent, and I lifted our heads in the direction of the entrance to see the silhouettes of three individuals outside my tent. There was a bit of an argument, most of which was performed by a familiar female voice, but after a handful of seconds, Helena burst into the tent with Gaius and Marcus following behind her.

"I'm sorry, Legate, but she…" Gaius started.

I cut him off with an upheld hand. "It's all right, Gaius."

The man nodded and glanced at Marcus, both of whom looked more uncomfortable than I'd ever seen them before.

They were my friends, and I owed them my life, and I'm sure I'd repaid the favor once or twice as well. We shared a close bond, just as they did with everyone else, but they were also legionnaires. And they were also Praetorians. With my advancement to the rank of legate, they'd practically demanded that they step in and act as bodyguards. They knew as well as I that I hardly needed such a personal protection detail, but their Roman stubbornness had eked out a victory for them. But that also meant they had to do things they might find uncomfortable, like barring entrance to my tent from even Helena, who had never needed a reason to enter my *praetorium* before.

Then again, she *was* interrupting a command level meeting.

I flicked my hand, and Gaius and Marcus saluted before vacating the tent. Helena watched them go angrily, but her anger didn't seem directed toward them. She seemed exasperated, but I didn't know why. She knew the protocols as well as anyone.

When they were gone, she turned a frustrated expression on me.

I clasped my hands behind my back. "What is it, Helena?"

"Jacob, we're…"

"*Legate*," I said, cutting her off. "I'm on duty, remember?"

Helena stared at me, but seemed to understand, although she made an obnoxious show of it.

"Legate... *Hunter*," she said, her voice dripping with sarcasm. "It seems that we're under attack. Maybe you'd like to do something about it?"

My eyes narrowed angrily at the fact that I hadn't been told sooner, and stormed my way toward the entrance. Vincent and Minicius followed, but Vincent stopped beside Helena as I exited the tent. I missed their conversation, but I doubted it was important.

However, an attack by the shadow force most certainly was.

Luckily, we still had a few tricks up our sleeves.

***

I emerged from my *praetorium* calmly, but my nerves were bubbling with excitement and adrenaline. I hadn't had a good rush since Alexandria, and I was itching to release some built up tension.

The camp was a roiling ocean of controlled chaos as I took a moment to get my bearings. Legionnaires were scattering to man their defensive positions and Bordeaux and Wang were jogging to the right flank where Bordeaux could set up his Mk 48 machine gun to lay down a base of suppressing fire, and I almost laughed at the thought of a man with a machine gun suppressing barbarian Celts, dissuading them from casting *spears*. It was a wonder we hadn't taken over the world by now, and the nagging idea that we probably should have had been a recent, but persistent, thought of mine.

Santino and Stryker moved off to the left flank while Brewster and Archer held themselves back. Artie was nowhere to be seen, probably in her tent where she belonged. A moment later, Helena and Vincent popped out of my *praetorium* and moved to stand on either side of me, both of them tracking their eyes toward the coming field of battle.

Two hundred and thirty meters from the camp, just before the tree line we'd marched through earlier tonight, stood Celtic warriors primed for battle. They were too far away for me to discern any further detail about them, but their battle line stretched maybe four times as long as our camp was wide, and I had no idea how deep it ran. With the natural barrier of the river to our backs, they would be incapable of surrounding us completely, but they could easily pin us against the river, although I was confident my legionnaires could handle them.

I twisted at my waist and looked up to Cuyler perched in our LP/OP. He held his binoculars to his eyes as he scanned the tree line, his sniper rifle cradled in his lap.

"What's your headcount, Eagle Eye?" I called up to him. "Five thousand? Six?"

Cuyler pulled his binoculars away from his eyes and glanced down at me, ready to answer, but before he did, he looked at me oddly, and returned his attention to the enemy troops. I waited impatiently for another ten seconds before he finally looked back down at me again.

"I count no more than fifteen hundred," he reported.

He sounded serious but either his mathematical skill was as horrible as his gear was primitive... or mine was.

I straightened and returned my eyes to the enemy, and noticed that Cuyler was right. Not only had my initial estimate of six thousand enemy troops been far from wrong, but the enemy had shifted positions since I'd turned away as well. The width of their battle lines had narrowed by at least half.

I glanced at Vincent. "Did they just maneuver their people into a tighter formation?"

He glanced at Helena, and I could see Helena drop her chin just slightly out of the corner of my eye. After an obvious delay, his eyes finally shifted to meet mine. "They haven't moved... *Legate*."

My head tilted back in surprise. Maybe Santino had rubbed off on Vincent, and he'd developed a penchant for inappropriate jokes in inappropriate situations, and had decided to pull a fast one on me, as there was simply no way the barbarians *hadn't* shifted their formation.

Choosing instead to accept Vincent's little joke for now, I turned back to Cuyler.

"Give me a description of what you're seeing, Eagle Eye," I ordered. "Armaments. Transportation. Siege equipment."

The man shook his head as he continued to glass our perimeter. "No siege equipment or chariots that I can see, Legate. Standard Celtic kit for the foot soldiers. Two spears, a shield, and maybe half the contingent carry swords. Light to no armor. Basic animal skins for clothing. Minimal cold weather gear." He paused and I could see him lean forward, as if the movement could help offer him a better view of what he was seeing. "Maybe a quarter of them are female."

I nodded. Female Celts fighting in battle wasn't necessarily the norm, but they were still capable fighters. Most circumstances that saw them raising arms was when their tribe's back was up against a wall and every able bodied member was needed to fight. Front line combat wasn't as common, but perhaps an advanced party such as this one would have a greater place for women. Their slighter frames and agility would be invaluable tools for a scouting or shadow party. We still hadn't determined which this particular one was yet, but I had no doubt these people were the same ones who had tracked us since Camulodunum. That told me that they meant business, and while I didn't know why they'd chosen now to fight, a fight tonight would suit me just fine.

I relayed Cuyler's intelligence to Minicius and requested his tactical appraisal.

"They caught us off guard, Legate," he started, "but they took too long organizing their forces. They should have struck quickly or waited until the early morning, because our legionnaires are already on line and ready to defend the camp or advance forward." He paused and craned his neck for a better view, but didn't hesitate for long. "In either situation, our forces could easily overwhelm them. Had they outnumbered us four to one we could have defeated them with minimal losses; but evenly matched, prepared to receive them, and behind our defensive barricades, I suspect they will break off after our first *pila* volley."

I nodded. "Very good, Centurion. Order the legionnaires to hold their ground until the enemy are in range of their *pila*. Order one volley at that time. Should they continue to advance, my people will attempt to further dissuade them. If they're persistent, send the legionnaires forward."

"Your orders are sound, Legate. I obey."

He saluted and moved off to put my orders into action. I watched him go and clenched my teeth. Unless something disastrous occurred, there was little else to do but kick back, relax, and enjoy the show.

Even with more than two football fields between us, I could hear the roars and warlike chants coming from the opposing Celts. They were riling themselves up for battle as most barbarians did, but my legionnaires held themselves back in patient silence, a coiled cobra ready to strike, not an ape pounding his chest to intimidate a foe, and they were far more dangerous because of it.

Seconds later the roars and chants abated, and the enemy pushed forward. I grinned, feeling the excitement in my chest grow and grow, and I decided I couldn't just sit back and play the arm-chair general. I spun around and marched toward my *praetorium*.

Helena turned and tracked my movement. "Where are you going?"

"Getting Penelope," I answered over my shoulder.

"Why?" She asked as I disappeared into my tent and moved to my equipment chest. My left hand brushed against my foot locker and I had a thought to retrieve something within, but the thought was gone in an instant so I ignored it.

Within my equipment chest was all my combat gear, including my MOLLE vest and other pieces of my kit. I already had my pistol strapped to my right thigh, but there hadn't been a need to be fully kitted up earlier, so I reached in gently and removed Penelope, giving her a quick wipe with my sleeve to remove a smudge on her collapsible stock. I pulled back the cocking lever to reveal the ejection port on its right side and blew into it to expel any dust or dirt that may have collected there. I hadn't had an opportunity to use the old girl since our battle with Agrippina, so my anticipation only grew at the thought of using her now.

"Ready to get back in the fight?" I asked Penelope. I twisted her around so that her barrel pointed at my face before tilting her up and down quickly like a dog agreeing with his master. "Oh, yes you are," I squealed. "Yes you are."

I smiled at Penelope and wrapped her sling around my shoulder. I reached back into the chest and retrieved two loaded magazines and stuffed them into a cargo pocket, not needing my

MOLLE vest tonight. Finally, I swapped out the reflex sight currently sitting atop my trusty HK 416 assault rifle for my night vision equipped ACOG scope.

Once all was ready, I stood and turned, only to find my way blocked by Helena, who held her arms crossed against her chest and above ever expanding baby bump. My smile grew as I noticed it and took a step forward to put my hand against her stomach.

She didn't flinch or move her arms at my touch.

"How's my little guy doing?" I asked.

"Put it away, Jacob," Helena said.

"Put what away?"

"Penelope. You don't need it."

"Lay off, Helena. I need this."

She uncrossed her arms and gripped my hand against her stomach, but instead of holding it lovingly, she ripped it away and threw it aside.

"Since when have you needed to blow off steam by murdering people!?"

"This isn't murder, Helena," I said. "This is war. Now get out of my way!"

I pushed past her roughly, but she barely even flinched at the contact. I stormed my way out of the tent with Helena in quick pursuit. Once outside, I noticed the advancing Celts had halved the distance between our two forces, and swore under my breath that I was losing time.

"Jacob, don't do this," Helena said as she followed me around to the back of my *praetorium*. "Don't you realize what you're doing?"

I ignored her and called up to Cuyler atop his LP/OP. "Get on the line, Gunny. I'll take it from here."

Sergeant Cuyler looked down at me in confusion with his binoculars still held in place. "Sir?"

"Down," I ordered.

The man rarely hesitated, but he made up for it by acting instantly this time. He shouldered his rifle and climbed down the observation platform before dropping to the ground. He stood there, his confused expression still on his face, and he glanced at Helena for information. She stood beside him, hugging herself, but didn't look at him as I started my ascent.

"We have contingency plans for a fight like this, Jacob," she called up to me. "You developed them months ago. We don't need to fight a force this small."

I ignored her as I reached my perch. There was a small chair situated atop the platform with a footrest near its opposite edge. I sunk into the hard, wooden seat and tried to get comfortable, propping my left foot up on the footrest. With my left leg slightly elevated, I shouldered my rifle, placing my left elbow against my thigh for support and sighted through my ACOG. It was completely dark so I flicked on its night vision capabilities and the advancing troops materialized in my scope like they were right in front of me.

I could have fired in that moment, but I decided to at least see what would happen once the legionnaires cast their first volley, but the Celts were smart, and paused just out of range to continue their taunts and shows of force. I smiled through my scope and mimicked firing my rifle in quick succession, pretending each shot to be a kill shot.

"Who are you?"

I heard the voice at the outreaches of my hearing, and didn't think much of it at first, knowing it was Helena's and suspecting it must have been directed at someone else. But when silence followed her choice few words, I looked down, and saw her staring up at me intently, Cuyler still at her side. I found his disobedience infuriating.

How like him.

"I said get on the line, Cuyler," I ordered down at him.

He hesitated again, and with obvious reluctance, looked back at Helena for support but she was too focused on me. He didn't seem to know what to do, but then he took his leave to join Archer and Brewster. Helena didn't move, so I turned my attention back to her.

"Go find Artie and keep her company, Helena."

Her jaw dropped at my comment, but instead of anger in her eyes, all I saw was sadness and a sudden determination. Such an expression surprised me, but what was she going to do?

In answer to my silent question, I saw her grind her teeth together and move away from the LP/OP as she reached into her pocket to retrieve her radio. Confused, but interested, I placed my own radio's ear bud in my ear to listen in.

"3-3, this is 3-2. Come in," Helena transmitted.

"Santino at your service, sexy pants."

"I'm countermanding 3-1's orders. Have Minicius order all troops to stand down unless directly threatened, and prepare to initiate protocol alpha."

"I don't think you have the authority to do that," Santino replied, and I smiled proudly, "but I call you sexy pants for a reason, so give me a second."

"Copy, meet me at Minicius' position in two mikes."

There was a double click over the radio, and this time it was my turn to open my mouth in shock. I scrambled down off my perch, noticing Helena enter my *praetorium*, which also happened to be where she still kept her things as well. I dropped five feet to the ground and sprinted to my tent, flinging myself through the entrance to discover Helena rummaging through her equipment container.

"What the hell are you doing??" I demanded as I stepped forward. "We can't have these barbarians harrying us all the way to Anglesey. They could recruit more numbers or find better ground to attack us from. What are you..."

As I was about to ask my final question, I placed my hand roughly on Helena's shoulder. I hadn't meant to hurt her or even intimidate her with the gesture, but that's when, in her search through our gear, she opened my footlocker. An immediate feeling of anger and jealousy overcame me as her frantic search ended with the discovery of something I didn't want her to find.

"Jacob... what is..."

I squeezed my hand against her shoulder tightly as realization set in. She flinched at the grip, but she reacted so quickly that I barely had time to understand what happened next.

Reaching across her body, she took my hand in her own and wrenched it to the side so forcefully that I doubled over instinctively to keep her from breaking my arm in half. She spun around in the opposite direction to get behind me, and kicked the back of my knee a half second later. I fell to my knees and turned my head to plead for her to stop so that we could talk, but before I had the chance, her left hand was already cutting through the air faster than I could track. It smashed into my jaw and I saw stars flash before my eyes as she let go of my hand and let me fall to the floor.

She screamed in pain and shook her hand, but didn't waste any time before retreating from our fight, yelling, "I can't believe you would hide that from me! How could you betray me like that??" Her words were angry and distant, like she was talking to herself rather than to me. She stumbled from the tent, but before she was gone, I heard her say, "I just hope that knocked some goddamned sense into you!"

Three emotions and feelings swirled within me in that moment as I rested upon the ground, my head having fallen to rest atop the footlocker that Helena had slammed shut before punching me. The first was of course anger – lots of it – but it was quickly, and interestingly, replaced with pride. I felt a smile creep onto my face as I remembered my first meeting with Helena, and how she'd nearly punched a hole in my face then as well.

But then the third feeling crept in: pain, and with it came something else.

Like a stopper released from a drain, a swell of negativity and darkness flowed into my body from some unknown source. It was as if every negative thought and memory to ever cross my mind suddenly invaded my consciousness all at one moment, and all the pressure and responsibility I'd accumulated over the years whispered to me, coercing me to do something about it, clouding my better judgment.

I squeezed my eyes shut to push out the thoughts, but a blue light seemed to shine through my eyelids, and I no longer wished to push the darkness away. With the light returned my anger, which fueled my body's ability to channel the pain I felt in my jaw to revitalize me, and with a quick blink of my eyes, I felt powerful again.

Punching the earth beside my head with both of my fists, I pushed upwards and got to my knees. I shook my head to fully abolish the cobwebs in my mind from Helena's assault and prepared to stand, but before I could, an ominous red glare bathed my tent in a sea of color, followed moments later by the deafening sound of an explosion.

There was a massive cry of fear, but no cries of pain, and in a surge of awareness, I knew the battle was already over. I gritted my teeth and stood, straightening the warm jacket I wore. I put my mask of leadership back on my face and steeled myself, and walked briskly toward the exit, ready to confront the inevitable, unaware that deep within me something was stirring.

Something glorious.

***

I emerged from my *praetorium* calmly for the second time tonight. Whatever anger that had consumed me a minute ago was contained now, sequestered away like a massive bubble in my chest that was ready to burst. I felt immense pressure there now, pressing tightly against my lungs and heart, a sensation that made it difficult to think without the interference of my emotions, but I let it simmer for now, no longer needing that anger to drive me.

Around me, the collective calmness from the legionnaires had dissipated, replaced instead with shouts of good cheer at their bloodless victory. I smiled as well as I strolled toward them, my hands clasped behind my back. It would have been more beneficial to our cause had these interlopers been dealt with more permanently, but a victory was a victory.

Many legionnaires stood around our perimeter throwing taunts and jeers at the retreating enemy, but those nearest to the center of the camp had Santino hefted in the air, tossing him up and down in jubilation. Santino in turn was of course eating it up, whooping and hollering in celebration along with the Romans, waving his arms like a bird, enticing them to throw him higher and higher.

Vincent and Archer stood aloof from the show, but Wang, Bordeaux, Gaius, Marcus, Stryker, and Brewster laughed and clapped as Santino slipped through the grips of those who'd launched him into the air and landed hard on the ground with a thump. He looked up at them angrily, but they didn't even seem to notice as they picked him back up and continued their fun.

I watched them as I slipped in between Vincent and Archer, who like any good commanders, stood aside, choosing instead to participate silently and distantly. Both men parted to allow me access between them, but both seemed to add excessive distance between us as well. I ignored them as I noticed Helena standing away from the frivolity as well with Cuyler nearby. He watched Santino rise and fall with his usual expressionless neutrality, but I couldn't help but notice how close the two stood near each other. They weren't quite touching, but it was clear that Helena had sought someone for comfort after what had just occurred between us.

I managed to quarantine the jealousy I felt at the sight of them into my chest along with my anger, putting it there for later use.

I turned to Vincent, jutting my chin out toward Santino as well. "What'd he do?"

"He and Helena enacted Operation..." he paused and rolled his eyes, "...Operation: Dissuade the Shit out of Them. Protocol alpha."

I nodded. Santino and I had come up with the name during our time on the Mediterranean.

During better times.

The operation was meant to do just as it said: spook the natives by launching an eerie red flare into the sky, followed by sending up a small bit of C-4 to explode and truly scare the shit out of them. Santino had retrofitted a basic Roman sling to accept the small brick of C-4, but it was a two person operation, with one person launching the flare, followed by the second person slinging the C-4 into the air, and completed by the first person remotely detonating it from a safe distance. It was a dangerous operation and required precise timing to make sure the C-4 wasn't detonated too early or too late, but it had obviously worked just as we'd hoped.

"Helena didn't wait around for the legionnaires to notice who'd enacted the operation," Vincent explained, although his voice had no humor in it, "but Santino... well, you know how he is."

"Of course I do," I replied. "Think it'll work again?"

"Perhaps once more on the same group," he answered. "Easily again on a different group, but also one I would prefer to try every time we encounter an enemy until it fails to be effective."

I eyed him angrily. "You know the reason I didn't want to use this tactic immediately was because I didn't want to give it away so early in our journey, right?"

"As you say," he said, his tone unchanged.

"Like Minicius said," I argued, "the barbarians would have broken off after a single *pila* volley. It would have been the natural course of such an engagement, even without our presence."

Finally, Vincent turned, the smaller man having to look up just a bit to meet my eye. "Is that why you needlessly retrieved your rifle and set up atop the LP/OP?"

I recoiled at the insinuation. "I can't help but notice you have your pistol as well, Vincent," I countered harshly. "These barbarians are tough, and may have broken through our lines. If not for me being up there, the barbarians could have..."

"In all the time I have known you," Vincent interrupted, his remaining hand held up in a silencing gesture, "I have never, not *once*, heard you use the word 'barbarian' to reference those we encounter, even *without* the modern, negative connotation, yet I wonder why it is so readily on the tip of your tongue now..." He leaned in closer to me for a few last words before leaving. "Have you forgotten, Hunter, that you, too, cannot speak Greek?"

Vincent turned and left, and I scoffed at his retort, turning to Archer to make an off handed comment at Vincent's expense, but my old SEAL buddy had escaped as well, leaving me alone. I glanced around, wondering where everyone had gone, realizing that not only was I alone, but I was *really* alone. There was no one around me in any direction, not at any conversational distance anyway.

I looked up, noticing that Bordeaux and Stryker had contributed their considerable strength to the Santino-tossing effort, and wondered if they were still throwing him out of happiness for his efforts, or if they were simply testing how far he could fall before he got hurt.

I decided to seek out Helena, but while Cuyler remained, a smile on his face now at the Santino-antics, Helena was gone. I swiveled my head around and searched for her, but she was nowhere to be found. My first thought was that she'd retreated back to my *praetorium* to rest after the night's exertions, but when I turned to walk toward it, I had to pull up short so that I didn't knock Artie over, who had been standing just behind me unexpectedly, her arms crossed.

"Artie," I said. "Sorry. Didn't see you there. Glad to see you're okay though. Where've you been these days?"

She offered me a sneer of a smile, one completely without humor. "I'm happy you're so concerned for my wellbeing, Jacob."

I looked at her curiously. "I *was* concerned."

"I know you were."

"Is there a problem, Diana?"

"I don't know. Is there?"

"Are we going to do this all night?" I asked, growing annoyed at her silliness. "Because I really don't have time for it."

"No, I'm done," she answered. "Don't worry."

"Good," I said as I maneuvered around her to approach my *praetorium.*

"You're lucky," Artie called from behind me just before I could enter.

I stopped and twisted at the waist to look at her. "Lucky for what?"

"That you have an *image* of leadership to maintain."

I spun all the way around so that I faced her. "And why's that?"

She took a defiant few steps forward and poked a finger into my chest. "Because you'd be sleeping in the latrines tonight if not for the fact that those impressionable toy soldiers out there expect you to be their leader, and you are therefore given the privilege of sleeping in *that* tent."

I pushed new anger into my chest so that I kept myself from striking her. "Enough with the riddles, Diana! Get to the point."

"Stay away from her, Jacob," Artie said in a tone I'd never heard from her before. "I'm warning you. Stay. Away."

She started to walk away, but I took a step forward and reached for her arm. "Stay away from who…"

But before I could finish, she whirled around and threw both hands into my chest, pushing me backward. I stumbled but kept my footing, but the tears in her eyes now only made me feel worse, making it impossible for me to draw on the anger in my chest to direct against her.

"Stay away from *us*, Jacob," she said threateningly with a finger pointed in my direction, tears dripping from her chin. "You say Archer doesn't know who you are but the fact is that *nobody* knows who you are anymore!"

She sniffed, spun away, and ran toward her tent. I let her go without another word, watching as she found the small tent she'd occupied by herself these past few months. Nothing else and no one else came to my attention as I stared unblinkingly in her direction, so when it became painfully obvious that I was alone again, I glanced back at my friends, thinking that perhaps they would come join me for some wine in celebration of our victory, but they weren't anywhere to be found either.

I frowned as I pushed down my feeling of loneliness to join the anger and jealousy that already occupied the emotional storage unit I'd constructed within my ribcage. As it joined together with the others, the pressure in my chest only increased, and I staggered a bit as I walked back to my *praetorium*, the pressure I felt there a distracting but familiar sensation. It was a combination of many I felt quite often, as I imagined everyone else in the universe did as well, but never had I felt it as intensely as I did now.

It was a nervous feeling, like the budding kind I would experience back in high school as waited for the results of a test I'd forgotten to study for.

It pressed against my ribcage like the eternal dread of a first date, a feeling that grew and grew as the date wore on in anticipation of a first kiss.

It hit suddenly deep inside me like when the expectation for bad news was confirmed, like when I'd returned a call from Artie all those years ago, learning that not only had I been unaware of my mother's passing while in the field, but that I had also missed her funeral.

It also left my heart feeling just as empty as it did when a beloved character was unexpectedly killed from a favorite TV show, never to return again and for reasons not quite clear.

What I felt now were pieces of each of these moments and so many more, acting as a degenerative sickness that slowly abated my soul, all rolled up into one massive bout of emotion that threatened to burst through my upper body like a grenade lodged between my lungs. I doubled over at its intensity and fell into my tent, knowing that Helena would notice my discomfort and come to my aid, ready and willing to soothe away every ache and pain like she always did.

But when I collapsed to the ground, no help came.

The test did not magically have a B- on it.

The date did not end with a kiss, not even on the cheek.

The phone call did not end with shared tears that allowed my sister and me to console each other.

The TV show did not bring that character back from the dead, even in a dream sequence.

And Helena did not come to my side to take the pain away.

I was alone, and the pain lingered.

I clenched my teeth and forced myself to crawl to my cot. It seemed to take hours, but eventually, I found myself atop my wonderfully soft bed, sweating bullets and unable to shake the chills that stabbed at me like icicles at the same time. Every other time I'd come to this bed since setting out from Camulodunum, I'd found some level of comfort, but not tonight. Tonight, the pain was only intensifying, driving my mind through a maelstrom of negativity.

It was almost too much to contain in my chest, as it wasn't nearly big enough, but then another feeling snuck its way into my mind, something soothing, something calming. It was coming from the side of my bed, so I rolled to the right and fell from the low perch, not knowing what I was doing or caring what would happen. I simply craved relief, something to take the pain away, and I found it in my footlocker. I didn't know who had blessed it with such healing properties, but someone obviously had, because as I wrapped my arms around it and laid my head upon its lid, I felt immediately better. All the sorrow and torment my body and mind had felt was gone. Like a wondrous drug that could take away all pain, I'd found my salvation.

I was asleep seconds later, but in an odd way.

Instead of the peace that normally accompanied sleep's sweet embrace, I drifted off with a billion thoughts surging through my mind, over and over, with trillions of answers and possibilities. It was enough to drive a man insane, but it only comforted me now as I finally fell asleep, too exhausted to realize that someone had left a blue tinted flashlight aimed directly at my face.

VIII
Anglesey

Western Britannia
December, 42 A.D.

It had been two days since Helena and Santino initiated Operation: Dissuade the Shit out of Them, and we were now deep into modern day Wales, only a day out from the Isle of Mona. In that time, little of consequence had happened, and we had made excellent progress through bare and frozen but dense forests. More importantly, I no longer felt bogged down by inane thoughts out of my control, and I found myself focused. Even though I spent my nights alone now, Vincent no longer attended my nightly mission briefings, and most of my team seemed to go out of their way to avoid me, I felt peaceful, almost happy. Only at night did I find my mind whirring out of control, but slumber came easily now and I would awake more refreshed than ever.

It was a good feeling, one I didn't want to see interrupted.

We hadn't yet made any further contact with the indigenous population, but our Celtic shadow force still paced us at a distance. They seemed cautious now, sending fewer of their forces into visual range, apparently more inclined to simply watch instead of challenge us. It left many uneasy just knowing they were out there, but it took more than a few thousand barbarians to spook the Romans, and I, too, was unconcerned.

It was late in the day as I rode atop Felix near the vanguard of our formation, alone and cold, as had become the norm recently, but nothing clouded my mind besides our destination. And even then, I was less worried about the possibilities of what could happen there, and was more focused instead on simply getting there.

Which was when Wang rode up from the rear of our formation to ride with me.

I looked at him in surprise and offered him a nod in greeting which was returned in kind, but our interaction ended there, so I ignored him and shifted my attention back to the path before us.

Two minutes later, Wang finally turned to me. "Something on your mind, mate?"

"Actually…" I said, without turning. "No, nothing in particular."

"Really?" He asked.

"I know," I replied. "It's pretty nice not to have any thoughts in my head. This must be how the rest of you people live your lives…"

Wang adjusted his seat, and returned his attention forward. "I've actually had quite a bit to think about lately."

"Wait…" I said, confused, "…you're coming to *me* to talk about *you*?"

"Blimey, it's right embarrassing, but yes."

"Interesting," I said, legitimately so. "Been thinking about the fight a few days ago?"

"No," he replied. "Archer deserved it for sure, even if it was bloody stupid of you, but no, I've been thinking about home mostly. Not about how to get home, but memories of home, my parents, Cardiff, school friends, my chums in the SAS. Even thoughts of fighting a real war instead of the bloody mess we've gotten ourselves into here make me feel better, and even remembering McDougal brings on happy memories."

I frowned at the mention of our one-time, and far too brief, commanding officer who had died before even reaching Ancient Rome. His death had been my fault, but unlike everything else that was my fault, I was at peace with what had happened to him. There were far too many other deaths for me to feel responsible for, and his had come on the field of battle during an operation that had been sanctioned by my commanding officers in a theatre of war openly engaged against me.

Unfortunately, the rules were different now.

"So being here has been melancholic for you then, is that it?" I asked.

He nodded. "I don't know what your deal is these days, but at least you're still sharp. I'll give you that."

"I guess I'll take it."

"Take it if you will," Wang said, without humor, "but you are right. There's something about Anglesey that's always bothered me, only I didn't really remember until recently."

"So what's on your mind then?"

He looked over his shoulder, left and then right. "This place doesn't feel that different from home really. Oh, it's missing the roads and towns and pubs, but if I didn't know any better, I'd say we were taking a stroll through the country back home."

"Sounds nice actually."

"Aye, it is," he confirmed, "but I didn't come here to waffle on about memories of home." He fidgeted atop his horse to find a more comfortable sitting position, which was in turn making me feel the opposite. When he was successful, he turned back to me. "Ever since Alexandria, I've been thinking about some looney stuff…"

"Just fucking tell me, Wang!" I said, exasperated that it was taking him so long to get to the point.

"Crikey Moses, Hunter, give me a moment. I thought you were supposed to be the patient one…"

"What little patience I have left is waning quickly, believe me."

Wang sighed. "Well, I'd better start then, because I won't blame you for losing it completely once I'm done. It's just that ever since Rumella told us to come here, to Britain, to Wales, I've been thinking a lot about things like magic, time travel, orbs, Druids, fairy tales, epic quests to save the world… it's all pretty fantastical rubbish but believe me, me mum will believe every detail of all this when I get back to tell her about it."

I looked at him, suddenly curious. "Yeah? Why's that?"

"You know my family history," he said, "about me dad's parents coming from China after The Great Revolution and him marrying a local lass and all that, but when I say *local*, I mean her family is *old* local. Her family's been in Wales since… well, now, I suppose. I wouldn't be surprised if I ran into some ancestor of mine, actually."

I didn't bother explaining to him that the chances of that were surprisingly high.

He laughed for a second. "Me mum's dad never seemed happy that she married a *Chinaman*, as he always called me dad, but it turned into more of a loving nickname as they never fought, and granddad always spoiled the knickers off me. I love that man. He *never* got along with me dad's dad though. I think the language barrier was just too much for him."

I actually found myself smiling, always finding family drama that wasn't my own humorous. Family dynamics and how members of extended families and in-laws treated each other had always been fascinating to me. Both sets of my grandparents had died well before I was even in middle school, and my own family life had never been particularly enjoyable, so I'd never really gotten to experience the pangs of having a big family on my own.

"Sorry, Hunter, didn't mean to go off on a tangent like that."

"So *that's* what it feels like," I said, feeling surprisingly cheerful in the moment.

"Aye, now you know how the rest of us poor nutters feel most of the time."

"Just get to the point," I ordered.

"Crikey, now *you* sound like Helena," he said, cutting off my retort with a smirk, "but you're right. As I was saying, me lovely mum's family has been in Wales forever, and as you may know, many Welsh are a superstitious folk. Some do all sorts of nutty things, and me mum was very into it. Told me lots of stories as a lad. Most were more terrifying than spooky-fun like your American fairy tales. Was the Brothers Grimm shit they were, extra grim, and for some reason they always had a lot of fairies in them..."

"Seriously, Wang. Cut the shit. What are you trying to say?"

"Bloody Christ, Hunter, I'm just saying that I always thought mum was off her trolley about all that stuff! She was right barmy about it, I thought."

"For crying out loud, Wang, I left my ridiculous British slang dictionary back in the 21st century! Speak. Real. English!"

He fidgeted in his saddle again, seeming just as annoyed with me as I was with him.

"She seemed nuts, okay?" He asked in his best American accent, which sounded distinctly Southern. "She was convinced the local folklore was real. She thought Wales in particular had some legitimate connections with magic and the supernatural. She thought Wales actually was the *home of fairies*!"

"So what's your point?" I asked, my patience and curiosity returning.

He shrugged. "I'm not sure yet, Hunter, I'm not. All I know is that we should be careful. I can't shake this feeling that we've entered into some unknown realm of necromancy. I think that was a word me mum used once. Black magic maybe. Something evil. I know you're going to want to grill these Druids for information, but I don't know if that's so wise. You might not like what you learn."

I chuckled. "Thanks for the warning, James, but unless we run into a three headed giant, a fire breathing dragon, or hot chicks in sexy nerd-envisioned armor that can cast level twelve frost spells, I think we'll be just fine."

"I wouldn't joke about that, Hunter. I wouldn't. No, mate, I would not."

"We'll be fine," I snapped, annoyed again.

The last thing I needed right now was talk of magic and fairies and shit like that. There was no need to complicate things any more than they already were, and there was certainly no need to throw in more challenges to overcome. I really couldn't deal with a fight against a dragon right now. I really couldn't. And if we encountered a troll or an elf or a fairy or a demon or a wizard... I truly was bound to go off my own trolley.

***

The next day, I stood with my bootless feet in the water that made up the narrow straight that separated mainland Wales from the Isle of Mona. The distance between shores was not that great, and the great expanse of the island was laid out before me like a large, flat chunk of earth that looked like it had been gently lowered into the water by some ancient mythological hero. Judging distances was something I was good at thanks to my sniper training, and it took me no more than a few seconds to determine that the opposing shore was only four hundred and twenty five meters away.

I turned to Wang who stood beside me. "So, have you ever been here before?"

"Once," he answered. "When I was a lad. No more than nine, and thought the place was right creepy. It's flatter and emptier than Santino's personality, and even back home the area was very sparse and not very developed. Lots of sheep. Even a small city like Cambridge probably had twice the population of the entire island."

I looked at the water and immediately felt I could easily swim across it, even though the current seemed rather choppy.

Wang noticed my scrutiny and pointed out over the water. "I wouldn't think about it, mate. The current is worse than it looks. I remembered seeing whirlpools in the straight as a kid, and dad told me that they were more common than most would think here. Besides, the water is bloody freezing, so I'd advise you to step out it, you git."

I looked down at my feet, noticing for the first time since I'd stepped in that they had gone numb. I hadn't even noticed the cold when I'd first slipped into the water, but I stepped out and sat on the shore so that I could more easily dry them off.

"You're risking hypothermia or frostbite if you keep that up," Wang said.

"I'll keep that in mind," I replied, as I started the process of tying my left boot, jutting my chin in the direction of the island. "How big would you say the island is anyway?"

"Not big. We could probably walk to the end and back again before the week is out."

I nodded. "Good to know." I switched to my other foot and looked up at Wang again. "Anything else you want to tell me about this island? What is it that's got you so spooked?"

Wang looked away again but said nothing, and I rolled my eyes at his brooding.

But Wang wasn't the only guy spooked around here. I'd only noticed Vincent's displeasure at being in the area yesterday, after we'd crossed the vast mountain range that helped conceal the island from the mainland. I would often catch him and Wang talking together about topics they hadn't shared with me, and I'd constantly seen Vincent looking over his shoulders or snapping his head around at an odd sound. Wang too.

What was it about this island that had them acting like frightened cub scouts telling scary stories around a camp fire?

I had no idea, and that was part of the problem. I hated not knowing something when someone else did. All I knew about the Isle of Mona was that it had been a bastion of Druidic resistance against the Romans that had been wiped out because they'd been so feared. As for the Druids, I wasn't quite sure what the big deal was. While legends tell that they'd once possessed mystical powers to manipulate nature, it was pretty clear that by Roman times – these times – they were nothing more than spiritual, tribal, and economic leaders.

The historian in me remembered that there was certainly the chance that modern scholars knew far less about Druids than was actual reality, since Druids had been practitioners of an oral tradition, much like the Greeks in Homer's time, and hadn't recorded their histories and stories by writing them down, so with their demise came the loss of all their history and tradition as well.

Vincent had once told me that those in the modern age associated what they thought of as "druids" with a seventeenth or eighteenth century romanticized version of the group, and that version had very little, if anything, to do with their ancient precursors, but it was heavily assumed that they were a very naturalistic society, worshiping gods associated with the Earth and nature. While it was certainly possible that the Romans, in their lust to eliminate all aspects of Druidic culture, had purposefully omitted the details of their supernatural abilities, I couldn't yet bring myself to accept the idea that Druids had ever had any power worth censoring at all.

Still… there was the orb to think about. Hence the possibility.

Finished with my boots, I held a hand up to Wang so that he could help me up, but he didn't seem to notice. I grumbled and climbed to my feet, and took a step forward to stand beside my quiet companion and looked out at the island.

"It's a shame we don't have the whole legion with us," I commented. "They could have built us a bridge in a less than a week to get over there."

"The boats they're making will be done in a day or two," Wang countered.

"True, but I have an odd feeling that whenever we leave Anglesey, there'll be something symbolic about burning a bridge behind us, both literal and figurative."

I turned and left Wang to ponder on my comment and whatever the fuck it was that bothered him, allowing him to wallow in his own musings. It seemed well past time for someone else to do it, and I took immense pleasure at the thought that both

Wang and Vincent were finally in positions to actually worry about something.

I didn't care that Vincent had created a life here in Ancient Rome, one that he had abandoned to aid me. It didn't matter to me that he too must have had a lot on his mind because he had left his young son, Brian Wilson Glabrio, with no one else but his mother and *maybe* Titus if he had arrived in the Middle East by now with Madrina.

It was about fucking time, and I let that hateful elation alleviate some of the pressure I felt in my chest, as it seemed to do. The act gave me a slight buzz, or a mellow high, and I considered letting myself take pleasure in everyone else's displeasures more often, realizing there certainly was something to all this *schadenfreude*.

I strolled back to the freshly erected legion camp, this one a little bit more defensible and permanent than all the ones they'd built since leaving Camulodunum. Despite Anglesey's small size, we might be there for a while, and while it would have been nice to bring the entire reconnaissance force with us, Vincent felt it might also antagonize the natives. I'd agreed, so they would be left here to guard our exit strategy while Gaius, Marcus, every single time traveler, and a century or two of Romans would cross the narrow straight that separated us from yet another piece of the puzzle.

And I could barely contain my excitement.

***

We'd made the short journey across the narrow straight earlier this morning, two days after arriving on the shore that separated us from the mysterious island beyond. Dozens of slender but sturdy boats had carried us all, with me at the spear point of our party, and I had almost felt like standing up and propping my foot up on the prow of my boat to emulate the famous painting of George Washington crossing the Delaware River. It had seemed like an appropriate thing to do at the time, especially since the landscape mimicked the environmental conditions depicted in that painting almost perfectly, but Wang had been all too right about how rough the water was.

The crossing had only taken minutes, but I had nearly been jostled from the boat a handful of times, and three legionnaires had in fact been pitched into the frigid waters. They'd been able to swim shore, and would be fine, but were lucky Wang had been there to treat them for mild hypothermia.

So far, that had been the only mishap of the day, and our stroll across the Isle of Mona had been uneventful, even relaxing. We'd landed near the southernmost tip of the island and had been traveling up its western coast for over seven hours, a trip that seemed more like a hike with friends rather than a precision legion march, but that image was tarnished by the lack of amiability amongst the entire group.

Everyone seemed to be on edge.

While the legionnaires were always tense and ready to encounter an enemy force, my time traveling companions seemed nervous, and their body language told the tale quite unmistakably. Santino, Cuyler, Helena, and Artie hiked about as far away as they could from me while still maintaining a safe distance in case of attack. Since Helena had abandoned me that night after the barbarian attack, I hadn't once thought about approaching her or seeing how she was doing. She seemed almost an alien entity to me over the past few days, and search in my heart as I did, I couldn't find a reason to go talk to her. I just didn't care and I felt the same about Artie.

I did miss Santino. He seemed too serious these days, and I found his new formed friendship with Stryker annoying. Cuyler's overprotection of Helena and Artie was also disturbing, and while Wang and Vincent also walked together, usually in companionable silence, they often conversed in hushed tones. I didn't like them keeping secrets from me, especially if it was information crucial to the successful completion of our quest, but I also wasn't sure I trusted them anymore. The oddest pairing, perhaps, was Brewster and Bordeaux, more for the extreme size differential between them than anything else, and I wondered if Bordeaux was trying to sneak a little action in with her on the side.

New time travelers and old had come together in recent days, and had formed deep bonds of camaraderie I hadn't yet experienced, but I was fine with that. I didn't need any more relationships that would only get in the way of doing what needed doing.

Only Archer marched anywhere near my position at the forefront of our group, and he watched me like a hawk. Every time I glanced at him, I had no need to seek his attention for it was already on me, and we would simply stare at one another until I was forced to turn away before I tripped over a root or stepped in a deep patch of snow.

To hell with him.

All of them.

The Romans, at least, had been happy to follow my orders. They didn't know where we were going, or why, but were proud that they had been chosen by their legate to follow him into unknown territory. In their minds, those left behind were simply not worthy of the task, something those who remained would also consider, driving them to prove otherwise in the future.

I couldn't understand why the rest of my companions didn't think the same way.

It didn't matter. Once we were home, I would consider accepting each and every one of their apologies. Maybe then they'd recognize how hard I had worked and how much I had suffered for all for them.

Maybe then I'd get the respect I deserved.

But until then, I still had more work to do.

I bounced my backpack against my back to lessen the load momentarily as I walked. It was heavier than normal, since I'd decided to pack my small footlocker for whatever reason, but it hadn't yet become a burden, so I simply readjusted the pack's straps and pushed on across the barren island.

A frozen landscape of desolate, flat, and lifeless terrain relieved by sporadic patches of empty trees were our constant traveling companions, along with the view of the coastline to the west and north. The Isle of Mona was just as vacant as I expected it to be, but there was something particularly isolating about this place that seemed as level and endless as a Kansas plain in January. Even the sight of wild animals had eluded us, offering the illusion that we were entirely isolated upon this empty chunk of land surrounded by ocean. Perhaps they were simply hibernating for the winter, but I couldn't shake the feeling that somehow they were purposefully avoiding us. We'd brought enough food to last more than a week, so the lack of large game wasn't particularly disconcerting, but there was something off-putting about it nonetheless.

A lesser man may have been deterred by it, but I simply pushed forward, one step in front of the other. While I hadn't a clue where I was going, if the island was as small as Wang had described, I didn't think it mattered. If I had to explore every single nook and cranny for what I was looking for, whatever that was, I would.

But for now, it was time for a break.

I turned to Archer, who again was already looking right at me, just as I assumed he would be. I pointed off into the distance to a small area of trees down the shallow hill we were currently marching on. The wooded area seemed no bigger than half a football field, but it seemed as good a place to rest as any other.

"Time for a break," I told him. "Let everyone know where we're going."

He responded neither physically nor verbally. Instead, all he did was cease his forward movement and continue staring at me as I veered off toward the tree line. I watched him until I could no longer see him in my peripheral vision, but before I lost sight of him completely, the others had caught up to him and he pointed to the trees and said something.

Just before I lost sight of them all, I couldn't help but notice that the distance between the rest of my group and I was greater than it had ever been in the past five years. I hadn't been this far apart from another living, breathing soul in as long as I could remember. I wanted to stop and let them catch up, but something was forcing me forward, driving me into further seclusion on this already isolating island, like it was purposefully trying to keep me away from my friends.

And I let it.

***

It was early in the evening when I called for the break.

We'd been hiking since morning, and while we could have kept marching straight through until nightfall, I didn't see any reason to rush our trek across the island. If for some reason we encountered a hostile indigenous population, I wanted us energized and ready to receive it.

The day remained unusually sunny, but frigid, so Santino had built a fire for us to huddle around, while the Romans stood scattered around our perimeter or sat resting. There wasn't much room to gather around our small fire, so my team was forced to place themselves in close proximity to me for the first time in days. And they didn't seem particularly companionable right now because of it, each and every one of them basically keeping to themselves while Brewster distributed some of the packed food.

Like kindergarteners, we sat there passing the small packages to the next person beside us until everyone had their own. I was somewhere in the middle of the line, squeezed in between Vincent and Archer, and took a moment to inspect the small box held in my hands. We'd run out of our emergency Meals-Ready-to-Eat long ago, but Archer's team had brought hundreds of prepackaged packs of food along with them as well, but this was the first time we'd had the need to consume them.

I'd always found the MREs issued to us in the military to be quite tasty, with at least *one* exception. After eighty years of trial and error, military food scientists – or who-the-fuck-ever – had managed to prepare a number of palatable and mostly nutritional meals that kept active service men and women energized when in the field. Whether they were necessarily healthy was anyone's guess, but they'd served their purpose.

Sadly, those delicatessens were long gone, and I didn't know what in the name of God Archer's team had brought with them, but the only thing comparable to them that I could think of were K-rations.

World War II era K-rations.

I turned the box over in my hand before opening it, looking at the ridiculously retro color palette and font that screamed something out of the 1950s, making me once again try to imagine what their world had looked like. I failed completely, even with the images from Brewster's textbook in my mind to help, but unfortunately, the textbook would never be able to help me again, since I'd pitched it into the water during our boat ride to Anglesey, and I hadn't even thought twice about it.

I glanced at Vincent beside me, who also had yet to open his box of mystery food. He seemed just as reluctant as I was, and I could see that Wang, Santino, Bordeaux, and Helena were likewise skeptical about consuming such fare.

I glanced at Vincent. "Ever had one of these before?"

He looked at me, but seemed unenthusiastic about his answer. He stared with wide, open eyes before taking a quick breath while shaking his head. "I'm not *that* old, Hunter," he said, turning back to regard the K-ration before returning his eyes to mine again. "But back when I was with the Swiss military thirty years ago they didn't have much better…"

I grimaced and looked away, and saw Stryker sloppily shoving some kind of sausage covered in a thick, dark sauce into his mouth. Gnawing on it like a cow, he noticed my attention and gave me a sympathetic shrug.

"You get used to them," he said before swallowing.

"Yeah, but I don't want to," I heard Santino say as he opened a small, round can and hovered it below his nose. It wrinkled in disgust and Helena beside him slapped a hand over her mouth and suppressed a gag reflex as she turned away from him. He noticed her disproval and stuck the can closer to her face, but she recoiled again and smacked it out of his hand, sending it flying through the air.

"Hey!" He whined. "I was gonna eat that!"

He stood and went scrambling for his lost meal, finding it a few feet behind him in the snow. He retrieved it and returned to his spot, looked at it reluctantly, and sighed. He reached back into the box container and retrieved a set of plastic silverware, and then suddenly his eyes bugged open in surprise and I heard a sharp intake of breath come from him. At first I thought he'd noticed something dangerous on the perimeter, but then I saw him hold up an eating utensil in one hand and point a finger at it with the other.

He turned to me and opened his mouth to speak, but then he paused and seemed to think better of it, and turned to Stryker instead. "TJ! Look! A spork! I fucking *love* sporks!"

He then reached behind Helena, who ignored him, and grabbed Brewster's shoulder and shook her, causing her to spill her small cup of steaming coffee into her lap. She yelped and batted at her pants, but Santino hardly noticed as he continued to shake her.

"See Brewster!" He exclaimed. "It's like a fork and a spoon all at the same time. See!" Santino plunged the spork into his meal and pulled it out with a piece of meat on the tip and juice pooled in the spoon part. "Oh man, I never thought I'd ever see a spork again!"

Archer glanced at me while Stryker and Cuyler too shared a look as Santino continued to hold up his spork triumphantly. Everyone from my timeline simply ignored him, knowing there was absolutely nothing to worry about. Archer and his troops, however, hadn't quite gotten used to him and his antics even after all this time. Living with Santino was an experience, and it wasn't something someone could get used to in a matter of months.

Understanding Santino took a lifetime.

"He's fine," Helena managed around yet another gag, noticing their attention.

Archer didn't seem so convinced, but he went back to his meal anyway.

I, too, decided to open my K-ration and retrieve the hidden wonders within. I found a small can of... something – it was unlabeled – but there were also a number of unwrapped crackers, some sweet others salty, a cheese spread package, a small bar of chocolate, coffee powder, lemon beverage powder, a mini pack of cigarettes, matches, floss, and a few other goodies. I didn't know if the contents I'd just discovered would have been historically accurate fare for American GIs in World War II, but I had to imagine it was close.

I turned to Archer. "I can't believe they still put cigarettes in these things."

"What do you mean *still*," he asked. "They only just developed these rations a few years ago."

Only a few years ago... I mouthed silently, but shook my head to dislodge the thought, thinking of another instead. "But you guys don't even smoke."

He nodded as he chewed one of his crackers. "Most of us in the Special Forces don't. We spend too much time behind enemy lines to rely on supply lines to fulfill nicotine addictions, but front line troops had grown addicted to them before these rations were even a thought in someone's mind. Generations of fighting will do that to even the most health conscious of us."

I winced, hating it when I heard tidbits like that.

"I see," I said quietly as I fiddled with the canned entree.

Once I managed to tear the metal lid from the container like a can of tuna, I finally glanced inside but nearly threw up at what I saw. Within was a gelatinous patty of meat floating lazily in a fatty, viscous fluid that reeked of bad body odor.

I turned back to Archer again. "What the fuck is this?"

He peeked over the rim of my can and laughed. "Tough luck, Hunter." He turned to look at Cuyler sitting off to his right, and jerked his head at me. "He got the beef patty substitute."

Cuyler laughed, perhaps for the first time since I'd met him, as did all the rest of Archer's team. Archer shook his head as his chuckles subsided, and went back to his meal, ignoring my discomfort, and I looked back at the beef patty substitute in disgust. Even the fucking god of prepackaged military food seemed out to get me. As if my old nemesis the beef patty hadn't been bad enough, whatever deceitful, vengeful asshole who controlled such an industry had decided to provide me now with beef patty fucking *substitute*.

There was no way...

To my left, Vincent glanced over and pointed his spork at it. "Are you going to eat that?"

I thrust it at him as quickly as I could. "Knock yourself out."

He accepted it thankfully, and dug in. I looked at him like I would a man eating human feces. It was like watching a train wreck, and I just couldn't bring myself to look away. I held a hand over my mouth, but inadvertently caught Helena's eye. It was the first time I'd seen those glowing green eyes in days, and I was mildly surprised that when she noticed my attention, she simply smirked and shook her head, obviously amused that the "plight of the dreaded meat patty" continued, but her look didn't linger long as she went back to her meal.

She grimaced with every bite, and I had to smile as well.

I felt pretty good in that moment.

But happiness grown from good things didn't last long anymore.

Life just didn't let it.

When I looked away from Helena, I randomly saw four individuals to my left standing behind Bordeaux, Wang, Stryker, and Santino. Three males and one female. I made eye contact with one of the males, noted his presence and appearance, but then looked away, thinking nothing of him. A moment passed when something clicked in my mind and I shot them another look, but before my mind caught up with my suspicions, Brewster, Cuyler, and Archer were already rolling away to acquire their weapons and take up better firing positions. I rose to my feet as well, my mind still playing catch up to my actions, and the four time travelers with their backs to these newcomers seemed confused at our behavior. I was almost fully upright when all four strangers held up their hands innocently and the woman spoke.

"Wait!" She yelled in heavily accented Latin that was completely unfamiliar to me.

The four time travelers who sat just below them finally reacted, but Archer, Cuyler, and Brewster already had rifles trained on the strangers while Vincent had moved off to my left with his pistol pointed in their direction as well. I couldn't tell if the intruders recognized what my friends held as weapons or not, but they didn't make any sudden movements either, although they didn't appear particularly hostile anyway.

Despite the cold climate, they wore little clothing. Weakly constructed furs covered the men from the waist down to their knees and they wore some kind of moccasins that rose to their skirts. Over their shoulders they wore what looked like suspenders made from some kind of woodland creature. The woman was dressed similarly from the waist down, but instead of the suspender like apparatuses coming over and down her shoulders like the men, she wore a type of furry tube top that covered her stomach and breasts, but leaving her shoulders and arms exposed.

Neither the men nor the woman seemed particularly well dressed for the climate, but they weren't shivering either. At their feet, I noticed large fur coats pooled around their legs, and I assumed they must have shrugged out of them earlier to appear less threatening; however, the large blades they wore along their backs certainly were. They were sheathed, but it was not difficult to see that they were large and pointy, perhaps some early iteration of the claymore so often seen in places like Scotland during its medieval years.

By now, even the legionnaires had become aware of the intruders, and moved to gather arms and call in the sentry units that had somehow let these four individuals slip through their net, an impressive feat and one worth noting. When our pickets arrived, they moved in on them aggressively, but Vincent held up his hand.

"Stop!" He ordered. "They do not seem belligerent."

Archer beside me had his primitive looking distant cousin of the M-16 assault rifle shouldered and pointing in their direction.

"For now..." he said, and I had to agree.

Every instinct inside me screamed out to kill them and get the hell out of here before more of their friends arrived, but I beat back such thoughts. It wasn't easy, and the standoff continued, but Vincent distracted me when he took a step forward and looked over his shoulder at me.

"Want to step in, Hunter, or should I question them?"

I nodded reluctantly and took a step forward. To my right, I noticed that Helena had joined the others and had her shotgun held in a hand and pointed toward the intruders, and I saw Artie hiding behind her shoulder. It was reassuring to see that they were safe, but I thought little of it as I returned my attention to the quartet of individuals.

The men were forgettable, but clearly well suited for warfare. They all had light hair and eccentric mustaches that ranged from blond to red and each were tall and well built, especially when compared to the Romans, but their cold, light colored eyes indicated they didn't want to be here anymore than the rest of us. The woman, on the other hand, was far more noteworthy. Not simply because there was a woman with a sword before us, but because she looked like she certainly knew how to use it.

She appeared no older than nineteen or twenty, but she was already inches taller than Helena, which is where the similarities between the two ended. While Helena's skin always seemed perpetually bronze, this woman was as pale as a ghost. Helena's hair was jet black, while this woman's was as red as a particularly colorful sunset. Their eyes were more similar but while Helena's were piercingly green, this woman's were icily blue, almost silver in appearance.

And she was built.

Like Schwarzenegger built.

Helena was as tough a woman as I'd ever known, but she'd always maintained her feminine curves and grace. The redheaded woman on the other hand could have been an amateur body builder back home, a woman who spent far more time in the free weights section than the cardio area at the gym. Although her feminine frame was still obvious, her muscle definition rivaled Wang's but her build was more like Bordeaux's, and she carried herself with immense confidence while simultaneously maintaining body language that made her seem like an official dignitary, diplomat, or ambassador.

Unless I was off my trolley again, I was convinced she could be royalty of some kind.

I stepped around the fire and walked up to her, guessing that she was the leader somehow. I looked her up and down like a piece meat, sizing her up rather than checking her out, letting on like I wasn't impressed and wasn't someone to be trifled with.

Which I damn well wasn't.

"Who are you?" I demanded.

"We come not to harm," was all the woman said, her accent making her sound like she was speaking Klingon with a mouth full of marbles – and like a Klingon, I wondered if the only thing this gargantuan woman would understand from me was a show of force.

"We have been watching you for some time," she continued, "and have waited patiently for a suitable opportunity to meet you."

"Don't listen to her," Santino said from across the fire. "That's what they always say in the movies before they stab you in the back."

I ignored him but not his advice.

He was right.

"Why?" I asked her.

"I have been sent to aid you on your quest, Cernunnos."

Santino wasn't often right about things, but he was now. Warning lights were going off in the back of my head like a Christmas tree, but I was rarely able to rein in my curiosity.

I narrowed my eyes and crossed my arms. "What did you call me?"

She looked to the sky and held her arms over her head. "In a vision I was shown an image of the god Cernunnos floating above a Roman symbol swathed in brilliant red light."

"In a vision?" I asked skeptically, my right eyebrow rising instinctively.

Vincent stepped up beside me. "She's talking about the battle two days ago."

I nodded and took a second to think before deciding this whole story was getting far too ridiculous. I waved a hand in her direction in a shooing gesture.

"You're lucky I don't crucify you for attacking us," I said angrily, "but I'm feeling magnanimous tonight, so leave before I change my mind. What you saw wasn't a vision, it really happened, and I've got enough superstitious people tagging along as it is."

Her expression didn't change as I turned to leave. Vincent looked at me with his mouth open wide, but I didn't care. If these people were a part of the shadow force that had been tailing us since Camulodunum, I wasn't concerned. If they wanted a fight they were more than welcome to one. I would be more than happy to oblige them and send them to their premature deaths right here and now if they pushed me.

But before I could take another step, the fiery redhead pushed past Vincent and put a hand on my shoulder. With even more strength than I expected, she twirled me around to face her.

"The vision came before the battle, Cernunnos, not after. That is why I ordered my horde back to keep them from slaughtering you."

"Uh-huh," I replied, "sure you did."

Surprisingly, Wang stepped beside me timidly, looking particularly spooked and frightened. "Hunter, I think you should listen to her."

I looked down at him at the same moment as the powerful woman before me did, and I noticed her look him up and down just as I had her earlier. Only, her expression indicated she was doing exactly what I hadn't, namely, checking him out instead of sizing him up as a possible adversary. She towered over him, and Wang never risked a look at her so he never saw how she looked at him, which did not seem platonic in the slightest.

I smacked him on the shoulder, and he jerked in surprise, but managed to look up at me.

"What the hell is your problem, Wang?" I demanded.

He responded by shaking his head like a person with severe mental deficiencies.

"Why should I listen to her?" I asked, trying another route

"Because of your name!" He spat out finally, his eyes wide with unfocused fear. "Your name, Hunter!"

"What about it?" I asked, legitimately concerned my old friend was falling off his own trolley.

How odd it would be if I wasn't actually the first...

Wang looked back at the ground and mumbled his next words. "Your name. Hunter. Cernunnos. Fucking Welsh mythology and fairy tales class in high school. Who knew I'd actually use it. I can't believe it. I..."

"Wang!" I said sharply, gripping the man by the shoulder. "Snap out of it. What about my name is so important?"

He looked shaken but met my eyes. "Cernunnos is an old Celtic god that is sometimes referred to as The Lord of the Hunt, Hunter. *Hunt*! *Hunter*! *Hunt*! *Hunter*! That can't be a coincidence. It just can't!"

I looked away from him, no longer thinking him insane. There did seem something odd going on here that was beyond my control, beyond anyone's control. Wang was totally right. There was no way such a word association could have been a coincidence. My head shifted nervously back to the woman who had no way of knowing me, but somehow did.

"Who are you?" I asked nervously.

She smiled proudly and pumped out her chest. "I am Boudicca, Cernunnos. Sworn wife to Prasutagus, king of the Iceni people, defender of all Celtic lands."

***

There was an audible gasp from behind me, one I knew had to have come from Helena, who now stood face to face with one of the very heroes she'd learned about in university. I looked over my shoulder to see her with a hand covering her mouth, her eyes wide in surprise.

I turned back to the young redhead. "Say again?"

"My name is Boudicca, Cernunnos. Sworn wife to..."

"Yeah, yeah, I got all that," I said with an upraised hand, extraordinarily amused at this particular woman's presence, mostly because I was not at all surprised that she was here.

How many historical figures had we randomly bumped into during our time in Antiquity? It was like a supreme being had placed us on a path that allowed us to continue meeting these people. Even Josephus' father back in Caesarea had seemed almost predestined. The prominent historian, Josephus himself, had been too young to help us or influence our journey, but his father had been a good substitute, but unlike Josephus, while the very young woman before us was also much younger than the prominent figure history remembered, she seemed fully capable and able to help us, if that was in fact her mission here. Perhaps with history as fucked up as it was, she was no longer destined for a place in the history books, no longer predetermined to leave a mark on this planet to remember her by. Maybe, only through her involvement with us – an anomalous outlier in the timeline – could she regain that position of historical significance, and something was driving her toward it.

Hence why she was here.

Maybe.

After everything I'd experienced recently, I was no longer adamant in my stance that there *wasn't* some form of divine, supernatural, or just superior presence pushing us along in a specific direction. It would certainly explain a lot. It seemed completely possible that fate was doing everything it could to reorient the timeline away from the one that resulted in Artie 2.0's world. While it hadn't succeeded before when the Other Me had died, when Artie 2.0 and company showed up, fate had been given additional variables to play with to make things right.

Or... it was simply an interesting coincidence.

"Cernunnos?"

The voice of the woman claiming to be Boudicca interrupted my thoughts and I suddenly forgot what it was I had been thinking about.

I jerked my head and looked at her. "What?"

"You seemed very far away just now," she answered.

I shook my head again and tried to understand her presence. I was still figuring it out when Vincent walked up beside me and eyed the tall woman as he whispered in my ear.

"Maybe you should have everyone stand down, Hunter..."

I kept my eyes on Boudicca suspiciously as I slowly turned to face our gathered force at his suggestion. Her eyes never left mine but at least they seemed neutral in presentation, nothing treacherous, deceitful, or even lustful present behind them – the latter of which being a pleasant surprise for me when encountering women in antiquity.

"Stand down," I finally ordered my team with a wave of my hand.

They looked at each other nervously, but all of them lowered their weapons and grew more relaxed. I scanned my eyes across each of their faces, noticing that while their defensive postures were lowered, they didn't appear very welcoming as they milled about cautiously, their movements suggesting they were taking up better positions to contain Boudicca and her men.

Only Wang and Vincent remained at my side, but Wang was forced to do everything he could to avoid Boudicca's roaming gaze. After a while, he didn't seem able to take it any longer, so he awkwardly strolled away, but Boudicca never took her eyes off of him.

"Where does he hail from?" She asked, having to look over my shoulder now as Wang continued to beat his retreat.

"Who Wang?" I asked as I hooked a thumb over my shoulder in his direction. "He's a local actually. Born and raised just south of here."

"You lie, Cernunnos," she said with a challenging tone, finally returning her attention to me.

She looked at me with an angry look, but I nodded at her reassuringly. "I don't actually, but I can't blame you for not believing me. He's single by the way."

Her eyes squinted briefly in surprise. "Of course he is just one man, Cernunnos."

"Never mind," I said, no longer annoyed that these people couldn't understand a simply idiom. "But stop calling me Cernunnos. I'm not a god."

Not yet, came a random thought.

"I know this," Boudicca said, "but it is how you were presented to me in my vision."

"Just call me Hunter," I said.

"*Hoont-her*," she said slowly with her crude accent. "What does it mean?"

"In my language the word 'hunt' means to stalk and kill prey," I explained in Latin but using the English term so that she could get the gist, "and a 'hunter' is someone who does this."

"I see. A good name then. I too am a... hunter," she said, pronouncing it reasonably better than she had most of her Latin words.

I smiled and patted her arm but quickly yanked it away, freaked out by how hard and beefy it was. "Great. Then we should get along just fine."

The men under her command tensed at the contact but she shooed them away with the flick of her chin. They obeyed and moved off in silence.

"That is good Hunter, for we have much to accomplish."

"Why do people always say things like that?" I mumbled to myself, but held out my hand to lead her toward our fire. She understood and stepped forward. The two of us took a seat upon fallen logs cattycorner to each other, and I couldn't help but get a pretty impressive show of the muscles on her legs and upper back as she moved and sat. She cut an impressive figure, and while the rest of us were certainly no slouches, I couldn't help but make a mental note not to mess with her.

Once the two of us were comfortable, Vincent, Archer, Gaius, and Marcus came to sit near us as well while everyone else scattered. Wang was nowhere in sight, and I could see Santino and Artie walk off together toward somewhere, but they were out of sight before I could see where. To my right, I saw Helena sitting with her back to a tree, only her side profile visible, her hand resting upon her protruding stomach. Her head was tilted back against the tree and her eyes were cast upwards, looking at God knew what.

I ignored her.

I turned to Vincent who sat nearest me. "Feel free to jump in whenever you want, Vincent, but make sure you translate for Archer so he can keep up."

He nodded but didn't say anything. Archer's Latin had grown... serviceable, but wasn't nearly good enough to completely follow a conversation.

I turned to Boudicca, who was already staring back at me and seemed to have something on her mind.

"Curious about something?" I asked.

She shook her head. "It's just that your appearance and weaponry is mystifying. I did not expect such things from my vision. Also, there are women with you. I knew not that Rome employed female warriors. It is all most confusing..."

"We're what you would call unique," I explained. "Don't expect to see anyone else look like us around here."

She nodded. "I would expect not. My vision made it clear that I was to embark on a most particular task, and that I should expect to experience much I did not understand."

"Let's talk about this vision," I said, and waited for her to explain, but when she remained silent, I spoke again. "Give me details."

She looked surprised by my line of inquiry, but did not hesitate. "The night after my warband was repulsed outside the city you call Camulodunum nearly two weeks ago, I was gifted with a vision as I slept about how I was to continue my struggle against Roman aggression."

I glanced at Vincent, who shrugged. He'd been a pretty pious Catholic for as long as I'd known him, and I assumed he still was – although we didn't talk about it much anymore – and I knew he wouldn't necessarily rule out the idea of a "vision from God."

I was a little more skeptical, but who was I to judge anymore?

"Go on," I prompted.

"I was told to come here," she explained. "To the Isle of Mona where I would meet a powerful man who had the ability to control the fate of the entire world. It was shown to me that I would be made aware of him before reaching the isle, accompanied by a red light in the sky and the raining of fire. At first, we thought your contingent of Romans were a raiding force, but when we saw the light, I ordered my warriors back. I knew then that within your group was the man I sought, although I did not know who I was looking for specifically until just now."

"Your vision was so detailed?" Vincent asked.

She turned to him and nodded. "More so than even I have the ability to explain. It was because it was so that I accepted it. It was no mere dream. I assure you."

Vincent turned to me. "I don't know, Hunter. It's hard to deny this woman's claim after everything we've been through, and there *is* historical precedent. Figures like Constantine have claimed similar stories to great effect."

"I was just thinking the same thing," I agreed.

"Who is this Constantine?" Boudicca asked.

"Don't worry about him," I said with a smirk. "He's someone you'll *never* have to worry about. Trust me."

Vincent actually allowed himself a small smile at the comment as well.

"Was there anything else in your vision?" He asked.

She nodded. "There was. A voice. It was an old voice, almost ancient in my mind. It spoke with authority but quite unlike any other voice my ears have ever heard, and while his words were completely alien, his meaning was quite clear."

"What did it say?" This comment was from Marcus, who sat there like someone at a personal book reading by their favorite author.

"Little. Only that I was to protect this man," she said, gesturing toward me, "and..." she paused, "to guide him safely to him."

"To him?" I asked. "To who?"

"*Him*," she said unhelpfully. "The voice."

"Who was it?" Vincent asked, just as interested now as Marcus was.

"I know not," she said, "but I suspect it is someone with great power. Great power."

"Okay, great," I said cheerfully, feeling everything but as I slapped my thighs and stood up. I reached down and offered the famed warrior-queen a hand to help her up. She took it and I could feel the immense strength and weight to her well before I even started to pull. "We welcome you with open arms, Boudicca, but if you will excuse us, we have much to discuss. I think we'll camp here for the night and continue on tomorrow."

She tilted her head down. "Very well, Hunter. I believe I will seek out your fellow female warriors and speak with them."

"Find the tall, dark haired one," I said. "She'd love to speak to you."

"I thank you."

I watched her go for half a second before turning back to Vincent, throwing my arms out to the side at the same time. "What the fuck is going on here, Vincent??"

He shook his head slowly as he stared at the ground. "I haven't a clue. This story went well over my head back in Rome five years ago when you were trying to explain time travel to me, but this… this is something beyond me entirely."

"She can't be serious, can she?" Asked Archer, perplexed as well. "Can she?"

I threw my hands in the air again. "She seemed serious to me!"

"What is it that confuses you all?" Gaius asked calmly.

"What is it that…" I started, wildly confused. "How about everything? How about the idea that she was talking about communing with… a god! Or something!"

"What is so odd about that?" Marcus asked this time.

I looked at him blankly. "Don't act like you have conversations with Mars every other Saturday or something, Marcus. I know that you don't."

"Of course I do not," he answered, humored by my comment. "But there are many stories concerning such occurrences. Many. Gods have interfered in the lives of mortals for centuries, doing so on a divine whim. Why is it so odd that one would approach this woman then?"

I rolled my eyes. "When have you ever seen a god, Marcus? Really?"

"Just because you haven't experienced something doesn't meant it does not exist," Gaius answered for him. "It simply means you have been lucky enough avoid such an entanglements… until now apparently."

"That's just fucking great, Gaius," I mumbled. "Thanks…"

"You have to understand," Vincent jumped in, "that where we come from, the idea of gods or supernatural beings interacting on the mortal plain of existence has grown rather unpopular and, frankly, dated. The stories remain, but the idea that such instances are commonplace or anything but parables has long since abandoned most cultures."

"That does not mean they are untrue," Gaius continued to argue. "Even today in our more modern times, we hear fewer of these stories, but that is not to say that at one time, they were not in fact more commonplace."

I sighed. "So you're convinced a god spoke to her?"

Both he and Marcus shook their heads, but it was who Gaius continued speaking. "I know not that it was a god who spoke with her, Hunter. I simply believe that there is more to this world than what we see. I am surprised you are not so open to this possibility yourself after your interactions with the orb. I would think that it alone would have been enough to sway your judgment on such matters."

Marcus nodded in silent support of his friend before the two of them wandered away.

I pinched my nose and squeezed my eyes shut. "I need a vacation… I really do."

"Nobody's arguing with that," Archer replied snidely.

I lowered my hand and turned back to Vincent. "What do you think?"

He thought for a moment before answering. "I think it would be unwise not to learn more about her. If anything, she speaks the language of her tribe, and while I assume she doesn't speak the local language, it is certainly possible that one of the Druids here will speak hers. She could be invaluable as a translator."

"Good point," I answered, "but what about this 'vision' of hers?"

"I don't know, Hunter, I don't. But I wouldn't so easily discount it if I were you, and I would certainly council you to seek the perspectives of as many of us as you can… *if* you can."

He left those as his parting words and moved off to join Gaius and Marcus, leaving me alone with Archer.

"So what do you think?" I asked, not particularly interested.

"Fuck if I know, Hunter, but I will say that I think you've managed to alienate the last few perspectives available to you, and that you'd better work damn hard getting your friends back."

Archer's own parting words echoed Vincent's, but I decided I'd already wasted precious seconds of my life asking for his opinion anyway, so there was no point wasting even more trying to comprehend it.

***

The woman named Boudicca didn't speak much as she led our contingent along the western border of Anglesey the next morning. She was a very stoic individual, and hadn't had much to say, except to continually reassure me that she was leading us to "him" – whoever the fuck "him" was.

Then again, while I was certainly skeptical about everything this woman had told us so far, her story was still more believable than not. Since meeting her, I no longer thought I understood the nature of the world so clearly. Denying the involvement of some unknown or supernatural force accompanying us along our journey was no longer so odd a concept. Whether that force was fate, God, gods, or… fucking magic even, was anyone's guess, but I didn't think anyone felt alone out here anymore.

It only fueled the questions in my mind about affecting history, changing timelines, fixing past mistakes, and working toward better futures, but those thoughts no longer distracted me. It felt refreshing, and I wasn't about to fall back into that routine now, so I pushed forward toward answers instead of dwelling on the past.

We hadn't been traveling long this morning, but I'd quickly grown bored now that my mind was no longer as occupied as it used to be, and since my team still seemed wrapped up in their own little worlds that didn't included me, I was left with little to do. No one had wished me a good morning and not a one had decided to walk with me on this bitingly cold morning.

Each of them, from Helena to Archer, walked alone or in small groups, and few spoke to even each other. A pall of unease had encompassed our group and a lack of enthusiasm for what we were doing had taken root. No one seemed particularly confident anymore and even though both Archer and Vincent had suggested I seek everyone's individual council on the situation, I found it insulting that none had seemed interested in offering it, so I didn't bother.

At least Boudicca still seemed interested in what I was doing and where I was going, and I actually appreciated her silent companionship along the way. She'd asked only the briefest of questions concerning the manner of our clothing and the origins of English, and had not seemed rebuffed when I told her some things were better kept secret. She actually seemed to understand, and hadn't pressed the point. I was even getting used to all those muscles of hers. She wasn't nearly as intimidating anymore, and she did have a rather lovely face, so as traveling companions went, I could do far worse. I was tired of Santino's whining, Vincent's righteous superiority, Wang's superstitious nervousness, Helena's judgmental attitude, and Archer in general, so I was quite happy to have her around.

But while Boudicca wasn't the worst traveling companion, the air was still cold, the wind blistering, and the sun morbidly obscured by heavy clouds. We were all lucky that most of our cold-weather gear had held up well after all these years, unlike our electronic gear, and I was also lucky that I hadn't yet broken my favorite pair of glacier glasses, which were working perfectly now atop this island that seemed more like a barren sheet of ice than anything else.

I'd just about fallen asleep from boredom mid-step when Boudicca stopped just as she crested a small hill that had blocked our view of the landscape north of us, causing our entire contingent to halt abruptly. Everyone shifted their attention left to right nervously, anticipating trouble, but the sight of something over the hill and off in the distance drew my attention, as did the sound of Wang whispering, "Bloody hell..."

I barely heard him because I was mesmerized by the sight before us. It was clearly an island just off the coast of the island we were on now, but a small one, at least relatively so. It was so astounding a sight because its flat surface seemed to lift itself out of the water like a shallow ramp growing higher and higher as it extended northwards. Off in the distance, the island's western coast may have been a two hundred foot cliff to the water below.

Beyond that was a small mountain near its northern edge. The entire island was covered in snow and blanketed with fog that curled and wisped from the edges of the cliff sides to fall into the sea, disappearing long before they reached the water.

It was a haunting view that I couldn't tear my eyes from.

Boudicca pointed toward it.

"There, Hunter," she said unwaveringly. "That is where we must go."

I squinted at it. "An island off the coast of an island?"

She nodded. "Indeed. It is a foreign land to me as well, but where we must go nonetheless."

I turned to her with a distrustful look on my face. "You got all this from your vision?"

She met my eye but didn't say anything, not needing to because her determined expression was more than enough.

I looked back at the island. "Does it have a name?"

"I know not its local name," she replied, "but in my vision, I felt it known as: Holy Island."

Within my chest of constantly growing jealousy, anger, and anxiety, I felt my heart literally skip a beat – an actual, momentary cessation of its primary bodily function. A bit of pain filled the chasm that was my chest at that moment, but the feeling subsided quickly and I was simply left with the reality of Boudicca's words.

It wasn't that she had referred to the island as "Holy Island" that bothered me.

It was that she'd spoken the name in heavily accented, but near perfect English.

"Holy Island," I whispered.

In English.

Behind me, I heard Wang say under his breath, "This shite is going to give me a heart attack…"

***

We camped for the night in the shadow of the island, but early the next morning we crossed the narrow straight that separated Holy Island from the Isle of Mona, and hiked toward the mountain in the north that Wang had explained was called Holyhead Mountain – although prying that information from him had been like pulling a kid's first tooth. He was more disturbed than ever, as he remembered traveling to Holy Island during a childhood visit to Anglesey, but hadn't explained much more than that.

And Vincent wasn't any more helpful.

It was like living with a pair of ghost hunters too afraid to do their jobs.

Luckily, neither of them attempted to impede our progress, and I appreciated people like Santino and Stryker chiding the two of them into action. Even Vincent had a sense of pride, and didn't want to be thought a coward because he was spooked by an island.

Two hours into our march across Holy Island, we came to its narrowmost section, so narrow that my contingent of Romans, a few dozen shy of two hundred men, could have held hands and stretched from coast to coast. We were also clearly much higher than sea level now, but it seemed like we were only bound to climb higher. Holyhead Mountain dominated the horizon now, but didn't seem like a challenging climb even at this distance, although it remained the most discernible landmark on the island.

After a few more hours of relentless hiking, we arrived to within a few hundred meters of the mountain and the village that was now visible at its base. Constructed out of mud and sticks, the village was made up of huts that looked like something out of a Monty Python movie – a humorous exaggeration of what actual primitive people would live in, but it was hard to argue with my own two eyes. Its most troubling feature, however, was that it seemed like every single member of the village had come out to greet us as we grew closer. A few hundred individuals total, they appeared quite healthy and vibrant, except for the creepy, zombie-like expressions they turned on us, made all the more disturbing by the fact that they had already formed a tunnel of human bodies that directed us toward and up the mountain.

I turned to Boudicca to find out what the hell was going on, but she ignored me as she led us toward the opening that would allow us entrance between the two lines of people. The Romans behind me seemed unperturbed by our odd surroundings, but the rest of my party was another story. I looked over my shoulder and noticed Vincent a few people back and waved for him to catch up, noticing that Wang was sweating despite the cold, mumbling repeatedly to himself that we shouldn't be here.

"Thoughts?" I asked when Vincent finally caught up.

Before answering, he took a moment to study the ritualistic manner in which the people here had gathered.

"Well," he said, wiping a hand nervously across his brow, "if I had to imagine a scene of Druidic rituals and practices, this would be fairly accurate."

"Yeah," I replied, agreeing completely. "Think they're hostile?"

He shook his head. "They do not seem to be, and I do not believe they would pose a threat regardless. Their numbers are not large, unless they are hiding people behind the mountain, although they … they *may* possess other abilities."

I sighed dejectedly, sick and tired of how superstitious he had become.

"Even so, I think you should hold the Romans back," Vincent advised.

"Right when we might need them most?"

"It would be a sign of good faith."

I shook my head. "I'd rather have them and not need them than the other way around."

He did not reply, too lost in his own thoughts.

If this village was anything like what the Romans had encountered twenty years from now in my timeline, then it was quite reasonable to assume these people to be the foundation of the last real bastion of Druidic life in Europe. As Vincent had pointed out, they didn't seem hostile, but I couldn't shake the nagging feeling that there was more to these people than history remembered.

I turned to Boudicca. "Thoughts?"

"This is where I was to lead you," she answered immediately, but left it at that.

I took in her words, and concluded again that Boudicca was the true solidifying factor in all this. Had she not shown up as conveniently as she had, questions would have remained in my mind, but her simple presence seemed enough to prove that there definitely was more to all this. What that was, I couldn't yet say, but it was there, and the only way I'd find the answers I was looking for was to push on.

I waved a hand and my contingent fell into step behind me. Passing morbid faces and sullen expressions, we marched between the gathered throng of people. I studied them as I marched, noting that almost all those gathered here were middle aged or older. There were few individuals my own age, and I only saw two whom I would have thought in their twenties. Boudicca, in fact, seemed the youngest of them all. The demographics of this gathering in no way suggested a stable population, but Druidism was ancient, so I knew their children and young people had to be somewhere.

The somber crowd ushered us silently, the only noise coming from the clinking of armor and weapons from the Romans behind me, but by the time we reached the base of the mountain, I realized it was unrealistic to have them follow. I signaled for them to hang back, as I surveyed the trail.

It appeared steep, although manageable, and the path was clear of debris or obstacles within the tunnel of villagers. It all seemed very set up, and as we climbed the mountain, I couldn't help but feel our trip had been designed to take longer than normal. But then we finally crested a small slope of the trail alongside the mountain and found ourselves on a type of circular ledge that jutted out from it, appearing much like a helicopter landing pad.

"This... shouldn't be here," Wang muttered nervously.

I ignored him. Two thousand years was a long time for geographic details to change, but my eyes grew wide when I noticed a number of stone monuments arrayed around the perimeter of the clearing and the half dozen elderly men in robes, not completely unlike the ones worn by romanticized versions of druids back home, but also distinctly different and contemporary. They had no hoods and their sleeves weren't nearly as baggy as the ones depicted from old stories or fantasy artwork, but something about their appearance reassured me.

This is where we needed to be.

After all this time.

Finally.

What drew my attention next, however, was the crude altar that they congregated around, one that looked oddly familiar, but not because I was Catholic. It looked nothing like a church altar, as it had three legs arrayed like a tripod, and was roughly carved from a large stone in the shape of half an egg with its surface carved flat but its bottom half left round.

I turned to find Vincent staring at the altar intently.

"What?" I asked.

"I... believe I've seen that altar before," he said hesitantly. "I believe... I believe it is a duplicate of the one we found in Rome."

I looked at him in confusion. "When did we find an altar in Rome?"

He finally shifted his attention away from the altar as he answered. "The one we found beneath the Temple of Lupercal. The one in the cave when we first arrived in Ancient Rome."

I didn't remember, but I tightened my lips and nodded at the information. "Then it looks like we're on the right track."

Abruptly, one of the Druids held up a hand, signaling for us to stop. We did, but when the Druid lowered his hand a moment later, I took a challenging step forward. No further indication that we should stay back emanated from the gathered Druids, so I turned around to face those behind me.

"Stay here," I ordered, but then met Boudicca's eye. "You come with me."

She nodded and fell into step behind me as the two of us closed the distance. Our destination was only a few dozen meters away, but it seemed to go on forever, giving me time to study the gathered Druids. Each of them were old, ancient really, with sun dried faces and white, stringy hair, but they also carried themselves confidently, and there was determination in their eyes. None of them batted an eyelash at me or seemed surprised at the fact that I wore clothing and carried weaponry none of them had ever seen before...

That is, unless they *had* seen me before.

There were seven of them arrayed in a semi-circle around the altar, but it was clear that the man in the center was the guy in charge. He was an elderly chap with a long gray beard and a nasty scar that vertically bisected his left eye. He was also taller than the rest, and was the only one to take a step forward as I stepped up to the altar.

He eyed me evenly, his face blank, and when he spoke, his words came out in a gravelly, old voice that reminded me of an old Classics professor I'd had a lifetime ago. In fact, as I peered closer, I saw that he even resembled my old Classics professor as well. This man's beard was longer and thinner, but the set of his eyes, size of his nose, and shape of his mouth were all quite similar.

I'd spent a lot of time with that particular professor while at Dartmouth, wasting much of his time during office hours discussing ancient history and being ridiculed by him for my inability to pick up Greek as easily as I had Latin. He'd been a mentor to me, at least until I'd dropped Greek after only one semester my junior year. It had been too much of a time consumer, as I'd found myself literally having to translate lines of Greek every Saturday night in between beer pong throws. Our relationship had soured after that, and while he'd always been my closest mentor, he no longer looked at me as one of his protégés, as he most certainly had when I'd been an underclassman.

And like most first time students of my old Classics professor, I hadn't a clue as to what the man had just said.

I turned to Boudicca. "Did you understand him?"

She nodded. "He indicated that what you seek is not here."

I looked back at the old man, but then did a double take, and looked back at Boudicca. "Wait, did he say *what* I seek or *who*?"

"It is not entirely clear," she answered. "This is not a language I have heard in many years."

I nodded in understanding and gestured toward my old Classics professor whom I knew couldn't possibly be my old Classics professor. "Can you communicate with him?"

"I believe so, yes," she answered confidently.

"Good," I said. "Just translate everything as we go so that I don't have to ask for translations all the time, okay?"

"As you say, Hunter."

I nodded and turned back to the old, craggy, scarred man, searching my mind for the right words to receive the information I needed as quickly as possible. As I searched and formulated questions, only one thing came to mind, and I realized that I hadn't thought about the orb in months, and for the first time in as long as I could remember, wondered where Helena had hid it.

"Do you know of the orb?" I asked.

Boudicca translated and the man nodded in affirmation.

"Were you expecting us?"

Another nod.

So far so good. Time to muck things up then.

"If what I seek isn't here, why did I come here at all? Why did all the clues lead here?"

"If you had known where to go," the man said, "then you would have not needed to come here."

So this conversation was going to be like that then... great.

"Helpful..." I muttered, but held the man's stare. "Then where do I need to go?"

"That is for you to learn, and we to never know."

I glanced at the sky and mumbled in English, "God, help me; I'm going to kill this guy."

"Hunter?" Boudicca asked.

"Nothing," I snapped, dropping my head again. "Are you a Druid?"

Another nod.

"Was coming here a mistake?"

This time the response was a negative.

I was just about to ask another question when behind me, I heard Santino yell out, "Borrrr-ing. Enough with the twenty questions already, Hunter! Get us outta here!"

I threw a hand over my shoulder to shut him up, my eyes never parting from the elder Druid.

"Tell me what I have to do," I said.

I braced myself, waiting for what I knew would be a series of tasks, trials, and tests that would take us to the ends of the Earth to recover lost artifacts, uncover hidden clues, and slay any number of beasts before completing our quest. So far, our so-called adventure had been rather dull, but I knew it was only a matter of time before it kicked into high gear. It would be an adventure straight from mythology, like the ones Odysseus or Jason had experienced. We were in the land of Druids and fairies, after all!

It was only a matter of time...

The old man pointed the way we'd came and spoke softly. "Leave the island and follow the coast north. There you will find what you seek."

I stared at him dumbly. "That's it? Really? Just get the fuck out of here and keep going north? Just do what we were already doing? Except that we had to take a pit stop here for you to simply tell me to go north?? Go to this mystical and magical island that has two of my best and brightest guys spooked out of their minds just for you to stand there and tell me to go fucking *north*? How about some specifics or is north all I need? North??"

Boudicca had stopped translating long before I'd finished my rant but I hardly cared. I was fuming, enraged, and before I knew it, I had my hand on my pistol before I even knew my arm had moved at all. It was already out of my holster when a voice stopped me mid motion.

"Don't, Jacob!"

It was Helena's, and my pistol seemed to snap back into place on its own. As my weapon was returned to its sheath, my boiling blood reduced to a simmer and I forced myself to growl out my next inquiries more slowly.

"So go north then?"

Nod.

"How will I know where to go? What to find?"

"In time, you will know."

"Yeah, thanks, Yoda," I mumbled.

Boudicca didn't bother asking for clarification this time.

"Fine then," I said with a weary sigh, glancing to my left and seeing the great expanse of Holyhead Island and Anglesey before it. It was quite the view, but I didn't let myself take any pleasure from it as I turned back to the Druid. "Can we stay here for the night at least?"

"You are most welcome here, Jacob Hunter," the man said.

I didn't even bother asking how he knew my name.

"Great," I said, already leaving.

***

Later that evening, with the legionnaires bunked down in their bare bones Roman camp near the base of Holyhead Mountain and the rest of my team doing whatever it was they did these days, I decided to take a stroll around the island. The sun had come out a few hours ago, so a walk seemed like a great idea. It was a cold but beautiful evening as the sun was just beginning to make its daily descent into the sea, so I'd traveled south, but about an hour into my walk, I found Vincent sitting atop a cliff that rested so high above the waterline that a fall into the water would have killed him instantly. Staring death in the face quite literally, I walked over and plopped myself down beside him to let my legs dangle over the ledge, deciding that maybe the two of us could come to terms and go back to the way things used to be. I leaned forward to catch his attention as he sat beside me but he didn't flinch, his mind clearly occupied. His amputated arm hung uselessly beside him, his eyes fixed on the southern horizon intently.

I followed his gaze and squinted, seeing nothing off in the distance besides the coast of Mona off to my left, along with a bit of western Wales past that, creating an enormous bay of water with a tiny speck of an island at the very edge of the visible land.

I placed my hands on the ground beside me and leaned forward, stretching the muscles in my arms and shoulders.

"Not exactly what I was expecting," I said, hoping to make small talk.

"Nor I," Vincent answered.

"I just don't get it, Vincent," I said with a shake of my head. "This story makes less and less sense the deeper we get into it, and the mystery isn't developing, just growing more confusing. If the Druid we seek isn't here, where is he? North? Big help that is. And they know about the orb but won't tell me anything about it? Some adventure this turned out to be…"

Vincent's eyes hardly twitched. "Leading Roman legionnaires into unexplored country isn't adventurous enough for you?"

I shrugged. "Yeah, I guess, but it hasn't been very exciting. How am I going to script this into a movie when we get home if nothing happens during the middle of it?"

Still his eyes remained fixed, but now he closed them and kept them closed.

"You really have no idea where we are, do you, Jacob?"

"Anglesey?"

"Yes, but don't you know anything about this island?"

"The history classes I took about Britain started around the Reformation," I pointed out.

"No mythology? No history from the Dark Ages?"

"Mostly stuck to my Romans, Vincent. My schooling was cut short, remember?"

"I remember," he said, "I simply find it implausible that we would find ourselves in a place such as this, and you know nothing about it."

Annoyance was beginning to set it. "Enlighten me then, Vincent. I could use direction here."

"That's another question my mind has been struggling with, Hunter. I'm not so sure the best course of action here is to enlighten you about anything."

"Why's that?" I said, the anger growing.

"I have my reasons," he whispered.

"What reasons could you possibly have?" I demanded. "I need information here. Direction! I…"

"Do you see that island on the horizon?" Vincent asked, interrupting me, his finger stretched out before him pointing south.

I squinted. "Yeah, barely."

"It's known as Bardsey Island back home. Have you heard of it?"

"You know I haven't."

Finally, he turned his head in my direction but didn't look at me. "It's simply that I cannot believe that it's there… and that we're here as well."

"Why, Vincent? Just tell me."

"I can't," he said, and with that, he stood to leave me alone on the edge of the cliff.

I watched him go for half a minute before glancing out again at this mysterious Bardsey Island that sat just barely in my line of sight. Had the evening weather not cleared up as nicely as it had, it probably wouldn't even have been visible on the horizon. This thought mixed with Vincent's odd proclamation and apprehension about the island sent a chill down my spine.

If only I had access to the internet I could just look it up.

But then I guess that would ruin the surprise.

Where was the fun in that?

***

The next morning I awoke to the sounds of screams and the roars of pandemonium, unsure where I was.

Since command level officers entitled to a *praetorium* rarely accommodated so small a scouting force, the Romans under my command hadn't constructed one for me, but I was okay with that. It hadn't been that long ago when I'd pitched my own tent every single evening, the same one I'd used since going on the run with Helena and Santino all those years ago.

The only difference now was that Helena stayed with Artie instead.

And it was Artie who awoke me, as neither the screams nor sounds of panic had roused me from my slumber. She unzipped my tent roughly, the first sign of disturbance, and jumped on me like she used to do as kids at six in the morning on Christmas day, a tradition she'd continued well into my college years.

"Jacob!" She cried.

"What?" I asked still half asleep. "Is it Christmas yet?"

Actually, Christmas had been just a week ago. I'd barely noticed.

"It's the legionnaires!! They're burning the village!"

"What?" I asked, leaning up on an elbow so that I could more easily rub sleep from my eyes.

She grabbed my bare shoulders and shook me. "The legionnaires are murdering the villagers, Jacob! They're burning the village down with them in it!"

I sighed and rose to my feet, strapping on my web belt and holster and slipping into my jacket.

"Let's go take a look then," I said, pushing my way past her and her gaping mouth.

I stopped just outside my tent and looked at the chaos before me.

The small village was completely ablaze, turning the mountain behind it into a flickering wall of shapes and colors, a beautiful image against the pre-dawn light. I placed my hands on my hips and noted the rampaging legionnaires that put down men and women alike as they attempted to flee the blaze.

I waited for the scene before me to change like it always seemed to do these days, but when I closed my eyes and then reopened them, it remained.

Artie emerged from the tent, hot on my heels. "Stop them, Jacob!"

I didn't look at her. "What do you want me to do, Artie?"

She looked at me, a mixture of anger and terror splashed against her face. "Tell them to stop!"

"I can't," I said, "Their adrenaline is surging. They'd kill me just as quickly as these villagers if I tried to stop them. You don't see Santino or Archer interfering, do you?"

I pointed to the two men who stood near each other off to the left, staring at the chaos before them as well. They weren't nearly as worked up over it as Artie, but the horror on even their regular tough guy faces was clearly evident. Around me, former friends were stumbling out of their tents, also awakened by the screams. Their expressions were mixed, some simply staring in confusion while others wore looks of abject horror.

I turned away from them and returned my attention to the show and shifted in place, narrowing my eyes in confusion as I felt an unexpected object that seemed to have found itself in my pants. Glancing down, I reached a hand toward a cargo pocket and discovered that the object seemed large, hard, and round. Not remembering putting anything there the night before, I cautiously reached in and retrieved the object in question.

I smiled as my hand came into contact with it, knowing what it was well before I saw it in the light given off from the blaze. I pulled it out slowly and brought it to eye level, and then took a bite out of the apple and chewed.

I'd always loved apples, especially the green ones.

Very sweet and...

"Jacob!"

I glanced back at Artie, my mouth full of half chewed apple. "What?"

Her eyes were a mix of emotion. "Do something!"

I rolled my eyes, making an overt display of annoyance, and made my way toward the town and the legionnaires that surrounded it. My progress was slow and lacking in energy for the task ahead, each stride mimicking how unenthusiastic I felt. I'd just taken another bite from my apple when a dark figure stepped in front of me, cutting me off just steps away from Minicius. All I could make out in the early dawn light were a pair of tiny green orbs looking up at me.

"Tell me you had nothing to do with this, Jacob."

I chose to ignore the fact that *those* were the first words she'd decided to speak to me in days, and instead decided to play nice and answer the question.

"Does it look like I had anything to do with this?"

She looked at me intensely, studiously, and waited patiently for me to react to her scrutiny but I didn't flinch. In turn, I felt patience surge within me and I knew I could stand there under her gaze for days if I had to, but luckily, I didn't. With one last glance at me, she walked away, and I found myself pleasantly alone again. With another bite from my apple, I watched her go for the briefest of seconds before continuing my search for Minicius.

I found him a minute later, his spear deep in the chest of an elderly woman who had taken a chance at fleeing. Her arms were stretched out in Minicius' direction, her fingers extended like the claws of a wild animal, her face a mixture of shock and pain. I half expected lightning bolts to fling themselves at him from her fingertips, but when the centurion withdrew his spear and looked up, he simply nodded as the woman died. I spit out a seed and watched it land at her feet, thinking little of her or the village I'd ordered burned to the ground before turning in for the night.

"Anyone escape?" I asked Minicius.

"No, Legate," he answered quickly. "The village is contained. Most of these demons chose to burn within rather than risk escape. I will never understand the minds of these sorcerers."

I smiled and took another bite, speaking my next statement around a mouthful of apple. "Don't even bother, Minicius. I've been trying for years."

He nodded and returned his attention to the blaze, biding his time for another potential escapee. I waited and watched as well, but not to intercept an escaping Druid hoping to reveal our secrets to the world, but because I was simply enthralled by the village as it slowly burned to nothing. As I stood there transfixed by the flames, I wondered if this was how those guys back in Vietnam had felt watching random Podunk villages reduced to ashes. Was there really a unique aroma to napalm that smelled better in the morning? Were there actual spirits dancing in the flames that entranced a man to the point where he no longer cared that there were people burning alive within the wall of fire?

I neither knew, nor cared. I simply waited for the tidal wave of screams to cease, a cessation I didn't have to wait long for. From the moment Artie had awakened me in my tent to this moment right now, only eight minutes had passed, but the elapsed time had felt like hours as I stood with the silent sentinel, Minicius. When all the excitement seemed to die down completely, I felt a sudden emptiness in my chest, upset that it was over so soon.

I sighed and went for another bite of my apple but my teeth met nothing but core. I scowled at the depleted fruit angrily and hurled it into the flames. It seemed to catch fire the moment it interacted with the fire, bursting into an impressive and unanticipated fireball that left me wondering if the Druidic magic that apparently permeated this ground had somehow left me with some final warning or act of defiance.

But like much in this world, I hadn't a clue, nor was it explained.

I placed a hand on Minicius' shoulder and gave him a nod of approval when he turned to regard me. He dipped his head in acknowledgment but went back to his passive sentry duty around what was left of the village, too disciplined to assume the job was finished until I said it was. I dropped my hand, turned, and made my way back to my tent, passing and ignoring a dozen mixed expressions from the other people who had once traveled back in time as well, their disapproval, frustration, and anger meaningless to me. They didn't have to understand let alone care what I was doing; all they needed to do was fall in line and follow.

This was my story.

I was their Moses, destined to lead them from the desert to the Promised Land. That was *my* job. Only I could get their sorry asses home and they either knew that now, or they'd better understand that soon. I was done playing nice and trying to fit in with the denizens of the past, and so, unlike Moses, I wasn't about to give the Egyptians any chance of following me, Red Sea or no. I was going home, and I was prepared to burn the world down around me to ensure I got there.

No more Mr. Nice Hunter.

Part Three

IX
Northward

Northern Britannia
January, 48 A.D.

It was hard to believe that less than a year had gone by since I'd sent Bordeaux in search of Wang and Vincent, initiating my plan to kidnap Agrippina's son Nero and place Vespasian on the throne. It seemed like a lifetime ago, two even, but with the passing of the New Year, I was reminded that it had only been a matter of months, nine to be exact.

Almost a term of pregnancy.

And it had all seemed so simple then. Stage a coup and put a competent ruler on the throne that was supposed to be there, albeit thirty years earlier than expected, although that part hadn't concerned me. Rome was an empire ruled by emperors who were supposed to rule for a long time, and Vespasian would need all he could get to put his house back in order after Agrippina had spent the past four years dismantling it.

It was a tall order but I'd had complete faith in the man.

But the following nine months had been filled with failure after failure, something I wasn't used to. Sure I'd failed with the ladies a number of times in my younger days and had bombed exams because I'd forgotten to – or had been distracted from – studying, but never had I outright failed so many times when I'd set out to succeed. Agrippina had outplayed me at every turn, and while I was happy to still be alive, I was sick of losing.

I wasn't going to lose again, whether at Agrippina's hands or anyone else's.

Never again, and the past two weeks – maybe three –since leaving the Isle of Mona had given me plenty of time to prepare for the future.

We'd followed the western coast of modern day Northern England, keeping the soon-to-be-named Irish Sea on our left, possibly finding ourselves about as far north as modern day Carlisle, in a place Wang had called Cumbria. It had been a tedious trip, one filled with plenty of time to think alone, ponder our situation, and dream of the orb, which now seemed to invade my thoughts every minute of every day.

It was a divisive topic of thought in my mind. A part of me continued to fear its influence, but a growing sensation had taken hold of me that actively considered finding the orb and... experimenting with it. There had to be a way to use it more tactically than how it had already been used. It was just a matter of finding out how.

My only worry was that my former friends would try to stop me, as I was sure they plotted to do every day since leaving Anglesey. I could sense their future betrayal looming, but they dared not move against me when I had fifteen hundred legionnaires at my back. Even with all their advanced weaponry, they wouldn't stand a chance against so many.

And I still had Penelope, the only person besides Felix who would never let me down.

I smiled as I glanced down at my trusty rifle, resting lazily in my lap, riding contentedly as she waited for her moment to be put to work. HK416s were particularly reliable rifles, but even Penelope was something special. While Santino's had failed him on a handful of occasions since coming to Rome, Penelope had not once misfired or failed me. Her reliability was the result of all the care and love I'd shown her, having given her a name, a personality, and having dutifully cleaned and maintained her daily.

She'd never let me down, because I'd never let *her* down.

Like loyal Felix beneath me, we shared a connection, and neither of them would ever fail me. It didn't matter who I trained Penelope on, whether friend or foe, she'd never let me down. Unlike the rest of them – Vincent, Santino, Helena, whoever – Penelope would always be there for me.

Always.

***

And then there were the grumblings beginning to circulate within the camp.

The pace I'd set since leaving Anglesey had been intense, even by the Romans' already extreme standards. Their normal marching order called for a dawn wakeup call followed by breakfast, the breaking down of camp, and an all-day march that ended at sunset. Our current protocol, however, called for an even earlier wake up time and the end of the day came well after dusk now. It was an arduous pace, even for campaigning legionnaires. They weren't accustomed to marching during the winter, especially not one as unforgiving as this one had become.

It was late January, and the days were naturally short, but I wasn't about to lose time because nature had decided to hurl everything in its arsenal at us, from snow to ice and everything in between. It was tough going, but if our final destination was as far north as Scotland, which would be just my luck, I'd rather get there sooner rather than later. The Roman Empire was still fracturing, and my lack of involvement wasn't helping. I'd promised Vespasian that I would help Galba settle the turbulent Britons, but I would do it on my terms. It seemed best to handle my own shit first before diving back into the political and military situation Rome now found itself in.

Only when I had my answers, would I get involved again.

And when that happened, things would be different this time.

But the legionnaires didn't seem to understand that. All they understood was that their legate was working them far harder than any other legate had before, and they weren't happy about it. Under my old first file Fabius' professional and stalwart command, his subordinates would have been able to keep their underlings in check, but he was back with Galba. While Minicius was tough, and his men respected him, he was no first file centurion. He could keep dissident legionnaires in line for now, but I wasn't sure how long his authority would last.

Only Boudicca seemed unperturbed by our pace. Nor was she hesitant about speaking with me, because as the days wore on, she only became more curious. She knew less about the orb than the others, and didn't suspect my involvement in the slaughter of the Druids' village, so she didn't distrust me either. She was simply curious, a quirk I could appreciate, and her questions, while endless, had been appropriate.

She wanted to know more about me, the others, and most importantly, the nature of our quest. Her curiosity was quite endearing actually, and the fierceness she displayed when I would answer a question in a roundabout way or avoid it all together left quite an impression. It was not hard to see the defiant and charismatic queen she was destined to become in the young woman before me.

It left me feeling oddly attracted to her. All those muscles aside, I found myself growing giddy at the sight of her riding up from the marching column to ride by my side. I wasn't sure if the emotions came from a growing sense of isolation, loneliness, or misplaced infatuation, but whatever the source, it was unfortunate that she didn't seem to reciprocate that attraction. She'd ride and talk with me for most of any given day, but she was always business.

Wang, on the other hand, seemed to have her full attention. When she wasn't with me, most of her time was spent with him. The small framed Brit looked like an ant next to the exceptionally built woman, and his lack of interest in her made the scene quite humorous. The two would often ride side by side, saying nothing, Wang doing everything in his power to avoid eye contact with her while she, on the other hand, would constantly sneak glances at him only to look pouty when he refused to return them.

Despite everything, it made for an amusing scene to draw some enjoyment from.

As for the rest of them, they continued to plot and scheme against me in private. While some were less overt about it and would occasionally ride in sight of me, the others would travel out of sight – but not out of mind. I hadn't even seen Helena or Artie since linking back up with the rest of our legionnaires near the straight that separated mainland Wales from the Isle of Mona weeks ago. I also saw little of Santino or his new buddies, and Bordeaux and Vincent never came around anymore either. I no longer understood why the latter two didn't just leave and go back to their families, since it was clear they didn't want to be here, nor would I miss either one of them if they did.

They'd all created a distrustful cloud of apprehension around me, and I could feel in my gut that it was only a matter of time before they all turned on me. I'd spent the past two weeks trying to come up with a plan to ditch them somehow, but I couldn't think of a way that kept everyone alive. I was certain my force of legionnaires could overwhelm them if necessary, but I couldn't guarantee I'd even be left with a century at the end of the engagement.

And it may end with all of them dead as well.

It hadn't yet come to that.

It was growing late in the day as I thought about this possible outcome.

There was too much at stake here to throw away lives senselessly, and it was with that thought in mind that I realized it was time to provide a show of good faith to the Romans. I glanced at my watch, still functional despite a large crack that ran through its center, but I could already tell by the dimming sky that dusk was settling in. Deciding to give the legionnaires a break tonight, I called for a scouting force to locate a suitable camp site instead of continuing our march for a few more hours, as had become the norm.

I caught Minicius' eye and signaled with a hand gesture for him to assign a scouting party. He nodded and peeled off from his marching position and shouted orders. A timid cheer rang through the nearby legionnaires, but I returned my attention to the snowy path that had been our trail for the past five days – little more than a narrow gap between trees that twisted and bent sinisterly, each and every one a distant cousin of that creepy tree from *Poltergeist*.

No one had any idea where we were going, where we were, or who exactly the natives in the region were. We were in uncharted territory, and even Boudicca, who'd sent her contingent of troops home, had never ventured this far north before. Nary a soul had we seen since leaving the Isle of Mona, and the local wildlife had abandoned us as well. Not only had fresh game like rabbits and deer disappeared, which wasn't necessarily a problem since the legionnaires were well provisioned for months, but also anything that creeped, crawled, swam, or flew. At night, the sounds of the wilderness were startling silent, with little more than the howling of wind through bare branches to keep us company.

It had more than just my former friends worried now, as some of the legionnaires began suspecting that the murdered Druids back on Holy Island had somehow cursed us, and that their vengeful spirits were harrying us in an attempt to lead us toward a grisly end. I was fairly certain such superstition was just that, but even I couldn't completely shake the feeling that we were being watched, tracked, corralled... or worse. There was undoubtedly some form of energy in this winter wonderland that I couldn't quite understand. At night it could be quite terrifying, especially alone and isolated inside my *praetorium*. Every time a horse neighed or a legionnaire swore loudly, cutting through the silence of night, I would jolt out of bed or up from my desk for fear of some ghastly spirit haunting us. Other random cries of fear or wails for comfort would come from the camp, either joining my own or in response to some other calamitous occurrence. It left the camp a ghostly, ominous place, and made it difficult to fall asleep at all for fear of the boogeyman.

Even thinking about it now had my heart racing, acting like a pump that continuously fed the growing reservoir of negative emotion in my chest. Always growing, never shrinking, and always on the verge of bursting, I forced myself to calm down when I noticed a pair of centurions pass by me at a quick trot with a handful of legionnaires and engineers behind them. As always, they would run ahead and get to work making camp wherever they saw fit before sending back a man or two to lead us to our final destination. While suitable terrain had grown more difficult to find the further north we travelled, the routine nature of their assigned task gave me a sense of calm and I felt immediately better.

I settled myself, both physically and mentally, and waited for their return, but then a centurion hit the dirt in a sprawl a few dozen meters in front of me, a pair of arrows lodged through his neck, crisscrossing each other at its center. There was a brief pause when his companions processed what had happened to him, but then they too were perforated by a barrage of arrows that came at them from all directions.

"Defensive formation!" Minicius yelled, understanding the situation before anyone else.

To their credit, the legionnaires were quick to respond. Raising shields and locking them into place, my legionnaires flawlessly shifted their marching order into their famous *testudo* formation. Acting like the shell of turtle, their overlapping shields created a defensive barrier that protected them from incoming missiles that approached from any direction. As long as the spirits who taunted us didn't raise spears from below our feet, the Romans could withstand any missile barrage.

Unfortunately, Felix and I were significantly less protected, a fact Felix quickly discovered when an arrow found itself lodged in his rump. I wasn't sure how or why the single arrow had missed me to bury itself into my horse's ass instead, but it must have been some form of signal, because it wasn't long before hundreds more joined it.

Arrows came at me from all directions except from ahead, but I was saved by Felix who wasn't stupid enough to stick around and play the part of a stationary target dummy. He took off like a drag car gunning it off the line and galloped toward the clump of fallen legionnaires a few dozen meters ahead of me. I glanced behind me in time to see maybe three dozen arrows protruding from the ground Felix had just vacated, clustered in a neat little circle almost too accurate to believe.

My attention was directed forward again when Felix leapt over the bodies of my fallen men. He came down roughly and I was jerked forward, another random and inadvertent motion that saved my life when I felt a number of arrows whiz past the back of my neck and others, too many to count, plink off my body armor. It also allowed me to see the five men and two women who ran out in front of us, their spears held before them threateningly.

But like most horses, Felix was too smart to go blindly running into a clump of sharp sticks. He quickly veered to the left but his forward momentum kept him moving in his original direction, and he very nearly tripped over himself. To compensate, he dug his hoofs into the snow but started to slide toward the enemy on a patch of ice like a souped-up street racer performing a power slide. In that same moment, I instinctively drew my pistol, extended my arm, and with controlled squeezes of the trigger, fired off seven rounds in quick succession.

As I fired, the ice beneath Felix must have disappeared, because he suddenly jerked to a stop, nearly pitching me off of him again. He started hopping in place and spinning about in fear and pain, so without thinking, I reached back and snapped the arrow in his rump. I knew there wasn't much of a point to the action, but it would at least shorten the length of the arrow to help it from snagging on something and causing further torment to poor Felix.

He reared at the action but to my surprise, calmed down. I patted his mane and finally remembered the enemy combatants I had just shot.

I turned, expecting them to still be alive and advancing on me, but I found each of them sprawled out on the ground. Half were dead, while most of the rest were writhing in the throes of death, but one was on his feet, clutching a wound at his shoulder, his face awash in confusion at what I had just done to him. The two of us locked eyes for only a second, before he sprinted toward me, his spear hefted over his good shoulder. I lifted my pistol into a firing position near my waist and fired at the man like a cowboy in a shootout. The bullet clipped him in the neck, nicking his jugular and causing a weak spray of arterial blood to gush from the wound. I was lucky enough to avoid being sprayed as the man fell to the ground steps away, one hand clutching his neck the other grasping for me.

Whether he was continuing his assault or seeking aide I didn't know.

"Why did you attack us??" I growled in Latin.

The man gurgled with blood in his mouth, and I couldn't tell if he could even understand me. I glared at him and deftly reloaded my pistol without a thought toward the action. Once I had a full magazine in place I aimed for the man's forehead, intending to put him out of his misery.

Our eyes never parted, and I saw understanding dawn in his own. He'd seen my pistol in action twice now, and knew that it had the capability of putting him out of his torment.

But I didn't fire.

I simply held the pistol there, my mind and body in conflict over what to do. My instincts told me to end his pain or call for a medic, but my mind told me to let him suffer. I waited there in silent internal debate for what seemed like an hour before I finally returned my weapon to its thigh holster and urged Felix back toward the ambush. I could hear the man pleading incoherently below me, his intentions as clear is if he'd been politely asking me to pass the salt, but I didn't look back.

I now found myself alone, our attackers apparently thinking a simple seven man element of spearmen able to handle me, but my Romans were already engaged in close quarters combat with an uncountable number of barbarian Britons. They were surrounded but holding easily, although there seemed an endless stream of attackers behind those already engaged.

I smiled and felt Penelope already in my right hand, my left holding Felix's reins. I gave him a solid kick and he bolted forward again, obediently obeying my command. Like I'd been instructed to do all those years ago, I kept my feet firmly planted in his flanks for stability as we took off, leaving the lone Briton at my feet to die slowly in a puddle of his own blood.

But instead of riding toward the legionnaires' immediate aid, I guided Felix into a thicker portion of the twisting trees to swoop behind our attackers to my right, only to find the area empty. I was alone again within the forest of bare, ugly trees, but I took my time searching the woods, creeping Felix along with the sounds of battle off to my left. I wasn't in a hurry, knowing the legionnaires could hold the line all day if need be, but there was the chance that a leadership element may still lurk in the rear with hidden reinforcements. That could be a problem if left unchecked, but I again found nothing, just the remnants of a former human presence in the form of broken branches, random garbage, footprints in the snow, and smoldering campfires.

Had they been waiting for us?

A loud bang to my left shifted my attention back to the battle. It had been the first rifle shot I'd heard throughout the engagement, and I wondered why I hadn't heard any before, and what this one in particular meant. I figured I'd find out soon enough as I kicked Felix back into a trot and toward the battle, but I didn't have far to go, and it didn't take long before I arrived to find...

Nothing.

I jerked my head left and right as I pulled Felix to a halt, searching for the legionnaires but saw no one. I kicked Felix into gear again and the two of us galloped a hundred meters in the direction I thought we'd come from. We crested a small hill that had blocked my line of sight, but found nothing in that direction either. Neither the Romans, enemy Britons, nor my former friends · were anywhere in sight. My eyes furrowed in confusion and I turned my head around to look in the opposite direction, but again found myself alone.

I decided to send Felix back to where we'd started.

Still nothing.

I scratched my head and scanned the ground, unable to locate any form of evidence to suggest I *wasn't* alone here. There were no bodies or weaponry, nor blood or footsteps. A thought sparked in my mind and I immediately patted my body down, but my suspicion that I'd somehow time traveled to an earlier point in history came up as empty as my pockets. I searched my backpack and the pair of saddle bags straddling Felix but they too did not contain the orb.

I let out a confused grunt, Felix echoing the sound almost exactly.

I reached down and patted his neck. "You have anything to do with this, big guy?"

He neighed and shook his head as though actually responding to my question with a resounding negative.

I wheeled him around again and urged him toward the scene where I'd been ambushed by the spearmen. As we grew closer, their bodies seemed to shimmer into existence, looking almost like they were being beamed in by the *U.S.S. Enterprise*. Six were sprawled out in a semicircle right where I'd dropped them a dozen meters away, but the seventh appeared just in front of me. I glanced down at him – the one I'd shot in the neck – noting that he seemed just as dead as the rest. I half expected him to open his eyes and speak to me like something out of a demonic exorcism or zombie movie, but he remained quite dead and motionless.

A noise from behind me spun me around again, but the setting sun washed out my vision as it kissed the horizon, and a figure materialized upon the path before me, silhouetted by the setting sun behind it. The figure's details were shrouded in darkness, but I could tell that the figure was a man and that he wore robes that gave his body little shape, along with some kind of triangular hat atop his head. The first thought that came to mind was that of a KKK clansman but something about that didn't seem to fit the theme of what was going on here.

I started to kick Felix toward him when I was distracted by a voice from behind me.

"Jacob…"

The voice was feminine and familiar, so I wheeled around again, only to find myself plunged into the deep darkness of night.

The suddenness of how dark it had just become didn't make any sense, since I'd thought the sun had only just set, but I then realized this darkness wasn't the result of nightfall. I knew this because there were in fact no stars in the sky, nor could I see the moon, and not because they were concealed behind a thick layer of clouds. The sky was jet black and smooth, completely without light and depth, although snow still fell lightly around me in thick flakes.

I looked back down, and in the same moment, the path before me was illuminated by an unknown light source, like a spotlight from the rafters of a film studio.

Just then, the shape of a woman appeared out of the darkness, clad in a formfitting, but not tight, white dress. She materialized too far away for me to immediately recognize her, but as she strutted toward me, details began to emerge. When she finally moved to stand beside Felix, I saw blond hair and sharp features that revealed the woman to be none other than Agrippina.

I drew my pistol from its leg sheath and without thinking, fired a bullet through Agrippina's forehead, but the apparition merely smiled at me as the neat little hole in her skull knitted itself back together as bloodlessly as Wiley E. Coyote plugging a hole in his stomach after he'd accidently shot himself with an ACME cannon.

Now fear started to settle in, but Agrippina didn't seem threatening, nor was she coming on to me with her usual shtick of seduction. Instead, she simply smiled at me and the hand she placed on my thigh just sat there instead of acting in an inappropriate manner. It was more like a gesture of comfort than anything, and my fears evaporated, only to be replaced with confusion again.

Her smile was entrancing, as were her bright blue eyes that looked up at me like a happy puppy dog's, and I felt like I could sit there and stare at her for the rest of my life, an idea that seemed a peacefully oblivious way to spend eternity.

But my trance was interrupted when Agrippina reached up with her hand that wasn't already on my leg. She extended it toward the back of my neck and gently pulled me toward her. At first I thought she was bringing me in for a kiss, but then the hand that had just been upon my leg came up to cover my eyes, and I was pitched into darkness again.

"Who are you?" I asked. "What do you want from me?"

"From you, Jacob?" The spectral form of Agrippina asked. "Nothing. And everything."

A burst of clarity overcame me, and I asked, "What's happening to me?"

"Nothing that cannot be reversed."

"Why me?"

"It is no fault of your own, Jacob."

"Then what..."

"Continue your journey, Jacob."

"But..."

"Hunter?"

"I'm here."

"Hunter??"

"What?"

"Wake up, Jacob!"

More confused than ever, I realized that my eyes were closed.

Carefully, I opened them to discover that I was no longer atop Felix and that Agrippina had disappeared. My head felt heavy as I determined that I was lying on my back, half buried in a snow drift, and that I was staring up at the trees above me. Looming over me were the faces of Wang, Boudicca, Vincent, and another female figure that I didn't immediately recognize.

I had to blink away the fuzziness in my vision before I finally identified the fourth figure as Helena, her eyes confirming her identity well before anything else, but then I understood why she'd been so hard to identify earlier: she'd cut her hair, and it wasn't just a trim.

She'd grown her lush hair out over the past five years to the point where it had extended well past her waist. She'd always kept it tucked in behind her MOLLE vest to keep it out of the way during combat, but it had been one of her most alluring features when she let it out, something she apparently wouldn't need to worry about doing for years.

Not only had she cut it so short that even my own brown wavy locks seemed longer now, but that it looked like someone had gone at it with a knife, pulling at random strands and then just cutting it off with no thought to style or evenness. Only a few inches long at its longest, it stuck out or laid flat in a series of patchwork clumps of varying lengths.

I processed all of this in a second, and found that it was all I could focus on.

"Your hair…"

She didn't say anything, but at least the look in her eyes suggested she was, for the moment, concerned and not angry.

"How do you feel?"

This question came from Wang, and I shifted my head left to look at him. I stretched my neck carefully so that my face tipped upwards, and wiggled my fingers, trying to determine an honest answer for the medic.

"Bit cold, but functional," I admitted, just as surprised as he looked. "What happened?"

"We were ambushed," Vincent answered.

"Oh, thank God," I mumbled, dropping my head back to the ground.

"Hunter?" Vincent asked slowly.

I lifted my head up again. "Long story. Thought I was going crazy there for a second."

Wang, Vincent, and Helena traded nervous glances and I looked between them in turn. They ignored me so I decided to sit up, an action I struggled with until Boudicca reached out and assisted me with her strong arms. I nodded my thanks but returned my attention to Helena. She was staring at me now, her eyes full of sadness and concern, with large dark bags beneath them. I looked closer and noticed for the first time that age lines were beginning to take shape at the corners of her eyes as well, blemishes that really stood out against her otherwise clear complexion.

After a moment of silence, she turned away and dropped her head. She sat there for a few seconds as though deciding something of great importance, but it wasn't long before she finally rose to her feet. She struggled for half a second and my first thought was that she was experiencing one of her old pain attacks, but then she straightened, and I could see the real source of her struggles.

Her stomach was enormous, standing out clearly against her otherwise slender but strong frame. I was amazed at how much she'd grown recently, almost to the point of disbelief.

When she noticed my attention, she looked down at me again, almost reluctantly. I met her eyes and reached a hand up toward her stomach, and for the briefest of seconds she seemed ready to grab my hand with her own and guide it, but with a suddenness almost too quick to comprehend, she whirled around and retreated.

I watched her go, noticing that without being able to see her stomach and without her long hair, I couldn't recognize her at all as she walked away. I turned back to the remaining trio of people at my side, to find Wang and Vincent staring awkwardly at the ground. Boudicca had her eyes locked on mine with a look that lacked any understanding at all.

"So what happened?" I asked.

Vincent and Wang ended their inspection of the ground and raised their heads. They glanced at each other to see who would respond, but Vincent placed a hand on Wang's shoulder and took the lead.

"What do you remember?" He asked.

I shook my head as I tried to piece together what had happened. "I called for a scouting party to locate tonight's camp location, but they were shot to pieces. Felix got spooked and took off, saving me I think." I paused, trying to remember the rest of it. "It all gets a little fuzzy after that."

Vincent nodded. "That's how it started. We were then attacked on both sides by a considerably larger force. Casualties were sustained and..."

"Is Felix all right??" I asked, my sudden concern hitting me like a freight train.

Vincent blinked. "He's... fine. Just an arrow to his rump. It's been removed."

"Whew," I said. "Close one."

Vincent traded glances with Wang again before continuing. "We sustained nearly two hundred casualties. All legionnaires. Stryker took a sword to the arm, but it's just a flesh wound."

I nodded. "That's it? Not too bad then."

Vincent shook his head. "How can you say that? What's happened to..."

"Let's focus, Vincent," I interrupted. "What happened to me?"

He glared at me but I barely noticed. "This is how we found you... an hour ago." I blinked at the announcement of how much time had gone by, but didn't say anything, so Vincent continued. "There are corpses over there that suggest you were attacked, and we also found a spent pistol magazine on the ground and shell casings, but nobody saw what happened."

I checked my arms and legs for fresh cuts in my combat fatigues but besides the few that I hadn't yet been able to patch up, I couldn't find any new ones.

I turned to Wang. "Was I poisoned?"

He shook his head. "Not likely. Unless you ingested it somehow. Are you certain your head doesn't hurt?"

I reached up to grip the back of my skull. "Feels fine."

"Then I'm at a loss. Maybe you fainted."

"I didn't faint!" I shouted, and Wang held up his hands defensively.

"Did you experience anything while unconscious?" Vincent asked knowingly, but none too kindly.

I considered telling him that I had seen something, although my memory of what exactly it had been was already fading, but he hadn't asked nicely.

"Not a thing," I replied.

He shook his head, stood abruptly, and left without another word, leaving Wang, Boudicca, and I alone. Boudicca lifted me to my feet, help that I accepted gratefully.

"Anything else to report?" I asked.

Wang pointed off toward a cluster of legionnaires that also contained Archer, Brewster, and Santino. "We captured a few of the blokes and are in the middle of questioning them. They aren't saying much and seem a bit dodgy, but there doesn't seem anything special about them. Just a band of local warriors defending their territory, or so they say."

"All right," I said, taking a step toward them. "Let's see if I can speed up the process a little."

Wang shot his hand out and gripped my arm, stopping me in my tracks. "Hold it, Hunter. Are you sure you're all right? I'm debating keeping you under medical supervision."

I didn't try to throw his hand off, knowing it would be a futile effort.

"I'm fine. Why don't you take Boudicca here out to lunch or something?"

The comment, spoken purposefully in Latin, had the desired effect, surprising Wang long enough for him to loosen his grip on my arm so that I could slip away. I took off with an amused jaunt in my step, hearing Boudicca behind me mention how she would be happy to hunt some game for the two of them to share. I had no idea where she would find any in this desolate chunk of Britain, but she was more than welcome to knock herself out trying.

The first thing I did before joining the interrogation was find Felix, who wasn't too far away and seemed in pretty good shape despite the bandage on his rump. I gave him a pat and reached into my saddle bag to retrieve one of the last few carrots I had that hadn't rotted away by now. Luckily, the cold kept them pretty well preserved and it wasn't like Felix was picky about his carrots.

I scratched behind his ear as I finagled Penelope out of the safety strap that attached her to the makeshift saddle I had equipped Felix with. It was a simple task, and in quick order I was fully armed and heading toward the circle of interrogators.

I was steps away when Santino noticed my approach, his naturally acute situational awareness ensuring no one could ever sneak up on him. He stood beside Archer, the two of them holding stalwart stances as they watched a pair of legionnaires work the interrogation. Archer turned as well when he noticed Santino's shifted attention, and both of them took a step to intercept me. Santino stuck out an arm and placed it against my chest.

"Whoa, wait a second, Hunter," he said. "Where do you think you're going with that?"

He asked his question with a finger directed toward Penelope.

I shrugged. "The interrogation's taken long enough. We need to get moving."

Archer shook his head. "Let them do their jobs, Hunter. We're already setting up camp a half mile from here so there's no rush."

I looked between the two men in disbelief. "What are you two, best buddies all of a sudden?" I looked at Santino accusingly.

"You abandoning me so quickly, bestie? Some friend you turned out to be."

"You're out of your mind," Santino accused, his voice steady.

"Excuse me?"

"You fucking heard me, Hunter," Santino said, jabbing a finger into my chest. "No one else has the balls to say it, but you're nuts. Wigging the fuck out. You'd better take a cold shower one of these days because you're on a downward spiral toward crazy tow…"

I whacked his arm with one of my own, dislodging his hand from my chest.

"Quit you're fucking whining, Santino," I said. "Now let me through."

I pushed past him swiftly, the two of them too slow to stop me. With another step I was through the circle of legionnaires who loomed over their captives threateningly, while two of their comrades did the actual questioning. One noticed me as I stepped through the perimeter and moved out of the way, making a show of bowing to my authority and command – quick thinking that elevated the good cop/bad cop charade he might have been going for.

I reached down and grabbed the nearest captive by his animal skin top, hauling him to his feet. He was a very large man but I was drawing on a strength fueled by determination and energies beyond my understanding. I pulled him up as easily as picking up a feather and thrust my nose into his face as I pressed him against a tree.

"We gave you no cause to attack us, so why?"

The man showed no fear but shook his head nonetheless. I turned to the legionnaire who had been the chief interrogator.

"Translate," I ordered.

He did so but still the man refused to answer. I dropped him back to the ground and looked around. Beside the fallen man were four other individuals, two of them female who looked as fierce and capable as the men. Neither were as strikingly attractive from the head up as Boudicca, nor as impressive physically from the neck down either, but they certainly appeared to be able fighters in their own right. The one directly beside the man I'd initially questioned seemed to shift closer to him almost inadvertently, and I also noticed she happened to be the prettier of the two as well.

I flicked my head in her direction but kept my eyes on the man. "Is this one yours?"

The legionnaire translated.

The man didn't answer but his face provided all the answers I needed. I frowned at the man. "You leave me no choice then."

The legionnaire was in the midst of translating as I drew Penelope, aimed her at the woman's forehead and –

"Jacob, no!" Santino cried.

– squeezed the trigger.

By the time his words registered in my mind, my finger had already tightened, but all that emanated from Penelope was a slight "clicking" noise – the kind associated with a misfire. I looked at my rifle questioningly, not understanding what exactly had happened. Since Penelope had never misfired before I wasn't quite sure how to react. I ejected the bullet from the rifle's ejection port and caught it clumsily. I looked at it curiously but couldn't find a flaw in its craftsmanship. It was possible it had gotten exceptionally wet and was rendered useless or was just a simple dud. I dropped it into a pocket and released the magazine from its well and blew on the lead bullet before slapping the magazine back into place, all the while our hapless prisoners watched in confusion.

I aimed at the woman again and squeezed the trigger, but again nothing happened.

I ejected the magazine and slapped home a fresh one, but still the rifle did not fire. Frustration was beginning to grow in me like a weed, clawing its way from my chest and into my mind like a vengeful spirit. Over and over and over, I pulled the trigger only to have nothing happen, leaving nothing more than a series of bullet shaped holes in the snow beside me.

What had just happened was more than impossible.

There was simply no way that many bullets could just misfire without cause.

It was a miracle.

Unless the problem was with Penelope.

I looked at her and slapped in yet another fresh magazine but it too failed to fire. Round after round after round would not ignite, and a thought in the back of my mind convinced me my pistol would do no better.

Deep in my chest, where all this time I'd subconsciously contained all my negativity, something snapped. It wasn't a bone or an artery or a valve, but something in there broke open, and I could no longer contain the swell of emotion that I'd been carrying with me for years.

With the maniac clumsiness of someone who'd completely lost control, I struggled to unclip Penelope from the sling around my neck, but when I did, I gripped my rifle by the barrel, and flung it over my head at the nearest tree like a Viking hurling an ax. It hit with such force that I was sure it would snap in half, but it stubbornly remained intact. Perhaps a little scratched and dented but little more.

Its durability only made things worse.

I scrambled toward it, only dimly aware of the surprised expressions on the faces of all those around me, and retrieved it, only one thing to say coming to mind before I summarily bashed it against the trunk of the tree over and over and over again.

"*Et tu?*"

With the words spoken, the evisceration began, and I had no plans of stopping until my rifle was crushed to a fine powder in my hands. Finally, the silence among the men was broken by the sound of Santino yelling for the legionnaires to get out of his way. They apparently had no problem with it now because seconds later, Santino's powerful grip was pulling on my shoulder. The suddenness of the motion caused me to drop the rifle and it fell at the base of the tree in a clatter of pieces and parts, joining all the rest that had already broken free.

"What have you done, Jacob?" Santino asked with a tone that suggested I had just murdered my own mother instead of a worthless piece of junk well past its prime.

The two of us looked down at the mangled mess that had once been my beloved rifle, but the sight of it only served to lift a heavy weight from my shoulders. Its broken presence beneath my feet seemed to alleviate every bit of tension I'd ever felt, replacing those dark emotions with a freshness, satisfaction, and with the soothing reminder that similar acts in the future would make me feel the same. The death of Penelope and the joy I'd felt at it symbolized the solidification of my focus on the orb and its secrets. I no longer needed a thing from my former life, just the resolve and determination to continue onward.

"What have you done?" Santino whispered again, but I was hardly listening as I turned back to the original man I'd questioned.

"Why did you attack us?" The question came out calmly and evenly despite the sweat gleaming on my forehead and my chest heaving after my earlier exertion.

The man seemed terrified now, maybe wondering what I would do to him considering what I'd just done to an inanimate fucking object, perhaps wondering if I'd start torturing him now instead of killing him outright.

His answer came slowly in his ancient, guttural language, and I waited for the legionnaire to translate, which he did cautiously.

"He says we attacked them first."

"Ridiculous," I said, the legionnaire translating. "You're the first locals we've encountered in weeks. We were just moving through."

The man responded totteringly, and even though I couldn't understand him, it wasn't hard to detect that he was repeating the same few lines over and over.

The legionnaire shook his head as he translated. "He keeps repeating that we attacked his tribe first, Legate, but there is an undertone of vengeance in what he's saying. He seems to think that we did something horrible to his people."

I nodded slowly and straightened to loom over the captured individuals. I glanced behind me to see Santino carefully sifting through the snow, collecting the pieces of my broken rifle. During my quick look, I noticed Archer moving to help. I shook my head and returned my attention to the legionnaire.

"Kill them," I ordered evenly. "Leave this guy for last."

"Legate?" He asked.

"Do it," I snapped.

Before the words were even out of my mouth, I heard the sound of cold steel piercing flesh followed by the piercing shriek of a woman too surprised to really feel the true effect of pain. Within seconds the scream subsided into silence but not before a handful of others had joined it only to die out in turn. I'd already turned away and started walking from the scene when I heard the last man cry out, his lingering far longer than the others.

We'd already wasted too much time here.

***

Nothing seemed to change in this wintery shithole that was Ancient Britain, just an endless ocean of empty, eerie trees and narrow passageways between them. The sea was still somewhere off to our left and countless miles of land to our right. Wildlife continued to elude us and though the legionnaires preferred a wholly vegetarian diet while on the march to keep them energized and light on their feet, the occasional reward of spit-fired meat had escaped them for far too long, which combined with continued forced marches allowed poor morale to fester. My centurions were working extra hard keeping them in line, but I didn't have time to worry about a rebellion, because we were almost there.

I could feel it.

I felt a lot of things these days. Some bad, some good, others exhilarating, most unexplainable. My mind worked in overdrive as thoughts came and went, flying through my consciousness at a rate I could barely process. Thoughts darted in and out so quickly that at times I'd find myself staring at nothing in particular for minutes on end with no recollection of the passage of time. Yesterday, Boudicca had found me slumped in my saddle in a position she said I'd held for over an hour. She said she'd thought me to be meditating, but I hadn't remembered a second of it had I been.

Other times I would mumble to myself endlessly to the point where my mouth would grow completely parched. Felix especially got most of my attention as I found myself talking to him more and more, and I was growing more comfortable with the fact that he seemed to reply, although we hadn't done much talking lately.

It was too damn cold for talking.

The temperature had dropped precipitously in the past few days to hover well below freezing, and I had been forced to supplement my warmest cold weather gear with a blanket just to keep myself from freezing to death. Felix, too, was bundled up like an Eskimo, and we rode in plodding silence, but as a strong gust of wind whistled through the tree branches above me, I snapped my head up and around at the sound, grimacing in pain at the movement. It must have been hours since I'd last moved my head, and the sudden twisting of my neck combined with the cold left it feeling like I'd just attempted to tear it from my shoulders.

I groaned as the action of returning my head to its forward facing position felt no better. Once I was settled again, I began a series of exercises of rolling my head around in a circle and tilting it against each shoulder, stretching out its kinks and warming it up, and I decided it would be a good time to flex my toes within my booted feet as well. Each foot may have been covered in three socks surrounded by a heavy duty boot, but my socks weren't much better off than my boxer shorts these days, and I wasn't sure I had any left that didn't have at least one hole in it. It was an odd issue to have, made worse by the fact that I couldn't buy anymore socks, and I was certain I'd cut off both my feet for a fucking Target and its endless supplies of them right about now.

Without socks, would I be forced to wrap my feet in the linens worn by the legionnaires to keep my feet warm? Would my feet even fit in my boots anymore? How much longer did my boots even have?

I jerked my legs angrily like a toddler stamping his feet at not getting his way, and Felix dropped his head back in preparation for an increase in speed. I reached out quickly to pat his neck, pulling back on the reins with the other.

"Don't bother, Felix," I whispered close to his ear. "We'll be there soon enough."

Felix answered with another of his all-too-knowing neighs and immediately settled down.

I nodded in satisfaction and sat back, ready to reluctantly endure a thousand more years of riding through this winter wasteland as long as my answers were still out there. I settled in and bundled my blanket under my chin again, shivering around the cold but remembering to bend my neck and wiggle my toes every few minutes.

I was just about relaxed when a runner plodded through the snow in my direction.

My immediate instinct was to draw on him but then I noticed he was one of the legionnaires normally assigned to flanking duty. I raised a fist in the air, wincing again this time because I'd neglected to stretch my arms and shoulders as well, but at my signal, Minicius tiredly called for a halt, and the entire contingent of legionnaires stopped on a dime.

I waited impatiently for the man to reach my side, setting my posture so that I sat commandingly atop Felix and put on my business face. When he arrived, I was immediately upset that he'd taken as long as he had since emerging from the brush. He wasn't out of breath or perspiring but still he took a moment to compose himself.

"Speak!" I demanded.

The man blinked in surprise but then shook his head as though clearing it from a stupor and answered. "Legate, we have found something."

I fidgeted angrily. "If your next words don't explain what it is you've found, I will sentence you to the *fustuarium*!"

The man cringed at the threat, not wanting to suffer the march through a tunnel of his fellow legionnaires ordered to beat and stone him to death as he ran the gauntlet. Even if he survived, and had therefore escaped further punishment, he would still be banished from the legion.

"My apologies, Legate," the man said politely, but my expression wasn't impressed. The man quickly understood and hurried to his next point, realizing that his last words hadn't actually been an explanation. "A Roman legion fort has been erected a short march from here."

"What?"

The man nodded vigorously to reiterate his point. "It is as I say, Legate. There is a Roman fort not too far from here. Its size indicates there may be as many as two legions within. We cannot explain it."

I sat there silently, waiting patiently with my eyes closed.

Almost two minutes passed while the legionnaire stood there, shivering in the cold, waiting for me to say something before he finally grew the balls to interrupt my thoughts.

"Legate?"

I opened my eyes, and sighed at the sight of him. "I was hoping you'd disappear."

"Legate?"

I ignored him and turned to Minicius. "Organize a scouting party, Centurion. Lead the party yourself and get to the bottom of this."

Minicius looked confused. "The bottom of what, sir?"

I smiled, finding that I was starting to enjoy myself whenever I confused these local yokels with my fancy talk. "Just find out who calls the fort home and make sure they're friendly."

He saluted crisply. "At once, Legate!"

***

Three hours had passed and I was growing frustrated.

I'd ordered the legionnaires to make temporary camp as we waited for Minicius to return, a rest that was much welcomed. They'd cheered and applauded the call for a break, but I'd shot the nearest legionnaires a venomous look and those in the immediate area quickly focused on erecting temporary barricades instead of cheering. It hadn't taken more than a handful of seconds before the remaining legionnaires got the point and did the same.

The local vegetation was sparse, just a few shrubs and trees that made up a forest so thinly populated that I could barely refer to it as a forest at all. It allowed for clear sight lines in all directions but also a few trees to sit back and relax against, as I was doing just now against a tree barely out of its sapling years. It was thin and flexible, which I found quite comfortable to lean against. Before me was a small fire and Felix stood munching on something he'd found in the snow just beside me.

Besides Felix, I was completely alone. The nearest clump of legionnaires sat maybe two dozen meters from my position and I couldn't even see my former friends. Even my rifle was gone, left to rot in a forest till the end of its days, destined to be found by some kid digging in the dirt two thousand years from now, a relic of a bygone era that no one will understand and even fewer will believe. It made me think of that kid Xenophon back in Byzantium and his possession of my butterfly knife. Because of Archer, I knew the knife would become some ancient, unsolved mystery that would stump scientists and archeologists for millennia, a thought I recently found hilarious.

I chuckled to myself, but the chuckles quickly changed to coughs. I hacked and sputtered for half a minute before settling down, and sniffed away built up mucus in my nose.

I thought I'd been getting a cold for a couple of days now, but hadn't been sure until just now. It was an odd sensation since I'd always been a pretty healthy guy, rarely ever experiencing bouts of sickness. While the exterior of my body was beat to shit, with more scars than I could begin to count, my internals had always worked just fine.

Until now, it seemed.

I grunted and retrieved my water containing CamelBak. I held it out and looked at it, noticing the duct tape that patched up the hose and bladder in a number of places, and it seemed that my CamelBak too was on its last legs.

I put the hose to my lips to take a swig only to realize that the water within had frozen solid. I tried again, straining myself as I tried to suck up a single drop of the liquid, but it was a fruitless endeavor, one that surged the rage within me, and I swung the CamelBak against the tree beside me, causing the hose to break away from it. I looked at the broken hose still in my hand, noting that we'd run out of duct tape weeks ago and there was no hope of fixing it.

"Fuck it!" I yelled and hurled it off into the distance.

Felix grumbled at my outburst, but I paid him no mind as I drew my knees against my chest and wrapped my arms around them to keep warm, settling in to await Minicius' return. I shifted my body to attain a comfortable sitting position, and for the first time in weeks, felt a sense of isolation overwhelm me. I might as well have been all alone out here, for all the companionship I'd had of late. I no longer cared that my former friends were lost to me, nor did I mind having the fate of the universe precariously balanced on my shoulders anymore, but the idea of dying out here and most likely being left to rot in a hole somewhere was not comforting.

I shuddered at the thought and pulled my blanket around my shoulders more tightly, but was immediately interrupted by a loud trumpet sounding off in the distance. I craned my neck to the left and saw Minicius returning with his scouting unit, and with another contingent of legionnaires behind him.

It took a concerted effort for me to rise to my feet, but when I was finally upright, I set out at a leisurely pace in their direction. The sound of hoofs crunching in snow drew my attention behind me, and I saw Vincent, Archer, and Santino riding up on their horses only to draw up short of where I stood. They eyed me cautiously and I didn't even bother welcoming them. I turned back and continued toward Minicius, the three of them falling in behind me atop their horses.

As our two groups grew closer, I tried to discern any details I could about the legionnaires that travelled behind Minicius and his men. Nothing seemed off about them or out of the ordinary, but because of their unexpected presence so far north, I half expected them to be some kind of parallel reality version of a Roman legion, one with horns and tails and fire discharging eyes, or at the very least, some kind of local tribe masquerading as legionnaires.

The last thing I expected to see was just another group of legionnaires, no different than the ones in their camp behind me.

"Hunter…"

The voice came from behind me and sounded like Vincent's, but I ignored him and continued walking.

The only discernible difference between these new guys and the legionnaires behind me was that, on a whole, these newcomers seemed older and more mature than the Romans under my command.

"Hunter…"

This voice could have been Archer's but it seemed farther away than Vincent's had earlier. He was the last person I wanted to speak with right now, and I was too distracted by another odd feature of the approaching legionnaires as well. Behind their first few lines, all I could see was a shifting pattern of darkness that I couldn't quite make out on this overcast day. My earlier thoughts of demonic alternate…

"Hunter…"

This voice was clearly from Santino, even though it sounded even farther away than Archer's had, so I finally turned to see what the fuss was about.

"What!?" I screamed, only to discover they hadn't been marching with me for the past thirty meters or so. They'd stopped long ago, leaving me alone between them and the returning legionnaires.

I cocked my head to the side quizzically as I looked at them. "What?"

But they didn't respond, so I turned back around only to find that the legionnaires had halted their forward progress as well. I looked to Minicius who marched on the right side of the approaching formation, but he didn't even glance in my direction. His face was hard and his eyes were averted.

I was about to start demanding answers when the formation before me split open right down the center. Half of the legionnaires stepped left, the other half right, opening up a tunnel between the two halves. The split ran about ten rows deep before a figure cut between them and strutted right toward me.

Recognition came almost immediately, and by the time the figure was only a few steps away, I was already planting the palm of my right hand firmly against my forehead. I dragged my hand down my face, and through fingers spread across my eyes, I saw the ironically angelic looking blond woman stop little more than a few steps away, cock her hip out to the side, and place a hand on it.

She looked me dead in the eye with a wonderfully self-righteous smile on her lips.

I chuckled and shook my head as the woman spoke.

"By my power as Empress of Rome," Agrippina the Younger said commandingly, "I place you under arrest, Jacob Hunter, for the attempted abduction of my son, murder of my person, and usurpation of my empire."

My chuckles turned to outright laughter, but ended quickly when a dark blur out of the corner of my eye swung something heavy at my head.

Then everything went black.

Again.

X
Facepalm

Northern Britannia
January, 44 A.D.

I was surprised at how much pain there was.

Besides my slight cold, I hadn't felt any kind of discomfort, mental or physical, in weeks, at least since my time in Anglesey. There'd been moments for such things since, of course, like when an errant tree branch would occasionally scratch my hand or when Felix accidently stepped on my toe, but I'd always been able to override and ignore the pain, fueled as I was by my determination. And I'd been hit over the head more times than I cared to remember in the past, so I knew what it felt like, and while I wasn't sure how many more I could suffer before I started losing my mind, this one seemed particularly bad.

My head felt heavy and clouded, and there was a rhythmic pounding in the back of my skull like the worst of hangovers. I could tell without opening my eyes that my head was dipped forward so that my chin propped it up against my chest, but I forced myself to lift it painfully, allowing it to loll and bob aimlessly around my shoulders before I could bring it to a standstill. Once I had it level and stationary, I aimed to open my eyes, a task not nearly as easy as it sounded. Failing on my first attempt, I decided to forgo eyesight for the time being to focus on my other senses.

My ass told me I was seated on a hard, wooden chair and my wrists and shoulders indicated my hands were tied with a coarse rope behind my back. Interestingly, my ankles seemed unsecured to the wooden legs of the chair but I assumed that could have been because my boots blocked me from feeling the sensation. It was also freezing cold but while I could hear the wind, I couldn't feel it, suggesting I was in an enclosed space. I could also hear the sounds of many men moving around me in all directions, indicating I was possibly in a camp. Finally, my nose was picking up the aromas of freshly baked bread and something... more pungent and flowery, and in closer proximity.

There was something else going on inside me as well, but there was too much physical discomfort at the moment for me to understand exactly what it was.

As I grew more aware of my surroundings, the earlier mystery of why my vision had failed solved itself, as I could now feel a blindfold tied across my eyes. I almost smiled at the scenario, but I wasn't sure my jaw had the strength to form the gesture, although I was smiling on the inside, knowing that the upcoming torture and/or interrogation scene was going to be pretty interesting.

"You awoke much quicker than last time," a voice said from somewhere in the room.

I let my head dip toward my right shoulder as I looked toward the ceiling. "I've had a lot of practice at it lately."

"It does seem to happen quite often to you," she said, her voice sounding well humored.

I cocked my head to the other side. "Eh, I feel like people have been unfairly judging me lately."

"Unfairly, is it?"

I looked blindly at the source of the voice. "You know, it may be hard to believe, but where I come from, people actually like me."

Before the words were completely out of my mouth, the blindfold was ripped roughly from my head and I found that my eyes worked just fine, although slightly blurry, although my aching head didn't help my ability to focus. But standing above me was none other than Agrippina herself, wearing more clothing than I'd ever seen her wear before, but looking just as lovely as always.

I looked up at her and finally found my smile. "I miss the cleavage."

She stared down at me, her expression no longer amused, and leaned in. "Do friends where you come from make a habit of abandoning each other?"

I glared at her. "What?"

She leaned back and crossed her arms over her chest. "Your friends. They do not seem to care about you anymore. Three simply watched as my Praetorian clubbed you unconscious and they have yet to move against me. Even your Amazon seems not to care."

"Haters gonna hate," I replied, but the comment felt wrong to say.

Why would I say something like that? I didn't want my friends to hate me.

"An interesting expression," she said, "but I am curious about the source of such hate? What ever happened to the Cult of Hunter that once followed you so devoutly? Not too long ago, those people seemed willing to follow you into the depths of Tartarus itself had you asked it of them, but no longer."

I looked away, frustrated at myself over my lack of focus under Agrippina's interrogation. "What does it matter anymore? You've caught me. Again. You have the rest of them under guard as well, I'm sure. Just kill us and get it over with."

"Now that isn't like you, Jacob," she said, lowering her arms and placing her hands on her hips. "Besides, what reasons do I have to justify such action?"

I looked back at her. "Every time we've met, you've schemed to either have me captured or killed... including now."

She cocked her head to the side. "In response to you attacking me, seeking to kidnap my son, or stealing from me."

"Enough with your games!" I snapped. "We all know you had Caligula killed for no other reason than to further your own ambition, and you've been responsible for everything that's happened to me since and you know it. Don't act like you're innocent in all this."

"And so what if I did?" She asked, turning away and tossing a hand over her shoulder. "Am I so different from anyone else with ambition who came before me? Or after? You should know."

I narrowed my eyes and looked away. "I suppose not, but I don't for an instant believe that everything you've done to me has simply been in response to what I tried to do to you. Remember, I know all about you. I studied your entire life before you were even born. I know what kind of person you are."

"And what kind of person am I, Jacob?"

"You..." I fought for an appropriate response, searching my memory for a gripping retort that would prove my point true, but nothing came to me. She'd been a bitch of a wife to her husbands, an adulteress, a diabolical schemer extraordinaire, and vengeful social climber, but she had a point that she hadn't been very different from any other Roman that had come before her, and she always did have her Nero's best interests at heart. Sure she'd backed herself into a corner when her son had turned out to be just as crazy as Caligula had been, but even the best laid plans weren't so easy to pull off sometimes.

I would know.

"Are you still thinking, Jacob?" Agrippina asked easily, no hint of concern in her voice. "Because while I know not what I am to be tomorrow, I am quite familiar with who I am today, so please forgive me for not seeing myself as so dastardly a person."

"You've been trying to murder Helena for years!" I accused, unable to think of anything else to say.

"I've been trying to kill *you* for years, Jacob. Torturing your Amazon has simply been an entertaining way to go about it. Besides, I owe you for this."

She punctuated her point by turning to the side and lifting the long, warm cloaks that covered her lower half up past her hips. Beneath was bare skin and her bare behind, where I could clearly see the wedge shaped remnants of a serious burn inflicted on her right butt cheek, right where I'd burned her when questioning her upon her barge last year.

She lowered her clothing without embarrassment and I grew concerned at her outright admittance that she'd always had it in for me. Was she really going to do it now?

"Listen to yourself," I countered, perhaps a little defensively. "What kind of person says something like that?"

Before the question was even completely out of my mouth, Agrippina surged forward and smacked my face with an open palm, her normally beautiful face obscured by a vengeful scowl. I tried to recoil from the strike but was too slow, taking the full force of it directly on the cheek. It hurt almost as much as Helena's punches did, and I now found myself having to deal with an entirely new kind of pain.

She pulled her hand back quickly and kneaded it with her other, her face infuriated. "I can say such things!" She screamed, her demeanor completely changed. "Because you are anything but human! You are evil! A demon sent here by the gods to ruin us all! A *thing* that doesn't belong, one who took everything I held dear away from me and threatened to take even more. You are not human. Your Amazon is not human. You are nothing!"

Oddly I didn't feel anger at her slap despite the blood I tasted in my mouth. Only interested in the things she'd said.

"What are you talking about? I never did anything to you," I said, but paused a second to spit a mouthful of blood from my mouth. "What could I possibly have taken from you?"

Her anger shifted to pure disbelief as a frown spread across her face. "How can you not know, when you already know so much? How can you not understand the very reason for why I loathe you?"

I shook my head. "You hate me because I can use the orb and manipulate time, something you can't do. I have power that you'll never have."

Her eyes widened even further, but instead of growing even angrier, she simply looked defeated, as if coming to a sudden realization. Her head drooped and she turned away slowly, something akin to sadness in her eyes now, and I grew only more confused.

A moment later, she flicked her eyes toward me, but kept her head angled away. "That is honestly all you believe?"

"Of course, Agrippina," I pleaded. "What else could there possibly be?"

I was about to dig deeper into this most recent of mysteries, when Agrippina whirled around and rushed from the tent.

I spit out a bit more blood from my mouth, but shifted my attention to the tent's entrance when I heard a scuffle going on just beyond it. I could see shadows against the tent wall created by a fire behind them, and a scene of two people struggling to move a third figure toward the tent with a fourth just beside them became clear, but the shadow puppetry ended quickly when a pair of Praetorians burst into the tent dragging a struggling woman with a hood over her head between them. Agrippina followed, all serious.

Finally, after a few seconds of struggling, the two Praetorians managed to force the woman to her knees, and it was then that I realized her to be Helena, thanks to her enlarged stomach. Unlike the last time I'd noticed how big she had become, I felt something now. I felt angry at myself for not spending every waking moment with her and our unborn child, and was infuriated at Agrippina for threatening them both. I opened my mouth to shout at her, but when Agrippina walked up to Helena quickly and put a knife to her throat, all I could think to yell was, "Don't!"

Agrippina snapped her head at me in what seemed like surprise at my quick response, but Helena's reaction was still a mystery, her shrouded head jerking left, right, up, and down repeatedly in confusion.

"Say it again," Agrippina ordered.

"Don't," I said in a manner that failed to convey the confidence I'd hoped it would.

Agrippina turned back to Helena and moved the knife threateningly, but not dangerously, around her neck.

"What do you see here?" She asked.

"What?" I asked in return.

"What do you see??" She yelled angrily.

"I don't under…"

"Oh for…" Agrippina started to say, and I feared this was the moment when she would finally slit Helena's throat, but instead she took two long and imposing steps toward me and placed her knife against my groin. I jumped in my chair at the contact but she didn't press the point.

Literally – thank God.

"You see the woman you love, don't you?" Agrippina asked, her voice silky smooth.

"Ye…" I struggled to come up with the answer, but something inside me was beginning to believe Agrippina's announcement, and found it odd that I needed her of all people to remind me that I did in fact love Helena with all my heart. I looked up at her. "Yes, I do."

"You do," she confirmed. "You put a baby in her belly, and that is proof enough for me."

"What's your point?" I asked, confused.

"You asked what you possibly could have taken from me to make me hate you," she said before shifting to the side so that I could more clearly see Helena. Agrippina looked at me as she pointed her knife at Helena. "That's what you took from me!"

I looked at Helena's hooded head again, not understanding what Agrippina was trying to say, but when I looked back at the enraged empress of Rome, I saw in her eyes such anger and hate that I immediately understood what she meant.

"Caligula," I said.

Her expression went from angry to stern to disgusted confusion in a heartbeat.

"Caligula??" She asked with disdain. "My brother Caligula?? The man I despised? How dare you even say his name!"

I shook my head again. "I... I don't understand. Really, I don't."

Her brow was creased and her eyes blazed, and I wasn't sure if she was angry with me or simply exasperated. Finally, her demeanor softened and all the frustration and built up ire simply melted from her face. She sighed deeply and closed her eyes, whispering just one word:

"Claudius."

"Claudius?" I asked, still confused.

"You love this woman," she said, pointing her knife meekly at Helena again, "and I loved Claudius."

"You did? Your uncle?" I asked rudely, and I winced at my tone.

"Since I was girl," she answered softly as she crouched beside me, placing a hand on my knee almost distractedly. "It was a child's crush at first, an infatuation with an older man who seemed like a god to me. He had always been so handsome and vibrant and he always took an interest in me. He taught me Etruscan and tutored me in politics, economics, and history, and always taught me to use every tool I had at my disposal to get what I wanted, and to stop at nothing to achieve my dreams.

"He was always so clever, he was. Before you arrived in Rome, he'd even developed a ruse to make himself appear feeble and inept in order to convince others to underestimate him. He'd gone to great lengths to rewrite history and convince those around him he'd been as he was for decades, but only in me had he confided the truth. But then you arrived and murdered my dear Claudius, the father of my son... so *of course* I despise you, Jacob Hunter!"

"Father?!" I exclaimed, so much information being thrown at me that it was easy to misinterpret context and come to muddied conclusions, but the historian in me was always on hand to tackle historical inaccuracies. "But Nero is your husband's son, not Claudius'."

She scoffed. "My useless husband Gnaeus couldn't impregnate a bitch in heat under a spell woven by Venus herself, but Claudius... oh, what a man he was!"

I cringed at the thought of an uncle and niece doing such things, but I suppose that was better than a sister and brother doing the deed.

Barely.

I shook my head to push the historian away. "But I didn't kill Claudius, Ca..."

"Caligula did," she finished, "and my brother's fate was well deserved."

"But..." I started, but then I saw everything she was driving at as clearly as if I'd said it myself. Because I *had* said it myself. I'd said it to myself over and over and over again for the past five years. I already knew why she hated me because it was the same reason I hated myself.

"Everything's my fault," I whispered.

She nodded. "Indeed. You are correct. Everything that has happened since your arrival has been your fault, Jacob Hunter, and while the rest of your friends are not entirely without blame, you were the catalyst, the facilitator, and therefore the only one I care about. Without *you*, Caligula never would have murdered the man I loved, and none of us would be here today."

As her words trailed off, I barely had time to remember how guilty I felt over how truthful her words were, as her sexual aggression suddenly returned and her entire demeanor transformed once again. She leapt forward and mounted me, wrapping her long, strong legs around my waist tightly, and reached out a hand to grip my head. With a quick pull, she burrowed my face into her chest, while at the same time I felt her bare lower section sitting warmly atop my thighs, and I felt an unwilling sense of arousal seep into me.

"Claudius always knew what to say or do to intimidate and manipulate those around him," she said as ground against me, her movements growing ever more intense and arousing. I closed my eyes and tried to think of anything else but this gorgeous creature seated upon me, but it was hopelessly impossible as she continued.

"And he taught me everything I know. There isn't a thing I won't do to see those who set out to destroy me destroyed in turn, and I will take every kind of pleasure I can as I go about it. In whatever way I can."

I barely heard a thing she said as she continued to thrust against me, but then she stopped almost as abruptly as she'd began. I opened my eyes as she pulled on my hair, craning my head back and my face up. She leaned in to place her mouth centimeters from my own, whispering, "I should do far more than just this to you, and have your Amazon watch just so I can take pleasure in both, *but...*"

Without finishing, she dismounted and took a step back and stared into my eyes as I slowly tilted my head down to its normal position, too frazzled to do much else. When I settled myself, Agrippina smirked and glanced down at my pants, flicking her eyebrows up and setting her mouth in a way that suggested she was impressed.

"It appears your integrity is more intact than I thought," she said. "Most men wouldn't have... maintained themselves so efficiently.

I didn't respond as the tension in the room dissipated, and I sat there as Agrippina studied me, Helena still gagged and silent. For the briefest of seconds, I thought Agrippina was done with me, that she'd made her point and that we'd somehow reached some kind of understanding. I almost thought she would just let us go, willing to let me wallow in my own self-disgust – which her affirmation of my responsibility for everything would surely exacerbate.

But then Agrippina rushed at Helena and the knife in her hand flicked out again as she thrust it toward Helena's throat. The love of my life couldn't possibly have seen it coming, but I did, and all I could do was yell out, already knowing there was nothing I could say that would stop Agrippina from doing what she must have been waiting all these years to do.

"Please!!" It was all I could think to say, but the knife flew straight and true, striking Helena's throat right at the jugular, and then the blood started to flow.

Agrippina and her Praetorians stood motionless, and Helena could do little but kneel with the knife at her throat, although she did not seem to feel any pain. The scene seemed frozen in time, like a sadistic still-life painting I had somehow walked into. No one moved, but then Agrippina straightened, her knife still buried in Helena's throat. She didn't say anything at first, and I sat there too stunned at the sight to wonder why there wasn't more blood.

Her hand steady and the knife remaining where it was, Agrippina looked at me. "I ask you to understand that I do this to prove what kind of person I *really* am, Jacob."

Tears welled in my eyes as I immediately knew what that meant, having known exactly what kind of person Agrippina was from the very first time I'd read about her back in college. She withdrew the knife from Helena's neck and I stared in disbelief, unable to understand why the bag over her head only had a single spot of blood upon it, but my tears flowed regardless.

"Perhaps you are human after all."

I heard Agrippina utter these words but hardly registered them and barely saw the nod she offered to her Praetorians. They seemed to understand, however, and removed the hood from over Helena's head and took the gag out from her mouth. Upon her neck was a pinprick of a wound, with only a single droplet of blood falling from it. As the blindfold came off, Helena already had her vibrant green eyes staring directly into my own, as though she had been able to see through the mask the entire time. But what surprised me was how distant they were, appearing so unemotional and rock hard that she didn't seem in the least bit concerned for her life...

As though she had been welcoming an end to it completely.

They suggested that she'd knelt there waiting and ready for the end, perhaps hoping it would come, and I knew exactly why. But then she saw me for the first time as well, and must have noticed the utter concern on my face and the tears streaming down it, because those perfect eyes of hers brightened, the set of her mouth softened, and I could see sympathy in those green gems now.

"And perhaps your Amazon has learned to forgive as well."

Helena looked at Agrippina angrily, but Agrippina held her gaze steadily like a mother offering her child a look that said, "I told you so." Once again, Helena's expression softened as she slowly looked away, but before either us could think on it more, Agrippina flicked her head toward the tent's exit.

"Escort her out and unbind her hands," she ordered. "Give her and the rest of them food and water and allow them to make camp with us. Treat them as friends."

Now it was Helena's turn to look at Agrippina in confusion. "Why?" She asked, her voice far steadier than I thought possible, but Agrippina's only answer was to close her eyes and shake her head.

The Praetorians seemed to understand again, and gently pulled Helena to her feet and ushered her from the tent. She looked over her shoulder at me before she disappeared, her short hair making her look almost childish, and there was a moment where again time seemed to slow and I saw her mouth three words very clearly:

I love you.

I smiled at her, feeling my chest swell with happiness instead of pain, elation instead of sorrow, peace instead of torment, and even more tears fell from my eyes. I was so happy in that moment that I forgot all about the pain and darkness that had gathered within me since the last time I'd come face to face with Agrippina, not caring where it had gone or what had released it.

When Helena was gone, Agrippina turned to face me, wearing a sad expression.

"The orb has affected you, has it not?"

My head jerked back at how random her question had seemed, but then it dropped against my chest as yet another realization finally set in. "It has."

"Negatively?"

"Yes," I whispered, vague memories in the form of scattered images materializing in my mind now.

"Do you wish to kill me?"

My response came surprisingly quick and honest as I lifted my head. "No…"

She nodded. "That is good, Jacob, because I no longer wish to kill you anymore either."

"You don't?"

"I do not."

"If you don't want to kill me, then… what? Work together?"

"Yes."

"Why?"

She didn't answer, but leaned down to place her head beside my own, her mouth just beside my left ear. She reached around me as though to hug me but instead of touching me, she simply used her knife to cut the bonds around my wrists.

"Because I have something to give you," she whispered into my ear.

"What?" I whispered back.

Without elaborating, she took my hands in her own and pulled me up. I felt weak under her grip, but she steadied me with surprisingly strong hands. I towered over her but not for an instant did I feel any power over her in that moment. She looked up at me with wide eyes that seemed almost giddy, eyes that could have been hopeful about something for the first time in a long time.

"Something you've sought since arriving here, Jacob," she said, a sweet smile forming at her lips before she pulled me toward the tent's exit. "Answers."

***

We emerged together from what I now realized had to have been Agrippina's *praetorium*, hand in hand, to the sight of every non-legionnaire from my contingent waiting for us with the exception of Helena, Artie, and Wang.

My eyes narrowed in curiosity that it was those three in particular who weren't present. Helena alone I could understand, Helena and Artie I could understand, but I wasn't sure why Wang was with them. I would have expected a third person with her to be either Santino or Cuyler, but both men stood a dozen meters away from me, waiting expectantly for my return.

At the sight of them all, Agrippina let go of my hand and I found myself wandering toward where Santino and Vincent stood. I stepped toward them as they stood with their arms crossed against their chests – at least, Vincent stood in the best approximation of the stance – identical stern expressions on their faces, although there was something off about Santino's.

They watched me approach intently, which I did slowly and silently, downtrodden, while everything inside me screamed to ignore them and do what I knew I really wanted to do: get my answers. But I fought away the feeling, ignoring it like I would a craving for something salty or sweet, knowing that eating it would taste great but wasn't something my body really needed. It wasn't an easy thing to do, but I felt my resolve tightening with every step I took.

I stopped when I arrived at a respectful distance and dropped my head. I felt like I was approaching a disciplinary review board made up of very important alumni, but finally, I lifted my eyes and looked at Vincent. We stood there like that for a very long time, before the most appropriate words that couldn't possibly do justice to how I really felt flowed from my mouth without the need to think them first.

"I'm… sorry."

My words were spoken softly, but not without conviction. I felt the truth in them as easily as the words themselves had come to my lips, although I still did not think they were enough. But it had not been a hollow statement, even if my mind could not conjure the appropriate memories for what exactly I was sorry for. In fact, the last month of my life seemed like a darkened room in my head with nothing but a weak nightlight to see by.

Perhaps the memories would return later.

Vincent uncrossed his arm and let it rest at his side. Santino did the same. I caught him glancing at Vincent out of the corner of his eye, but I wasn't sure why exactly. The two of them stood there silently for a few moments before Vincent lifted his hand and placed it on my shoulder.

"It's all right, Jacob."

I bit back an overwhelming surge of emotion.

Recent months had left me forgetting how much I looked up to this man, and how much I needed him for guidance and understanding. I'd always seen him as something of a father figure, and having his forgiveness now made it all seem right. Happiness swelled within me, but the tender moment was interrupted when Santino placed his own hand on my other shoulder. I looked at him, slightly upset that he'd interrupted my moment with Vincent, but he looked back with a seriousness I rarely saw in the man.

A few seconds passed, but then he said, "It's all right, Jacob."

Vincent looked at Santino and Santino looked at Vincent.

Vincent lowered his hand and Santino did the same.

"We don't have time..." Vincent said.

"We don't have time..." Santino said.

I was smiling by now, grinning in fact, something I hadn't done in a very long time, and it felt *good*. Vincent looked at Santino angrily and Santino looked back at Vincent just the same, but when Vincent threw his head in the air and rolled his eyes before storming off, Santino remained where he was. Vincent walked away, but not without another look in my direction that seemed more relieved than anything.

Santino looked at me out of the corner of his eye and raised an eyebrow.

"Find your sanity yet, or am I going to have to knock you out?" He asked.

My smiled returned again. I... think I did actually. Thanks..."

He lashed out and pulled me into a bear hug before I could finish, lifting me off the ground. "God, it's good to have you back, buddy!"

"I..."

"As for *you*," he said, releasing me quickly and turning to Agrippina, "if you're not busy, I'm pretty sure you're about due for another ride on the Santino-train later tonight. Just stop..."

"Go away, simpleton," Agrippina said without emotion.

"Don't have to tell me twice," he said in mid retreat, a movement that looked a lot like a cartoon character being yanked off stage by a giant hook. Some of my friends laughed at his display as the lot of them finally wandered away, and their spirits seemed higher than they'd been since Alexandria.

When they were gone I turned back to Agrippina. "He's not really a bad guy, you know."

"In comparison to who?" She asked. "You?"

"Good point..."

She shook her head. "Let us go, Jacob. You must be impatient for your answers."

I nodded, and went with my first instinct, which was to follow her, but I only made it three steps before I stopped and held my ground.

"Come, Jacob," Agrippina said, noticing my hesitation.

I wanted to but I couldn't move my feet. It was like my brain had lost its connection to them, and then those feelings of being hung over from earlier returned. I felt nauseous and sick, and the pounding in my head returned with a vengeance. I'd never had to cold turkey myself off of drugs before, but I had to imagine this to be about how it felt.

"Wait," I said through gritted teeth, leaning down to put my hands on my knees and support myself.

"Do you feel unwell?" Agrippina asked, placing a hand on my back consolingly.

"Yes... *urgh*, I'm not... no, definitely not well."

Within me, a struggle was taking place. It was an altercation I'd grown used to in recent time, as my mind, body, and soul fought over what one or the other intended to do. I couldn't explain it, but there could only be one thing responsible for what I was feeling.

"Where..." I clenched my mouth shut again, but forced it open, "...where... where is the orb?"

Agrippina nodded at me slowly. "It is quite safe, Jacob. And well away from you. We found it when searching your belongings, but your friends indicated it would be best if I removed it from your presence. Your centurion, Minicius I believe, has it in his possession."

Everything was beginning to make sense.

I *was* suffering from withdrawal...

I threw up with that revelation, expelling what miniscule amount of food I had left in my belly. It seemed my mind had thought my body could use a little flushing out in that moment, and I guess my soul had finally agreed, allowing them to play nice, apparently needing a clean slate from which to heal my badgered existence.

It was the only time vomiting had ever felt good.

"Do you need medical attention?" Agrippina asked.

I stood up wobbly, and threw her hand off my back, clarity returning and the pain ebbing. I waited while my head stopped swimming and took a moment to collect my bearings, understanding now that we were standing on the *via principalis* heading east, and I was wearing my night ops combat fatigues, boots, but I was completely naked from the waist up. I hadn't even noticed until just now, which in turn invited the cold to settle in.

"Where are my clothes?" I asked, rubbing my arms to stave off the chill.

Agrippina ran her eyes over my body unabashedly. "I removed them personally in preparation for our talk."

I rolled my eyes. "Enjoy that, did you?"

She shrugged. "Of course."

"It's freezing out here," I said, rubbing my arms more intensely now. "How do you expect me to go anywhere without a shirt?"

Agrippina pouted with impatience, perhaps eager as well for me to have my answers – whatever that meant – but she didn't seem upset. She looked up to the sky and at the stars before returning her attention to me.

"Perhaps it would be prudent to wait until morning," she said. "Our destination is not far but I suppose it would be best to arrive during the day."

"Best?"

She glanced away and then back at me. "It will be easier to understand if you to see for yourself."

"Yeah, I don't think so. I've seen too many movies to just blindly accept *that* as an answer," I said, interspersing the English term before I paused for a second, thinking. "In fact, I've seen too many movies to know better than to even fucking trust you at all, but yet," I opened my arms, "here I am, I guess."

She looked at me curiously. "Tell me about these *moo-wees*, Jacob. What are they?"

"Nope, nu-uh," I said, shaking my head. "Not gonna happen. I'm not about to start buddying up to you just because you didn't kill me. Seen too many movies. *Way* too many."

Her nose scrunched cutely in annoyance. "Is it rude where you come from to make references in front of others who clearly have no understanding of what it is you're referencing?"

I leaned in close. "Very rude."

"Fine," she said, "but you would do well to listen to what I'm about to say, even if you refuse to trust me."

I hugged my arms around my chest and dug my hands into my armpits. "Quickly. *Please*."

"I have not yet decided whether or not I will kill you at a later date," she said bluntly, before turning to return to her *praetorium*.

I gulped nervously, knowing she probably hadn't.

"Wait," I called out, and Agrippina stopped at the threshold of her tent. Unhappily, I tilted my head from side to side, unconvinced if my next words were a good idea or not, but finally decided it might be time for a little trust. "If I like your 'answers' tomorrow, I'll tell you what a movie is. Trust me. I can probably even still recite a few of them from memory for you."

Agrippina held my gaze, her lips pouting ever so slightly, but instead of answering, she reached up and unclipped a clasp from the furs wrapped around her shoulders. The heavy garments fell to the ground revealing little more than a sheer, see-through, Roman-style "nighty" that barely extended past her waist.

She jutted her chin past her *praetorium* and to the south. "Your Amazon was taken to that side of the camp. Or... you can stay with *me* tonight. I will keep you quite warm in all manner of ways, I assure you..."

I gulped again as she entered her tent, leaving me alone with nothing but the memory of her standing there in her scandalously revealing skivvies. Two Praetorians were nearby as well, ones who also must have seen Agrippina in her exposed outfit, but neither batted an eyelash at it.

And for more than a few moments, I considered her offer, the ache in my groin from earlier not making my decision any easier, but with a confident effort, I turned in the direction Agrippina had indicated and started walking.

I passed by a lot of individuals as I headed to the southern end of the camp, most of them Praetorians or camp administrators, and none of them outwardly friendly. When I stopped and asked for directions, I was met with either silence or spit on my boots. Both scenarios left me feeling unwanted, not to mention queasy in my already upset stomach, but one man, who I assumed was a Praetorian, had been vaguely helpful. After asking for directions he gave me the *digitus impudicus*, the always helpful middle finger, but at least he pointed it in a very general direction that seemed the right way to go. I waved my thanks only to have him raise his other finger to join the first, but I passed by him and walked toward the far end of the camp as my skin started turning a light shade of blue from the cold.

It took me a while to reach the fort's southeast corner, where it seemed Agrippina had allowed my friends to camp, but after ten minutes of wandering around, I finally found a series of tents that were most certainly not from around here. Those who occupied them were milling about, performing one task or another, none of them immediately noticing my arrival. I saw Brewster and Stryker sitting around a small fire together, not talking, but clearly guarding each other's backs. Cuyler was behind all the tents situated on a haphazardly built platform that offered a little extra elevation, while Santino and Bordeaux were busy crafting a small palisade of stakes to place around the small encampment.

I caught Archer's eye as he surveyed the others and he waved me over.

"I hear you're sane again," he said as I approached.

I knocked my head with the palm of a hand. "I hope so."

He nodded, his blond hair so long now that it fell into his face at the slight motion. He brushed it away before handing me my heavy winter jacket that he must have found after Agrippina and I had left her *praetorium*.

I took it from him and slipped it on.

"I know I've been playing catch up since getting here," he said as I zipped it tight, "but I think I understand that what you were going through wasn't exactly your choice."

"Not my choice, no," I agreed, "but my actions were still my own. The last few months are a little fuzzy, but I remember a few things. Bad things. I'm not sure..."

"Hunter," Archer warned, placing a surprisingly warm and consoling hand on my shoulder. "Try not to think about it."

"Yeah, I know... it's just that I don't think I've been magically cured," I warned. "It could happen again. I could relapse maybe. If the orb somehow finds its way back to me, I... well, I need you to be vigilant, Paul. Do whatever you need to."

He smiled and worked his jaw with a hand. "I do owe you a few punches..."

"Cash them in," I said hastily, realizing I was starting to like Archer again. "Whatever it takes."

"Agreed," he said.

I shifted my attention from him to survey the camp. "Where's Helena?" I asked, but Archer visibly hesitated. "It's all right, Paul. I'm okay. Really. Now, where is she?"

He slowly hooked a thumb over his shoulder toward the tent behind him.

"Thanks," I said, and walked past him, moving toward the tent.

It was large, one not meant for sleeping, but one we used for recreational use or team meetings. I leaned down to find the zipper that kept it closed, but had to take a second when a shiver rand down my spine, but it was a natural shiver, one born from the cold I'd only just now escaped and nothing more. But when it subsided, I remained unmoving, wondering if this was the right thing to do. The last month hadn't done anything for my relationship with Helena besides damage it, I was sure, and I wouldn't blame her if she didn't want anything to do with me at all anymore.

I took both a moment and a deep breath, but pushed into the tent.

"I told everyone to stay out!"

I heard Wang shout these words, but my eyes were drawn immediately to Helena laying on a table with her legs spread wide and Wang situated between them. This initial sight of horror was only slightly improved by the sight of Artie near Helena's head, facing Wang.

"I said that you'd better bloody well stay..." Wang started to say again as he turned around, but then stopped when he saw me. "Oh, it's you. You especially get the fuck..."

"No, it's all right, Wang," Helena said as she leaned up. I think he's better."

Wang shot to his feet before she could finish and moved on me threateningly. I took a step back and raised my hands innocently as he spoke, his hands balling themselves into tight fists.

"If you really are *better*," Wang challenged, "then tell me something only Hunter would know."

My head jerked back in confusion. "I was under the influence of some really rough drugs, Wang, not replaced by a clone..."

His aggressive expression softened and his fighting posture disappeared as he straightened. "Oh, right..." he muttered, glancing at the ground, "well, I suppose the other you wouldn't have been so patient with a question like that, so... welcome back, mate."

I rolled my eyes and gestured toward Helena. "What's going on here?"

"What do you think is going on here?" Artie said, but her voice had a challenging edge to it.

"Artie, just don't," I said as I returned her look, which she held with hard eyes until I couldn't help but look away.

Wang returned to Helena and lowered a sheet over her legs as he spoke again. "Not many lady-part doctors around here, Hunter. So I'm all she's got."

I looked at him, almost shocked. "And you're okay with that?" I turned to Helena. "And you?"

Wang answered first. "I may not be a doctor, but I took an oath, and Helena needed me. Besides, me mum was a nurse and helped deliver a thousand babies. I learned a lot from her."

"I trust him, Jacob," Helena said. "And he's been very gentle."

"He'd better have been."

Wang narrowed his eyes at me, but quickly took a deep breath and shook his head as he turned away to search for something in his bag.

"Would you like to see your baby, Hunter?" He asked.

My eyebrows rose at the suggestion. "What? How?"

"My portable ultrasound device still works," he indicated as he pulled a small, square device with an attached cord from his bag. "But barely. It'll be fuzzy, but Helena's far enough along that seeing him is quite easy."

I looked at Helena. "Him?"

She nodded and beamed at me. "We've known for a few weeks now."

I smiled, not even a hint of annoyance or anger present in my chest or heart or in my mind or anywhere at the news. All I felt was unabashed joy, the last month devolving into nothing more than a distant, painful memory, one that I pushed away to dwell on later. Now, I got to see my son for the very first time, and not even Agrippina or the orb could ruin that moment.

"I told you," I said, barely above a whisper, and Helena's grin grew and she tilted her head in acknowledgment that I had been the one to hope it was a boy. She waved me over and I moved to kneel beside her, which is when Artie pulled away from Helena and marched away in silence. I watched her go but then realized I couldn't just let her leave without saying something.

"Wait, Artie," I called out, shooting back to my feet and intercepting her by the tent's exit, and she stopped and turned to look up at me. She rarely had to look up at guys, but she always had with me, but I had never thought any less of her for it, and I certainly didn't now.

She stared into my eyes with a look of frustrated sadness that nearly broke my heart.

Carefully, I reached up and gripped her shoulders, and lowered my head toward her. "There's nothing I can really say to explain how sorry I am, Artie, but..."

As I spoke, she violently choked back tears as a fit of sobs overwhelmed her, which was when she broke down completely. She pulled herself against my chest as tears started to flow, but I hesitated before wrapping my arms around her, unsure if that's what she really wanted from me, but finally, I did.

I patted her head and let her cry.

"You have a lot to make up for, Jacob," she said around her tears. "You can't even imagine."

I felt my eyes close on their own. "No. I can't."

She lost her next words in another jolt of emotion, and I had to wait before she found it within herself to speak again. "I thought I'd lost you, big brother. People snap all the time, for no reason at all sometimes, but because of the orb I... I thought I'd have to watch one of our friends hurt you before you did... before you did..."

I squeezed her tighter as she failed to find the words she sought, and shushed her, feeling tears of my own form and fall at her words, realizing that I no longer cared about changed timelines and "2.0" monikers. If I'd ever doubted that the Artie before me was anyone but my real sister... I no longer did now.

She was.

"I'm so sorry, Artie. I wish I could say it wasn't my fault, but... I can't. I could have done something about it."

She pushed herself away finally, shaking her head as she wiped tears from her cheeks. "It's okay, Jacob. I think we all understand. I... I just need some time, okay?"

"I understand, little sister," I said, and she looked up at me and small smile formed on her lips at my use of my own pet name for her. The smile tightened a moment later, and after one last hug from her, she left, and I watched her go. I wiped away a tear as I stared at the empty space Artie had just occupied, my emotions threatening to overwhelm me, when I remembered why it was I'd come here.

I turned around and saw Wang awkwardly fiddling with the ultrasound device in his hands, while Helena still laid on the table, smiling at me. She reached out again and beckoned me toward her, so I complied and knelt beside her, taking her hand in both of my own.

"Thanks for that," I whispered.

"She's your *sister*, Jacob," Helena said. "And she's a great one."

I nodded slowly. "Has she been with you for these before?"

"Every one," Helena answered.

"God, I'm so sorry, Helena," I said, lowering my head to her hand, my earlier tears threatening to return. "How can you still love me after everything I've put you through? I should have been here for you! Should have been able to ignore orb. I..."

"Not now, Jacob," she said, her eyes supportive but with a frown.

"But..."

"Later..."

I nodded, but it didn't come easy.

Helena turned to Wang. "We're ready, Doctor."

I looked at the medic, some of my sadness leaving at the odd word choice. "Doctor?"

"Her idea," he said as he gave his device one last inspection, not missing a beat. "It made her feel more comfortable."

"Works for me..." I said, my facial muscle memory finally remembering how to form a smile, "...*doctor*."

He paused to give me an irritated look, but continued his preparation without pause. "Pull up your shirt, Helena," he ordered.

She did as she was told and lifted her shirt that may have belonged to Bordeaux a few weeks ago, to reveal her swollen belly. I looked at it in wonder, having had no idea how big she'd really gotten until just now.

"Don't look so disgusted, Jacob," she chided. "Other things are bigger as well."

"*Please...*" Wang said as he applied a gel to her stomach.

"Sorr... y!" Helena's voice rose sharply as the cold gel hit her. Wang ignored her and placed the wand against the gel and guided it along her belly. I watched in wonder as the image of a tiny child materialized almost immediately on the handheld screen Wang also held, and was amazed at how clearly details came into view. Bits and pieces of the little guy like arms and legs, fingers and toes, a torso and head were so plainly obvious on the screen that I couldn't believe what I was seeing. Even his face and nose were easy to detect despite the fuzziness from Wang's defunct device.

It was an awesome sight, in every definitive meaning of the word.

Without prompting, the little guy squirmed and kicked in a series of tumbles and karate moves. I sat there, mouth agape at what I saw, having never believed that seeing what I was seeing now could ever be so amazing and emotional. I'd never even been sure if I'd ever get to see something like this, but I couldn't be more thankful that I was now.

"My God," I said, raising a hand to my mouth to cover my amazement. "He's... perfect."

Wang nodded as he manipulated the device for a different view. "He does seem quite healthy, and his dimensions look good. I'm actually quite surprised considering the diet Helena's been forced on here and the stress she's been under. There's no way for me to perform a more detailed analysis, but it's my professional opinion that the lad looks aces."

"Helena's got great genes..." I whispered, barely understanding a word he'd said.

"You helped," Helena said.

"Hmm?" I asked. "What?"

She laughed and turned back to Wang. "One of us should really have taken that bet, James. He's taking this a lot better than we thought he would."

"Aye," he replied, "he is."

"I'm proud of you, Jacob," she said, turning back to me.

"Hmm?" I asked, my eyes never leaving the image of my son. "What?"

"Never mind."

I could have watched my boy tumble and enjoy life all day long if I could, but the screen flickered and cut out a second later.

"Bloody hell," Wang said, smacking the sensor against Helena's knee, but when he replaced it against her belly, nothing happened.

"What's wrong with it?" I asked.

"It's been wonky since the very beginning of Helena's pregnancy," he answered. "It's been used too often over the years for other things, and this cold certainly isn't helping."

"Can you repair it?" Helena asked.

"I'll try but don't expect much. I'm sorry."

I turned to her and she met my eye. "At least I got to see him."

She smiled. "I'm glad you did."

"Keep your chin up," Wang said as he packed up his things. "Helena's almost there. You'll see him again soon enough in all his wiggly glory."

I put a hand on Wang's shoulder and gripped it tightly. "I can't begin to thank you enough, James. You being there when I wasn't means more than you can possibly understand. I don't know how to even begin to…"

"Don't worry yourself, mate," he said as he raised his hands in front of him so that I could see them. "These are good hands. Believe me, I wouldn't have allowed any others to do… the things that needed doing, or… the things that are still to come."

He smiled at me but I glared at him, and he got the message. Gathering his things he rose to his feet and started for the exit, but turned back to Helena for one last bit of advice.

"Remember to keep your liquids up, Helena," he advised, "and don't exert yourself but stay active if you can. I'm sorry to say it, but it's going to get harder before it gets easier."

"Thanks, Doctor," she said.

He nodded and left, leaving the two of us alone. Slowly, I looked at her and she looked at me, and we simply stared at one another for a while before she dropped her chin and looked at her shoulder, clearly only one thing on her mind.

"Jacob, how did you find the orb?"

I too dropped my eyes to her shoulder. "How long have you known?"

"Only after leaving Camulodunum, remember? I found it in your footlocker."

I didn't remember.

"I didn't go looking for it, Helena!" I said hastily, perhaps defensively. "I didn't. It found me. It was just there one morning on our way to Alexandria, and when it was, I... I kept it. I didn't even realize what I was doing, but it was with me this whole time. That I remember now. It was in my footlocker, it..."

"Shh..." Helena breathed, reaching out to pull my head against her shoulder. "I believe you."

"There's so much I can't remember about the last few months, Helena," I said, resting my head against her shoulder and squeezing my eyes shut as though that would help force the memories to return. "I can see images, things like fire and people tied up and Penelope..."

"Don't think about it, Jacob," Helena soothed as she held me.

I reached up and grabbed her shirt near her other shoulder, and clung to it desperately. "I'm so sorry, Helena. I can't believe I let it happen. It all felt so right and it made me feel *so* good. I couldn't help it. I..."

She interrupted me by lifting my chin up with a finger. "No more apologies, Jacob. I don't need them. I don't want them. I'm the one who should be apologizing to you. I should have..."

"No!" I nearly yelled as I pulled away from her embrace to stare at her intently. "Promise me if I ever fall under the orb's influence again that you'll stay away from me. As far away as possible! Don't confront me! Don't even come near me! It make me... makes me dangerous! You can't possibly understand, but

I'm not sure I wouldn't have hurt you had you tried to intervene before."

"But, Jacob…"

"No, Helena! If it happens again, stay away. You have to! Do it for me."

Reluctantly, she nodded. "I'm still sorry."

"I understand. Completely. But you had the little guy to think about, and you did the right thing. My mom always told me that parenthood is all about sacrifice, doing what's best for the baby, even if it hurts you. You protected him, and I am so happy that you did." I paused and smiled. "I always knew you'd be a good mom."

She cocked her head to the side and reached up to stroke my hair. "Thanks you, Jacob. That means a lot. And I have to admit, such parental insightfulness is kind of a turn on…"

I smiled. "Oh, yeah? So where would you like me to start?"

I placed my hand against her bare thigh and stroked it lightly, but she laughed and pushed it away. "I'm hardly in the mood for *that*, Lieutenant Hunter! Look at me! I'm hideous!"

"You're beautiful."

She looked genuinely happy at my comment, and reached out to cup my cheek with a hand. "I suppose there's hope for you yet, Jacob Hunter, but if you really want to impress me, you can start by getting me another pillow. My back is killing me!"

I chuckled. "Well that I can do. Always was good at finding things."

She offered me a sly smile. "Oh, you certainly were, but there will be time enough to see if you've still got it later."

I smirked and found the pillow she needed, and placed it behind her head, noticing her short, disheveled hair again and found myself staring.

Helena noticed my attention. "Problem?"

"It's just that your hair is…"

"I didn't necessarily want to do it, Jacob."

I sighed. No, she probably hadn't.

"It's just that it…" she gave me a look as I started, so I rethought my words. "No, it looks good. Really. Like an 80s pop star or something. It's very sexy."

She chuckled. "Hope indeed."

I pumped a fist in the air lightly in triumph, but couldn't think of anything else to say, although I was content not to say anything at all so that I could simply enjoy the moment. But then a sudden and urgent thought entered my brain, one so dire I nearly shouted at Helena as I spoke.

"Wait! We need to pick a name!"

She belted out a quick laugh, probably surprised by the randomness of my comment. "I did have a few in…"

"Augustus!"

"Uh… no."

"Julius!"

"*No…*"

"Galba?"

"Really, Jacob?"

"What about Jacob?"

"Well, it was on my list…"

"Oh… I got it! What about Romulus Remus van Strauss Hunter! It's got a ring to it…"

"*Jacob…*"

"How about…"

***

"Well you look as pleased as peaches this morning, Mister," Santino said from beside me.

I glanced to my right and over at my friend as the two of us rode side by side, unsurprised to notice that there was a smile on his face. I felt like returning it, but didn't want to give him the acknowledgment that he was in fact quite right.

I *was* as pleased as peaches this morning.

Emotions still whirled within me, anger, guilt, and shame all still there and many more, but I no longer felt alienated and lonely, nor did I feel unwanted or hated by those who called me their friend or from those who loved me. I felt my old, self-deprecating, bearing-the-world-on-my-shoulders self again, but that was okay, because that's who I was, and that also meant I had the love and friendship that defined me as well. Everyone carried negativity around with them, perhaps me more than many others, but that was a burden all of humanity shared. It was only by the ways we dealt with those emotions that gave us our own unique individuality – that is, unless under the influence of the orb.

I'd had a lot of time to think about it last night, and I was certain I understood it now.

It was a simple drug, one that seemed to work by taking all of a person's pain, his anger, his darkness, and all of his unrealized negative intentions for use as fuel to power the body's impulses. Personal values were rendered moot, replaced with a sense of confidence and superiority, but at a grave risk. With the loss of inhibitions came the loss of good judgment, and the orb only magnified that loss, replacing clear headed thinking with something much worse.

No one had yet told me what I'd done while under the orb's influence, but I knew it hadn't been good. In fact, I knew I'd done horrible things, but the entire experience had given me perspective. Carrying around all my negativity was a part of who I was. It defined me as equally as my positive attributes did, but it was through the help of friends and loved ones that those issues could be dealt with and contained, something made all the more clear to me after spending the entire night with Helena, to whom I felt closer than any other person throughout my entire life, a bond made all the more inseparable by her inability to abandon me even after everything I had done. No person really deserved that kind of love, but I would take it and hold onto it for as long as I possibly could.

That still did not explain the orb's other apparent ability to drive men insane, but I figure such a stage would have only been just around the corner had I not been parted from it.

"Don't give him a hard time, John," Artie said from my other side. "He's been through a lot."

"He's been through a lot?" Santino demanded. "*He's* been through a lot?? *I* was the one who had to deal with a best friend who'd gone crazy! Me! Not him!"

"And I'm just *so* sorry to have let that happen," I said, happier than I could possibly describe just by being here with them.

"You'd damn well better be," Santino responded, but then he sighed and seemed to grow sad.

"What's wrong?" I asked.

"Oh, it's nothing," he answered, clearly not in a mood to talk about it until a half second later when he was clearly in the mood to do just that. "It's just that you weren't any fun when you were crazy and Helena's pregnancy has taken all the fun out of my jokes."

"Excuse me?"

"There's just no fun in the sexual innuendoes anymore, man! Kinda gross actually, but that was my thing!"

"Yeah," I said gratingly. "I remember."

"It's just not funny anymore when I say something that references Helena and…"

"Shut it, John!" Artie scolded. "You shouldn't be thinking about those things anyway. Ever! You should be thinking about m…"

Artie's voice trailed off and I snapped my head to the left to see what it was that had kept her from finishing. She seemed fine but her eyes were looking past me and toward Santino. I snapped my head around but found my friend staring off into the distance, not paying either one of us any mind. I eyed him suspiciously before turning back to Artie.

"Mind finishing that thought?" I asked.

She flushed red. "Um, no, not really."

"Uh-huh…" I said, giving her an equally uncertain look. "That's what I thought."

She smiled at me awkwardly but didn't turn to face me, settling instead with simply glancing at me out of the corner of her eyes. I sighed but realized that if the two of them were messing around there was little I could do about it. At least they had the common decency to try and keep it from me.

"I can't believe I'm actually saying this," I said, "but I think I'd rather go ride with Agrippina for a while."

"Oh, Agrippina," Santino said lustfully. "How I cherish those memor…"

He too cut himself off midsentence, but instead of wasting time glancing at him first, I looked to Artie instead, but she didn't seem even the least bit curious about what he'd said. Slowly, I turned back to Santino, who was also looking away, inspecting a dead branch from a tree as he rode by.

I looked away from them both, frowned, and noticed Boudicca riding silently in front of us beside Archer. She hadn't understood a word of our conversation, but she didn't seem to mind either. She simply rode in silent contemplation, content with simply being here, but not needing to get involved. She was my stalwart protector it seemed, and while I didn't think I needed her, I appreciated the gesture.

Besides, Wang wasn't here, so she was her usual dour self when he wasn't around.

I shook my head and pressed Felix to surge past them all. He picked up speed and I found myself approaching Agrippina's position near the head of our tiny marching formation. Only thirty individuals had set forth from the camp an hour ago, two hours after dawn, including Archer, Vincent, Santino, Artie, Boudicca, myself, Agrippina, and the rest of our party consisted of her Praetorians. Agrippina hadn't indicated where we were going, only that it wasn't far and that it was of vital importance. In fact, she'd been rather cryptic about the whole thing, but I supposed I couldn't blame her for being just as distrusting of us as we were of her. Our temporary partnership was of mutual interest to both parties, although I wasn't sure what exactly she hoped to get out of it yet.

As I rode up to her position, I thought of a dozen different questions to ask her, but foremost in my mine was the notion that finally, after months of growing fuzziness, I could suddenly think clearly again. As we left the orb behind us, I could feel its presence less and less, and while I still felt a pang of longing for it, I wasn't nearly as overwhelmed by it as I once was. Its presence persisted within me, a distant reminder of its power and potential, but for now it was, literally, out of sight and out of mind.

Felix snorted obnoxiously, causing a thick cloud of mist to dissipate around me as I passed through it, but also serving to alert Agrippina of our approach. She twisted her head just slightly, and while I knew she couldn't yet see us, the slim smile tugging at her lips suggested she knew exactly who was approaching.

"Come for questions, Jacob?"

I grunted silently under the noise of Felix's stomping feet as I came up alongside Agrippina. She rode a startlingly white mare of ample size, its blank coat blending in with the snow so well that

Agrippina seemed to float in midair. She wore heavy robes that cascaded down her body in numerous, thick layers, but I could see that she had chosen to wear trousers as well.

"If you don't mind," I answered.

She lowered her chin. "I suppose you deserve them."

"Do I?"

"You do," she said, lifting her head. "You may be the source of a great many negative things, but I am willing to accept that they were done inadvertently and out of your control, but that is why I have an inkling that your presence is essential to the task ahead."

"What task?" I asked, almost pleading for answers. "Where exactly are we? And how did you even end up here? How is it that I'm on the most aimless, directionless journey of my life, and yet I end up bumping into *you* of all people?"

She smiled. "It seems pertinent to answer your third question first."

I jerked my head at her impatiently, prompting her to continue.

She looked away, almost distractedly. "Quite simply, Britain was always where I intended to go."

I looked at her suspiciously. "Why?"

"I will get to that," she replied, "but first, after the incident between us in Syria, I led my Praetorians north to deal with the Parthian insurrection. Our reports indicated they were quite ready to invade Anatolia and push through Byzantium and into the West, but such claims were rather farfetched. One particular upstart princeling had decided that Rome was in a more vulnerable state than reality reflected, and raised a rather sizable force against us, but when facing my Praetorians on the field of battle, with Vespasian having arrived to lead them, most turned and ran. The rest held their ground, but I was able to… personally convince their general to head back to Parthia and never raise arms against Rome again."

"Yeah," I muttered. "*Convinced*?"

She shrugged. "I can be quite convincing at times, can I not, Jacob?"

I gulped and didn't answering, knowing she certainly could be.

"What happened to Vespasian?" I asked, curious about the man.

"He returned to Germany where I left a sizable portion of my Praetorian force to help with hostilities."

"He didn't want to come here? With you?"

"No. What cause would he have?"

"No cause, I guess," I said quickly to cover my suspicious tone. "But that doesn't answer why you came to Britain."

"Most astute of you, Jacob," she said and I forced myself not to roll my eyes. "As I was saying, the Parthian threat was dealt with quickly, so I took my Praetorians west almost immediately. There were still the Germans to deal with, and Gaul and Iberia were acting recalcitrant as well, but as we arrived in Dalmatia, one of my spies returned from Alexandria."

I grimaced at the memory and immediately rubbed my leg where the arrow had hit me when chasing Agrippina's ninjas to the coast. She noticed my action and pointed at my leg.

"They reported wounding one of you."

"They sure did," I said, the memory of my warped vision surfacing. "I've had worse, but it still hurts sometimes."

Agrippina continued to look at my leg for a moment before she settled back on her horse and jerked herself forward in a manner that suggested she was exceptionally frustrated with something.

"By the gods, Jacob, I do not wish for this feud between us to continue! There has already been too much death and pain. My feelings, as I explained them to you last night, still ring true, but I have thought long on you and those with you for many months, and I truthfully do wish to end hostilities between us."

"For just how many months have you been thinking about it?" I asked. "Because you seemed quite content to torture and murder me the last time we met."

She looked angry for a moment but then seemed to push it away, but not easily. "I am not without my faults; I more than anyone understand this character deficit. I am quick to anger and I am not averse to violence with permanent ramifications, but such actions have begun to haunt even me in recent..."

"Does Varus' death haunt you?" I snapped. "Because it haunts the hell out of me!"

"It does," she admitted quickly, "but I was not without reason in killing him. He had committed treason and was an enemy of the state. That, and I'd learned he had been able to manipulate the orb and was unwilling to use it in a way that aided me. Again, treason alone may have not been reason enough to have him killed, but…"

She trailed off and I understood.

It wasn't that I understood her reasoning, but that I understood that she'd simply had him killed because she was an angry, venomous bitch. But as our conversation moved to revolve around the orb, I couldn't understand why it hadn't affected her when she'd had two of them? It had affected both Claudius and Caligula, and was apparently affecting me, so why not her?

I cleared my head, hoping that I might find an answer to that question soon.

I turned back to her. "Treason?"

She didn't immediately answer, but when she turned to meet my eye, her face almost looked apologetic. "My Praetorians found the note he'd left telling you to come to Britain."

"So that's how you knew," I surmised stupidly, as if the answer hadn't been obvious all along.

"Yes."

"But how did you end up here?" I asked, gesturing out to the bare trees we rode between. It wasn't a thick forest, but it was still the densest one we'd encountered in days.

"My spy indicated your destination was the Isle of Mona, so we marched straight there, only to be told that we needed to continue venturing north…" she answered with a smile, playfully reaching out to grab my arm in a teasing gesture. "Were you not confused as to why the Druids were expecting you?"

I looked at my arm for a moment before plucking her hand off of it. "Wait, you told them I was coming?"

"I even gave them your name," she said, giggling like a little girl. "I am not without a sense of humor, Jacob."

"Yeah, like the Joker's," I murmured.

"Who?"

"A demented clown."

"A what?"

"Never mind," I said with a chuckle, unable to help myself. And here I thought the Druids back on Anglesey had possessed supernatural powers of precognition, divination, or any other kind of *-tion* associated with black magic. Instead, they'd simply been told we were coming ahead of time, by someone who'd even given them my name…

It was almost funny.

Except for the indistinct memory of something bad happening to them.

"Something wrong?" Agrippina asked, seemingly as observant as Helena was.

"Everything's wrong," I said quickly, the memory trying to knit itself back together in my mind. "Remember?"

"I do, but it is also good that you are willing to acknowledge such a truth. I must admit that I grievously misjudged you before."

"Yeah…" I whispered, memories of Helena dying in my arms, Bordeaux's skull being shattered to pieces, Titus crushed in half, Vincent's severed arm, the sight of Santino hanging from a cross, all memories I had because of nothing but Agrippina's *misjudgment*, "…no biggie."

"I had thought the orb to have completely warped your mind," Agrippina continued. "However, I am glad such a suspicion has been proven untrue. I believe you would have been most difficult to work with had I been right."

I supposed she had a point.

"So how much further?" I asked.

She held out a hand. "We are already here, Jacob Hunter. Behold."

I could tell from my peripheral vision that we had just reached the edge of a clearing, but I was suddenly too nervous to turn my head and look. In my mind, I envisioned a dozen different things that could be there in that clearing: something that looked like Stonehenge, some piece of long lost technology, an alien being, a time machine of some kind, and so many more. My imagination was running wild as I forced myself to turn toward the clearing and discover what I'd waited all these years to find.

I moved slowly, but eventually my eyes met the clearing and saw what it contained.

My eyebrows rose in complete amazement, shock, and surprise.

It was a simple cottage.

***

I looked at it skeptically before looking at Agrippina, back to the cottage, then back to Agrippina, but I wasn't the first to voice my disproval.

"That's it??" Santino asked angrily with a pointed arm as he came up beside me. "A dinky little house? That's what was so important?"

Agrippina simply smiled. "Come with me."

Reluctantly, we did as we were told and followed Agrippina off to the left. We rode for a few minutes around the perimeter of the cottage before she stopped abruptly and gestured back toward the structure.

"Behold," she said.

I turned more quickly this time, half expecting the cottage to have disappeared and be replaced with one of my earlier predictions, but nothing had changed. The cottage remained in its original, uninspiring, and mundane form.

I turned to my friends. "See anything special?"

Archer shook his head and Santino shrugged while Boudicca too seemed confused, but Vincent seemed to be looking at it intently.

"What?" I asked.

He shook his head. "I don't see anything out of the ordinary, but the architecture of the building doesn't seem contemporary with this time period."

I returned my attention to the cottage and noticed what Vincent was talking about. There was an oddly distinctive medieval look to the cottage, straight down to the roof that looked to be made from an entire field of thatched reeds or wheat stalks, making it look like it belonged in *Braveheart* rather than *Gladiator*.

I shrugged. "Familiar with British housing structures circa 40 A.D.?"

He glanced at me, at a loss. "Not really."

"Me neither."

Only Artie looked at the cottage with any kind of real interest, but even then, she didn't offer an opinion so I left her to think. Instead, I turned back to Agrippina.

"We've long ago established that you like to play games, Agrippina. How about we just skip to the end of this one."

Her smile returned once again, a beautiful and beaming one. "Do not concern yourself, Jacob, for this is not a game I am playing on you this time. It took us quite a while to understand as well. Come."

She started forward again, and I couldn't help but sigh and follow, the rest of my friends falling in behind me. Once again, our ride didn't last particularly long, but it ended when we reached the opposite end of the cottage from where we arrived. I didn't even bother to wait for Agrippina's "behold" as I looked back at the cottage, noticing her Praetorians standing opposite us on the other side of the building.

But again, nothing seemed to have changed, and the cottage looked exactly as it had before. Just a small, round building with a sloped, thatched roof. I glanced at my friends, but while Archer and Santino continued to look just as confused as I was, Vincent now stared at it as though he was trying to piece together some complex puzzle in his mind, while Artie's eyes were wide and clearly surprised at something.

"Artie?" I asked. "What is it?"

She raised a hand to cover her mouth and slowly turned to look at me. "It... Jacob, look!"

I did, but again didn't see anything out of the ordinary.

I turned back to Artie. "*What?*"

This time she gave me a frustrated look. "Look at the door!"

I did, and at the same time heard Vincent whisper, "My God..." and seconds later, Santino say, "Holy shit..."

Now I was growing frustrated that my usually keen ability to notice details had apparently eluded me. I was about to speak up and yell at Artie or Vincent or even Santino to just tell me what the fuck they'd seen, but then I noticed it.

The door.

There wasn't anything particularly interesting about the façade. It was boring and lacked any kind of detail or personal touch, but it wasn't the door itself that was of interest. What I found interesting was that even though we had completed half of a rotation around the structure, now standing opposite the position we'd originally occupied, the face of the door was still there.

Every single time we'd moved to look at the cottage, the door had moved with us.

"Huh," I breathed. "Well, that's a thing."

***

I looked at Santino. "John, ride back to the Praetorians and let me know if you see the door."

It seemed like a stretch of a concept, but it was the first thing I thought to do, and I wasn't sure anything could possibly seem like a stretch anymore.

"Yeah," he whispered, still amazed. "I think I'll go do that."

He kicked his horse and rode around the cottage, giving it an exceptionally wide berth as he returned to the Praetorians. When he arrived, he didn't even bother using his radio.

"There's a fucking door over here!" He yelled

I didn't reply but waved a hand indicating he should come back.

"Has it always been like that?" I asked Agrippina.

"Ever since we arrived at least," she confirmed. "It is quite amazing, is it not? Were you to walk around the cottage, never taking your eyes off of it, you would observe the door rotating around the structure with you, but your mind would hardly even notice the oddity of it, or even be aware of it."

"I'll take your word for it," I mumbled, unable to tear my eyes from the door. "Have you tried going inside?"

She responded by kicking her horse into motion again. "Come."

Although I was starting to feel anxious at how odd the cottage seemed to be, I couldn't help but follow, my curiosity bound to doom me sooner or later.

So why not now?

It was a short trip to the door, but I felt a strange sensation of nausea overwhelm me when we grew closer. There was a light mist surrounding the cottage, obscuring the snowy ground, but I couldn't detect any odd smells or see anything ghastly that would make my stomach roil like it had.

"Your stomach will settle momentarily," Agrippina reported, and I found myself thankful that, for once, it wasn't just me being affected by some outside influence.

When we arrived at the door, I couldn't help but notice all but one of Agrippina's Praetorians stayed firmly where they were. Whether they were scared, superstitious, or simply planning something treacherous, I didn't know, but for some reason I envied them. This place was, simply put, odd.

Agrippina pointed at the door. "As you can see, the door is made of simple wooden planks arranged vertically. There is no handle or other form of entrance device, nor does it seem to be latched from the inside, but I assure you none of my men have been able to pry it open."

"No shit?" Santino whispered, amazed.

"And there is this…" Agrippina said.

Taking a torch from the Praetorian next to her, she threw it on the roof, but I barely had time to register the action, let alone stop her, before it was sailing through the air.

"Why the hell would you…" but then the torch landed on the roof and did…

Nothing.

The seemingly flammable material that made up the cottage's roof didn't even spark. Not a reed or branch or whatever it was seemed to even notice. The torch simply sat atop the roof and burned itself but nothing else.

"That's impossible," Artie whispered.

"Yeah," Santino said, "but so is time travel."

We all turned to look at him nervously but no one said anything. My mind was blank at the moment and I found myself speechless, and my friends didn't seem much better off.

Finally, after minutes of silence, I turned to Agrippina. "Is it okay if I speak privately with my friends for a few minutes?"

She gestured toward them with a hand. "Please."

I shook my head at her politeness, still not quite believing this wasn't actually Agrippina's doppelganger – the good one. I reeled Felix around and faced my friends, but looked at Boudicca first.

"Do you mind?"

She simply nodded, clearly not happy about being left out of the conversation but perhaps understanding we couldn't completely trust Agrippina. I nodded my thanks and switched to English.

"So?" I asked.

"We've reached an all new low," Santino said helpfully.

"Won't get any argument from me," I mumbled.

"Who do you think is in there?" Archer asked. "Or what?"

I shrugged. "Could be anything. Or anyone. I mean, it could actually turn out to be some legitimate ancient Druid that still has some magical abilities that our modern world has simply forgotten. That or it could be…"

"My bet's on Yoda," Santino offered.

I rolled my eyes but I wasn't about to rule it out.

Archer just looked confused. "Who?"

Santino's eyes went wide and then sad. He placed a hand on Archer's shoulder consolingly. "There are times when I truly pity you, Archer. Truly pity you. Truly." He looked at Artie. "Did I mention truly?"

She chuckled. "You did."

I ignored them and thought, but then noticed only Vincent seemed aloof from the conversation, wrapped in his own thoughts. He'd been like that for too long, months really, that much I remembered while under the orb's influence, and I was now absolutely convinced he knew more than he was letting on.

"You have your suspicions, don't you, Vincent?" I asked.

It took a while before he finally nodded absently. "I do. Ever since Alexandria, learning the things that we've learned, seeing the things that we've seen, going to the places we've gone, it's like we've been acting out a story from a book I've already read before."

"So do you know who's in there?" I asked impatiently.

"I don't know anything, but as you said, I have my suspicions."

"And you still won't tell me?"

His smile grew wider. "Sorry, no spoilers."

Santino laughed hysterically and raised a hand in the air, which Vincent quickly high fived, something I never thought I'd ever live to see. He chuckled now himself, looking very much like an old man who was taking too much enjoyment out of knowing something his grandchildren simply could not understand, and thinking him crazy for it.

"I'm so confused," Archer chimed in.

I dropped my head, realizing none of them were going to be of any help. Whoever or whatever was in there didn't seem able to go anywhere without us knowing it, and the mystery wasn't going to solve itself, so I turned back to Agrippina. "So why bring me here?"

"Because I believe this to be the source of all your answers. Where Marcus Varus always intended for you to go. Where the Druids on Mona sent you. And where I believe your destiny lies."

"And what's it to you?" I finally asked.

She reeled back in annoyance before answering. "While I no longer feel the desire to destroy you, Jacob Hunter, the sooner I am rid of you the better. I wish you to go home just as much as you do."

"Mhmm," I hummed, still suspicious. She certainly was singing a different tune this time than when we'd last met. "I'm sure."

"Believe what you want," she said, "but I did bring you here, did I not?"

"I suppose you did," I answered, although that was hardly comforting. "So now what?"

"Go inside."

"Just like that?"

She glanced at the door. "I haven't any idea, but if my suspicions are correct, then going inside should be as easy as a... what was it you once said to me... a walk in the park for you."

I shook my head but hopped off Felix all the same. I looked at Agrippina as I walked past her toward the door. "I'll give you one thing. At least you pay attention to the things I say."

She smiled and lowered her head in acknowledgment of the compliment.

I looked away and thought to toss Felix's reins to Archer, but then another thought popped into my head. Sheepishly, I turned back to Agrippina and held out the reins for her to take. She looked at me knowingly, and accepted them

"Here," I said. "I... uh... want to thank you for loaning your horse to me. He's been the best."

Agrippina smiled and pulled Felix in close to her so that she could stroke his mane. "This one always had been my favorite, Jacob, but since you've 'owned' him longer than I by now, consider him a gift."

I was further surprised at her answer, but didn't want to risk changing her mind, so I glanced back at my friends and my sister one last time, each of them offering me gestures of reassurance. I nodded in thanks and turned back to the door.

It was close now, only an arm's span away, but I felt an unexpected energy around the door, like some kind of invisible barrier I had to force myself through. It didn't seem particularly resilient, but at the same time, it was like trying to push my way through Jell-O, and the more I pushed, the less progress I made.

It didn't hurt, but it seemed impenetrable.

I turned to look up at Agrippina, who had backed away considerably along with the rest of them.

"Good plan," I commented.

"I suspected it might not work," Agrippina said, "even for you, but there is one last thing I suggest trying before we abandon this place."

"What's that?"

She gestured to the Praetorian beside her, who then rode up to me and placed a round object in my hands. I accepted the gift but as soon as my hands made contact with it, I dropped it and recoiled away, shooting a venomous look at Agrippina.

"Why would you give that back to me!?" I demanded.

"A simple test," she said casually. "Tell me, Jacob, do you feel its draw now?"

My friends looked between us nervously, each of them knowing exactly what the orb could and probably would do to me if I reconnected with it, but Agrippina's question was an interesting one because I didn't actually feel anything. I glanced down at the object wrapped in cloth but felt nothing. Cautiously, I leaned down and picked it up, and carefully unwrapped the cloth from around it, finding that the orb seemed more inert than I'd ever seen it before.

"I don't actually," I finally replied, still looking at the orb.

"Then perhaps this structure is even more powerful than we suspected. And beneficial."

I looked back at her. "You gambled with something more powerful than even you know! I was *this* close to the edge last time!"

"It was an educated guess," she said without concern.

"Based on what?" I demanded, but she didn't answer.

Frustrated, I looked back at the orb and turned it over in my hands, noticing that it really did look like nothing more than a blue bowling ball lacking its telltale holes.

I whirled my head back toward the door, and with a surge of confidence, approached it once again, but my care was unwarranted. The door's defenses were down, and my hand moved towards its wooden planks without resistance until I felt the smooth contours and warmth of what felt like freshly cut wood.

I looked back at Agrippina. "Want to come?"

She shook her head. "I do not think I was meant to."

I craned my neck further to look at my friends. "And you guys?"

"Not on your fucking life," Santino muttered and Archer was nodding in agreement.

Boudicca remained behind them all, appearing upset, but perhaps understanding this wasn't her journey either.

I looked at Artie, and spoke to her in English. "You're just as connected to the orb as I am. This could be you just as easily as me."

"I... can't," she said, her voice quivering. "I'm terrified, Jacob. I'm terrified just being here. I can't believe how calm you are, but you always were the brave one. Stupidly brave, yeah, but still brave. I could never do what you do, and there's no way I can go in there now."

"*You're* afraid?" I jeered. "I thought you used to strap rockets to your ass and blast yourself into space all the time!"

Artie's eyes narrowed. "Space, Jacob? That's absurd."

I caught myself before I let my jaw hit the floor as I was once again reminded of how different Artie 2.0 was, and just little I actually knew about her even still. The idea of Artie not being an astronaut was almost too much to handle, but I did everything I could to pull myself back together.

"Are you sure you don't want to come?"

"Just be careful, Jacob," Artie said nervously.

I nodded and finally looked to Vincent. "Last chance, old man."

He smirked. "I'll silently echo Santino's sentiments on the matter, but I will at least give you this."

He tossed me a crumpled up piece of paper, which I caught in my left hand. I looked at it but didn't attempt to open it, looking back to Vincent instead.

"You'll know when to open it, Jacob," he said, his smile supportive and proud now.

"Will I be all right, Vincent?" I asked.

His smile vanished. "I think so. Just… remember Helena and your son, and you'll come back."

I nodded. Good enough for me.

I turned back to the door, and with a deep breath to steel my nerves, pushed it open and stepped inside.

***

The first sensation I felt was pain, the second nausea again.

I doubled over as my intestines seemed to knot themselves in a way that made them impossible to untangle, while my body attempted to expel them at the same time, but the only thing my stomach managed to lose was my breakfast. It came out unceremoniously and left a nasty taste in my mouth, but once it was gone, I felt immediately better. It was the second time I'd vomited in as many days, and both times had felt surprisingly wonderful.

Still doubled over, I gagged a couple of times and spit out whatever had gathered in my mouth to the ground. It was then that I noticed the floor wasn't exactly what I expected it to be. Instead of grass or snow, the floor was black, smooth, and slippery looking, so slick that it seemed a simple wrong step would send me sliding across the floor. I carefully tested this theory with a boot, but found that there was no risk of slippage at all.

"All right," I managed to say around gags and coughs. "Let's say I buy that…"

After one last cough, I found it within myself to straighten and look around. I tried to locate the door I'd literally just stepped through, but found it missing. Frantically, I looked everywhere for it, but all my search revealed was more darkness. In fact, I saw *literally* nothing, finally taking notice of the fact that it was completely dark in the cottage, not a single stray beam of light from outside penetrating within, obscuring even my hand in front of my face.

The peculiarity of my surroundings was making me nervous.

Oh, fuck it; it was terrifying me.

"Hello?" I called out, hoping my friends outside might hear me, but no reply came, only an echo that suggested this impossibly dark room was far larger than it seemed.

"Hello?" I repeated, but again received nothing in reply besides a series of echoes.

"God?" I called this time, recalling the last I'd thought I was dead. But again there was nothing. "Yahweh? Allah? Buddha? Thor, god of thunder! Zeus? Jove!! Oh, man, Venus maybe?"

Maybe I really was going crazy...

As I tallied off a few more divine names, I found the fear inside me shifting to utter annoyance. I was less concerned about the fact that this Druid was capable of playing such games with me, finding myself simply upset that he was instead. I knew I should have continued being scared at what I was experiencing, but I was startlingly calm.

Was I supposed to be impressed at his super dark hut?

Please...

But then there was a brilliant flash of light in front me, so bright that I threw up a hand to cover my eyes, but despite my precautions, I was blinded by its intensity, causing me to involuntarily take a few steps backward and fall on my ass. When my vision finally cleared, I saw that the light had formed into a cone, like a spotlight from a ceiling shining directly onto the floor beneath it. Centered within was a shadowy figure, little more than the silhouette of a bulbous, oddly man-shaped being. A mist billowed around him ominously and a series of colored lights flashed randomly and repeatedly.

The fear was returning again as I crawled backward, still unable to find the wall I'd expected three steps ago. I reached out behind me, blindly grasping for the door in a near state of panic, hoping beyond hope that this was just another one of the orbs dastardly side effects.

"Unfortunately that is not the case, Jacob Hunter," a booming voice said from no discernible location within the expansive space. "Your orb has no power here."

"Who are you??" I yelled, maybe a bit girlishly when my voice rose and cracked at the end, but I couldn't help it.

There was no answer, but then my eyes caught the shape of the silhouette again, and I saw that it was changing, not in form, but in detail. What was once just an amorphous man-blob was now becoming something far more familiar. Obviously human, he wore what seemed to be a long, puffy robe with only his head and hands visible. I couldn't tell what color his clothing was, or what his skin color was, or tell what he looked like in the slightest, but one detail was far more obvious than the rest: atop his head sat an object that was tall and came to a point at the tip, with what looked like a wide, floppy brim that encased it.

Thoughts were starting to form in my mind, coalescing themselves into ideas, but before they reveal anything to me, the light softened and I could see the man in vibrant detail now. He stepped forward to reveal an extremely old man with a bushy beard that fell to his navel. His robes were red, as was his hat, with the shapes of small half-moons woven into it the fabric.

I sat there dumbfounded, unable to form thoughts let alone words.

All except one.

"Dumbledore?"

The old man smiled not unkindly at me. It almost seemed warm as he leaned upon a long thick staff that I swore hadn't been there a second ago.

"A worthy guess," he said in a gravely but strong voice. "And a fine comparison if your mind holds the character true."

"Wh-what?" I asked through jittery teeth. "Who are the hell are you?"

The man sighed deeply and rested heavily on his staff. For a moment he seemed almost weak and brittle, but something told me he was anything but.

"I have gone by many names in my lifetime, Jacob Hunter, and will go by more in the years to come," he said, his voice suggesting he found this fact quite humorous, "but I suppose there is one still yet to come that you may be rather familiar with."

My eyes went wide as all of Wang and Vincent's cryptic words and fears about a lone British island in the middle of nowhere coalesced in my mind, along with an odd reference I now remembered my mom had made about Bardsey Island fifteen years ago.

The man smiled again. "You go it."

I gulped.

"Merlin."

XI
Answers

A Cottage in the Middle of Nowhere, Time/Space
January, 44 A.D.

My first instinct was to dig into my pocket and retrieve the note Vincent had left me. I straightened it and looked at the single word he'd written there:

Merlin.

I dropped the page and stared with wide eyes at the man before me.

He wore a bored expression with lazy eyes, like an old, laid up St. Bernard retired from a life of carrying rum around his neck, and he took a deep, impatient breath as the smoke and light show around him continued, a show that somehow seemed far less intimidating now.

When the man had first been revealed, the show had added mystique and awe, but now, as I looked at this man who claimed to be – of all people – *Merlin*, the smoke and light show simply looked like just that: a smoke and laser light show, like something out of a Kiss concert or lame haunted house or some damn thing.

As this realization set in, I found myself rising slowly to my feet, straightening carefully in case I had to react quickly to an attack. I analyzed the old man's face as I rose, studying his cold eyes, grizzled features, long beard, and his... reading glasses. At these I stared the longest, failing to understand where they'd come from. Last time I'd checked, glasses hadn't been invented yet. Not even close.

When I was able to finally focus on these details, the insanity of the situation became fully realized in my mind. I closed my eyes and looked again, the full picture before me clear now: Before me stood a man dressed like a wizard, with a low budget smoke machine and laser lights behind him, an appearance that reminded me of a professional wrestler making his entrance, just without his theme music.

With this thought came something else to the production.

Music.

It sounded like...

The Beach Boys?

Don't Worry Baby?

I glanced away from the man, and then back at him, the music playing around us. We locked eyes, and while mine narrowed in anger, his tightened in self-satisfied amusement. He cocked his head to the side, his smile lingering, and it was that look that caused me to rethink everything.

"No..." I muttered, shaking my head and waging a finger at him frantically. "No no no no, I don't think so. No. Nope, nuh-uh. Not buying it. No, sir." I pointed a finger over my shoulder. "I think I'm just going to go now."

I turned to leave and was surprised to see the cottage door right where I'd left it. I'd thought that it would have remained hidden but there it was. Surrounding it was nothing but a sea of darkness, an endless and invisible ocean of wall that stretched as far as my senses could discern. But through the cracks in the roughly created door I could see Agrippina and my friends beyond. They seemed to be waiting patiently, but they wouldn't have to wait much longer as I reached for the door.

"Are you really so willing to simply abandon all the answers you've sought for so long, Jacob?"

My fingers were inches from the door, but as the man finished his statement, my hand was already clenched into a fist. I looked down from the door to see it shaking on its own accord, but I lifted it to my forehead and squeezed my eyes shut, forcing the hand to calm down. I couldn't believe what was happening, but I also knew that if I wasn't actually hallucinating, that this was my only shot at answers.

My hand went still, and I gave those outside the door one last look, but then I turned to face... Merlin.

I looked at him, my expression betraying nothing and my eyes set determinedly, and noticed that the music had vanished. For Merlin's part, he didn't look the least bit impressed as he continued to lean heavily on his staff. My first instinct was to snap at him and demand answers immediately, but then the thought was gone, pushed from my mind by the rational logic I'd thought lost to me in recent months.

"You are most lucky that your mind is more durable that you might think," the man said.

I didn't take my eyes off of him. "Why don't we tackle that one right away then," I suggested. "What the hell do you mean?"

He shrugged. "All in good time, young man."

I really wanted to get mad, but something told me it wouldn't help.

"You are quite right," the man said.

"Stop that," I ordered.

"Stop what?"

I glared. "That!"

"What?"

"Reading my mind!" I snapped. "Or whatever the fuck it is you're doing."

The man nodded excitedly, his smile widening. "I am most excited for this, I must say, Jacob. This will be quite refreshing."

"What will be?" I asked, confused.

"In time," he said as he turned around, "but please, first come with me."

"Come with…" I started, taking a step toward him, "but we're in a tiny hut. Where are we go…" but before I was finished, Merlin stepped to the side to reveal another door opposite the one I'd entered. My feet took me closer on their own, as I couldn't believe my own eyes. There was no way the door had been there just seconds ago, but there it was. I looked behind me at the first door again, just for reassurance, but while it was still there, it seemed very far away.

"The choice is yours, Jacob," the old wizard said. "Take what time you need, but I would not tarry for long. I suspect you will be most excited for what is to come as well."

With that, the man stepped through his door, but I was unable to see anything beyond it before the door was shut, leaving me all alone in the pitch black room. All that was visible were the two doors.

I glanced between them again.

Like I really had a choice.

***

I approached the second door cautiously.

I felt naked without Penelope, but thoughts of my beloved lost rifle wouldn't help me now. The memory of how I'd destroyed her had come to me for the first time in a dream last night as I'd slept with Helena in my arms. It had been more like a nightmare than a dream, and I'd snapped awake with a jolt at the apex of the memory. Helena had slept through it, of course, and I hadn't had the heart to wake her to discuss it.

I looked at the orb in my hand now and frowned, hating it and everything it was capable of. A part of me still wanted to destroy it here and now, but since it had been the key to my entrance into this hut, I figured I may need it to leave as well. I placed it in the shoulder bag I had at my back and put it out of my mind.

The last thing I did before giving the second door another thought was to check the pistol at my thigh. My trusty old Sig P220 had seen me through plenty of tight spots over the years and I was glad to have it now. Although, there was an odd thought at the back of my mind that manifested itself from Santino's earlier prediction that I'd meet Yoda in here; about the wise Jedi master's warning to Luke that what he would find in that creepy-ass cave was only what he took with him. I never really understood what that meant as a kid, but as an adult, I'd realized how that one simple, poorly structured line of dialogue had been filled with a vast array of interesting philosophical and transcendent implications that for some reason resonated with me in this moment now.

But like Luke, I kept my weapons right where they were.

I looked up to inspect the door, noticing that it too was as odd as the man who had just stepped through it. Completely out of place in this ancient world, the door, which was actually two large double doors, had giant pane windows that dominated their upper halves, and had large, rectangular shaped door handles on each. Curious, I leaned even closer, again making note that while the doors looked like wood, they were in fact made out of another material, one that was quite adept at mimicking its appearance, if nothing else.

Plastic.

I snorted out a laugh at the sight. Not only was it impossible for these doors to exist in this time period, but I also felt like I'd seen them before, only I couldn't place from where. I had no idea what resided beyond them, but considering their appearance, I suspected the worst. Or the best. I wasn't sure yet.

Only one way to find out though.

I grunted reluctantly and once again debated whether to turn back or not, but instead of deciding I let my actions do my thinking for me. I reached out with both hands and pushed both doors wide open, and stepped through like a cowboy entering a saloon.

If only I felt as confident as the swagger suggested.

***

Stopping just past the threshold, I felt my heart drop into my stomach.

Not because I was feeling the orb's draw or the crushing pressure from all that I was responsible for, but because I had just stepped into a room I'd stepped into a thousand times before. It was a space more familiar to me than anywhere in Ancient Rome, but I hated it just the same.

The space was large and open, with a series of low walls spread throughout like a basic maze. To my right were a series of low couches and in front of me, a small podium, but the most prominent feature here were the low walls that created sectionalized rooms with booths, tables, and chairs arranged to seat people in an efficient manner. Narrow pathways connected these small sections, but only one of the four contained a large, U-shaped bar that dominated its center along with an innumerable number of bottles filled with alcohol.

Finally, scattered along the walls, ceiling, and pretty much everywhere else where stupid knickknacks could be crammed, were decorations and items that gave the entire room a distinct Western/Cowboy theme. Large pictures of desert locations or Native Americans, statues of desert creatures, and many other stupid things were everywhere, and a familiar resentment and sense of loathing swelled in my heart.

"Holy shit," I said, still not believing my eyes. "Is this my…"

"Do not say the name, Jacob," a voice that was becoming familiar said from beside me.

I turned to see the wizard Merlin standing there, still leaning heavily on his staff.

"Why not?" I asked.

He turned to meet my eye. "Don't give them the free advertisement."

I blinked twice. "What?"

Merlin smiled. "A jest, Jacob, little more."

"Yeah," I said. "Right. Sure."

I looked out over the restaurant again, memories I'd long since tried to forget flooding back into my mind as I stood there. The day after I'd turned sixteen, I'd applied for a part-time job at this place, after one of my best buddies had already been employed here for a few months. The two of us had thought it would be so much fun spending our time working part time as bus boys.

Boy had we been wrong.

I'd spent two years here in an oppressive and tyrannical environment, with dictatorial managers and bitchy waitresses who hated the two of us because even though we screwed around and had fun together, we still managed to be the two best damn bus boys in the joint. It was a thankless job, and the two of us had hated it within months, but had stayed on until we went off to college, probably because we thought we were sticking it to them somehow. I suppose the joke had been on us, however, because we'd actually done the restaurant a huge favor.

One of the managers even pleaded for us to stay when we had later quit together.

I honestly hadn't thought much about this place in recent time, even before arriving in Ancient Rome. A decade had elapsed between when I'd quit and when I'd ended up here, and between going to college, spending some time in grad school, and fighting in a bloody and devastating world war, I'd pretty much forgotten everything about my life from those happier years. Kids never really understood just how good life was until they finally grew up, and my friend and I had thought the two of us so damn clever, but we'd grown jaded over our silly, part time jobs, never really appreciating the simplicity of it all.

What I would give to go back to those times again.

"So am I dead?" I asked. "Because if I am, please tell me this isn't Heaven."

"Far from it," Merlin answered.

"Am I hallucinating?

"Not in the slightest."

"Dreaming?"

"Not quite."

"Being manipulated?"

"Aren't you always, Jacob?"

I coughed out a laugh, and raised a hand to encompass the restaurant before me.

"Good God, I spent so much time here in high school," I said, turning to offer Merlin a small smile, "but not as much as I was supposed to, you know. I was always trying to get out of work whenever I could."

Merlin nodded. "The youth often shirk their responsibilities. Quite normal, I think."

I returned the nod appreciatively, turning back to the restaurant. "In retrospect, I think I loved working here. It had helped that my best friend worked here too, but honestly, the managers only rarely put us on the schedule at the same time together. They always tried to keep us apart so that they kept their two best bussers spread out as much as possible. We despised them for it, and did everything we could to get back at them."

"In what ways?"

I shrugged. "Simple things, really. Only filling the peanut bins half full at the end of the night, loading the bathroom soap dispensers backward, stealing unused silverware off tables and then using them for our end of the night quota. You see, everyone always had to roll thirty sets of silverware before they could go home after their shift: a knife and fork within a cloth napkin. We fucking hated doing it, so we'd just take unused ones off tables as we bussed them, hide them on top of a cabinet in the back, and present them before going home. We were quite clever, you know."

"Apparently," Merlin said with a chuckle.

I laughed at the memory, unable to help myself, but when I looked out over the restaurant again, confusion returned. Something was out of place.

"What is it?" Merlin asked.

"It's just that I didn't get to see this place so empty very often," I said. "I rarely worked opening and closing shifts so I always saw this place filled with…"

And then, just like that, there were people everywhere. Patrons and staff both, and not just present, but alive and going about their lives or business like this was actual reality. I looked to the hostess station and...

I recoiled backward, my heart skipping a beat, almost panicking at what I saw.

Standing there was a teenage girl, no more than sixteen or seventeen years old. She had dark hair pulled back into a pair of pig tails, with dark freckles speckling her face. She had light colored skin and round, puffy cheeks. She wasn't overweight, but her face had always been a bit round, which I'd always thought made her look exceptionally cute.

I risked taking a step toward her, and glanced at her nametag, but I didn't need to.

"Suzie-Lu?" I asked, looking at the young girl that stood barely five feet tall.

She giggled and looked up at me with bashful eyes. "How did you know my friends call me that?" She asked with a sweet, high pitched voice that brought a grin to my lips. "It just says Susan on my name tag."

"Uh... just a good guess, I suppose."

"Yeah, I guess!" She said excitedly. She looked up at me in a way that made me somewhat uncomfortable, but performed her job flawlessly. "So how many are in your party?"

"Umm..."

But Merlin stepped up and answered for me. "Two, miss, but I think we'll sit at the bar."

"Oh, okay," she said, perhaps sadly, but then she perked up. "Well help yourself. Our drink specials are on the wall beneath the TVs."

"Thank you," Merlin answered as he turned back to me. "Come, Jacob. I hear the cinnamon butter here is amazing."

I was still staring at little Suzie-Lu, the girl I'd lost my virginity to sometime around what seemed to be now, and wondered why she'd looked at me like that when she was supposed to be teenage-me's girlfriend. I didn't have long to ponder as Merlin grasped my arm with a strong hand that belied his age, and I stumbled after him, Suzie-Lu watching us go.

Reluctantly, I tore my eyes off of her to see where I was going, not that I needed eyes to know my way around.

I could walk around this restaurant blindfolded.

I glanced to my right and noticed the cook's station behind a display case of meats. Those faces were certainly familiar, but I hadn't interacted with them much, so I couldn't place their names. They'd been druggies and real losers and they hadn't thought much better of me either.

We took the first left and then a quick right and found ourselves in the bar section of the restaurant. As we walked, I caught sight of another hostess, a six foot tall stunning blond, who in some ways now reminded me of Agrippina, and I almost looked away out of sheer motor reflex. I forget her name, but she'd been eighteen when I'd started at sixteen, and had been an aspiring model, and damn, she'd had the potential. Hell, even now I thought she had potential. The two of us had flirted occasionally, but I hadn't been much of a playboy back then – not that I'd ever been much of one – and had often been too nervous to even look at her.

I hadn't thought myself a particularly desirable catch as a teenager. I was young, had acne, and wasn't nearly as fit as I was today. In fact, Suzie-Lu had often referred to me as "pleasantly plump." I had been tall however, like the blond hostess, and I think she'd simply been jealous that I'd fallen for little, cute Suzie-Lu, instead of a "Victoria's Secret Angel to be," as she'd certainly seemed.

I'd fallen out of touch with the blond after I'd quit, much like everybody from this restaurant, and had no idea what she had been up to prior to my arrival in Rome, but I'd never seen her on any of the Victoria's Secret catwalk shows I'd always tried to catch back home on TV. I always looked out for her, just in case, hoping to *never* see her because I would have killed myself for missing the chance to date someone who would later become a Victoria's Secret Angel.

So as Merlin and I walked toward the bar, I kept my eyes off of her, but surreptitiously sneaked a glance only to find her already looking at me as well. I smiled awkwardly and she winked back. Shyness set in again, and I quickly turned away.

I was saved by the bar.

I took a seat atop a tall stool and leaned my elbows upon the wooden bar, burying my face into my hands as I tried to think of a rational explanation for all of this. It was all too familiar, but this shit was impossible to believe.

I looked to Merlin accusingly, who stood by an empty stool. "It was you."

He smiled smugly at me. "It was I, what?"

"Oh, fuck you," I said. "I know you already know. I know it was you who sent Boudicca the vision to help me, and it was you who sent that vision of Agrippina a few days ago."

He shrugged. "Guilty. I wanted to prepare you as well as I could."

"And the Druids back on Angle..."

"Friends of mine," Merlin said quickly as he jumped in place impatiently, glancing over his shoulders frantically. "Very nice people, but just people. I asked them a few years ago to send you looking for me when you arrived.

"But how could you even..."

Merlin interrupted me, asking, "Where's the bathroom, Jacob?"

I pointed immediately over his shoulder and toward a back corner of the restaurant.

"Thanks!" He said, and took off.

I looked at him with wide eyes. "Wait you can't just leave me here! Where the hell are you going?"

He paused to look at me but pointed in the other direction. "Little boy's room. Let's hope your friend put the soap in the right way this time."

I looked around the restaurant, hoping to see him. "He's here??"

"Try to calm down, Jacob. Relax. Order yourself a drink."

He rushed off toward the bathroom, looking completely out of place in his disproportionately large red robes and pointy hat. I stared at him, still unable to understand any of this. Who was this guy? Really? Was he the elder sage character in the "hero's quest" story arc, the one put in the story for no other reason than to provide integral plot details and exposition about something too confusing for the writer to explain naturally?

What a lame plot device.

Or was he really just the Druid I was looking for all along?

I was never going to get away with this when…

"What can I get you, handsome?"

Like everything else in this restaurant, the voice was very familiar. Slowly, I lowered my hands and turned to the bartender, but when I saw her, my jaw nearly hit the floor.

"*Foxtrot Alpha…*" I whispered under my breath, struggling to say even that.

While the Victoria's Secret Angel may have been the hottest girl at the restaurant, Foxtrot Alpha was easily the most desirable. Probably in her late twenties when my friend and I started working here, she had been gorgeous, with dark, curly brown hair and the biggest brown eyes I had ever seen, along with the largest pair of breasts our teenage eyes had ever seen as well.

My friend and I had worked out a system of referring to all the hotties that worked here with the code name "foxtrot" and then designated them in order from hottest to least hot using the Greek alphabet. It was a thing only the mind of a sixteen year old boy could spawn, but we'd been bored, pretentious, and a bit chauvinistic, so what else were we going to do? I wasn't even sure I'd known Foxtrot Alpha's name back when I'd worked here, but it didn't matter, because then and forever, she would always be Foxtrot Alpha to me.

I looked into her dark, sultry eyes but couldn't help but glance down at her purposefully low cut shirt, confirming that her breasts were just as voluptuous as I'd always remembered. When I glanced back up, she didn't seem displeased that I'd just checked her out, just impatient that I was wasting her time.

"Let's just keep those eyes up here," she said, leveling her own eyes at me.

I continued to stare, managing only to whisper again, "Foxtrot Alpha…"

She shook her head, confused. "I'm not familiar with that drink. What's in it?"

"It… you…" Finally, I shook my head and tried to focus, which wasn't nearly as easy as it should have been. All of this really was just too much. "I'm sorry. It's just that I haven't been here in a very long time, so coming back has been kind of surreal. I used to work here actually."

"Really?" She asked skeptically. "Are you sure? I've worked here since the place opened a few years back and I'm pretty sure I'd recognize a good looking guy like you."

"I..." but I couldn't think of anything else to say. Deciding to go with another line of thought, I pulled myself up and leaned heavily on my arms that rested on the bar. "Look, how about a Long Island Iced Tea, but could you do me a favor and put triple of everything in there?"

"Triple?" She said in surprise. "I'm not sure I'm allowed to do that..."

"I swear I'm not a crazy drunk or anything," I pleaded. "It's just been a rough few months and I could really, *really*, use a drink."

She looked deeply into my eyes in a way she'd never done when I was a kid.

"Well," she said, "you seem harmless enough... and I'm *sure* you're a good tipper. Am I right?"

She asked her last question in a way that suggested there was only one answer.

"Right," I said with a smile.

She smacked the bar excitedly and got to work.

I sat back on my stool, my smile still in place, and drank in the moment, ignoring how much I hated the country music blaring from the speakers in the background. Based on the song that was playing right now, I knew immediately what the next two would be, starting with *The Devil went Down to Georgia*. They played on a loop, and it had nearly driven me insane back in the day, but now I found it somehow relaxing. I glanced at the TV and saw football was on, and I grew even happier.

That drink couldn't come soon enough.

A moment later I heard a toilet flush and I glanced at the bathroom. An elderly man with a short, neat white beard, wearing obnoxiously short cargo shorts, a Hawaiian shirt, and knee high white socks came sauntering from the bathroom like a man proud of his latest achievement in there, but it wasn't Merlin so I turned back to the TV. Seconds later, I was joined at the bar by someone, which seemed odd since it was only a quarter full and most patrons sat on their own.

I turned and saw the old man who'd emerged from the bathroom moments ago. I analyzed him, looking at him from head to toe. He looked every bit the tourist, complete with everything from his casual summer apparel to the fanny pack he wore around his waist. He looked nothing like the old wizard who'd indicated he'd needed to use the bathroom a few minutes ago.

"Merlin?" I asked, barely believing my own guess.

"What?" He asked back, but not because he'd misheard me.

I sighed and turned back to the TV. "Feel better?"

The old man who looked like pretty much anyone's goofy grandfather simply nodded. "I do actually, thanks for asking."

"Soap dispense all right?"

"You know what?" He asked, turning back to the bathroom. "It did. Perhaps your friend isn't working tonight after all."

"What day is it?"

"What day do you want it to be?"

"Monday."

"Then Monday it is."

"Then he's not working today."

"Well that's a relief," Merlin said thankfully. "I may have splashed myself a little."

I dropped my head and shook it. "Let's drop the shit here, Merlin, or whoever-the-fuck-you-are. I've bought into this little fantasy of yours long enough. I don't have time for this. I want answers. Now."

Before answering, he removed his glasses and wiped them with the edge of his shirt.

"This isn't my fantasy, Jacob," he answered. "It's yours."

"Yeah I got that," I said, glancing back to the hostess station and noticing little Suzie-Lu and Victoria's Secret talking to each other and giggling in my direction. I smiled, finding myself growing more confident, and waved, but they spun away in embarrassment, but then their giggles continued. I looked back at Merlin. "That said, I've got to admit that I'm enjoying this quite a bit. Quite. A. Bit."

"I thought you would," Merlin remarked, "but we've only just gotten started."

"What do you mea..." but I was interrupted by Foxtrot Alpha placing my drink before me.

"There you go, handsome," she said with a wink. "Try not to drink it too quickly."

I smiled thankfully and lifted the large glass off the coaster, placed the straw in my mouth, and drank deeply. My mouth was awash with flavor, everything from the tea to the sheer quantity of alcohol that clearly made up the majority of the drink. I pulled away from the straw and coughed violently as the alcohol burned its way down.

I caught Foxtrot Alpha's eye on the other side of the bar as she entered another drink order into the computer.

"I told you to go slow," she said with a wry smile.

I looked back down at the drink and gave it a wide eyed and impressed look.

"Wow!" I exclaimed. "Now that's a drink!"

"I'm glad you enjoy it, Jacob," Merlin commented.

I ignored him and took another long pull, ready for the alcohol this time, and felt the burn go down far more easily. I sat back contentedly, and then looked over at Merlin who leaned atop the bar from his seated position, looking back at me over his shoulder.

"You don't understand, Merlin," I exclaimed. "I haven't had anything even remotely like this in half a decade! All I've had to drink around here is this nasty wine the Romans have! I'd almost forgotten what something like this could taste like!"

"Oh, I understand, Jacob. Believe me."

I ignored him and leaned in for another gulp, and had just about drained half the drink when I noticed something beneath it. Curious, I lifted the large mug off the coaster and peered at it. Written there was a phone number, followed by the name: Tiffany. I glanced up and caught the lovely bartender's eyes, and she answered my unspoken question by lifting her hand to her head in the ubiquitous "call me" gesture.

I laughed and turned back to Merlin. "Well, now I know I'm dreaming."

"Bartenders don't usually give out their numbers, do they?" He answered for me.

"Not usually," I answered. "Believe me. At least not on an asshole's first visit."

"Maybe she recognizes you in some way," Merlin suggested. "Sees something in you that she appreciates or likes. Correct me if

I'm wrong, but despite those roaming eyes you've always had, didn't you always go out of your way to help her when she needed it?"

I thought about his statement, having honestly forgotten. But he was right. I had always been ready and willing to help her when she'd needed it, and not in a creepy kind of way. She'd always been very nice to me, one of the few people here who had been, and I'd always been very willing to lend her a hand because of it. Now that I thought about, she'd almost been something of a... friend.

Merlin nodded. "It's one of your more admirable qualities, Jacob. One of your many admirable qualities, in fact. Always willing to help those in need. It's a shame then that you have so many others that are not quite as venerable."

I turned an angry look on him, intending to yell at him for saying such a thing, but then thought better of it.

"A good decision, Jacob."

"Stop that," I snapped, but then curiosity set in. "How are you doing that anyway?"

"I'm a wizard, remember? I can do lots of cool things."

I was about to yell at him for real this time, but then little Suzie-Lu walked up to me with a basket of freshly baked rolls and a container of cinnamon butter. She set it down and Merlin eagerly dived into them, but I was distracted by her lingering stare.

I returned her look evenly. "Something wrong?"

She snapped out of her daze and shook her head. "No, of course not, it's just that you look super familiar. Do you have a younger brother or something?"

"No," I answered. "I do have a younger sister though."

"Are you sure?" She asked skeptically.

"Yeah," I replied. "Pretty sure."

She worked her mouth from side to side in confusion, but then turned away abruptly and rushed back to the hostess station. I turned back to Merlin, feeling suddenly sad for Suzie-Lu. I tried to remember what had driven us apart all those years ago, but like much from that time of my life, I couldn't remember.

As my stool swiveled around, I discovered that the older man had a spoon filled with cinnamon butter in one hand and a roll in the other, his mouth chewing vigorously. When he swallowed, he bit into the fresh roll and stuck the spoon of butter into his mouth. It was clean when he removed it.

I cringed. "You're supposed to spread the butter on the roll and *then* eat it."

He shook his head vigorously. "Too inefficient. This is much better. *So* much better."

I stared at him, deadpanned. "Seriously, just who the fuck are you?"

He stopped chewing at the question and breathed a deep sigh, glancing absentmindedly at the coolers filled with beer behind the bar. I followed his eye, the alcohol from my drink settling in, and I knew immediately what I had to order next, but I was distracted by the sound of Merlin struggling to gulp down what was left of his roll. I watched as he spooned another glop of the cinnamon butter into his mouth and pick up another roll, but before he bit into it, he turned to me and spoke with his mouth full of butter.

"I'd order another drink if I were you," he suggested. "Because we're going to be here for a while. Kick back, relax, and block off some time. This chapter's going to be a long one..."

***

I'd taken his suggestion to heart and ordered a beer. Not just any beer, however, but a beer that I knew could never possibly exist in this restaurant. It was a beer brewed by Augustinian monks in a small brewery/monastery in Austria. I'd studied abroad in Italy during my junior year in college, but my friends and I had taken more than a few trips up into the rest of Europe. One in particular had found us finding this small little brewery in the middle of nowhere outside Salzburg. The monks had invited us in politely, and had offered us their finest of brews.

And it had been the most amazing beer ever.

There was no way to truly describe it, except as perfect. It had the ideal blend of hops, fruitiness, and spices, and my friends and I had drank gallons of it. The saddest part of that entire semester had been the moment we'd left with the knowledge that the monks didn't export their beer.

Anywhere.

But when I'd placed my beer order just now, asking for a tall one from the Augustinian Brewery – if that's even what it was called – Foxtrot Alpha had simply smiled, moved over to the tap, and poured me a beer. She handed it to me, brushing her hand against mine as she handed it off, and I smiled at her, but it wasn't until the beer touched my lips that I decided that I was never leaving this fantasy world.

Never ever.

"Unfortunately, Jacob, that is not possible."

I pulled the beer away from my lips, slopping a bit at the abrupt motion, but took another long pull before setting it down carefully. I looked at it longingly, but then snapped my head around to look at Merlin.

"Answers," I ordered. "Now."

Glumly, Merlin looked down at the basket of rolls before him – his third – and reluctantly pushed it away. He wiped his mouth and neat beard with a napkin before shifting in his seat to face me. He gripped his hands together and dropped them into his lap, causing me to notice how his cargo shorts rode *way* too high up his thighs when he sat down.

"What do you want to know?" He asked.

"Do you know about the orb?"

"Of course."

"Is it a time machine?"

"If such a moniker makes you more able to understand what it does, then yes."

I set my shoulders and pressed on, each of his answers building my confidence and alleviating years of tension.

"Is it yours?"

"It was mine once, yes."

"Are you a Druid?"

He smiled. "No… but also yes."

"Explain."

"Not right now, Jacob. Continue with your questions first."

"Did you give it to Remus?"

"Ah, well, that answer would also be best left for later."

I rolled my eyes angrily, but I couldn't stop now. "The first time I used it, when I connected with Varus' orb and it brought me to Ancient Rome, was it merely an accident or was there some kind of... greater power at work?"

Merlin smiled and spread his hands wide. "A happy accident, Jacob. I, at least, am enjoying this immensely."

"Was the way we used it the right way?"

"What defines, 'right,' Jacob? You used it and it did something. What more is needed?"

"But did we fuck it up or something? Did we break it? Did we do something wrong?"

"No to the first two questions, but your last seems like a matter of perspective to me."

I ground my teeth, steeling myself for my final three questions.

"Is it driving me insane?"

The answer came immediately. "Yes."

I grimaced.

"How?" I asked, fearing the answer.

"You've figured that one out quite easily on your own, Jacob," Merlin answered. "Your visions were merely the first step in your addiction as the orb took control. In your lowest moments, when you were at your most tired or vulnerable, it infiltrated your subconscious until it had complete control of your mind. It then worked as the drug you so aptly compared it to, as it offered you alleviations to cravings it had provided in the form of emotions, and you learned to associate those negative emotions and dark choices with pleasure and happiness. This association may have lasted for quite a while, but I assure you that by the time the orb was finished with you, it would have twisted your mind into something beastly and evil. Quite fascinating, is it not?"

I stared at him, thinking of a new question. "Why give me such a straightforward, if melodramatic, answer to *that* question, but none of the others?"

He shrugged. "You asked a straight forward question, so I gave you a straight forward answer."

I gritted my teeth again, but pushed on and forced my final, two-part question from my mouth, dreading the answer.

"Can we use the orb to go home? Our real home?"

Merlin didn't answer immediately. He looked at me with a hint of sadness in his eyes.

Finally, he answered. "No."

My heart sunk again and I closed my eyes. I dropped my head and felt like falling asleep, perhaps more because of the alcohol than his answer, but I forced myself to look up.

When I opened my eyes, the scene before me had changed.

No longer was the restaurant a bustling eatery with patrons and staff eating or working. Instead, it was completely empty. I looked over the bar, but even Foxtrot Alpha had disappeared. I glanced down, looking for the coaster with her number on it, but it too was gone. The number written there eluded me as well, but her name, Tiffany, remained.

I looked back at Merlin, but his head was turned to the right, looking off toward another section of tables near the middle of the restaurant. I followed his look and noticed a young man moving through the central aisle, a wide push broom in his hands as he swept a sea of peanut shells from the ground.

I stood and moved over to him, recognizing him immediately.

It was me at sixteen, zits and extra body fat and all. Although not quite as tall as I was now, his facial features were all the same, only softened by youth, inexperience, and too much fast food. I'd always been a bit of a baby face, even throughout my early college years, and it hadn't been until I started working out and getting serious about my image that I'd morphed into the man I was today – only minus the last five years of stress and scars, I suppose.

He didn't even notice me as I walked up to him, but I could see the anger in his eyes and subtle movement of his lips as he muttered to himself. I couldn't exactly make out what he was saying, but I was sure it had something to do with being put on to close the restaurant when I wasn't normally scheduled to do that.

"You were always such an angry child, Jacob," Merlin said from behind me. "It wasn't all your fault, and I think you grew out of it quite nicely as you aged, but ever since, you have carried with you a jaded sense of mistrust, anger, and superiority because of it. Most unfortunate."

I reached out to touch my younger self's shoulder, but even though I made contact with him, he didn't flinch. I squeezed his arm reassuringly but something told me he had no idea I was there at all.

"Who are you?" I asked Merlin again as I stared at my younger self. "Tell me."

"You already know, Jacob."

I whirled away from my younger self, but when I turned, I found the scene had once again changed. Instead of the restaurant, I was in my old home, the one I'd spent my entire teenage life in and the one I'd always come back to during college vacations and shore leaves. My initial reaction was a bout of joy at seeing it exactly the way I remembered it, but then a sense of homesickness set in, followed by anger at Merlin if he did what I thought he was about to do.

"Don't you show her!" I yelled at him. "Don't you dare! I don't want to see her. If you do, I'll…"

"You'll what, Jacob? Shoot me?"

On instinct, I reached for my pistol, but it wasn't there. In fact, I wasn't clothed in my combat fatigues at all, but in a pair of professional looking khakis and a colored dress shirt with a tie around my neck. It was exactly what I'd worn nearly every day during high school.

"I know the pain you feel surrounding your mother and her death, Jacob," Merlin said, snapping my attention back to him. "And I would never do anything to purposefully hurt you, so I assure you, the home is empty and will remain that way if you choose. Now, please, sit down."

He gestured to a large and uncomfortable looking chair, one I also recognized.

My parents had never been wealthy, but they'd always had some money, and my mom had been as thrifty as any good mom could be, but she'd had a taste for the fancy, elegant life as well. She'd always been the cultured one in our family, and always expecting nice things, so she'd outfitted our small den to look like an eighteenth century British study or library. It had always seemed sophisticated and quaint, and while everything looked authentic enough, I knew that she'd only managed it by scouring a thousand garage sales and thrift stores, making do with what she could find.

Cautiously, I walked over to the large, high-backed sage green chair, a duplicate of the one Merlin now sat in. The fireplace across from us was ablaze, and the room was dark besides the light emanating from the flames. Outside the window I could see the sun was still out, but the shades were drawn, giving the room a cozy and decadent appearance, just the way mom had always liked it.

I sat down and glanced at the chess board that sat between the two chairs. It was one of the fancier and more expensive items my mom had splurged on, and I had to admit that it had always been a stunning centerpiece. Elaborate and handcrafted, it looked more artistic than functional, but I knew that it was. At least once a week after school, my mom and I would sit down and play a match atop this very table. While the time between matches had lengthened as I'd grown older, my mom and I had always tried to fit in at least one match every time I came home.

And she had kicked my ass at it nearly every time.

I studied the pieces, finding myself unsurprised that they were the same ones we had always played with. In lieu of a fancy, traditional chess set with your generic pawns, knights, castles, and the rest, my mother had allowed me to purchase a rather unique set of pieces when I was eleven. It consisted of mythological figures from a number of time periods and cultures, and instead of the pieces being black or white as a traditional chess set might be, these armies were distinguished by the colors red and blue.

I smiled as I looked at my loyal blue army, its pieces completely different from its opposing color's equivalent since it was a Monsters versus. Heroes set. I picked up one of my pawns, represented in this set by a ferocious naga – some kind of aggressive sea monster that carried a trident and had long, sharp teeth and appeared much like a serpent. My mother's equivalent red pawns were a line of Greek warriors, who she always liked to think of as a squad of Myrmidons, the army Achilles had brought with him to Troy.

I set my pawn down when something else caught my eye. I reached over and picked up my mother's bishop. It was a wizard who appeared much like Merlin had upon our first meeting, right down to his red colored robes with small half-moons stitched into them.

I held it up to him and smirked.

"Friend of yours?" I asked.

He returned the smile warmly, and gestured at the piece from his seated position with his elbow still on the armrest. "I had hoped such an appearance would have been of some comfort to you."

"Well, I guess you succeeded," I said as I put the wizard back in its appropriate spot.

I looked back at my army and nodded appreciatively, crossing my arms and tightening them around my stomach comfortingly. "God, I used to love this chess set," I said. "I always thought it was so cool. Monster versus heroes! It can't get much better than that, right?"

Merlin nodded. "To a young, curious mind, I can think of little else that could."

I picked up my king, easily the largest piece on the board, represented by an intimidating, fire breathing dragon. I held it in my hand and smiled, remembering my childhood self thinking it had been the most badass thing ever. I glanced at my mother's king, represented by none other than, and appropriately so, King Arthur himself.

"I know it's hard to believe," I said, rotating the dragon in front of my eyes carefully, "but this dragon got thrown against the wall quite often, and not because I was testing if he could fly or not. Your boy over there was a good king."

Merlin nodded slowly and reached out to pick up King Arthur. "He will be."

I rocked backward in surprise. "Wait... what?"

"He will be," Merlin repeated, still staring at the piece.

"How can you possibly know that?" I asked, but then another thought set in. "Wait a second, before you answer that, are you actually sitting her confirming to me that Arthur was a real guy?"

"Not yet, but he will be."

"How can you possibly know that?" I asked again, having forgotten I'd already asked the same thing.

Merlin sighed and looked at me patiently. He leaned back into his chair, still holding the piece in his lap. He sat there for a few moments, studying me, looking ridiculous in his old man's tourist outfit, but finally he placed Arthur down on the edge of the table.

"I can read your mind and conjure memories from it," he said, "and yet it surprises you that I can see the future?"

I looked at him, amazement finally settling in over the capabilities this man possessed, as well as their ramifications.

"If you can see the future, why can't you help me?"

He shook his head. "The only future I can see is my own, and sadly, that does not include you past today."

I sat there unimpressed. "Seems kind of limiting... aren't you supposed to be a wizard? What kind of magic is that?"

Merlin rolled his eyes and leaned in. "I know you've seen, read, and played enough fantasy tales to know that magic can, in fact, be very limiting."

"So are you confirming that the orb is magic based then?"

"I didn't say that."

"So its technology based then."

"I also know that you've seen, read, and played enough *science fiction* stories to know exactly what I'm getting at."

"Yeah, yeah," I said, indeed knowing pretty much exactly what he was getting at. "Arthur C. Clarke's Third Law: any sufficiently advanced technology is indistinguishable from magic. Blah blah blah. Give me a break..."

Merlin leaned back and sighed in contention with his eyes closed, waving a hand across his face. "A beautiful quote. Poetry to my ears, in fact. You have no idea how long it's been since I've heard someone speak with such clarity."

I was about to counter my own argument by stating that such a sentiment only applied to primitive beings with no knowledge of science or technology, and that it didn't apply to a smart guy like me from a time period with the very same science fiction author who coined that very quote, but then something in Merlin's wording caused me to stop and rethink what I was going to say. I waited for Merlin to interrupt me like he always seemed to do, but he simple sat there, gazing at me.

"Let's take a step back here," I said. "If you really are Merlin, *the* Merlin from the Arthurian legend everyone knows about back home, then there are actually a few things I know about you as well."

Merlin nodded. "Go on."

I wondered if there was even a point in saying what I was about to say, suspecting that he already knew what it was long before I even thought to say it, but I continued anyway.

"My Arthurian knowledge isn't super deep," I admitted. "My mother always had a big, old, English edition of *Le Morte d'Arthur* sitting on her booksh…"

I stopped myself, snapping my head to the shelf in question.

And there it was.

I stood and walked over to the floor to ceiling bookshelves that encased the entire wall leaving only the fireplace dead center as a spacer. Reaching up, I retrieved the large black tome entitled, *The Death of King Arthur*.

I sat back down.

"I never read it," I said with a hint of regret. "Too intimidating. And for some reason, I never really got into the lore because of it, even though it was one of my mother's favorites. I only really know a few tidbits that the general public gets wrong, mostly because she loved to lecture me on it endlessly; like when people assume the sword in the stone was actually Excalibur, when really they were two different swords and Arthur only later gets Excalibur later from the Lady in the Lake."

"It's actually Lady *of* the Lake," Merlin corrected.

I glanced up at him. "Another friend of yours?"

He nodded. "Nice lady."

I returned my attention to the book, trying not to think about that. "I know only a few other things, but I do know two in particular about you, oh great and powerful Merlin. First, that you died, but more importantly, that you knew exactly when and how you were going to die, and that you let it happen."

Merlin smiled. "And you were so surprised that I could see the future."

"Yeah, but…" I started to say, thinking, "you also said that all you could see was your own future, so if you can't see past your own death – which is cool for you I guess – I assume you can't see much past the Dark Ages."

The man nodded again, an action that was starting to aggravate me. It was beginning to seem condescending, as though he were a puppeteer stringing me along and controlling everything I was saying, all the while sitting there patiently waiting for me to catch up. But that was okay, because I was starting to make sense of everything myself, and it was starting to get interesting.

"But you can also read my mind," I continued, "however it is you do that… but that also means that everything I know, you now know too."

Merlin nodded again with an impish smile. "And now you understand why I have been so excited to meet you. The past five years have gone by far too slowly."

I slumped in my chair, quite shocked despite having pieced it together for myself. Had I just given what was obviously an exceptionally powerful man more knowledge than I should have? Had I just done more damage to the timeline by simply meeting him than I had through everything I'd done over the past half-decade? If he knew everything I knew, plus everything I've ever known and then forgotten apparently, he had quite an arsenal of *new* knowledge to draw on.

"You shouldn't worry yourself about such things, Jacob," Merlin said. "There was nothing you could do to avoid it, but if it makes you feel better, let's just say that you've given an old man that hasn't had much to do in a *very* long time, much to think about, and little more. For that, I am grateful."

"Please stop answering the questions in my head, Merlin," I asked politely. "It's rude, and I'm not used to having my internal monologues interrupted by anyone but myself."

He dipped his head. "My apologies, Jacob."

"It's fine," I replied, not really that annoyed. It was actually kind of nice having someone answer all my unspoken question for me. "But why did you have to wait five years? If you know your own future, then you should have already seen my presence here, and therefore been able to see this entire conversation from the beginning."

"Normally, you would be right. And, in fact, I did foresee your presence beyond my front door five years ago, but it wasn't until you stepped inside that things became much clearer."

"That really wasn't your actual front door, was it?" I asked, referring to the cottage door.

He shook his head. "No, not actually."

I rolled my eyes. "So how is that you hadn't already seen this conversation then?"

"Because there is an anomaly that you haven't yet thought of."

"The orb," I answered immediately.

Merlin's eyes furrowed in confusion.

"What?" I asked.

"Nothing," he replied, "but you are correct. The orb. It... muddies things."

"But you invented it! Didn't you build a failsafe or something? Or something that can better control it?"

"I never said I invented it," Merlin clarified.

"Then tell me more!" I demanded. "There's so much I need to know! How does it work? What is its origin? Why didn't Remus use it? Why would an ancient pre-Roman even have such a thing? If it can't send me home, then it must be able to send me somewhere! There has to be somewhere out there better than this! There has to be! I... I have a son to think about now."

Merlin looked at me, but his expression was soft, as though he empathized with my plight. "I will help you, Jacob, but in order for me to do so, you must be willing to help yourself."

"I'm beyond ready, Merlin."

"All right then," he responded. "So where shall I begin? I suppose the beginning is as..."

"Wait," I said, holding up a hand. "You're not just going to sit there and tell me everything I need to know in horrible expository dialogue like in that one *Matrix* movie, are you?"

"You aren't harboring any hopes of being referred to as *The One* referencing a movie like that, are you?"

I leaned back in my chair awkwardly and cleared my throat. "Of... course not?"

Merlin rolled his eyes. "Well fear not, my young friend. For you are most certainly not *the one* of anything. You and Varus were hardly the only people capable of utilizing the orb, merely the unluckiest. And, it grieves me to say, he was far unluckier than you."

I looked away, saddened at Merlin's reminder of Marcus Varus, but he didn't wait long before he stood abruptly and moved to leave the room. I watched him go, confused at his departure, and wasn't sure whether to stay or follow. I looked at the fireplace, the chess board, and the bookshelves, a part of me wanting to stay right here, in this very comforting part of my old life. Even without my mother here, I found this room nearly as protective and soothing as Helena's warm embraces.

But I stood, unable to let myself grow complacent. I had to see this through. For her sake and our son's if no one else's. When I turned to follow Merlin, I pulled up short. The back of the den did not appear as it should have, replaced instead with the original dark room I had first entered. I snapped my head to catch one last look of the fireplace, but it was gone in a flash.

I frowned and moved off into the darkness.

Merlin stood not too far away, dressed in his original red robes and pointy hat, a pair of doors standing on either side of him. He looked more morbid than earlier, but I continued to suspect that he didn't mean me any harm.

He raised his eyes and looked at me. "I suppose you are right, Jacob. A simple explanation will hardly do what really transpired justice, nor will it be very interesting for your future books and movies, so instead, I shall show you. But where we go from here is completely up to you, as two paths now lay before you, one with answers and one without." As he spoke he held out his hands to either side of him, one toward the door on his left, the other the door on his right. "Either choice has acceptable outcomes, but only one will lead to what you truly want."

I lifted a hand to my shoulder in a questioning gesture. "Where'd the other Merlin go? I liked him better. He was more Gandalf the Grey than Gandalf the White."

Merlin smiled, but his form did not change. "Then let's spice things up a little, shall we?"

I wasn't exactly sure what that meant, and I was doubly certain that I would probably regret it later, but then the door to Merlin's left opened. It was a large door, ornate in appearance, with a pair of Corinthian columns flanking it on either side. It only opened a crack, but the first thing to come through was a human leg.

A bare, shapely, woman's leg.

It extended itself in a kick before snapping back to a bent position, but then disappeared completely behind the door. I craned my neck to see where it went, but then a female figure sauntered through the opening, wearing nothing but a bikini. I tracked my gaze up her body slowly and my mouth hung open when the figure revealed herself to be none other than Agrippina.

Her bikini was white and stringy, setting off her pale skin alluringly, and her golden hair cascaded past her shoulders in thick curls that swayed with the rhythm of her body. She pranced around the door like a stripper, clawing her way up and down Merlin like he was a pole. When she was finished, she returned to the door and stood beside it like game show girl. She set her head low before tossing it back, looking at me seductively, all the while saying nothing.

Which was probably the best thing about the whole show.

Merlin gestured toward her. "Door number one."

I crossed my arms and grinned. "Is this your idea of providing more stimulating visual aids to spice things up, Merlin?"

"It was hardly my idea, Jacob. It did come from *your* mind... for better or worse, I suppose," Merlin commented. "Now, door number two."

He held out his hand toward the other door, and another leg kicked itself out before retreating just like Agrippina's had, but while Agrippina's was pale, this leg was a light bronze and slightly more muscular. Again, like before, a long lean female body emerged, and I was not surprised to discover that it was Helena. Pre-pregnancy and without any of her scars, instead of a string bikini she wore a bright green one-piece swimsuit like the kind from the 90s that rode way up high on the hips, with the addition of a deep V that went just past her bellybutton.

She strutted toward me like a catwalk model, her eyes locked on mine. She reached out and placed her hand on my chest, staring deeply into my eyes as she circled around me, her hand never leaving my body. My grin widened as I watched her dance around me, but when she completed only a single revolution, she leaned in and kissed the air inches from my nose.

With a wet smack from her lips, she twirled around and made her way toward Agrippina. The two of them reached toward each other with scandalous intent in their eyes, but Merlin slammed his staff into the ground, distracting them. Helena pouted at the rebuke and waved at Agrippina sadly before returning to her door, where she stood beside it just like Agrippina did her own.

"Oh come on, Merlin!" I shouted, throwing my hands out wide.

"That's the mother of your unborn child, Jacob!" He countered, pointing, but he sounded more amused than angry.

"Yeah," I said, staring at Helena as she gyrated seductively by the door like she could just barely contain herself and was just dying to jump me. I glanced at Agrippina, who was biting her lips and beckoning me with an outstretched hand, and I pointed at her. "But she isn't! And... I mean... this is *my* fantasy, man! Come on! When am I ever going to get the two of them wearing outfits like that in the same room together again?"

"Probably never, Jacob, and believe me, that is for the best."

I crossed my arms and pouted. "Fine. So that's it, then? Just two options?"

"Would you like a third? I suppose I could arrange that."

He clapped his hands and a third door appeared from nowhere, and again a leg popped out, this one just as sexy and shapely as the first two, but when the figure emerged, I saw that the leg belonged to a red bikini clad Artie.

I threw up a hand to cover her from view. "No! That's okay! Just two is fine!"

"Are you sure, Jacob? Perhaps four would be best?"

And again, a fourth door emerged, and a fourth leg appeared, but this one was hardly feminine, at least not by my standards. Out emerged Boudicca, looking everything like a female version of Arnold Schwarzenegger, striking show poses in her black thong bikini.

I threw up my other hand to cover Boudicca now, but placed extra effort in keeping Artie blocked. I tried to focus on Helena, who was now bending over and running her hands up her legs slowly, Agrippina doing the same, only turned around.

"All right, all right, enough! I get it!" I shouted, squeezing my eyes shut and turning away. When I opened them seconds later, all four women had thankfully disappeared along with the last two doors.

I sighed in relief and put my hands down, looking at Merlin angrily. "Some spirit guide you are."

"Whoever said I was, Jacob?"

"Fine," I said as I stepped forward, looking toward the door the Helena apparition had recently abandoned. It was a copy of the cottage's original entrance door, and one I assumed would lead to the outside world.

"What happens if I choose this one?" I asked, not taking my eyes off of it.

"You will leave, never to see me again. While I cannot speak with any certainty, I believe if you were to choose this door, you could convince Agrippina to leave you alone as long as you stayed as far from Rome as possible. You would be able to live out your days with Helena and your children."

"Children?" I asked. "As in more than one? I thought you couldn't see anyone's future but your own."

"I speak simply with an intuition that I have honed over a great many years, Jacob."

"I see," I said, deciding to finally look at him. "Could we be happy?"

"You could. Very happy, I would think."

I gestured toward Agrippina's door with a hand. "And this one?"

"Your answers, Jacob. Nothing more."

I was at a crossroads, but even with all the doubt my mind could surely come up with, there really only seemed one door I could possibly consider.

I stepped forward and reached out to grip the handle of Agrippina's door and looked back for Merlin, but he had disappeared, only to be replaced once again by Helena. She was still wearing that wonderful green one piece swimsuit with the deep V, but she wasn't exuding any of the slutty qualities she had earlier.

I stepped away from the door and moved toward her, but she held out a hand and stopped me.

"Don't, Jacob," she said.

"But…"

"It's all right, my love," she said, her eyes practically shining like green lensed flashlights against the color of her swimsuit. "This decision was yours, but right or wrong, I'm here to remind you that I will always support you. I know you may not believe me after what happened because of the orb, but you have to believe it in yourself before you can believe it in anyone else. Just remember that I'll always be there for you. No matter what."

And with that, she winked out of existence, leaving me with little more than the memory of her in the swimsuit and the idea that I knew she was right. Helena would always be there for me. As long as I remembered that, I would never have to doubt anything ever again.

I turned and faced Agrippina's door, took the handle firmly in my hand, and tugged it open.

With a deep breath, I stepped through.

***

My first thought upon crossing the threshold was that nothing had happened. Even before the door had closed behind me, I could tell that this room was exactly like the last one. Bathed in a sea of darkness, I wouldn't have even been able to see my hand in front of my face if not for the light coming off the door behind me. I turned to see that it was still there, a reassuring presence, my mind convinced I could at least go back if I wanted.

I shook my head at it, the motion causing me to catch something else out of the corner of my eye. I looked to the right and saw the other door there, the one Helena had presented and the one that would have supposedly led me out of this mad house. I cocked my head at it, confused at its presence, when Merlin's voice interrupted my inspection from behind me.

"Did you really think I'd give you the opportunity to pick the wrong door?" He asked. "It isn't like you are not, in fact, solely responsible for the systematic destruction of the entire space/time continuum."

My eyes grew wide, every single one of my fears emerging at once at the statement. "I am??"

"No, not even close," he said playfully, "but you aren't exactly doing anyone any favors by staying here."

I turned to face him. "But you said Helena and I could be happy here."

He angled his head away from me. "Let's just say you're not doing anyone *else* any favors then."

I shook my head, closed my eyes, and allowed my heart rate to slow itself. "So I didn't really have any choice at all, did I?"

"You did, Jacob," he said. "This is merely a representation of how little a choice it was to *you*. In your mind's eye, as some might say."

My frustration at all his games continued to grow, but when I opened my eyes, I found myself in a new location, with Merlin nowhere to be found again. I didn't even bother looking behind me this time, knowing that it too would have been filled with the same expanse of nature that lay before me now.

The transition from the claustrophobic black room to this outdoor space was jarring. I threw a hand up to shield my eyes from the sun's intensity, but I wasn't nearly fast enough to stop it from washing out my eyesight. I clenched my eyes shut again, but after a few moments, reopened them. I didn't focus on anything right away, giving them the time they needed to adjust, but when they did, the view in which they took in was simply breathtaking.

I stood atop a low hill with a series of other hills spread out in front of me, and small clumps of tree scattered off in the distance. Judging by their foliage, I figured it was summertime, but it didn't seem excessively warm, even though the sun was shining brilliantly with only a few puffy clouds spattering the sky. Off to my left, a large group of birds fluttered off, briefly silhouetted by the sun before disappearing out of view. It was like a painting – the large ones with beautiful rolling vistas the size of entire walls found mostly in art museums.

I took in a sharp breath of air, more enthralled than surprised at what I was seeing. After what seemed like endless months of desolate, wintry Britain, this locale was awe inspiring. I wasn't even sure I'd seen anything like it in all the years of my life. I looked down, finally taking notice of a small settlement located at the center of two hills. Without a thought, I took my first step toward it, deciding there was no point in waiting for Merlin.

On my way down I noticed my feet below me, and saw that I was again wearing my combat boots. I checked the rest of my body and found that I was back in my old outfit. I sent my left hand into its corresponding cargo pocket and dug around for my glacier glasses. Luckily, they were still there, and I fitted them over my eyes.

"Does wearing your sunglasses make you feel like a badass, Jacob?"

I turned to see Merlin walking beside me, back in his old man tourist outfit, now complete with a wide, circular brimmed straw hat.

"Only at night," I said. "Now, however, I just want to protect my eyes from the sun's deadly, dastardly radiation. Wouldn't you?"

"But would it surprise you to learn that those aren't really your eyes you are using to perceive this world?

I rolled my head toward Merlin and lowered my glasses with a finger to look over them. "I think you should know by now that I'm past surprises."

"You do seem to be pretty perceptive."

"Damn straight," I said, pushing my glasses back to cover my eyes. "So where are we? Scratch that… when are we?"

"I believe I can answer both questions by simply replying with: the founding of Rome."

"No shit?" I said, more excited than surprised, glancing at the little settlement between two of the landscape's handful of hills. In a moment of clarity I tried to count them, including the one Merlin and I were descending, and tallied seven in total. "Well, shit."

Merlin chuckled beside me as we sauntered down the hill. "This really is all very stimulating for me as well, Jacob. To borrow one of your many wonderful expressions, I thank you from the bottom of my heart."

I turned to look at him. "You like all those, huh? I'm so happy for you. Really, I am. It's not every day that a simple human can have his mind invaded by an alien creature against his will and forced into some kind of vision quest that, while it does have its perks in the form of near naked ladies, has been something of a trip. And not a good one at that. So I'm really glad I could help you out, Merlin."

"Are you fishing for the truth behind who or what I am?" He asked.

"For a guy who doesn't even need a Vulcan mind meld to read my mind, I would think you should already know."

"Oh, *Star Trek*!" He exclaimed. "A wonderful series. I only wished you'd watched more of the spin off shows or read the supplemental books. A little more depth to that universe would have been fascinating!"

I shook my head at him, almost horrified at what he was saying. "So what exactly did you do to me? Download my entire mind onto a hard drive and then watch every single thing I've ever experienced in super fast forward, absorbing everything I've ever seen or done, even the things I can't remember?"

"You really have seen too many movies, Jacob."

"That isn't an answer!" I growled.

"Do you really need one, at this point?"

I turned back to the settlement which was just coming into focus as we grew closer. "I suppose not. It's just that you could have asked first, you know?"

"I apologize," Merlin said with a chuckle. "Next time, I'll be sure to ask."

"Yeah, you do that," I said, knowing that if there ever was a next time I was pretty sure I'd run like hell away from him. But for now, I had to work with the man, so I gestured toward the settlement, and turned to him. "I assume this is still a part of my vision quest then, and that we didn't actually travel back in time?"

"I wish you would stop referring to it as that, but yes, you are basically correct. Do not worry about interference, for they won't even sense our presence."

"Oh, wonderful," I said glumly. "I always wanted to be part of an extreme interpretation of Dickens' classic Christmas tale... I just didn't know it'd be *this* extreme. Just don't turn into the Ghost of Christmas Future on me, Merlin. That guy was terrifying."

"I'll keep that in mind," he answered, and I rolled my eyes as I watched him marching beside me, his arms swinging wildly with each step, a large closed lipped smile permanently plastered to his face.

"By the way," I said, "you looking fucking ridiculous in that outfit."

Merlin looked offended. "You clearly have no sense of style, Jacob. This fanny pack is perhaps the most amazing invention I've ever seen in all my years. Observe." He paused for a second so that he could twist the pack to the front of his body and unzip it. "There is ample storage space within this compartment and its location around my abdomen is most comfortable and convenient. I can place a great many objects in here. See... I have here my magic wand, a packet of pixie dust, a deck of tarot cards, a travel-sized crystal ball, a pocket edition of the Necronomicon, my passport..."

"Let me see that!" I yelled, reaching for it but he backed away.

"That's protected information, Jacob. You wouldn't want the State Department knocking on your door, would you? Oh! And finally, there's even enough room for a ham sandwich. Everything a wizard on the go could possible need."

I shook my head. "It's becoming harder and harder to take you seriously, Merlin."

He shrugged. "You'll try anything to look and feel young when you reach my age, believe me."

"Which is?"

"Nice try, Mr. Hunter."

I sighed. "Why couldn't it have been Santino who activated the orb? The two of you would have been perfect for each other."

"Why indeed?" Merlin lamented. "But better you than your sister. She seems a little... boring."

I ignored him, wondering if the last few hours of my life wasn't just further proof of my steady slip into insanity, but I pushed the thought away and tried to get a better sense of what we were walking into. If Merlin wasn't exaggerating, and that we really were about to witness the "founding of Rome," then I was about to witness the actual events lost to history that were later replaced with bed time stories and mythology.

The way I remembered it – and there are, of course, varying accounts – Romulus and Remus each had opposing views as to which hill was best to found their city upon. Romulus preferred the Palatine Hill, while Remus preferred another. I only remembered the Palatine Hill as Romulus' choice because he was in fact the eventual victor, which subsequently led to Remus' later murder.

"It was the Aventine Hill that Remus preferred," Merlin supplied.

I nodded appreciatively. "You see, that's the right way to read my mind. Telling me things I can't remember. Hot damn, I really could have used you back in college, Merlin."

His smile remained in place but he didn't respond, which seemed odd since he seemed to take great joy in always getting in the last word. I wondered if it had something to do with what we were about to observe in the coming minutes, that is, if mythology had it right. After everything I'd seen and all the history historians had either gotten wrong, or were purposefully misled to interpret as wrong, I was ready to see just about anything...

Except for what I *actually* saw the moment we entered the small encampment.

Merlin and I squeezed between a pair of tents, and found ourselves at the perimeter of a large central area. Within was a raised platform at the very center, surrounded by a large crowd of screaming, shouting, fist pumping...

Muppets?

I tore my glasses off and squinted at the anthropomorphized crowd of puppets that looked so much like the Muppets from the beloved children's show that the scene before me was borderline copyright infringement. There wasn't any string dangling from their forms, nor did I see any hands shoved up their asses, but still, the puppets before me leapt and shouted and were very obviously alive and worked up over something going on at their center. Not believing my own eyes, I was half tempted to look up and search for Statler and Waldorf yelling insults from their viewing box, but I refrained. Instead, I looked to the center stage to see two large puppets wrestling each other.

I turned to glare at Merlin, who did little more than watch them as he spoke. "Do not blame me, Jacob," he said casually. "You know as well as I that *The Muppet Christmas Carol* is your favorite version of the story."

I looked up at the sky in annoyance. "Change it..."

"But it really is a wonderful metaphor for the childlike..."

"Change it!!"

"Spoil sport..."

And in the blink of an eye, the chaotic mess of puppet on puppet action vanished, replaced with normal looking humans acting in very human ways. I sighed in relief, almost worried that the people of this time period actually had been puppets.

"Come," Merlin ordered. "We'll have a better view over here."

I nodded and followed as he wove his way around the mob of sweaty, shirtless, men who cheered for one of the two individuals atop the platform. As we crept around back, I took notice of the wrestling duo, an odd sense of déjà vu setting in as I recalled the moment when I'd first met Wang and Bordeaux when they'd been boxing in our secret subterranean hideout beneath the Vatican back in 2021.

However, while Wang and Bordeaux were polar opposites in terms of their physicality and fighting style, it was clearly evident, even from this distance, that these two wrestlers were nearly identical in size and build. Additionally, while I couldn't yet make out their facial features, both had mops of long, thick, black hair atop their heads that flung beads of sweat in all directions as they grappled with one another.

It didn't take a genius to deduce that these two young lads had to be none other than Romulus and Remus, but instead of feeling excited or elated at the fact that I was actually witnessing the mythological founders of Rome fighting each other, I simply felt sad that this was really only just a dream, and that I'd never be able to get their autographs.

But I wasn't about to let something so trivial bring me down completely. Reality or fantasy, if this vision really was accurate, then I was seeing the actual events played out by Romulus and Remus.

Romulus and Remus!

Remus and fucking Romulus!

I couldn't wait to get back to Helena and explain all of this in as much detail as I could remember. I had no doubt that she'd absolutely love every single second of it, but I would be doing her a disservice if I didn't make an effort to discover as many details as I could.

Feeling that giddy excitement the historian in me always felt when discovering new parts of history, I turned to Merlin. "How about a little background information? At what point in their lives is this?"

"There's no point offering you today's date, but what's important is that Romulus and Remus have just thrown off the shackles of their great uncle, Amulius, and have restored their grandfather, Numitor, to the throne of Alba Longa."

"Which they could have taken for themselves had they wanted, right?"

"You know your mythology well, but they never would have. They were far too industrious and ambitious to simply settle for inheriting someone else's kingdom. They wanted to forge their own destinies."

"Yeah..." I said, the fact that he was speaking of them as though he knew them not really registering in my mind. "We are actually talking about *the* Romulus and Remus here, right? Romulus *and* Remus?"

"Yes, Jacob. We are."

I threw out a finger and pointed it toward the young wrestlers. "Those guys??"

He chuckled. "Those guys."

"Amazing," I said in complete disbelief. "I honestly can't believe it."

"I could always send you back through the door, Jacob," Merlin suggested. "I'm sure if you really wanted I could conjure up Helena and Agrippina again as well."

"Oh, don't you play games with me, Merlin," I joked. "Don't you put something as tempting as that between a man and his need to learn himself some history."

"I'd never think of it. Believe me."

I smiled at the jovial tone of our latest interchange, and while I was certain I didn't trust Merlin even a little, I was beginning to realize that I certainly liked the guy.

"So how do you even know so much about them?" I asked.

"Let's find out," Merlin said, raising a hand toward the platform. "Observe."

By now the two of us were standing just beside the raised platform, which only came up to about my midsection. I was able to see the two young men very clearly now, and I was rather impressed at what I saw. Both men, and I use that term lightly, stood as tall as I and were broad shouldered and very well-muscled. The maturity in their physical form was offset, however, by their very youthful faces, which barely seemed able to grow peach fuzz. But despite this limitation, there was something strangely alluring about the two of them, something charismatic and otherworldly. Even now, as I watched them rise to their feet after one had successfully pinned the other, I felt drawn to them, like I would do anything for them, even if that meant stepping in front a thrown spear for them.

I wondered if such an aura came from simple genetic luck, or if there really was something to the story concerning their patronage, since supposedly the god of war himself, Mars, had been their father.

I turned to Merlin. "There isn't really anything to that part of the story, is there? It's just a coincidence, right?"

"*Shh*," Merlin hushed. "The best part's coming up."

I bobbed my head in a silent apology and turned back to the stage. The twins were on their feet now, the victor consoling the loser while at the same time rubbing it in, just the way I always thought a pair of brothers would treat each other. There didn't seem any animosity between them or anything that suggested one was capable of murdering the other, even though that's the way the story continued.

The losing brother looked downtrodden as the victorious one clapped him on the back, sending a wave of sweat to fly out into the crowd, who cheered and roared as the little droplets struck them like it was actual mana of the gods.

The two were shaking hands when a third figure ascended a small flight of stairs to join them atop the platform. He was robed from head to toe, and his face was concealed from view, but when he took center stage, the crowd of manly warriors grew quiet and still. Not a soul stirred or even breathed as the stranger stood above them all, waiting.

I was the only person who dared move, simply shifting my weight off of my left leg to my right, but was quite surprised when the hooded figure seemed to shift his attention directly at me.

I leaned in closer to Merlin and whispered, "I thought they couldn't..."

"*Shhhh!*"

I gave him a sour look but did as I was told. The robed man slowly rotated away from me and I let out a thankful breath. As I did, he threw his arms up into the air on either side of his head, causing his loose sleeves to fall past his elbows, showing skinny white arms. A moment passed, but then he lowered them ever so slowly to clasp the hood over his head, and in one quick motion threw it back.

I was almost surprised at who the action revealed.

Almost.

"Hey," I whispered. "It's you! I honestly didn't see that one coming."

"Shush, Jacob," Merlin scolded and I wondered what his deal suddenly was.

"Well, at least you aged well," I remarked, but then closed my mouth. In fact, judging from the other Merlin's appearance, he hadn't seemed to age at all. "Or were you just born this old?"

"I will not tell you again to be quiet," Merlin snapped, so I took the hint. Something stank about this, but now seemed like a good time to behave, so I stayed quiet and observed the show.

"A fine match!" The Merlin on stage shouted so that all before him could easily hear. "But as it is with any show of dominance, there must always be a victor and there must always be a loser. In this showing, your victor..." He paused so that he could reach out and grip the arm of one of the twins. He raised it up like a referee would the winner of a boxing bout. "...Remus!!"

A cheer went out from the crowd, but it wasn't hard to see that only half of those gathered seemed particularly joyous, although unlike a very typical and usually divisive U.S. Congress, it wasn't like the crowd was distinctively separated in half. And unlike the polite but obviously forced applause that would emanate from the congressmen not actually agreeing with the sentiment announced, even those who were clearly not in Remus' camp seemed genuinely happy, clapping their brothers-in-arms on the back in congratulation, passing coin money around, and wore proud and happy smiles.

I nodded appreciatively. If these men represented the shepherds turned soldiers that Romulus and Remus had led into battle against their great uncle, then legend had it that half would have been loyal to one brother, and the rest to the other. Yet, there seemed nothing to suggest animosity between the two factions, which reflected the attitude shared between the two brothers themselves, and I was impressed that such a feat was even possible.

Remus raised his other arm and clenched his hands into fists, and punched them in the air victoriously. Romulus, meanwhile, clapped happily and led his men through example by actually being happy for his brother.

Now that I knew the twins apart and had a better look at their faces, details began to emerge.

They were obviously identical, with the same broad forehead, high cheekbones, strong jaw, and prominent noses. They were handsome young men with faces that would grow hard in ensuing years, but in a way that would only make them more endearing to those who followed them. However, there were subtle differences in the set of their eyes and the way in which they composed themselves that distinguished one from the other.

Despite having just lost their wrestling match, Romulus seemed tougher and more physical than Remus, perhaps more aggressive and action-oriented too, while Remus seemed more introspective. It would not be difficult to imagine Remus as the general who devised the battle strategy while Romulus carried it out on the battlefield.

I couldn't exactly explain where these deductions were coming from, but I chalked it up to Merlin's influence. It was possible he was giving me the ability to read into the personal character of these two individuals for one reason or another for some future purpose.

That or they were just that transparent.

Or gods.

Either way, I filed the information away for further thought as the gathered men slowly calmed themselves and the other Merlin lowered Remus' arm. He turned to Romulus and reached for his arm now, and as one, lifted both twins' arms high in the air. As expected, the roar was even louder this time, and I had to wait a good ten minutes before it quieted again, and the other Merlin put their arms down together.

"And to the victors," the other Merlin shouted, "go the spoils."

"Really, Faustulus," Romulus said humbly, "that isn't necessary. I believe Remus would agree that the terms of our wager is award enough."

"Hey!" I whispered sharply. "They're speaking English!"

Merlin smacked me on the arm, but didn't say anything.

"Hush yourself, brother," Remus said. "Let our father revel in our glory a little more. I, for one, will accept his kind gift."

"Father?" I whispered again.

Either Merlin was Mars himself or their biological human father, a name that had escaped all history books, or perhaps he was just impersonating Faustulus, the human shepherd that had taken them from their suckling she-wolf and had raised them to be shepherds as well.

Again, there didn't seem a point in asking, so I simply crossed my arms and continued to watch.

The other Merlin turned an eye on young Romulus, who smiled meekly, which didn't seem in character for the tough looking lad, but gestured with his head that he was in agreement. There was a series of laughs and chuckles from the gathered men, but it wasn't chiding or insulting.

Such scenes must have been quite normal.

The other Merlin smiled proudly, truly like a father who saw real greatness in a beloved son destined to change the world, an expression I'd never seen on my own father's face, a thought that nearly caused me to miss what happened next. In the blink of an eye, the other Merlin reached his right hand into the billowing sleeve covering his left arm, and immediately pulled it free to reveal something in his hand.

It was the blue orb.

I felt the presence of my own orb resting comfortably against the small of my back, and a chill went down my spine as I thought about it, but seeing the orb in the other Merlin's hand seemed far more ominous.

"Steel yourself, Jacob," Merlin ordered commandingly. "Do not let its power touch you."

That was easy for him to say, but the concern seemed unnecessary. While the chill I'd felt hadn't been comforting, it also hadn't seemed associated with the dark emotional firestorm within me that normally preceded some kind of option to soothe it.

I shook my head to clear it just in time to see Remus reach out and take it from his "father's" grasp. He took it confidently and held it out before him, and stared into it longingly with an expression I had to think was a reflection of my own when I too looked at the orb, but then the last thing I expected happened. A brilliant blue flash burst from the orb, and I was certain everyone had been thrust into some distant, unknown land, much as my friends and I had been five years ago. I couldn't believe the other Merlin's recklessness by giving something so powerful to someone so primitive. It was extraordinarily irresponsible, and I braced myself for a Tyrannosaurus Rex storming into this assembly of men to swallow Remus whole, thus ending the mystery of his death.

Except, as the light dimmed and blinded eyes cleared, the gathered group, Merlin and myself included, remained where we were. Nothing had happened. No one moved, not even Romulus, but everyone else looked at Remus with odd expressions on their face. Odd because they weren't of stunned disbelief, but of inspired wonder, like they'd encountered such miracles all the time and were reverent of such occurrences.

And something about that was beginning to send more than just a chill down my spine. I was beginning to grow frightened at what was transpiring here. There was something not right here, something that smacked in the face of everything thought known about this time period and its residents.

"Merlin…" I whispered. "You've got to explain something to…"

"Just watch," he replied, but not angrily.

So I did.

Remus raised the orb over his head with both hands, tilting his head back to look up at it.

"A miraculous gift, father," he exclaimed. "I thought such devices lost to civilization generations ago. What does this one do?"

"Patience, young Remus," the other Merlin said happily, "for this gift is not yet complete. There is more…"

As he spoke, he shot his left hand into his right sleeve this time, and again pulled it free to reveal another object.

It was another orb, identical to the last…

…only…

…this one was red.

A billion questions flew through my mind, but it was in such a state of shock that I couldn't process anything of what I saw. Nor did the other Merlin give me much of a chance as he promptly handed the red orb to Romulus, who took it in a similar fashion as Remus had, but unlike his brother, seemed to have just as many questions as I did.

"But Faustulus," he said as he looked at the orb, "there have never been two at a single moment. Has there ever…"

"Hush, Romulus," the other Merlin scolded, much as my own Merlin had done with me. The other Merlin looked back to Remus, who had lowered his own orb and looked at Romulus jealously, but he looked away glumly when the other Merlin gave him a stern look and took the orb from him. The other Merlin looked back to Romulus, and took his orb as well.

He held one in each hand and brought them together so that the clinked off each other.

"The two of you represent an ideal," he said, glancing at Remus and then Romulus and back again. "Much has been lost in recent generations, but I see such greatness in the two of you that I foresee a time for the return of old things. You've each been bestowed with a great gift," he said as he carefully returned each orb to the proper twin's grasp. "Used in conjunction, the two of you can achieve wondrous things that will bring about a resounding peace to the land for thousands of generations."

The boys looked at each other nervously, but it was Remus who turned to Other Merlin. "How do we operate them?"

Merlin looked up at the large and intimidating boy, and smiled. "In good time, young Remus, but for now, your true reward. It is time to choose a location for the capital of your new empire. Come. Remus, I believe you have earned first choice."

I expected the other Merlin to lead the young twins from the stage and out onto the hills of what would soon be the land that becomes Rome, but instead, everything around me winked out of existence and changed. Merlin and I had returned to my old restaurant, and we were already seated at the bar.

"You look like you could use another beer," Foxtrot Alpha said as she stood on a stool at the far end of the bar, reaching for a replacement bottle of liquor that I knew was stored up there.

Normally, my young self would have done that for her, but he wasn't anywhere to be found.

"Make it a tall one," I said, barely even hearing my own words, "and a double shot of whatever will fuck me up the quickest."

***

Merlin sat beside me patiently for the few minutes it took Foxtrot Alpha to prepare my order, watching me curiously. When she finally returned with my beer and shot, she seemed rebuffed by my lack of interest in her as I unceremoniously drained a quarter of my beer in one hard pull. Without skipping a beat, I picked up the shot, dropped it in, and with little effort, drained every last drop of liquid before slamming the glass down and belching loudly.

"Impressive," Merlin commented from beside me.

My head rotated on its own, and I glared at him.

"I suppose you have a lot of questions…" he said, trailing off, perhaps expecting me to interrupt him, but I didn't. I simply sat there, frustration coursing through every vein in my body, rightfully so for once I thought. He flicked his eyes to the side nervously at my silence. "Where would you like me to start?"

I ignored him and signaled for Foxtrot Alpha to bring me another round. I waited patiently, and when she returned, I repeated what I'd done with the first drink, managing to belch more loudly this time. A young couple in a nearby booth looked at me in disgust. I glowered at them and hurled my glass squarely at the man's face, but it simply bounced of his forehead and crashed to the ground without him even flinching. He shook his head and went back to his date.

"Asshole," I muttered, turning back to the bar. After all that alcohol, I didn't feel even remotely drunk. Just mad. I picked up a nearby steak knife and started carving into the bar distractedly.

"I don't believe a thing you just showed me," I said. "Not a bit of it. This is a dream. A hallucination. Or if it's not, you're just fucking around with me for your own sick enjoyment. I don't have a clue as to who or what you really are, and I couldn't really care less anymore."

I stabbed my knife into the bar and pushed myself away, leaving it to wobble in place as I made my way into the back of the restaurant, where all the business happened. I took an immediate right upon entering and found a high cabinet with a gap between it and the ceiling. Having to stand on my tip toes, I reached up and found exactly what I was looking for. Gathering them in a bundle beneath my arm, I marched back to Merlin, and threw what I'd found on the bar in front of him.

"There's my thirty rolled silverware. I'm ready to clock out and go home now."

I twirled on the heel of my foot, and made for the exit. I passed by the hostess station in a hurry, not even giving Victoria's Secret, who stood there rearranging a seating order, another glance.

She looked up at my passing. "Thanks for coming to the..."

"What home exactly are you going back to, Jacob?"

The voice was Merlin's, from just behind me, and I stopped. I looked at the restaurant's outer doors, at their windows specifically, and saw Agrippina and my group of friends still diligently waiting for me outside of Merlin's cottage. Like before, they still seemed suspended in time, but just seeing them gave me cause to rethink my decision.

What home did I have?

I hadn't had one in half a decade, but still I remained stubborn. "Home is where the heart is," I said, dropping my chin against my chest, "and my heart is with Helena."

"A touching sentiment, Jacob, but you know as well as I how little it means when you are cut off and removed from everything else you hold dear."

I looked up, noticing that the windows had reverted to their actual form, and that I could see Merlin behind me in the reflection. "Is that another subtle hint at your origin story?"

He spread his arms wide. "I've already shown you far more than I ever should have, but yes, it is. I, much like you, do not belong here."

I turned to face him, taking a step forward. "Then why the dog and pony show? What's the point of all this?"

"Because I believe you can succeed where they failed."

"I don't understand. Succeed where? How? All I want to do is go home and you already told me the orb can't do that."

"No," Merlin said with a nod, "the blue orb cannot. At least not by itself."

His sudden seriousness was infectious.

"Show me."

***

It was night now as we again walked through Romulus and Remus' settlement.

A busy night, it was filled with raucous story-telling and heavy drinking, punctuated by the shouts from one man or another waged in a friendly bout of fisticuffs. It was an unruly camp, scattered and unorganized, lacking in noise discipline and security measures, completely unlike the Roman legions that would, apparently, be the spiritual successors of this army, but I wasn't necessarily surprised. I'd only seen a miniscule part of this world, so small that my observations were barely worth anything at all, but since seeing Rome as nothing more than a series of rolling hills, it wasn't hard to imagine this world was so vast and underpopulated that entire armies could go weeks or months without encountering anyone worth fighting. In a world like this, I supposed there wasn't much of a need for security or mission discipline. It was only in a world like Agrippina's, or the world that I was trying so hard to return to, where a lack of discipline could get you killed as easily as being on a long sea voyage without vitamin C.

But operational security was the last thing on my mind as we walked toward a large tent near the center of the haphazardly constructed camp. It was four times as large as any other dwelling, appearing much like a miniature circus tent, complete with an opening at its apex, and smoke billowing from it much like a chimney.

I gazed at the smoke for only a moment before dropping my head and quickening my pace. Merlin seemed unconcerned by my impatience and determination, and said nothing as he matched me step for step until we reached the entrance. I paused, wondering for a moment if I really wanted to see what Merlin brought me here to see, but immediately decided that I did.

We entered quietly, a precaution that seemed hardly necessary upon witnessing the scene before us. The other Merlin or Faustulus or Mars or Whoever The Fuck He Was, stood between Romulus and Remus near the fire at the center of the tent. Arranged around them were cushions and rugs scattered throughout, with spoils of war piled everywhere – everything from coinage to weaponry. It looked much like an Arab Sheik's tent might in the late nineteenth century, but everything was far less opulent and splendid.

Of all the spoils however, two stood out easily. The other Merlin again held the pair of orbs in his hands, holding the blue one near Remus and the red one near Romulus. The twins stared at their respective orbs intently, eagerly, while the other Merlin glanced between them casually. None seemed poised to speak in that moment, but then the other Merlin opened his mouth wide, as though preparing to bellow a great oration.

But then he stopped mid motion.

Or, more accurately, time stopped around him.

"I apologize, Jacob, but I have to interject here," Merlin said beside me.

"Why?" I asked.

"Because I have to explain what the orbs do."

I was too excited by his proclamation to ask why the other Merlin couldn't just do the same, as I assumed he was about to do, so I simply nodded vigorously and enticed him to explain. He sighed, and I couldn't help but feel like he was still in contention with himself over everything he was showing me. I continued to wonder why, but wasn't about to interrupt him now.

"The blue orb you understand..." Merlin said finally, "... to some extent at least. With it, a user can travel through time. It is quite simply – perhaps *too* simply – a time machine."

He paused, so I felt it was okay to ask a question.

"But why a ball?" I asked, but then thought of a better question. "I mean, *how* a ball? It's a ball!"

"Would you prefer this, perhaps?" Merlin asked as he gestured off to my right. I looked, and saw what looked exactly like a perfectly functional DeLorean, but not just any DeLorean, but the exact one from *Back to the Future II*, complete with Mr. Fusion and everything.

I turned back to Merlin, my mouth open wide. "Can I actually use that?"

"Unfortunately, no. In this case, the DeLorean there really is nothing more than a figment of your imagination."

"Shoot."

"Indeed," Merlin said as he gestured behind me. "Perhaps you'll enjoy this as well?"

I turned quickly, but saw nothing more than an empty phone booth.

"A phone booth?"

"Bill and Ted?" Merlin asked, leading me on.

"Oh right!" I exclaimed. "A little before my time, but I remember."

"Perhaps this then?" He said with a flick of his hand to my right.

I looked and saw a large, blue box that said POLICE BOX near the top on all four corners.

I tried to think as I gazed at it. "That's the thing from *Dr. Who*, right?"

"Correct."

I shook my head. "Never could get into it."

"A pity. I myself enjoyed the reboot pilot."

He waved his hand and all three objects disappeared, and I felt the little kid in me vanish along with them. I turned back to Merlin, looking dejected, but determined to understand.

Merlin started to pace. "You recognize each of those things as time machines because you come from an era when the idea of time travel has become enriched in modern pop culture. The fictional understanding of it has become quite commonplace in your world, and I place considerable emphasis on the word *fictional*, but in this age, the idea of time travel is nearly non-existent. Imagination, quite bluntly, is rather limited."

"So you created as simple a time machine as possible," I deduced.

Merlin shook his head. "I already told you that I did not create the device itself, but I crafted the orb as a physical analog for it so that the people of this time could understand it. Simplicity, as you stated, was key."

"An *analog...*" I said as I thought. "... so the orb is just a physical representation of something else? Just a façade? So you're saying your time machine really could be anything?"

"*Not* mine," Merlin uttered, sounding frustrated.

"But how? Where's the actual time machine?"

"The mechanics are quite beyond you, Jacob," Merlin said, recovering. "You are neither an engineer nor a scientist, just an amateur who watches way too much TV – not that a scientist or engineer from your world would make much sense of it anyway. Besides, knowing would do you no good, and we are running short on time. I must return you to your friends soon or else too much time will have passed."

I glanced at my watch, wondering if such an action actually meant anything in this odd place. When I caught the time, I was surprised to learn that I'd only been in Merlin's company for the better part of an hour, although it already felt like a lifetime.

I shrugged. "I've only been here an hour. Trust me, my friends won't miss me. I'm kind of on their shit list lately."

Merlin didn't answer, and only gazed at me with a hint of sadness in his eye. He let the silence continue, so I kept up with the questions.

"So the blue orb is a time machine," I explained to myself. "It itself isn't exactly a time machine, but that's what it does because of some vague explanation about analogs. Fine, I get it. Let's move on. Then what does the red orb do?"

Merlin remained silent, his expression suggesting he was still deeply lost in thought.

"Merlin?"

Finally, he turned to me, looking like he'd never seen me before.

"The red orb?" I prompted.

Without hesitation, but without any excitement, he said, "It allows you to travel into other dimensions."

I processed this new information very slowly. I wasn't sure I'd heard him right. "Say again?"

"The red orb allows a user to travel to parallel worlds, Jacob."

"I'm..." I started, still processing, "...I'm not sure I understand."

"You do understand, Jacob. This is a popular concept in your culture as well. The red orb allows its user to tap into the Multiverse, as some might call it."

"I... but..." I uttered, my mind whirling at the implications. I looked down at my left hand and raised it to shoulder height. "The blue orb controls time." I looked at my right hand and watched as it rose to shoulder height all on its own. "The red orb controls... space?"

"Quite right," Merlin said. "Since time immemorial, every decision made at every nanosecond, in every place within the universe simultaneously has created an alternate timeline in which life takes different paths. Uncountable, infinite, beyond even the scope of my imagination, these timelines, dimensions, parallel worlds, whatever you choose to call them, *exist*, and are quite accessible with the red orb."

I looked back at my left hand, and jerked it up. "Time."

I turned to my right hand, and jerked it as well. "Space. Dimensions." Finally, I returned my eyes to Merlin. "Whoever controls both would be unstoppable!"

Merlin nodded, very much in agreement. "Alone, each is quite formidable. Blue is time. Red reality. But together... well, together a person could go anywhere and do anything."

"With that kind of untapped potential," I pondered out loud, "a tyrant could alter the past, control alternate civilizations, steal technology from the future, and strip mine parallel Earths to the bone, leaving them empty husks, all the while keeping his Earth pristine."

The words streamed from my mouth without thought, years of thinking and contemplation on the effects and abilities associated with time travel had finally coming to fruition. With the addition of multi-dimensional travel thrown into the mix, everything was beginning to become crystal clear.

With my arms at my sides, it was an easy task to lash out and grab Merlin by the shoulders. "You'd better hope somebody like OPEC doesn't get ahold of the red orb one day!"

"I do not think that will be a problem," Merlin said, but before I could seek clarification, he continued. "But while you immediately assume the worst in man, I saw the orbs as an opportunity."

I dropped my arms and backed away. "An opportunity for what?"

Merlin looked to the twins and his double, as though embarrassed, and it seemed to take a great strain of will for him to gather his thoughts and speak again. He'd seemed so flakey throughout this latest experience, and it was also becoming very clear that Merlin regretted much and was still struggling with implications that were beyond me.

"In the right hands," he explained, "the orbs could allow great leaders to do great things. Rewrite wrongs, ensure prosperity, and build empires that would throw off the negative connotation of the word 'empire.' In the right hands, users of the orbs could be true paragons of virtue and empathy. Benevolent masters of the universe that would right all the wrongs of the past and... ensure *certain* futures never came about. They could do great things."

I took a step toward the fire and threw a hand out toward Romulus and Remus, still suspended in time like a paused movie. "Who, these knuckleheads??"

Merlin shook his head and closed his eyes. He seemed frustrated. "You do not understand..."

"Then help me understand!"

He looked to the twins, held his eyes on them for a few moments, then turned back to me. "I've shown you too much as it is."

"Quit it with that shit!" I yelled. "Don't cop out on me, Merlin. Don't think you can bring me this far and then just leave me with shit like, 'I've shown you too much as it is. Telling you more could potentially destroy the space/time continuum. Blah blah blah.' That isn't fair! I'm going to have to explain all this to my friends sooner or later and I don't think they're going to settle for just that."

"No," Merlin said firmly with a single shake of his head. "No. It is too much. Even for you."

"Just give me something then," I pleaded, craving every iota of information I could get. "Anything."

Merlin closed his eyes, his strain still evident. "The world was different in their time... very different, in ways you would both understand and be completely incapable of understanding."

"Try me."

"I will not. As I have already said, it is too much and too irrelevant to your situation. I have done enough harm and I will not do more by attempting to satiate your insatiable curiosity."

I almost smiled. "People always tell me I'm too curious for my own good."

"An admirable character trait in many instances; it's just one that will do you no good today."

I sighed. "Fine, but can't you give me something? At least tell me how the twins are so big and why they're so charismatic."

"You have a vivid imagination, Jacob. I believe, in time, you will come to understand on your own. Just remember that sometimes the simplest answers are the right ones."

I really hoped that didn't mean what I thought it did; that my initial random thought – the same one shared by mythologists the world over – was actually correct. The one that stated that the twins were in fact descended from gods. Mars in particular. Mars of the Gray Eyes, like his sister Athena, eyes like mine, and...

I looked at the twins.

They had gray eyes as well

I glanced quickly at Merlin, hoping to catch some kind of affirmation in his expression, knowing he could read my mind quite easily, but his face was neutral. I suppose he was too good at all this to just give up that piece of information so easily.

"Will I ever learn the truth?" I asked

"In time, perhaps, but not from me."

"More of your centuries of honed intuition at work?"

He smiled. "Who said anything about centuries?"

I shook my head as I gestured back toward the frozen trio. "You were right about one thing, Merlin. This had gone on *way* too long, and I'm starting to lose attention."

Merlin nodded in understanding and raised a hand toward his more ancient counterpart, but then he hesitated. "You realize it won't be hard to cut this part down a little when you write your book, right? Just have Helena edit it."

"Just fucking start the movie again!" I yelled, throwing a hand toward the twins.

"All right, all right. I don't know how she puts up with you..."

I glared at him, but his smile simply widened to look just like one of Santino's as the show finally resumed.

"Wait!" I called out as something came to mind.

The scene paused again, and now it was Merlin's turn to look at me impatiently. "What is it?"

"Why did you need to pause it at all? Why not let the other you explain all this to them?"

Merlin looked at me steadily. "Because they already knew enough."

Before I had even a second to think on that revelation, the scene restarted.

"Faustulus... father..." Romulus stammered, "...but such power, so easily accessible... It is a great responsibility."

"It is," the other Merlin confirmed, "which is why I entrust it to you, my sons. Such potential I see in you, more than I've seen in over four hundred years..."

I shot Merlin a look, and he flicked an embarrassed face at me, but didn't say anything. I shook my head and turned back to the focus of this particular story.

"...but I do not bestow these gifts on you easily, which is why I offer each of you only one half of the old god's third power. Alone you have been given something powerful, but only together will you change the universe."

"Old 'god'..." I whispered. "Singular?"

Merlin didn't say anything.

Romulus clutched his red orb to his chest like a newborn, dropping his eyes to study it intently before meeting his father's eyes steadily. There was love in their eyes, the kind shared between a father and son who respected each other greatly, and understood each other more than any other two people. There was no question that Merlin had legitimate feelings for these boys, it was only a question of the source of that love that eluded me.

Unlike his brother, however, Remus seemed less pleased with their situation. He held his orb in a single, massive hand down near his leg, like it was something that didn't really concern him or was something of menial importance. Interrupting the moment Romulus and the other Merlin were sharing, Remus took an imposing step toward his "father" and spoke.

"But Faustulus, why not grant each of us complete power? It would be more efficient that way. The two of us, acting independently, could do far more simultaneously than if were we restricted to working together."

The other Merlin turned his head, opened his mouth to speak, but then stood suspended in time again. I turned back to my Merlin who looked as sad as I'd yet seen him yet look.

"I should have known then and there."

"Known what?" I asked.

He replied simply with an upraised arm. I followed the arm, unsurprised to find that we were no longer in the tent of Romulus and Remus. The scene had shifted again, and Merlin and I now stood out on one of the great hills of Rome with the sun shining down on us brilliantly. I retrieved my sunglasses once again and placed them over my eyes, the sudden shift to daylight nearly blinding me again.

"One month later..." Merlin whispered, his voice acting much like a subtitle in a movie indicating the very same thing.

I saw nothing in my immediate field of vision, so I turned around, but when I did, I took a step back in surprise at what I saw. Where little more than a camp of tents had stood no more than a month ago, the makings of a city stood just beside it on a hill. Small but lavish buildings and paved streets dominated the area, carefully organized in a tight, neat grid. The city was not quite recognizable, but something about it made me instantly understand that this must have been Rome.

I turned to Merlin. "All of this in just one month?"

"With great power..." Merlin uttered, again in a whisper.

I looked back toward the city and shook my head in wonder. What I saw before me was beyond amazing. It was an engineering feat unparalleled even in the modern world. There, this city would still be little more than a field of grass, as it would have taken them years just to plan the city, let alone begin the process of hiring workers and gathering resources.

Truly amazing.

On an impulse, I started walking toward the ancient beyond ancient city of Rome. Merlin, as always, fell into step beside me. As we grew closer, I was able to notice a wall being erected around the city. From this vantage point, I surmised that it was perhaps only half complete, but it, like the city behind it, was both opulent and seemed highly effective as defensive barricades go – at least it would be once it was complete.

I strode down the hill and toward the city with purpose, but pulled up just short of entering it when a commotion to my left drew my attention. I looked and saw Romulus standing atop a completed portion of the wall, thirty feet above the ground. He was looking away from the city with a hand held up and pointing in that direction, gripping his red orb with the other. I tracked his outstretched arm and saw Remus standing on the field before the wall, a good forty meters away. I took a step forward but something else caught my eye. A bird was only a foot away from me, suspended in motionless flight, an indication that the scene before me was paused again.

I turned to Merlin, waving an arm toward Romulus and Remus.

"Don't tell me this is actually going to happen."

"It is."

I shook my head in disbelief. "Amazing. Simply amazing."

"What is?" Merlin asked, his voice indicating he was curious.

"That historians could get so much just flat out wrong about Roman history," I replied, "but stories of Remus leaping over Romulus' wall, the key event that drove Romulus to murder his twin brother, or as certain legends go, managed to survive for almost three thousand years. That's what's going to happen, isn't it? Unless you're fucking around with me here…"

"I most certainly am not, Jacob."

"Amazing then," I muttered. "But that wall is thirty feet high!"

"Just watch," Merlin said.

I nodded and turned as time resumed, just in time to have the nearby bird fly right into my face. I batted my arms at it as it tried to claw my nose off, but was lucky to defeat it with minimal injury. I shot a glance at Merlin, spitting out a feather as I did.

"Sorry," he said.

I glared at him but the commotion between Romulus and Remus saved him from feeling the torment of my gaze.

"This is a fruitless argument!" Romulus shouted down at Remus from the wall. "You may have won the right to choose your choice of locations for our new city first, but *I* won the actual choice of where to build it!"

"An unfair decision, brother!" Remus shouted back. "It is no fault of my own that the mating pattern of birds precludes my chosen location as the superior one. It is of no surprise that you saw more than I!"

"Good grief," I muttered. "Did you really entrust the fate of the universe to a pair of kids who actually relied on augury to determine where they were going to build their city?"

"Hush," Merlin shot back.

I rolled my eyes but did as I was told.

"Silence your whining, brother!" Romulus shot back. "We both agreed on the terms. It was all the men would understand. Father assured us it was the best course of action."

"*Father...*" Remus grumbled, his voice dripping with disdain, "...I am not quite convinced of his impartiality in all of this as well."

"Again with your whining, Remus," Romulus said, clearly impatient. "I tell you, it grows old."

I crossed my arms but then held out a hand toward them. "Seriously, Merlin, these two schmucks?"

Merlin looked at the sky as he shook his head but didn't say anything. The two twins continued throwing jibes and insults at each other, and I was beginning to think this seemingly epic brawl was going to turn into nothing more than a pissing match between irritated brothers. My suspicions of just that grew with every passing moment, but then Remus pulled his orb from behind his back. It was a simple gesture but something about it seemed threatening.

"And my orb is useless!" Remus yelled, shaking his fist with one hand and waving the orb in the air with the other. "It serves me no purpose to revisit my own past and nothing more unless used in concert with your orb, while you can go off and play in other worlds without the need for me! I will not stand for it! We achieved everything to this point together, and I will not merely reside in your shadow now. I refuse!"

Romulus, to his credit, did not appear angry or upset. He simply stood patiently atop his wall and extended both hands to his sides, his right hand still gripping his orb. "You are my brother, Remus, but if you wish to challenge me, you are free to do so. I welcome you into my city by going through or around my wall, but if you attempt to go over it... you will be well met by me personally!"

I suddenly felt myself walking forward again, too interested in what was to come to realize what I was doing. The air was as still as I'd ever experienced it before, and for a second I thought Merlin had stopped time again, but the distant rustling of leaves and the patter of feet off in the distance proved that not to be the case.

I looked to Romulus, still atop his wall, his arms spread wide, and then to Remus, who now knelt in the grass coiled like a viper. The man looked ready to jump, but even after everything I'd seen, I didn't for a second entertain the thought that he was about to jump thirty feet in the air and cross such a distance. Such athleticism was beyond even these impressive young men.

But then he did.

Like a flash of lightening, Remus no longer knelt in the grass but was sailing through the air directly toward Romulus. He wasn't flying, that much was clear, but the angle and approach of his path indicated he had, without a doubt, jumped, and looked to be on a course to clear the wall with room to spare. I watched the leap with an open mouth, viewing it like the slowest tennis volley ever hit, my head tracking Remus left to right as he flew. He looked so graceful in the air, like it was something he did all the time, but then his grace ended when he crashed into Romulus.

Even for a being I assumed equally powerful as the god-like Remus, the momentum behind his brother's leap was too much for Romulus to stop, and the pair of twins fell backward off the wall together. They dropped like stones but halfway before they impacted the street below, they winked out of existence.

They were gone.

I ran to about where they should have hit the ground, but found nothing. There wasn't a trace of their existence, let alone the orbs they carried. I looked to Merlin, who stood beside me as if he'd been there all along.

"Where did they go?" I asked in shock.

"In all honesty, Jacob, I do not know."

"How can you not know??"

"Because they went somewhere I could not follow."

The answer came to me immediately. "The orbs!"

Merlin nodded.

"But which one? The red or the blue? Did they go somewhere in time? Or into another dimension?"

"Again, I do not know."

I pulled back a few steps and surveyed the scene. If this was the moment in history where Romulus murdered his twin brother, igniting the chain of events that would lead Roman civilization down the path I'd learned about in school, then whatever had just happened, wasn't yet finished. I looked up suspiciously and confirmed that Merlin had stopped time again by seeing even more suspended birds frozen mid flap.

"What happens next?" I asked.

Merlin held out his hand to indicate the ground just to his right. "Back away, Jacob."

I did as I was told, moving to stand beside him, and when I arrived, time started again and the brothers immediately winked back into existence, but then I realized my eyes must have played a trick on me, because it became instantly clear that only Romulus had returned.

And he was no longer in possession of the red orb.

Instead, he held the blue one.

I stared down at him, gears in my mind continuing to churn, wondering how that was possible, when a movement to my left drew my attention away. The other Merlin stood beside me, and I found myself surrounded by Merlins. Romulus looked up at the other Merlin quickly, his eyes filled with terror, an emotion I hadn't expected. But there was something else in those gray eyes – eyes that I suspected actually were gray, instead of just light blue – something that suggested he had aged decades in the blink... of an eye.

"Father! Please!" He pleaded. "Give me access to Remus' orb! I can go back and stop him from attacking me. This will have never happened."

The other Merlin looked down at him sadly.

"You know I cannot do that, my son."

"But father!"

"I cannot..."

"But dad..."

"Son..."

"Come on, dad!"

"I told you no, and no means no."

"But dad I want to..."

"That's it, we're leaving, and no TV when we get home either."

"Noooooo..."

The interchange subsided, replaced by jerky vibrations that felt like someone was kicking my chair... that is, had I been sitting in a chair.

I shook my head, not exactly understanding why it was suddenly so dark and why the dialogue between Romulus and the other Merlin had changed so oddly. Finally, I realized that I had my eyes closed and that I still had my glacier glasses on. I pulled them off and opened my eyes, and discovered that we were back in my old restaurant, and that I was watching a father struggling to pull his young son from a booth. The kid held on stubbornly, wailing, and kicking the seat cushion, but finally the father managed to dislodge him and pick him up. Tossing the kid over a shoulder, he hastily made for the exit, the kid pounding against his back as they left.

I shook my head again and rubbed my temples with a pair of fingers on either hand, finally taking notice of Merlin sitting across from me.

I looked at him with wide eyes. "You really need to work on your transitions, my friend. They're pretty jarring."

"I'll do that," he said, amused.

I was just about to let out a string questions when I was interrupted by a busboy angrily throwing his busing tub into the recently vacated booth, swearing as he did. I looked up and noticed it was my younger self, preparing to bus the table. He slid into the seat, and I saw him eye a freshly rolled up set of silverware that sat upon the dirty table, and reach for it as he glanced around cautiously.

I smiled at the sight, forgetting all of my questions.

"Yo, Jacob," I called out.

My younger self dropped the silverware, jumping in surprise at my interruption.

"What?" He asked nervously, looking up at me.

I smiled as I stared at his face, remembering every contour of it vividly. In return, I was certain he wouldn't even recognize me at all as his older self. I hadn't had many opportunities to look into a mirror since arriving in Britain, but when I did, I wasn't very happy at what I saw staring back at me. I'd aged decades in just these past five years, so seeing myself so young and vibrant, even pudgy, was a happy sight.

I looked away for a moment to gather up four sets of silverware off my table.

"Here," I said, holding them out to him. He came over and reached out a hand, but I pulled them away before he could take them. "Just remember to switch up your dead drops. That shelf above the cabinets isn't going to stay a secret for long, believe me."

He stared at me intently, almost distrustfully, but then his face relaxed and he nodded as he reached for them again.

"And for crying out loud," I said, not letting go as he tried to pull away, "give yourself a break. Lighten up. Your life's good right now. *Very* good. Better than you deserve really, so enjoy it while you can."

I smiled as I thought to tell him that in at least one way, his life was going to get a million times better, but I decided to leave Helena out of it. A little mystery never hurt anyone.

"I'll... do that," he said with seeming honesty. "Thanks, whoever you are."

"No problem."

I nodded, let go of the silverware, and watched as he moved back to his booth slowly. He squeezed in and started the process of moving dirty dishes into his tub, when moments later, Suzie-Lu walked over and sat opposite him. It seemed like a slow night, so lengthy chats between us as tables were cleared had been quite common. I smiled as Suzie-Lu laughed at something young Jacob had said, and my grin grew into a proud one when he passed her the four sets of silverware I'd given him.

She had her own silverware quota as well.

"Way to go, me," I whispered.

She thanked him happily and winked as she exited the booth. She walked back to her hostess station, and the two of us watched her go, both of us sighing at the sight of her, but while I stayed seated, he stood seconds later and moved to the back of the restaurant with a full tub of dirty dishes, not giving me another glance.

I watched him go. "If only everyone could offer advice like that to their younger selves," I said to Merlin. "I think both younger and older versions would really get something out of it."

"I would have to agree," Merlin said.

When the younger me was out of sight, I leaned my head back to rest it comfortably against the booth, and closed my eyes. "It's a shame though, that this isn't actual reality, and that kid doesn't really exist."

"Are you quite sure of that?"

I tiled my head forward and opened my eyes. "Are you suggesting that this isn't a dream, and that this is actually happening in an alternate reality, one that we are actively affecting?"

"Do you think it is?" He asked.

"Not in the slightest."

"Why is that?"

"Because if this was an alternate reality, we wouldn't be here."

"Explain, please."

I took in a deep breath. "Because if it was, then that would mean you, Merlin, would have the ability to travel between realities. But you don't, because if you did, you would have simply gone to another reality seven hundred years ago where Romulus and Remus hadn't fought like that. Besides, you already said you couldn't."

Merlin smiled. "You really are pretty sharp."

"Oh, there's a shit ton more, buddy-pal," I said.

"Go on."

I leaned forward and folded my hands together atop the table. "In fact, I think you're lying to me about everything, because I don't think it's even possible to hop between realities. Maybe they don't even exist at all, because if there *was* someone capable of traveling between them, then there would, theoretically – and technically – be an infinite number of versions of the same guy who could do the same. With the ability to jump between realities, alternate versions of the same guy would constantly be bumping into one another, fighting, making peace, ignoring each other, forming alliances. It would be an enormous clusterfuck that could in no way *not* affect my own reality. In fact, there would be an infinite number of *me's* doing exactly what I'm doing right now, having this exact conversation with an infinite number of *you's*, and there would have to be at the very least *one* who could hop between universes and fuck with me.

"That's why I don't think the red orb you gave Romulus does anything like what you claim it does. If it did, somewhere along the infinite line of alternate realities there would be a version of *you* who used it for himself for nefarious means, let alone a Romulus who acted evilly as well. The clusterfuck would only continue, especially when you factor in realities where Romulus and Remus go rogue together and can control *time* as well. So there's just no way. Nope, not a chance. With an infinite amount of time thanks to the blue orb, there wouldn't be a version of reality left standing. They would have all just destroyed each other. Wham, bam, thank you, ma'am."

Merlin spread his arms wide upon the table. "I am extraordinarily impressed, Jacob Hunter. Your arguments are quite valid, if crude in presentation, and your logic is mostly sound..."

"But..." I said, sensing his hesitation.

"But your logic is also incomplete... through no fault of your own. You see, traveling through alternate realities is in fact quite possible. Alternate realities, parallel worlds, and the Multiverse all exist. But you are also very right. In the scenario you just described, the ability to travel between realities could in fact cause that exact level of chaos..."

"*But...*" I said again, not quite sure where he was going.

"But while logic would dictate that if an infinite number of realities existed within our universe, each an extension of an infinite amount of choices and decisions made by every single thing to ever exist since the beginning of time, you are correct in assuming that there could be an infinite number of individuals capable of jumping between them."

"I think you've lost even me."

"I apologize," Merlin said, "Allow me to come to the point then. While logic would dictate all of what I just said, the truth is that while there are in fact an infinite number of realities out there to travel between, there is in fact only *one* reality that had access to the red orb, and therefore the ability to channel that ability."

I shook my head, and my next words were spoken very slowly. "This... one...?

Merlin nodded. "At least up until the point when Romulus and Remus disappeared... and only Romulus returned."

I shot to my feet and out of the booth, banging my knee on the table in the process but barely feeling it. I hobbled away from Merlin and twirled a finger over my head as I retreated.

"Back to the bar, Merlin. If this acid trip of mine is going to turn me into an alcoholic, then I'm going for broke."

***

Foxtrot Alpha had just finished lining up ten double shots of tequila on the bar in front of me when she looked up at me with those large, dark eyes. "Are you sure about this? I'm not even sure I'm allowed to let this happen. This is a restaurant, not a dive..."

"Don't worry, I'm a big boy," I said.

She turned a skeptical look to Merlin. "Is he really?"

Merlin shrugged. "From time to time."

"Well, okay then," Foxtrot Alpha said nervously.

"Light me," I ordered, and Foxtrot Alpha complied, retrieving a stick lighter from behind the bar and setting each shot glass filled with liquid aflame. When she was finished, ten little glasses with flickering blue flames sat before me.

I turned to Merlin. "If I fuck this up, you'll fix me, right?"

"Sure, Jacob," Merlin answered. "Sure."

"Good enough for me," I said as I picked up the first glass and poured the flaming liquid down my throat.

I'd never done a flaming shot before, and had no idea if I was even doing it right, but something told me I couldn't die or even get hurt in a hallucination. And I seemed to be right. I knocked back each flaming glass of liquid one after the other, not noticing the burning fire for even a moment. Foxtrot Alpha stared at me in wonder, and as I slammed the last glass down in triumph, she started the process of cleaning up the mess.

"I'm not sure if I should be turned on right now or scared senseless," she said.

"Don't be scared," I said as I wiped my mouth with a sleeve, "but don't get yourself worked up either. I'm spoken for.

"She must be a lucky girl," Foxtrot Alpha said sadly.

"She's certainly a girl, at least," I muttered, turning back to Merlin. "Now explain. Everything."

"There are parts I can and others I cannot," Merlin said. "Think of it this way, Jacob, because while this is as basic of an explanation as I can give you, it should help you understand: In this universe, there is infinite time, infinite choices, and infinite realities. But even with all those infinite outcomes, there was only *one* choice that brought the power of the old god, as you heard it referred to, into existence.

"And he is?" I asked.

"Another tale for another day, Jacob. But don't take the name *too* literally. However, the point is that because there was only one choice in one dimension that brought that power into existence, the origination of the power was secluded to one reality, and one reality alone. This one."

"But…" I said, trying to think, "…once this "power" came into existence, shouldn't other realities begin popping up from there on out with the… *old god's* power?"

"You really are catching on," Merlin commented, "but again, you are incorrect through no fault of your own. With the old god, well before the time of Romulus and Remus, came an ultimate timeline, a prime dimension, one that could not be splintered, one in which choices did not create new realities."

"So I really am special?" I asked.

"No more special than all the other trillions of people who came before or will come after you in this reality."

"But are there other versions of me out there in other timelines?"

He shrugged. "Of course, although none with access to the orb."

"That doesn't make any sense!" I cried, not caring that the eyes of other patrons were being turned on me as I raved at Merlin. "How can there be any timelines even remotely like mine if this 'old god' asshole only showed up in one, and no others? All those other timelines without him and the orb in them would be *so* different!"

"Just accept it, Jacob," Merlin said unhelpfully. "You must realize that this story is far deeper than what even I have showed you. Perhaps you will come to understand in the future, but for now... you need not know."

I growled in frustration but knew it would be fruitless trying to extract more from him now. "So the orb doesn't exist in any other timeline then? Not a single one?"

"That was the case once," Merlin said. "Except..."

He trailed off again.

"Goddamned it," I exclaimed, "just tell me! Except what??"

He took in a breath. "Except for the timelines you've created when you used the orb with someone else. By using the orb with Artie and Varus, you have *created* new timelines with the orb in them, although like this one, those universes cannot naturally breed into the Multiverse. Only were someone to use the orbs in those timelines could new ones be created from them."

I blinked, only vaguely understanding what he was talking about. "This is a lot to take in, Merlin. Like... a lot a lot. How are my readers going to understand this if I can't even?"

"Write a lot of sequels," he suggested.

A slight chuckle escaped me, but I pushed on. "So all this means that Artie... that Artie *2.0's* timeline didn't even exist until I connected with Varus and came back to Rome. You're saying that I... *created* her?"

"Again, technically, it was you and Marcus in tandem that began the process."

"But… that means I'm responsible for everything that happened in her timeline! All the death and suffering! That means that I really did use the orb improperly and that I *am* responsible for fucking up *everything*!"

"You are also responsible for all the life and joy, as well, Jacob," Merlin said in a calm voice.

I shook my head, refusing to accept that, but my continued curiosity kept me from losing a handle on my emotions. "But how do you explain how different my timeline is from Artie 2.0's, yet Jacob 2.0 was almost exactly the same guy I am? Not to mention how so many other things, including my friends and family, are nearly the same as well, even though the course of world history skewed so differently."

Merlin shrugged. "I cannot explain it, Jacob, for I have never experienced the result of how you used the orbs. Perhaps time is a fickle thing and required you to exist in these new timelines so that time could repeat itself, therefore avoiding what you would call grandfather paradoxes from occurring. Events were manipulated so that at the very least, another *you* was created as similarly to you," he tapped a finger against my chest, "as you, yourself are. Or it may have been a simple coincidence, something some might call synchronicity, but unfortunately I do not have a clear answer to your conundrum."

"But what could control something like that? Fate? God? And I mean, *my* God, not your stupid *old god* bullshit?"

Merlin shrugged again but didn't say anything.

"Do you really believe any of that?"

"I believe anything is possible."

"Must be nice," I muttered, and suddenly thought about Jacob 2.0 again, the one who had gone back in time in her timeline that had sparked a rescue effort that only resulted in them finding the Other Me's body and journal. I wondered what had happened to Jacob 2.0. Had he connected with some alternate version of Varus? Varus 3.0? If he had, he probably wouldn't have lasted very long since it was clear that Artie 2.0's timeline had been completely unaware of the orb at all until they'd found the Other Me's body.

Or he may have become an emperor.

Actually, is more likely that he had found nothing in Syria and had simply died there. Just another casualty of war whose body had simply disappeared, much like what had happened to Archer in my own timeline. That, at least, would explain why he and I hadn't connected.

"There is no point speculating on that, Jacob," Merlin advised, "but enough about alternate realties and the Multiverse for now. I could draw timelines with pieces of silverware for days on end, and it would leave you no less confused. Such things are simply not important for your story to continue."

I coughed out a laugh. "Nice *Looper* reference."

Merlin smiled. "I appreciate that you have seen so many movies from which I can draw references. It makes all this much easier. Now... what else are you curious about?"

I kneaded my brow with a hand as I thought, finally remembering where the story had left off. "So what happened when Romulus returned? Could you have given him access to use the blue orb like he asked?"

Merlin nodded slowly. "I could have, but didn't. Looking down at him in that moment, I'd learned my lesson, realizing that they hadn't been ready. With Remus lost somewhere in time or space, alive or dead, alone and unable to use the red orb, and Romulus back in Rome with the blue orb, also unable to use it, the status quo had resumed. Neither boy could operate their orbs.

"I'd thought Romulus would kill me, to be quite honest, but instead he banished me for treason. He was devastated at his brother's loss, not upset or angry, but saddened beyond description. He was very emotional, as were their troops, and when I tried to take the blue orb back from him, his men struck me down. They thought me dead, but Romulus knew I was not so easily dispatched, and had me taken here, to Britain. When I awoke months later, I chose to remain in self-imposed exile."

"But why didn't you go back with an army and take it back? Obviously you still have power and resources at your disposal or I wouldn't be here."

"Because I could do neither. I was alone, and physically unable to return to Rome."

"What do you mean?"

"Rome is forever lost to me, a place I shall never return to."

By now, I understood that Merlin would have clarified had he had any intention of doing so, but since he hadn't, I knew it was a moot point, so I reluctantly moved on, once again placing my face in my hands as I tried to process everything I was learning. "But if Romulus could only control the red orb, how did he even return with the blue one?"

"An excellent question, and one I do not have an answer to, but one I am certain you will discover on your own."

I shook my head within my hands, once again realizing such a vague answer was going to be left as such.

My next question came out very softly. "How could you let all of this happen, Merlin?"

"I believe I already told you that the orbs muddy things. The powers of the old god are not one to be trifled with. They make things unclear to me. Disrupt things. They are, to use another of your wonderful sayings, a huge pain in my ass."

I smirked and lowered my hands. "Mine too, and theirs as well, it seems. You know, this is all kind of funny in a sick and twisted sort of way, because I always assumed Romulus would be the violent dickhead of the two. History remembers Remus as the victim in all this, but now I know it wasn't so black and white."

"They were twins," Merlin said. "Two sides of the same coin. They had their faults, but one always compensated for the other. They were perfect compliments, and very nearly the last of a generation that was so inherently... special. It's why I gave them joint access to the old god's power. I had no reason to suspect one would grow jealous of the other, and it was unfortunate that Remus never really had the opportunity to understand just how powerful his orb was, even on its own."

I nodded. "Seriously, although it's a shame that it's also a double edged sword, more likely to drive someone insane than help..."

I purposefully trailed off, hoping Merlin would get the hint for once.

"I was always planning to elaborate on that, Jacob," he said. "I assure you."

I didn't answer, letting my look of impatience do my speaking for me.

"I'm sorry, Jacob, I truly am," Merlin said. "The orbs were never meant to be wielded alone, and certainly not by anyone other than Romulus or Remus. When I separated its power, I separated its safeguards as well. The blue orb, as it is, affects the mind. The red, the body. Had you for some reason found the red orb, your body would have suffered instead. It may have seemed much like intense radiation sickness or, even worse, you could have developed extreme mutations, and no, not like the kind in comic books."

I flicked my eyes in the air. "I guess I got lucky then."

"No, I do not believe so," Merlin said. "The red orb may have killed you by now, but the blue orb will continue to warp your mind, worse and worse, day by day, but keep you alive."

"Like with Caligula and Claudius," I said, finally coming to a point in our discussions where I already understood the context.

"Exactly."

"But why didn't it happen to Varus? And why the four of us and no one else?"

"Pat yourself on the back, Jacob," Merlin said with the first bit of humor I'd heard in a while, "because you did get one thing right. You, Varus, Caligula, and Claudius all share a genetic link to Romulus and Remus, although only you and Varus share a direct lineage with Remus, hence your ability to use the orb. It's all in the eyes…"

"So Remus had children then before he disappeared?" I asked, cutting him off.

"Only one," Merlin answered.

"Really?"

"Really."

"Wow," I said, feeling giddy at the confirmation. "That's pretty cool."

Merlin smiled like a father enjoying his son's own enjoyment of something well beneath him. "I suppose it is."

"But, wait," I said, thinking out load. "Then that means Agrippina is in the same boat. So why hasn't it affected her? Or Varus, like I asked earlier?"

"Varus was a kindred spirit, Jacob," Merlin answered immediately. "He was a gentle man and one who was very focused and driven. He didn't let his mind wander into a quagmire of 'what ifs' and 'how comes' and he didn't let it grind him down through fear, pride, avarice, seduction, indecision, or conspiracy. The orb would have affected him eventually, but his mind was well defended against outside influences. The likes of Caligula and Claudius, while perhaps good men at heart, were not so capable. The orb is simply too powerful for a human mind to handle. Some are just more capable of handling it than others."

"But what about Agrippina?" I asked, not quite understanding. "She's the worst kind of person, always looking out for what's best for herself, no matter the cost."

"It's not about being good or bad, Jacob. It's about how capable the mind is. Agrippina is many things, but unlike her brothers, she is not plagued by things that weigh on her mind. She is a determined, mindful person. She achieves her goals and is completely confident in the manner in which she accomplishes them. Her mind is well guarded, perhaps even more than Varus' was."

"But..." I started to say, the implications of his words saddening me.

"But," Merlin said, his voice just as dour, "what does that mean for your own mind?

I dropped my head. "Yeah..."

"I'm sorry, Jacob. No one is perfect, but you know as well as I that your mind is a tortured one. It always has been," he finished, pointing off toward my younger self who I saw was leaning against a back wall now, banging his head into it repeatedly in boredom or frustration, maybe both. "You are a product of your upbringing and your lineage. Romulus and Remus were head strong and inquisitive as well, but they never lacked in confidence. You, however, have never had faith in anyone, let alone yourself, and it is that doubt that harms your mind and keeps it constantly thinking, constantly blaming itself for everything, and constantly underestimating itself."

"I can't help it, Merlin," I whispered.

"I know you can't, Jacob. Nobody can help who they are. Nobody, not even me, is perfect. I've made my mistakes as well."

I clenched my hands into fists and shook them above the bar before pounding them down upon it. "I just can't stop blaming myself, Merlin! This is all my fault, and I'm so goddamned angry because of it. All the time. If not for me, everything would be different. Artie 2.0 wouldn't exist and my friends and I would be home and not in this shit storm. I know life wasn't perfect back home but at least I wouldn't have been responsible for screwing up their lives and forcing this on them. And now, after everything I've done in the past few months under the orb's influence... how am I supposed to live with myself? How am I supposed to expect Helena to keep loving me? *How?*"

I felt like crying like the whiney, wimpy, self-absorbed baby that I knew I'd become, but then I felt Merlin's hand reach out and grip my arm consolingly. I turned to look into his eyes that were so supportive, so full of forgiveness and understanding that I wasn't sure he was the same man I'd been with all this time.

My first tear fell, but then Merlin's hand tightened. "You learn to live with yourself by realizing that none of this, *none of this*, is your fault. You must understand that."

He spoke his words with such force that they caused my tears to dry up completely, but still I was left unconvinced.

"Easy for you to say," I said.

"It is not easy for me to say, Jacob. Not at all. Because the fact is that all the fault you place in yourself should be directed at *me*. You see, the fault is mine. Mine, and mine alone."

"What?" I asked, choking back one last tear.

He pulled his hand away and dropped both into his lap.

"You blame yourself for bringing your friends here. I understand that. But you have to understand that it's my fault you encountered the orb at all. I gave both orbs to Romulus and Remus and because I allowed Romulus to maintain possession of the blue orb, it's my fault that it was locked away beneath the Temple of Lupercal, and my fault you and Varus connected through them, and, therefore, *my* fault you are now trapped here. I can't even begin to explain how sorry I am, because this responsibility has pained me equally as long as it has pained you."

My first thought was to punch him right between the eyes, but the punch never landed. In fact, I never let it go. Not because I didn't think it would be of any use, but because I realized that placing blame on Merlin wouldn't help anyone. Just hearing his admission of guilt seemed more poignant to me than all the years I'd spent trying to justify my actions, not because I now blamed him, but because I finally realized that there must have been something in Merlin's own past that had influenced the decision he'd made to give the orbs to Romulus and Remus in the first place. It may have happened all the way back at the advent of the Big Bang, or the creation of the old god or whoever the hell he was, but something had pushed him as well.

He wasn't really to blame either.

Merlin smiled. "A good start, Jacob. A very good start."

I finally wiped away the only tear to have fallen with a hand, and nodded with a smile of my own, feeling a hell of a lot better than I had just a minute ago, also feeling that perhaps when this was all over, I'd never feel quite so bad ever again.

"Thanks, Merlin," I said.

"You are very welcome, Jacob. Very. Your acceptance of this truth brings me great happiness as well."

I sniffed and tried not to think of anything in that moment, not really wanting to hear or understand any more. It really was all too much already. My eyes wandered around the bar area and I noticed that Foxtrot Alpha had left, possibly to grab a food order. I continued to look around when my attention landed on a big screen TV off to my left. Playing there was a football game between the Cleveland Browns and the Chicago Bears, with Cleveland leading by a touchdown at the two minute warning.

There were two minutes left in the game.

I turned back to Merlin, understanding. "We're almost done here, aren't we?"

He nodded. "You have already stayed far too long. I apologize for that in advance but I think we still have a little bit of time left. So, your final questions, please."

I sat there and thought, but I didn't need long. They were all there, right on the tip of my tongue, as if they'd been there all along.

"I need the red orb to get home, don't I?"

"Yes."

"Time and space," I whispered, a smile growing as everything become as clear and vibrant as the morning sun. "This timeline is shot to hell. Too many dead and too much changed. In this timeline, 2021 is completely different."

"Perhaps not completely," Merlin interjected.

I bounced my head in agreement. "Perhaps not, but different enough to have at least caused Artie and Archer's timeline to come about, although I guess that must have changed by now as well."

Merlin dipped his head in agreement.

I continued. "But with the red orb, I can find *my* timeline. My reality. Blue to get to the year 2021, Red to get to Earth 1.0. My Earth. I can even use it to send Artie, Archer, and the rest back to their home as well..."

Merlin leaned back and smacked the bar. "Nailed it."

But I wasn't exactly so cheery. Artie and Archer had come here to change their timeline back into something a lot less horrible, but it can't be changed. Their timeline, although recently created by me, was just one among an infinite number. I couldn't change their timeline and I couldn't send them to another because they wouldn't belong. I would have no choice but to send them back to the place to which they had no desire to return.

I wondered how Archer would take that news.

"What about the orb's radiation?" I asked, more worried about that in the short term. "How do I keep my sanity along the way?"

"The orb is just a device, nothing more. Its power isn't unlimited. You have not yet reached the point of no return, Jacob; just keep your distance from it and you will be fine."

"What happens when I need to use it though?"

"Reuniting the orbs is the only way of eliminating their individual radiations. Find the red orb and you can use them at will."

"But I'm a descendent of Remus, not Romulus, how can I even use the red orb if I find it at all?"

"After three thousand years of generations, would you really be so surprised to learn that you're actually descended from both?"

I thought about it and then grinned, everything beginning to come together in a surprisingly neat package. "How incestuous..."

Merlin barked out a laugh. After three thousand years? Hardly."

I laughed too, unable to help myself. "Of all those people out there, Merlin... all those people who must share similar genetic lineages... and I'm the one this happens to? How unlucky am I?

"Among the unluckiest I have ever met, Jacob," he said with further chuckles. "As I said, you are neither the hero of this story, nor *The One*. You are just an exceptionally unfortunate man now tasked with an arduous duty wrought with untellable danger. I really am sorry."

"Don't be," I said, meaning it. "I don't want to be predestined for anything. Too much… responsibility. Besides, if I actually remember any of this once you let me leave, I'll at least be able to say that I got to meet *you*. How many people get to meet Merlin the Magician, King Arthur's personal wizard?

He nodded in amusement. "Very few."

I mimicked the expression but then the reality of my situation sank in. "Wait a second. How am I even going to find the red orb? It's trapped in time and space somewhere! How did Romulus even get home with the blue orb if he couldn't control it?"

"He never explained," Merlin stated, "and I only have suspicions."

"But where should I even start looking for it?"

"What was it your father would tell you when you couldn't find something?"

I thought for a moment, memories about my dad not always so readily available. "To… look again in the last place I saw it?"

"There you go, Jacob. Perhaps you shouldn't be so hard on your father either."

"But where…" I started, but then it came to me. "Rome!"

"Seems like a good place to start to me," Merlin joked.

"So that's it then?" I asked, surprised at how easy it all seemed. "Get the red orb, use it and the blue orb together, and then go home? How am I even supposed to use them?"

"Going home is an… option, Jacob."

I looked at him curiously, forgetting he'd failed to answer my second question. "What do you mean?"

"Let me ask you something first," Merlin said.

"All right."

"If you succeed in retrieving both orbs, you will have all the power I had so stupidly given to Romulus and Remus, and you saw the kind of… men… they were. So what will *you* do with it?"

I leaned back in my stool in complete surprise. "Wow... I actually hadn't thought about that."

Merlin nodded and patted my knee. "That is exactly why I feel comfortable giving you this power. For all your faults, you are an admirable man. You may not always have all the right answers, you place far too much responsibility on your own shoulders, and you are often quick to anger and judgment, but you always try to do the right thing, often at the expense of what you want for yourself. Sometimes it is misguided, but at least you always have the best intentions at heart."

"But didn't you think the same of Romulus and Remus? I mean... they were like gods."

"Were that even true, you know mythology. 'Gods' are hardly perfect. You, on the other hand, have been through an experience they had not. Real gods or not, they were certainly gods among men, and while you are simply a man, you are a man who knows better. It is because of that fact alone that I think you will do the right thing."

I took comfort in his confidence, surprised at how much it meant to me. "But what did you mean about going home only being an option?"

"Think on it, Jacob," he said happily as he glanced at the TV behind me. "Looks like your game is over."

I didn't bother looking. "Who won?"

"Couldn't care less," Merlin said. "I find American football to be quite dull."

I smiled slyly. "You really have gone native, you redcoat, you."

He shrugged and stood from his stool. He stretched his arms over his head and twisted at the waist and I heard bones pop. When he was finished, he reached into his fanny pack and removed five hundred dollars and plopped it on the bar.

"That should cover us," he said and moved toward the restaurant's exit.

"I'll say," I said and once again looked for Foxtrot Alpha, but she was still in the back somewhere. I frowned, upset I wouldn't be able to say goodbye. As much as I'd lusted over her back in high school, she really had been the sweetest person here, and I'd often missed her during my time employed at various other jobs, wishing my other coworkers could have been more like her.

Taking a deep breath I pushed away from the bar, gave it one last melancholy look, and turned to leave as well. I walked past the few remaining booths in the bar area, a half full barrel of peanuts, and the kitchen to my left. As I approached the hostess' station, I noticed Suzie-Lu and Victoria's Secret dutifully manning their post. The night was still slow, so they had little to do but chat, and both perked up as I passed by. Victoria's Secret looked at me like a woman on a mission, flicking her eyebrows at me and pouting her lips, but I simply laughed at her and turned to Suzie-Lu. Victoria's Secret scoffed and retreated into the kitchen, leaving Suzie-Lu and me alone. She looked almost embarrassed that I'd pay her any attention at all while Victoria's Secret had been right there, but she had always been a professional hostess, even at such a young age, and easily recovered.

"Did you enjoy everything?" She asked, only a hint of discomfort in her voice.

I nodded happily. "More than you can possibly imagine."

"That much, huh?" She asked. "Well, good! We hope to see you back again soon."

I laughed lightly. "I'll do my best."

I turned to leave but stopped as a thought came to mind, and I looked back at Suzie-Lu. "Hey, I know this isn't any of my business, but you wouldn't happen to be dating one of the bus boys around here, would you?"

She glanced down at her seating chart and blushed. "Umm… yeah, why?"

"Oh, no reason really," I told her, raising my hands innocently. "I just wanted to say: be patient with him. He can be a bit of a jerk sometimes but that's just because he's got no idea what he's doing. He'll grow up some day."

"Uhh…" she said with an odd look on her face, "…okay? Thanks I guess."

"No sweat, Suzie-Lu. Take care of yourself."

I turned and made my way to the double set of large doors that acted as the entrance and exit to the restaurant. They showed me nothing of interest, just a reflection of the restaurant behind me, but I was confident in my decision to simply push through them and see what happened next.

***

I was back in the empty, dark room with no walls, the same one that offered me no evidence that I was actually in a physical space, but unlike before, I wasn't disoriented by its emptiness as I looked around for the door that would allow me to leave. I found it almost immediately to my right, and I moved toward it. The only difference in the door now was that I couldn't see anyone outside through its cracks, but the terrain looked exactly the same, and I figured Agrippina and my friends must have moved away to find a more comfortable place to await my return. Without another thought, I placed my hand against the door and prepared to leave.

"It was a real pleasure meeting you, Jacob Hunter," Merlin said from behind me.

I removed my hand and turned to face him. He was back in his dull red wizard robes with the half-moons on them, looking just like my mother's chess pieces. I smiled, generally happy to see him, almost nostalgic that it was already time to leave.

"Come to see me off?" I asked.

"I couldn't just let you go without saying goodbye."

I chuckled. "Was all this really real, Merlin?" I asked, still unsure even now. "It all just seems so convenient."

"It was more than real," he assured me. "And this was most certainly not forced on you. You brought yourself here of your own volition."

I shook my head and took a step toward him. "It's just that I never expected such a *deus ex machina* moment in all this, Merlin, but I guess I should just take it! I never thought I'd be given *any* help at all, let alone how much you showed me. I... I really don't know what to say. You've shown me so much and given me so much to think on, things actually *worth* thinking. Things I feel really special just knowing. But more importantly, you've given me direction, which I think I needed more than anything else."

Merlin smiled. "I am glad, Jacob, and I must be honest that you have given me much to think on as well. More than you can possibly imagine."

I nodded. "Good. I suppose I should be proud of myself for teaching an old dog a few new tricks then."

His smile widened. "You should be."

I lifted my arms and let them fall to slap against my thighs. "So what are you going to do now? I have to imagine your meeting me has changed your perspective on life at least a little."

"It has, but all that's in the cards for me now is to wait."

"For King Arthur and his valiant Knights of the Round Table?" I asked, striking a heroic poise with my right hand clenched in a fist against my heart.

He chuckled. "Yes, actually."

"Amazing," I muttered, still in disbelief, collapsing the pose. "Just amazing! The next thing you'll tell me is that you're waiting for them just so you can use Arthur to find the Holy Grail for you, because it…"

I trailed off as my own words caused new thoughts to pop into my head.

"Wait, you said earlier that Romulus and Remus were very *nearly* the last of a generation. Not *the* last. Does that mean… no way… are you telling me that King Arthur was just like them? 'Advanced' or whatever you called them? Are you…" And then another thought popped into my mind, "…and are you going to send him and his knights out in search of the Holy Grail because it's… it's… nothing more than the blue orb itself!?"

Merlin shook his head and sighed. "You really are a very perceptive man, Jacob. Your mother was not wrong about many things, but she certainly was when she thought all that television would rot your brain."

"But…" I started, "…I… You… Arthur…"

"Try not to think about it, Jacob. Remember what we talked about."

"I… I guess you're right, but Jesus Christ, Merlin! You really *are* Merlin! It's just that you were also so much more before historians ever thought you even existed. And they don't have any idea. What other historical figures were you as well?"

"Oh, I'm sure one or two of them do," Merlin said, once again ignoring the more important question. "There's always a fringe historian here or there who accidentally guesses right from time to time."

"I guess that's true," I said.

I was too shocked to really know what I was saying, but as my mind cleared, the two of us found ourselves standing there in companionable silence. I'm sure Merlin could have found something meaningful to say, but I, for one, was speechless. Words simply couldn't describe everything I felt in this moment. I looked at him awkwardly again and shrugged, my feet planted, unable to bring myself to do much of anything.

Merlin nodded comfortingly and opened his arms. "Let's just hug it out and send you on your way."

I nodded vigorously and stepped in to give him hug. I hadn't hugged many men in my time, but somehow this one felt right. It was how I'd always thought it would feel to hug my father, and I swore in that moment that if I ever found my way home again, that I'd do everything I could to repair our broken relationship.

Merlin held me there tightly, but after a quick moment, let me go. We looked at each other and he smiled again, giving my shoulders a quick pat. "Take care of yourself, Jacob Hunter. Just remember this: while your journey may seem like it's coming to an end, I assure you, it is only just beginning."

"What does that mean?"

"All in good time."

Unable to think of a response, I pulled away and headed toward the door. I held out my hand and made contact with it, ready to push it open, but then turned for one last question. I half expected Merlin to have vanished by the time I'd fully turned around, but he was still there.

"How can I ever thank you for all this?" I asked.

"Just make me proud."

Which was all he needed to say, exactly like my mom.

I ground my teeth together. "I'll try, Merlin. I promise."

"I know you will, Jacob," he said, but then his tone grew playful. "But, hey, if you don't, you could always just name your first born son after me instead."

I barked out a laugh. "Name him Merlin? Yeah right. Have you even met Helena? She'll never go for that."

"Probably not," Merlin admitted, "but after all this, I'm sure you'll be able to convince her."

"I'll do my best."

"You always do, Jacob," he said, and then winked out of existence.

My smile slowly disappeared and I wasted half a second wondering if all of this had in fact been nothing more than a nightmare, but I just as quickly dismissed it and kicked myself for even entertaining the notion.

This was everything but a nightmare.

This was a dream come true.

And I couldn't be happier.

I pushed open the door and stepped out into the snow covered field I'd left no more than a few hours ago.

***

I felt groggy. I felt cold. I felt wet. And I felt like I was lying on my back.

I wasn't sure why exactly, as I didn't remember falling after leaving the cottage, but I couldn't shake the feeling that I was in fact lying in the cold, wet snow. Nor could I explain why I felt so horrible, like I'd only had an hour of sleep after a night of heavy drinking, made worse because I couldn't feel my limbs or extremities. They felt stiff and unresponsive, and every little movement I attempted took a serious force of will, even just to wiggle my toes.

"Jacob!"

The voice sounded intense but distance, like I was being called to from very far away. Since I'd never find out who had called out to me if I didn't open my eyes, I decided now would be a good time to do just that. When I did, I found my vision to be fuzzy, but I could still make out what appeared to be a man kneeling above me. He called my name again, which sounded clearer and less distant now. I struggled to lift my head, failing at the attempt, but I felt him snake a hand beneath my neck and lift me into a sitting position, a movement that both hurt and felt damn good at the same time.

Once I was up, I struggled to keep myself upright. Much like a very young baby just learning to support himself, I almost fell over, but the man's strong hands kept me steady. I heard him call out again, but it was clearly not my name this time. I squeezed my eyes shut and flicked my head to the side, trying to dislodge my grogginess. Feeling slightly better, I opened my eyes again and while my vision remained unclear, I could now identify the man helping me as Bordeaux.

"Wh…" I tried to say, but my throat was dry and crackly from a lack of use. I gulped and tried to find my words. "Wh-where've you been, big guy? I feel like I haven't seen you in months."

The large Frenchman looked confused at my words as he shook his head. "Are you all right, *mon ami*?"

"It's good to hear you call me that, Jeanne…" I trailed off, my mind wandering and unfocused, "… Jeanne… Hey, isn't Jeanne a girl's name?"

Bordeaux looked cross at the suggestion. "Most people who remind me don't stay conscious long. Would you like to go back to sleep then?"

"No, I think I've slept long enough," I said quickly, feeling elated at once again being in the presence of one of my friends. "How long was I gone, anyway? Two hours? Three?"

Bordeaux opened his mouth again, but then a pair of new faces ran into view. Santino and Boudicca rushed over and knelt beside me, and I felt elated at seeing them, like I hadn't seen them in years.

"I had just the strangest dream…" I said in my best Judy Garland impersonation. "You weren't there and you weren't there either," I said, pointing at Santino and Bordeaux, but then I dropped my hand and shuddered when my finger landed on Boudicca. "But you were there… in a thong bikini."

Santino and Bordeaux exchanged glances before looking at Boudicca, who simply knelt there in confusion. Both men looked down at me, clearly concerned for my mental state.

"Just what kind of dream did you have, Hunter?" Santino asked.

"A fantastic one," I said. "Well, besides that part. I've got so much to tell you guys, and you're not going to believe any of it, but…"

I cut myself off when a burst of pain resonated from within my stomach. I tried to move a hand to hold my abdomen, but I could barely lift it.

"Damn, I'm fucking hungry!" I nearly shouted, realizing that was my problem. "I feel like I haven't eaten in days!"

Bordeaux and Santino traded glances again, but this time Boudicca joined in with the awkward looks as well.

"What?" I asked, noticing their odd behavior.

Bordeaux looked down at me first. "How long do you think you were gone again, Jacob?"

"I don't know. A couple hours? Feels like a lot longer though…"

Bordeaux looked up at Santino, but Santino didn't look away from me.

"Jacob," he said, "you've been gone thirty seven days. That's with a three and then a seven, buddy. That's over a month!"

XII
Decisions

Northern Britannia
March, 44 A.D.

The four of us hadn't spent long in the clearing after Santino's surprising announcement. I'd sat there quite shocked for a few seconds as realization for why I was so hungry and stiff started making sense. It was no wonder that Merlin felt so pressed for time there at the end. Two hours with him had been a month in the real world. It was a long time to be out of the loop and my first thoughts were of how my friends had interacted in such close proximity with Agrippina for all that time.

I could have spent another month wondering why and how such a time differentiation could have occurred, but if I'd learned anything from my time with Merlin, it was that sometimes it was best just to ignore the less important questions, which would have been easier to do had my friends given me some information of their own to mull on.

All they'd confirmed to me was that Helena hadn't yet given birth, but hadn't elaborated much more than that as Bordeaux and Boudicca picked me up, set me on a random horse, and helped me stay in the saddle as we rode back to camp. Santino joined us, but a fourth presence in the clearing, Minicius, lingered under orders to wait until he was certain we were back at camp before returning with the blue orb, but making sure he kept it as far away from me as possible.

It was with that order from Santino that I'd finally taken notice of the cottage's disappearance, replaced with nothing more than a very real looking dead log that simply sat in the snow. There was nothing there to indicate anything unnatural had been there at all. After asking my companions about this, Santino had some interesting things to say on it.

"We all watched you go inside, Jacob," he'd said as Bordeaux and Boudicca had lifted me atop the horse. "We watched the door close behind you, heard the sound of it clinking shut and everything, but then it just disappeared! Artie thought it had simply gone invisible, but Archer walked his horse right through the area. There was nothing there. Even the snow looked completely untouched. All we saw were your footprints leading to the door, and then... nothing."

I could tell my disappearance had affected him deeply, because his explanation had been as straight forward and devoid of stupidity as I'd ever heard from him. He'd gone on to explain that the initial contingent had waited for six hours before they'd decided to go home, sending shifts of two to four individuals to keep watch over the location and await my return. He'd also said that both the legionnaires and Praetorians had wanted to leave a month ago, but only at the insistence of both Helena and Agrippina had they stayed. Apparently, both women – for what I was sure were completely different reasons – had demanded that they remain indefinitely.

It was then that I'd asked for more information about Helena, but none had come. I'd then asked for an update on Agrippina, asking if she was treating them well. All they'd said was that she was, but it wasn't like she interacted with them much. I then asked about the status of the camp, which was met with very dour looks all around, but again, no explanation. I'd taken a deep breath, upset at their silence, but remembering Merlin's advice about not letting my thoughts eat away at me, and asked no further questions, understanding that an explanation would come soon enough.

I only hoped it came sooner rather than later because my absence from the real world had left me confused and disoriented. My body felt weak from a month of inactivity and my mind couldn't understand that. The more I thought about it, the more disconnected I felt, like my mind and my body had been separated and could no longer function optimally together. It was an odd feeling, made worse by the fact that I didn't understand why I wasn't dead.

A month of complete inactivity and a lack of food and water should have left me a withered husk, but my only conclusion was that Merlin had somehow provided my stomach with sustenance and my muscles with mild stimulation to keep them from atrophying completely, although it hadn't done much to keep my beard from growing out. Unwanted facial growth or not, I was thankful, because with the way my friends were acting, I was pretty sure I was going to need my body in working order sooner rather than later.

But despite how horrid my body felt and how drained my mind was, I was grateful for the simple fact that my friends hadn't abandoned me. After everything I'd done in the past few months, I wouldn't even have been upset had they simply forgotten about me and moved on. I'd done more than my fair share to earn their distrust and hate, done purposefully on my part or not, and I was grateful for their loyalty.

They'd never understand, but still I rode my nameless horse to where Santino rode his own, near the tip of our tiny formation. When I arrived, he glanced at me and nodded in welcome, but didn't seem nearly as cheery as he usually did.

"Got a minute, John?" I asked.

"I've got more than I know what to do with, Jacob," he said, leaning over to nudge me with an elbow. "All thanks to you."

"About that," I said, "I can't thank you enough. All of you. After everything I'd done, I'm surprised anyone cared enough…"

"Shut up with that shit, Hunter," Santino said, although he didn't sound overly angry. "We're not stupid. The orb is one hell of a drug. It fucked you up, and we weren't just going to abandon you. What kind of friends would abandon their crack addicted friend to get worse and worse and not doing anything about it?"

"I guess I never really thought about it…"

"Then of course there's Helena to think about," Santino continued. "Honestly, I'm pretty sure most of us would have just left your ass to the wolves after all the shit you did, but you know better than all of us just how scary she gets when she's angry, so we couldn't just leave you. She wouldn't let us."

I smirked, easily able to imagine a pregnant, and therefore very quick to anger, Helena.

"And Agrippina?"

"Oh that bitch wouldn't let us leave either," he said, fidgeting atop his horse. "She digs you, Jacob. Always has. I'll never understand what it is, but she's got a hard on for you, my friend."

I rolled my eyes. "After all this, you still don't know what…"

"Of course I know!" Santino exclaimed. "Shit, Jacob, I just wanted to describe her as having a hard on, is all. That's funny stuff."

I patted his shoulder.

"That's right, Jonathon… that's *very* funny stuff…"

"Damn right, but it's not like we saw her much while you were gone," he continued. "She stayed in her *praetorium* most of the time, only rarely coming to ask for an update on you."

"Who'd she talk to?"

"Archer mostly, to be honest, which we all found kind of odd. Sometimes Vincent. Once me, but that didn't end very well…"

"Was she ever in the same room with Helena?"

"Are you kidding?" He said with a quick laugh. "Do you honestly think Helena would ever voluntarily be caught dead in the same room with Agrippina? Hell no, especially not these days when it's not so easy for her to stab Agrippina in the throat anymore."

I nodded and joined him in laughter, although not quite so enthusiastically. The idea of Agrippina spending so much time with Archer worried me. What was her angle there? And the answer to why exactly she cared so much about me at all continued to elude me. I wasn't sure if she would be sticking around once I returned to camp, or what she would do when I told everyone what I'd experienced, and that uncertainty didn't exactly leave me feeling optimistic.

"Nothing's happened to anybody, right?" I asked after a moment. "Is Artie all right?"

He squinted at me. "What? No, she's fine. You think we wouldn't tell you if something had happened to her?"

I shrugged. "It's just that your entire sit rep has been lacking in information, Santino. I just want to know what's going on."

He scoffed. "Won't need us to tell you soon enough, buddy. Just find your inner chi or whatever and get ready for it."

There was no point in asking what the fuck that meant, so I tried to roll my shoulders, which I managed to do uncomfortably, and looked away. Something really big must be going on to have Santino acting this way, so I settled myself like he suggested and tried to clear my mind. I was still processing every single word Merlin had told me and every single image he'd shown me, trying to understand it, and use it to my benefit. If everything really was as simple as finding the red orb and using it and the blue orb in conjunction to get home, great, but I wasn't nearly ready to believe my life could ever be *that* easy.

Something was bound to go wrong with Merlin's plan, or he'd purposefully left something out of it, so I had to be ready. I had to stay focused and keep myself from being lulled into a false sense of complacency, but as we approached the edge of the forest, I discovered there would be little chance of that happening any time soon.

Agrippina's camp of Praetorians was under siege.

Maybe two miles off in the distance, her small camp was surrounded by an army of enemy soldiers. A trench system travelled the circumference of the camp, and fortifications dotted its long, circular line. It was an impressive sight of siege warfare, one I hadn't expected from whatever natives called this part of Britain home.

And there was a perfectly good explanation for that.

Because the besiegers were not native Britons at all.

They were Romans.

I dropped my head in defeat at the sight of it.

"Who'd I piss off this time?" I asked.

Santino chuckled. "Who do you think?"

I barely needed to. "Galba?"

"Galba."

"When did he show up?" I asked, lifting my head to better analyze Galba's forces.

"Little over a week ago," Santino replied. "And believe me, he didn't come bearing gifts."

I raised an arm and pointed toward his army. "What the hell's he even doing here?"

"He's come for Agrippina," Santino answered, but he didn't seem finished with his answer.

"And..." I prodded.

"Well, Jake, he's come for you too. Apparently, he's a little sore at how you treated him last time. But don't worry, he doesn't even blame you."

"He knows I was affected by the orb?"

"Oh, that? Fuck no. He doesn't know shit about that. No, he blames Vespasian for giving you so much power and shit to do. Seems Galba's about ready to march on Rome himself, take things over, use Agrippina as leverage, and... well you know, put Vespasian's head on a spike... right next to yours, of course."

I looked at Santino with a mixture of surprise and confusion. "He tell you all that?"

He shrugged. "Not in so many words, but you know Galba. He's about as blunt as my elbow and not nearly as eloquent. I got the gist."

"Yeesh," I said, more surprised than worried. "I didn't think the guy would take it so personally."

"He's a Roman," Santino said. "They take *everything* personally."

"Good point," I said, but then the worry started to settle in. "So how are we going to get through all that?"

Santino reached out and clapped me roughly on the back, so hard that I almost fell off my horse. "Why do you think Helena made me spend sixteen hours a day waiting for your sorry ass? For my health?"

***

To this day, I still found it surprising when I had to be reminded of how useful Santino could be. Sneaking into a hostile Roman encampment was never a very good idea, but unlike the last time I had to do it, at least Santino was around this time.

He led us around Galba's trench, giving it a wide berth as we snuck toward a section that seemed less dense. At least, that's what Santino told me was the reason why we spent an entire hour sneaking through the shadows provided by the tree line, but I didn't question him. I still felt slow and dazed, and my mind's lethargic state hadn't improved much since leaving the clearing. Galba's Romans could have been flying for all I knew, so I simply followed while Bordeaux and Boudicca did the same.

By the time we ran out of tree line to hide within, I started questioning Santino's entire plan, but then I watched as he dismounted from his horse and made his way toward a large clump of bushes hidden behind a denser part of the tree line. I watched him approach them and waited while he got down on his hands and knees, and crawled into the thicket. Moments later, he emerged dragging a large satchel behind him, swearing at the same time as he wiped a droplet of blood from his face from a wound he must have sustained in the bushes. Once he was clear, he stood and angrily threw the satchel in front of him. Bordeaux and Boudicca knelt beside it and pulled sets of legionary armor from within, followed by swords and other equipment.

I stared at it, not quite understanding at first, but Boudicca looked up at me and noticed my confusion.

"They will conceal our identities, Hunter. A disguise."

Santino knelt beside her and looked up at me. "What part of that didn't you get?"

I shook my head as though I was snapping myself from a day dream. "What? I got it. No problem."

"Are you certain you are well, Jacob?" Bordeaux asked.

"Hmm? Yeah. I feel fine. No problem."

Bordeaux and Santino traded glances as the latter stood, hefting a set of armor in his hands. He walked around Boudicca and threw it at me atop my horse. Unprepared for it, I made a sluggish grab for it, but managed only to slip from my horse and tumble to the ground in a heap. I hit roughly and meekly coiled into a ball, thinking to do nothing more than just lay there. I wasn't upset or sad or angry, I was just tired and confused, unable to get a grip on reality. I heard a slight crunching in the snow beside me, so I opened my eyes to see Santino looming over me. He placed his hands on his hips and shook his head at me.

"Jeez, Hunter, let's not make a big scene out of this," he said as he reached down to help me up. "This'll be an easy one, and I'll hold your hand the whole way. Don't worry your pretty little self one bit."

***

And Santino had been right, but at least he hadn't held my hand.

We'd waited until night, and then some, before beginning our infiltration of Galba's camp. At first, I'd wondered about Bordeaux and Boudicca, neither looking anything like your typical Roman because of their size. I was less concerned by Boudicca's femininity since she filled out her armor as well as any man I'd ever seen, but still she and Bordeaux, and myself as well for that matter, were far larger than the average Roman. Santino, who stood just shy of six feet, fit in well enough even though he was still a bit tall for your average legionnaire, but the rest of us stood out like a kiwi in a fruit basket...

Okay that probably wasn't the best analogy.

Boy I was out of it...

But, as Santino had assured, our little operation had gone off easily and quickly. Not a single legionnaire glanced twice at our quartet as we marched into the nearest fort strung along the entrenchment surrounding Agrippina's camp. We'd left our horses strung up near Santino's cache of legionary gear so it was just the four of us, and at least we looked the part. Once in the trenches, we simply walked toward a spot that Santino had identified long ago to be a weak point along their lines, and crawled our way toward Agrippina's fortifications. Once there, we crept along its perimeter, having already been identified by our own people thanks to an IR beacon Santino carried with him, and simply walked through the *porta praetoria.*

Once inside, I dropped every bit of extraneous gear I had and sprinted in the best approximation of the term toward where I remembered my friends had made camp. I passed by dozens, if not hundreds, of Praetorians and legionnaires as I ran, each pointing at me like they were seeing a ghost, knowing who I was but not expecting to ever see me again, I supposed. But none moved to stop me, not that any of them would have been able to as I barreled like a drunken bull in a china shop toward Helena.

I stumbled dozens of times as my head felt light or empty or heavy all at the same time, or as leg muscles would tense up and threaten to cramp on me, and I fell completely into the cold snow at least three times along the way, one time falling into a pair of my legionnaires as I careened into their tent. They helped me up, dazed and confused as to the fact that it was *me* who had fallen into their quarters, but had simply gotten out of the way as I shrugged them off and continued my trek.

My legs were starting to work properly again, but after another two minutes, I was left panting for breath as I finally arrived at our small community of displaced time travelers and reality hoppers. Arrayed around a fire situated at the center of our half-moon setup of tents were Vincent, Wang, Stryker, Cuyler, and

Artie. They sat discussing something in low tones with morbid body language, but it was Artie who noticed me first. She shot to her feet and stood there, gaping at me, while Vincent and Cuyler noticed her diverted attention and stood more slowly. Stryker and Wang were the last to understand what had distracted their companions, but Artie was already running toward me as realization set in.

Like M.J. in his prime, dunking from the three point line, she leapt into the air and threw her arms around me. I was momentarily distracted by her appearance, having been too focused on Helena to really understand who she was and why exactly she seemed so interested in my arrival. I nearly dropped her, my body still artificially weak, and while my first instinct was to throw her off and continue my search for Helena, I held onto her just as tightly as she clung to me. I found myself touched at how quickly Artie had responded to my arrival, even though it was also easier to remember now that she wasn't actually my sister.

But she was a pretty good substitute, I had to admit.

"Jacob!" She practically yelled into my ear as she hung off me. "What happened to you?? Where did you go??"

"It's a long story, Artie," I said as I reached a hand up to hold her head against my shoulder and pressed my cheek against her hair. "And an unbelievable one, but I have to see Helena first. Where is she?"

Artie pulled back but gripped my arms with her hands. She looked at me briefly, absentmindedly brushing my new beard with a hand, which was a grooming choice I wasn't sure she'd ever seen before, but then she looked toward the same tent I'd found her in with Helena and Wang a month ago.

She tossed her head toward it. "She's right where you left her, Jacob. I... I don't want to worry you but she hasn't been feeling well lately."

I looked toward the tent. "Is she okay? The baby?"

"It's... It's just that the past few weeks have been difficult."

"How difficult?" I asked, snapping my head back toward her.

"I don't want to say. I think it's best if you talk to Wang."

I moved my head to look around Artie and saw the small Brit standing apart from the others now, his expression no different than Artie's. I closed my eyes and nodded, their moods infecting my own, but then I gave Artie a supportive smile.

"It's all right, Artie. Everything will be fine."

She managed a small smile as well, but then she released my arms and stepped away. I watched her walk around me toward Santino, who reached out and gave her a small and innocent hug. It seemed just as brotherly a gesture as my own embrace with her a moment ago, but even if it hadn't been, I didn't think I minded anymore.

By the time I turned back around, Wang was already approaching me. I took a step toward him but he gestured toward Helena's tent and stepped to his left, angling us toward it. I walked with him but before he led me inside, he stopped me by clutching my forearm with a hand.

"Wait, Hunter," he said quietly. "Listen, Helena's okay, but the last few weeks have not been easy. She's very weak and I've forced her to stay in bed."

I nodded slowly, taking it all in. "And the baby?"

"I... I'm not sure," he admitted. "I haven't been able to get the ultrasound device working again and it's not like I can run blood work here, and..."

He trailed off, which wasn't something I wanted to hear.

"And?"

"His heartbeat is erratic. It goes in and out, but I don't like what I hear. There's a possibility she may deliver prematurely and there's nothing I can do if that happens. Or, and I'm rather worried about this, it may come down to a Caesarean section, and there isn't even a Roman or Celtic midwife around here to help if..."

Again, he didn't finish his thought, and I had to force myself to stiffen up and keep myself from falling apart then and there. This was the last thing I wanted to hear after everything I'd just been through, the last thing I even wanted to think could possibly happen, let alone learn *was* happening. It was too much, especially now, but I felt my mind hardening again and I surprised myself when I didn't crumble under Wang's news.

Instead, I was again surprised to find my hand rising of its own accord to grip my friend's shoulder. "It's okay, James. You've done everything you can. Helena's tough; she'll be fine."

Wang nodded. "I think so too, Hunter, but I just thought you should know."

"Thanks," I said, tightening my grip before letting go. "Can I see her now?"

"Of course, just try to keep her calm. Even the excitement of seeing you might be too much right now."

"Thanks, James," I said as I turned to the tent. "For everything."

"It wasn't a problem, mate. It was a priveledge."

"Even so," I said, giving him one last look. "Thanks."

Wang simply nodded and turned to leave while I returned my attention to the tent's entrance. I waited for a moment, making sure I was ready for this. It wouldn't do Helena any good for me to return to her in any kind of mood other than a positive one. It pained me inside immensely to think of her reduced to a bed, unable to care for herself, or take action in a time of need. Five years ago, I might not have been so upset over such a predicament, and in fact, Helena herself may not have seen it as a slight against her character either. But now Helena was as tough as nails and never one to back out of a fight or let someone else do her dirty work for her. She was as empathetic and understanding as anyone I'd ever met, but she'd also become hard over the years, unflinching in her devotion to the preservation of herself and those she loved.

All of this swam through my head as I stood there, unable to channel the courage needed to enter the tent and see what the Fates had reduced the woman I loved to. But I took a deep breath and tried to ignore myself, forcing my heavy hand up to reach for the tent's flap and pull it away, but just as I worked up the courage and desire to face Helena, a voice from behind me interrupted the action.

"Wait, Hunter!" It said, and I immediately knew it was Archer.

I stopped and turned to see my blond haired peer rushing toward me from somewhere within the Praetorian camp. His hair was longer than I'd ever seen it before now, almost to the point where he could tie it into a ponytail. I held out a hand to forestall his approach but he wasn't deterred.

"I don't have time for this, Paul," I said. "I have to see Helena."

"She doesn't even know you're here yet," he indicated as he pulled up just short of where I stood. "What's another few minutes? I need to know what you learned first. What information you gathered about the orb. Can you use it to change my world? Can you?"

I held up a hand and kneaded my brow. "Paul, I really don't have time to explain. It'll take a really long time and I have to see her. Can't you understand that?"

I turned to enter the tent but Archer lashed out and gripped my forearm with a powerful hand.

"Just you fucking wait, Hunter," he growled. "I remember your promise to help me fix my timeline. That's what I understand. You said you'd do everything you could, and I held you to that. Now can you help me or not, goddamn it!?"

The look he gave me was as intense as I'd ever seen from him before, his eyes furrowed in rage and his teeth grinding together causing his jaw bone to squirm behind its protective layer of skin. It was an interesting expression and a familiar one, one I must have worn a number of times as I attempted piece together the grand puzzle of the universe.

But I'd completed that puzzle now. Completed it, glued the pieces together, and framed it in my mother's den, just like she'd done with a dozen of her own completed puzzles. I knew exactly what I needed to get home and even where to look.

I had all of this knowledge.

All of this power.

But I didn't have enough of either to "fix" his home.

And he needed to know that soon.

"I'm sorry, Paul," I said meekly. "I don't think that I can. I'm sorry."

His expression tightened to seem even angrier, something I wasn't sure was possible. "What do you mean, you can't? Why not!?"

"I... I don't have time to explain," I repeated. "There's a lot of information and I'm too messed up right now to really think about it. I *have* to see Helena first."

In a burst of action he yanked on my arm and pulled me closer to him so that we stood nose to nose, his fingernails digging into my flesh.

"That's not good enough, Hunter!" He said, his mouth inches from my own. "You're responsible for my very existence! We're all just a byproduct of your fucking around with things you couldn't explain or control, and you promised me you would fix it! Don't tell me that you can't! I won't accept that!"

As the rage spewed from his lips like the saliva flying from his mouth, something inside my mind clicked. There was something in his words that confirmed a suspicion I'd had all along that he knew more than he was letting on. *You're responsible for my very existence.* These words did not imply that I had simply altered who he was, but that I had created him.

With this turn of phrase, I felt something else in me, the return of an old feeling I hadn't felt in quite a while: good old fashioned anger. Not the darkness fueled kind as a result of the orb and its manipulative power, but the kind I'd felt when an eighth grader stole my milk carton, or when the girl I'd wanted to date chose to go out with another guy, or when I got a B on a test, or when I failed in any other endeavor. It wasn't the kind of anger that made me want to exact revenge in a cruel, vengeful manner, but the kind that drove me to better myself and work harder.

It gave me a surge of energy, and I tore my arm free from Archer's grip and smashed both of my hands into his chest, pushing him so hard that he fell to the ground and slid backward in the snow. I looked down at him, but the anger was already fading, having done exactly what it had needed to do.

"I told you'd I'd help you, Archer," I said quite calmly, "and I will. If not for you, then at least for Artie. I just need time to process everything Merlin told me, so would you kindly fuck off for now?"

He stared at me angrily as he scrambled to his feet, but I was no longer intimidated by him, and while I still had to get the bottom of his subterfuge, that too could wait for another day.

"Merlin?"

The question came from behind me, and I turned and saw Vincent standing there with a smug grin on his face. I glanced back at Archer, but he was already rushing off toward the center of

Agrippina's camp, so I turned back to Vincent and returned his smile.

"Yeah, yeah," I said. "You're just so damn smart, aren't you, Vincent? Thanks for letting me in on that one, by the way. I really could have used the heads up."

"What was he like?" He asked, taking a small step forward excitedly.

"Great," I replied. "He was just great, but seriously, if you don't mind, I just laid out Archer for not letting me see Helena. Don't make me do the same to you."

The words were serious, but it was the last thing I wanted to do, and I was certain Vincent understood that from my tone alone.

"Jacob the last thing I want to do is to keep you from seeing her," he said, which I took as my cue to finally enter her tent, "but Galba is at the gate and he's demanding to see you. I don't think he's willing to wait long."

I wheeled around and took a quick step toward him. "Vincent you have to stall him. I can't do anything right now without seeing her first. I just can't. Stall him!"

"I don't know if I…"

"I'll help you." This voice came from behind Vincent, and I immediately identified it as Agrippina's. I looked over his shoulder and saw her standing well away from the two of us, her heavy cloaks wrapped tightly around her shoulders. She looked as somber and respectful as I'd ever seen her before, with her arms overlapping each other but encased in the sleeves of her robes. She flicked her eyes away, almost embarrassedly, as she continued. "He's here for me as much as for you, Jacob, so I'll go with Vincent and talk to him. I'm sure we can provide you with a few extra minutes."

I narrowed my eyes. "You'd do that?"

"Consider it a part of our continued reconciliation."

"I guess I will," I admitted, unable to think otherwise. "Thank you."

"You are welcome," she said. "Now come, Vincent. Let us go talk with the old curmudgeon."

He nodded over his shoulder at her but then looked back at me. "Take your time, Jacob. Galba may feel overwhelmed, but he's still a good man. I wouldn't think him capable of outright murder."

I clapped him on the shoulder. "Thanks, Vincent."

He placed his hand atop my own. "You are most welcome, my friend. Now go see her."

***

I entered the tent slowly, cautiously, not wanting to disturb the delicate balance that had been achieved here between Wang and Helena in my absence. I felt as though my very presence alone would be enough to disrupt whatever tenuous agreement the Fates had concocted to keep Helena and our baby alive through all this. I knew such superstition was silly, but the idea of the Fates as living, breathing creatures described as they were in mythology didn't seem so farfetched anymore, and the idea of fate, destiny, and predetermination didn't seem so alien either. Perhaps we all really were being controlled by some supreme being or force, and I didn't necessarily mean God or any god for that matter, but something far more malicious and completely real in the physical sense.

Then again, I certainly wasn't about to rule out *God* either at this point, but a lack of control and free will replaced with Divine Providence wasn't something I wanted to think about as I cleared the tent's entrance and saw Helena, which was when every thought in my mind evaporated.

She rested on her back atop a raised platform, her upper body angled upwards like it would on a medical bed in any hospital. Wang must have crafted some kind of cushioned wedge to place beneath her as she lay motionless, a blanket draped across her legs and bulbous baby bump, with her hands laying at her sides but above the sheet. She looked comfortable, almost peaceful, perhaps even just enjoying a deep sleep, but as I grew closer I could see the light sheen of perspiration across her forehead and how her skin was just the tiniest bit paler. Her skin always seemed perpetually sun kissed, even in the dead of winter, so I didn't for a moment suspect her current complexion was from a lack of sunlight.

Something was wrong.

I tip-toed closer, doing everything I could to remain silent, but by the time I was a step away from her bed, Helena's eyes snapped open and she turned weakly to look at me. Her eyes widened in surprise, but then they closed again and she looked away for a few moments before returning to me. They opened again and she looked at me more clearly now in recognition, and lifted a hand toward me.

Emotion overwhelmed me, and I leapt at her, grabbing her hand in both of mine. I lifted it and kissed it over and over in greeting and she smiled frailly at me.

"Are you really here?" She whispered.

"It's me, Helena," I assured. "I'm back. I promise."

Her eyes squinted in painful sadness and she looked away again. "What happened to you, Jacob? Why did you leave us for so long?"

"It wasn't exactly my idea," I told her, "and I had no idea so much time had passed."

She looked back at me with a bit of her patented anger in her eyes, as a few tears fell from them. "You were gone for so long. I... I didn't know what happened to you. I was afraid..."

I lifted her hand to my cheek and tried to calm her down. "It's okay, Helena. I'm here now."

I smiled for her benefit but it was a difficult expression to form. From my perspective, I'd only been gone a few hours, but I'd been gone over a month from Helena's. Ever since our first operation in Ancient Rome, when Caligula had sent a small team to assassinate a rival general, Helena and I had never been apart for more than a few days at a time, and such lengthy moments of separation had been very few and very long in between. A year ago, I'd thought our constant close proximity had drained some of the love from our relationship, but I'd later realized it had actually been the most intense bonding experience a couple could possibly go through. We'd been our own version of Bonnie and Clyde, with a little Santino thrown in I supposed, only our time together had been far more intense and impactful.

I couldn't even imagine how devastated she had been in that moment when Santino, Agrippina, Boudicca and all the rest had returned after I'd disappeared. What had gone through her mind and her heart when Vincent or Santino had reported my absence?

What had she thought when she was told I'd simply disappeared? How had she handled it when morning after morning she'd awakened alone and with no news of where I was or if I was even still alive? We'd been aloof from each other for quite some time since I'd obtained the blue orb, but that had been different, and I'd always been just a short walk away. But day after day, week after week had gone by without an inkling of where I'd been or what had happened to me.

The stress…

The sadness…

How had she handled it? The answer was: as well as any person, but even her strength wasn't infinite.

And it was all my fault.

The fault is mine. Mine, and mine alone

Merlin's admission floated into my mind, a reassuring reminder that steadied me. I had to remember what I'd learned in my time with him. Placing blame is a slippery slope. It was easy when confronted with no other option than to place that blame, but placing it is never that easy of a task. Like the creation of all the timelines, the very essence that made up the Multiverse, it was options, choices, events, and decisions crafted by billions of individuals that dictated the course of the future. Everything affected everything, from the beginning of time to the present, to the distant future. But even a being like Merlin found it difficult to accept this notion. Even he placed blame for what had happened to me and my friends on himself and no one else. Like my inadvertent action that brought us to Ancient Rome, it was his own innocent but wrongful action that had led to the series of events that put me in that situation.

Perhaps I was thinking too much about it, as Merlin advised I shouldn't.

Had Merlin thrown the orb at my face, the result of such an action being our arrival here in Ancient Rome, then he would have been directly responsible for us being here. Blame should be placed. But he didn't, and I hadn't mindfully abandoned Helena for over a month either.

I may have been to blame, but the fault wasn't mine.

I took solace in these thoughts as I leaned down and kissed Helena on her forehead, her nose, and then finally her mouth, a kiss that I allowed to linger far longer than I'd intended. When I finally pulled away, Helena looked up at me with a smile, and I could already see life finding its way back into her cold eyes. Maybe I was, again, thinking too much into it, but I had to take strength wherever I could.

We gazed at each other for a long time, Galba's presence drifting in the back of my mind, but I pushed it even deeper. He could wait until the fall of Rome for all I cared. This is the only place I wanted to be, but the spell was broken when Helena shifted her position on the bed to find a more comfortable one. I helped her by placing another pillow behind her head.

"Thank you," she said, her voice a little stronger now. She went silent again for a few seconds, but then asked, "Where did you go, Jacob? What happened? Why did you grow a beard?"

I chuckled. "I want to tell you, Helena, but you wouldn't believe me."

"I could try," she suggested, taking a long, hard gulp before continuing, "but is it going to be a long story? Another one of your epic rants?"

My smile grew wider. "Oh, yeah. Probably the longest I'll ever tell."

She smiled back at me. "Then you'd better get started, Lieutenant. This will probably be the only opportunity you'll ever have to rant to your heart's desires and have me actually want to hear about it."

I leaned in and kissed her again, drinking in every second.

I pulled away from her. "I don't think I could love you more than I do right now."

"Oh, I think I can find a way," she said with a small wink, "but you'd better get started. I'm already losing patience."

"Same old Helena," I said and settled in beside her to tell her everything I could about my time with Merlin. I was excited for this, knowing that once I'd told her I'd have to tell all the rest of them again, and I was certain this was going to be my greatest lecture yet. I...

"Jacob?"

I looked down at Helena, but she didn't look like she'd just said anything. In fact, her mouth was closed and she was looking around me toward the tent's entrance. I grimaced, having momentarily forgotten about Galba completely, realizing the interruption couldn't be about anything else.

I turned and saw Santino poking his head through the tent.

"What?" I asked.

"Sorry to interrupt," he said, "but Ol' Triple Chin is pretty grumpy. He told me to tell you that if he doesn't see you in the next three minutes, he'll kill Agrippina. I mentioned that I didn't think you'd care very much, but then I saw his flabby neck jiggling and I knew he was pretty serious. I think he means business."

I looked at Helena. "What do you think? Should I let him just kill her?"

"My vote's for yes," Santino offered helpfully from behind me.

Helena smiled. "I really can't think of anyone who should kill her more… besides me of course."

I bobbed my head in amused agreement, and my smile grew, but before I could say anything Helena sighed and continued her thoughts.

"Then again, she hasn't done anything threatening toward us since you disappeared. I guess it doesn't seem right."

I nodded in agreement but with a smirk. "Besides, you *really* want to be the one to kill her…"

"You're goddamned right I do."

I chuckled at her comment and heard Santino laughing behind me as well.

It felt like old times just now, when the three of us had been on the run in the wilderness of Europe, Africa, and the Middle East. We'd had some good times then, and they'd been some of the best years of my life, all because I'd had Santino and Helena there, especially Helena.

I picked up her hand and kissed her fingers. "God, I love you."

She reached up with her other hand, a movement that seemed strong and deliberate despite her weakness. "I know you do, Jacob. And I love you too. So very much."

I smiled but felt a swell of emotion in my chest, knowing I had to leave her.

"Will you be all right if I leave again for a few minutes?" I asked.

"Of course," she answered. "Just don't go getting yourself killed out there, Lieutenant. I've just started liking you again. Just… try to hurry back this time."

I grinned and leaned down for another wonderful, loving kiss.

I didn't want to pull away, but I forced myself to, and looked down at Helena. We held our eyes on each other, but we were interrupted by the sound of forced sniffles from behind us.

"I think I'm going to cry…" Santino whispered around fake sobs.

I rolled my eyes, taking my entire head with them. I leaned down, gave Helena one last kiss, and then thrust myself from the bed as she smiled at Santino's comment.

"No, I think you should stay, Hunter, really," Santino said as I marched toward him. "I think the power of true love is all we need to get us through this, really I do. Just wait. A powerful rainbow is about to burst from Helena's chest and hit Galba in the face like a leprechaun swinging a pot of gold, and then he's going to fall in love with Agrippina and everything will be just fine. He'll go back to Rome and find Vespasian and the three of them will love and love and love each other, together, and rule Rome jointly with compassion and care… just like those damn bears from that cartoon! It'll be great. Pure magic! The three of them will have great sex too, although Agrippina and Vespasian will force Galba to wear a bag over his head just to get through the process, but that's okay because it won't matter, because they'll be… in love! True love! Only through the power of lov…"

Just as he was about to finish, I reached a hand out toward the exit and covered his mouth with it, pushing him out of the tent in the same movement. He fell to the ground with a thud, but continued professing how only through the power of love could we overcome all our struggles. I tried to tune him out as I turned back to Helena.

She blew me a kiss, saying, "Go fix the universe."

I reached up and tipped an imaginary hat at her. "Yes, ma'am.

***

Santino was already running by the time I left the tent, so I did what I could to keep up. My month long absence from reality had done much to impair my former level of physical fitness, and I felt weak and slow as I ran, but I managed to catch up just before we reached the camp's northern most entrance.

"So how angry is he?" I asked.

"Pissed."

"Do you think he'd really kill Agrippina?"

"Probably, but I'm hardly the guy to ask."

That much at least was true, but I decided to shut up and conserve my energy as we ran through the gate and out into the field beyond the camp, where thousands of legionnaires sprang into view. Illuminated by just as many torches and fires, each of them stood comfortably near their trench system, some upon the ramparts, the rest arrayed on the field of battle, ready to advance. It was an awesome sight, and a claustrophobic one, contained as we were by the might of a Roman army.

I looked at Santino out of the corner of my eye, and he looked back at me.

"Not used to being on this end, are we?" I asked.

"They've been here over a week," he replied. "I've gotten pretty used to it."

"Right," I said as I spotted Galba and Agrippina with their gathered retinues, which included Vincent, Bordeaux, Archer, Stryker, a number of Agrippina's Praetorians, and Galba's first file Fabius. All except Fabius were seated atop horses, arrayed in a pair of half circles disjoined from each other. As we grew closer I could see Galba's fat and completely unhandsome face, easily discernible from all the hard, stoic Roman faces that surrounded him.

Santino and I slowed to a trot as we grew even closer, but just before we arrived, Santino picked up speed again and charged forward. A few of Galba's Romans moved to draw their swords nervously but Galba held up a hand to keep them calm. Seconds later, Santino slid on an apparently icy bit of ground with his hands out wide like an old timey dancer, looking up at Galba with a wide, open mouth show smile, his spirit fingers wiggling wildly.

"Heeeeeeere's, Hunter," he said in English, but then grew serious and hooked a thumb at me and switched to Latin. "But seriously, I brought, Hunter."

Agrippina and Vincent rolled their eyes but Galba appeared amused. He turned to the empress for a moment and smiled at her. "As much as I despise these people, this one at least entertains me."

Santino beamed at the compliment and took a bow, while Agrippina simply frowned and shook her head at the display. No one's attention seemed on me at the moment, which was good since I was drawing in gulps of air like I'd just sprinted a marathon, so I took the opportunity to move around behind my gathered forces to stand between Agrippina and Vincent.

Finally, Galba seemed to take notice of me and shifted his head around. "So, you have completed your ritual then?"

I nodded slowly, curious as to how he knew the details of what I had been doing. I was completely out of the loop here. I hadn't even known that Galba was aware I'd been gone at all, and not simply hiding in the camp. It seemed best to be upfront with him and tell him what I knew he wanted to hear.

"Yeah," I confirmed, "but more importantly, I learned how to send us home. We can leave and you'll never see us again."

Heads perked up at the announcement, and each of my friends seemed quite interested in further information.

"Then go," Galba said, twitching his jowls away from the camp. "Go and I will forget you ever existed. All I need is Agrippina so I can settle this with Vespasian."

"What's your problem with Vespasian anyway?" I asked. "What did he do?"

"You are my problem, Hunter!" He bellowed. "You have caused great strife since arriving here five years ago, but your decisions since coming to Britain have completely compromised the strategic situation our forces face in this theatre of war. Why I let you wander into the hinterlands of Britain, I do not know, but I am finished with you. And I blame Vespasian for placing so much trust in you, and since I already had no faith in Agrippina, I have taken it upon myself to deal with all three of you."

My heart sunk at his words, but I only grew more frustrated than upset. "Making a power grab then, is it?" I asked. "Not content with the life you have? What do you want? More authority? More power? A throne to sit upon?"

He stared down at me from atop his horse, a serviceable pedestal if I'd ever seen one, but his eyes hid the anger I knew must have been seething deep within him. Despite his unappealing appearance, he certainly exuded the confidence needed to make a good leader of men. It was why he'd always been such a good general, but good generalship didn't always make for good leadership in the civilian sector.

Just ask Ulysses S. Grant.

Great general, good guy, poor president.

I wondered if Galba would be different.

Did I even need to care anymore?

Along with everything else I'd learned from Merlin, I now knew I wasn't actually destroying or altering timelines at all. Just creating new ones, so who was I to alter this timeline's natural progression, influenced by me or not? But I couldn't just abandon Vespasian either. He was too good of a man, and had a proven track record. Also, he'd had faith in me when it seemed like no one else had. I couldn't just abandon him to Galba, who was less power hungry and more afraid of his empire crumbling around him. He thought himself in the right, and perhaps he was, but I wasn't too keen on the options he may leave me with when I told him I couldn't go home quite yet.

"So is that it, then?" I asked when he didn't answer. "Are you staging a coup? What are you going to do if you we don't just turn ourselves over to you? Storm our gates and slaughter us?"

"I am not so stupid as to send fifty *thousand* men against you and your ilk, Hunter," he said, thrusting his finger at me. "But I will starve you out if I have to."

"Just like that? After everything we've been through and everything we've told you?" I took a painful step forward, pointing over my shoulder toward our camp. "Helena is *this* close to giving birth to my son, Galba. If you think for even a second that I'll just roll over and let you starve us out, you're delusional. There isn't anywhere you can hide even remotely close to this camp. I can have you killed as easily as stepping on a bug right now if I wanted to, and you know it's true."

I took a deep breath and calmed myself, not wanting to let my anger take control or overplay my hand. Galba, for his part, at least looked uncomfortable at my words, and risked a look in the camp's direction.

"But I don't want to," I continued, returning my arm to my side. "You're a good man, Galba, and a real leader, but you've overstepped yourself. How could you just ignore everything we've told you? You're risking your very future here!"

"I risk it," Galba said evenly, "because of exactly what you once said to me. I make my own destiny, and so does Rome. We need not your presence here, and I've come to do what I should have done five years ago."

I nodded and kept nodding, unable to find the words I needed to sway Galba's mind.

Luckily, I wasn't alone in this.

"You are delusional, Galba," Agrippina chimed in. "You know nothing about what is needed to rule an empire. I have come to accept the errors I've committed in the past, and have sworn to better myself, but what I cannot do is simply hand over the power of Rome to an upstart general who sees himself as the next Julius Caesar!"

"Silence yourself, woman," Galba snapped, "before I end your life here and now. Your crimes go far beyond simple reconciliation and an admission to better oneself. You have more blood on your hands than even Hunter here."

I forced myself not to drop my head at his comment.

But it was difficult.

"You don't have to do this, General," Vincent said from beside me. "We've gathered new information. A new strategy can be formulated. We can help you set your world straight again."

Galba looked at him not unkindly. "I always found you a sound thinker, Vincent, and Caligula was most fond of your council when he was still alive, as I was as well, but you cannot possibly understand the pressure I am under to regain control of our situation. Rome's power over its empire hangs by little more than a thread. It is fractured, disjointed, and I need Agrippina to bring it back under control. Vespasian as well." He settled back in his horse, almost uncomfortably. "And I no longer desire your interference. You need not die here in this uncivilized wilderness, but you can no longer be allowed to meddle. I refuse to allow it."

I took a breath, unable to foresee a desirable end to this conversation.

Galba no longer cared about the orbs and wouldn't see our ability to harness them as an advantage he could use. All he wanted was for us to become a non-factor in his world, so that he could retake control of its direction. He no longer wanted to use us, or harness us. All he wanted was to push us into a corner where we couldn't affect anything.

And I couldn't blame him.

But we could go home now. All I needed was a little more time and the freedom to go back to Rome. But here was Galba, standing in our way, having just declared war on us. We'd probably beat him in a fight, even with his overwhelming numerical superiority, but there'd be a lot of dead bodies when the dust settled, and some of those bodies could be Santino's or Vincent's.

One of those bodies could be Helena's.

Or my own.

And Galba wasn't wrong in all this. That truth only made our situation worse. And even more horrible was that I couldn't think of anything I could say or do to change his mind or keep this from ending in death. Even with my mind as clear as it's been in months, I couldn't think of a way out of this. I couldn't think of a single thing to do.

Except one thing.

I looked at Galba, whose eyes were drilling into my own, and raised my arms. "We surrender, Galba. Give me your word that we won't be harmed and we'll step aside. We'll let you take us back to Rome under guard."

"What?!" Agrippina exclaimed, clearly surprised.

Galba, however, looked at me evenly but he didn't seem convinced. "You have rarely offered me a reason to trust you, Hunter. Why should I now?"

I shot an arm out to point at our camp again. "I've got a guy over there that could kill you right now if I wanted him to. You know that's true."

He sneered at me. "All too well."

"And yet you're still alive," I said. "Just trust me, Galba. You say I can't imagine the pressure you're under? Well, you can't even begin to imagine what I just experienced no more than a few hours ago. Everything is different now. I'm comfortable stepping aside and letting you do what you need to do. Just promise me we won't be harmed and that when the dust settles, you'll let us go."

"What are you…" Agrippina started to say, but I cut her off with an upraised hand.

Galba noticed the gesture and after a moment's thought, nodded.

"I cannot guarantee your release at a later date, but I can ensure your protection if you come willingly."

"We will. You have my word."

"You had best keep it this time, Hunter," Galba said as he wheeled his horse around. "You have until daybreak to prepare."

"Yes, sir," I said to his retreating back as he led his officers back to their lines, but only Fabius offered me a respectful nod before turning to leave.

"He'll be back…" Santino said in an excessively deep voice.

I smacked him on the arm, and he jumped at the contact as I turned and walked back to camp. Agrippina maneuvered her horse in my direction to fall in step.

"Have you completely lost control of your mind?" She demanded.

"Not this time actually," I said with a smirk as I strutted back toward the camp, pleased with my cool head and immediate acceptance of my own decision.

"You have sentenced me to death, Hunter!" She exclaimed. "Galba will no doubt try me for treason and have me crucified."

"Maybe," I replied, "maybe not."

"Explain."

"In a bit," I said. "Let's get the band back together again and have a little talk first."

***

Everyone but Helena was present as I explained everything. Everything.

Some of them made connections to things they'd known before, while others failed to associate their prior knowledge with anything I'd said at all, and some figured things out for the very first time, while even others came away more confused than before. Some were interested. Some were not. But by the time I was done, everyone wanted to know more.

"How are you going to find the red orb?" Cuyler asked first.

"Why would he give such power to children?" Bordeaux asked.

"Who or what is a Merlin?" Agrippina demanded with crossed arms, clearly the one to understand the least.

"The Multiverse! I knew it!" Artie exclaimed. "I just knew it!"

"It is difficult to believe how accurate Romulus and Remus' origin story is to the mythology," Vincent muttered.

"You can barely control the blue orb. How are you going to work both?" A good point from Stryker.

Gaius and Marcus shared knowing nods, both saying, "I told you gods were real."

"After all of that and you still can't help us??" Archer asked, shaking his fist at me.

"Describe the bikini part again," Santino demanded, and Artie smacked him.

"How could your vision have been so vivid?" Boudicca asked, almost as confused as Agrippina.

"You met Merlin? King Arthur's Merlin? Mum is never going to believer this…" Wang said, his head shaking side to side.

"How could a pair of balls have that kind of power?" Brewster wondered, a hand cupping her chin.

I barely heard any of these questions as they came at me all at once, followed by a string of more, coming fast and without pause. Everyone spoke over one another and certain people started picking fights with those closest to them who had differing opinions.

Agrippina was arguing with Vincent about what was known to the general public about Romulus and Remus' origin.

Archer continued to threaten me while Artie tried to placate him with her own explanations, derived from a sharp mind that naturally knew more than I about time travel and alternate realities than mine did.

Wang tried to convince Boudicca that western Britain was superior to eastern Britain, and that it alone had contributed to the mysticism I'd just experienced. Boudicca argued it had only aggravated our problem and was the home of superstitious pansies.

Stryker tried to convince Santino that Agrippina would look far better in a bikini than Artie – right in front of them both, not to mention me – but Santino wasn't hearing any of it.

Brewster tried to argue with anyone around her, but no one seemed to be listening.

Only Cuyler and Bordeaux kept to themselves, maybe understanding that they couldn't accomplish anything by speaking over each other. Cuyler seemed a pretty pensive guy anyway, but Bordeaux was perhaps less than enthused about the idea of our apparent newfound ability to go home. He, along with Vincent, had made a home here in antiquity, and was perhaps nervous about what the orbs meant for his ability to remain here with Madrina when this was all over.

I listened to them all, hearing their points, their counter points, their arguments and opinions, hearing their voices rise and grow angrier or more scared.

It was all becoming too much, and I rubbed my temples to try and soothe the pain that was growing in my mind. It had nothing to do with the orb, just simple fatigue and the stress and annoyance of a bunch of bickering friends too wrapped up in their own thoughts to tackle the real problem.

"*Enough!*" I yelled, literally at the top of my lungs.

Conversations died down all around me and faces turned to regard me. I looked at each and every one of them, taking my time before moving on to the next, trying to instill in them the idea that there was only one person who had actually met Merlin, and only one person who had seen and understood everything.

That person was me.

"Enough," I repeated, calmly this time. "Every one of your discussions is moot. Galba is going to take us in and we're just going to relax for a while."

"Unacceptable!" Agrippina snapped.

"We won't let him take you away from us," I assured. "I can't believe I'm saying this, but you're with us now. You're more than welcome to sit on the sidelines too."

She tightened her arms around her chest and nodded, but she did not look happy.

"I'm surprised at your decision, Jacob," Vincent said. "I didn't think you'd be so willing to surrender. Especially when we're so close now."

I grinned triumphantly, raising a hand in Cuyler's direction. "Gunny there asked a pretty good question. How do we find the red orb? Well, I'm not exactly sure, but I know where to start. Any guesses?"

There were none.

"Rome," I said.

Vincent smiled. "Ah."

I dipped my head, but Agrippina looked even more frustrated. "Were you baiting him from the beginning then?"

I shook my head. "Not at all, but it was a good assumption that he'd simply take us back to Rome since he needs to go there anyway if he's going to bring us to trial. Galba's a lot of things, but unpredictable he is not."

"It seems you weigh the risk placed on my life quite lightly in your decisions," she accused.

"After everything you've done to us, do you blame him?" Vincent asked steadily, a surprising rebuke from the normally understanding man.

Agrippina stared icily at him, but her gaze didn't linger long. With a twirl of her cloak she retreated from our small circle and back to her tent.

"Why do dramatic exits always make me nervous?" Wang asked.

It was a good question. One I should take to heart. Agrippina's done a lot in recent time to gain some trust in us, but it was risky to assume she was completely without ulterior motivations.

I heard Vincent take in a deep breath, and I turned to him.

"What is it?" I asked.

"I'm not sure," he said. "All this just seems a bit convenient, does it not?"

I smiled. "I said the same thing to Merlin. *Deus ex machina,* right?"

He nodded.

"Deus ex what?" Santino asked.

"It means 'god from the machine,'" Vincent explained. "An old Greek term, but also a literary plot device that describes something exceedingly convenient that happens to solve a seemingly unsolvable problem, usually in a contrived or vague way."

Santino smiled too. "Ah, well that sounds about right then."

"Yeah, but there are no writers here to back us into the proverbial corner," I mentioned. "All this Merlin stuff may seem convenient, but I'm willing to bet there's more to his story than he let on, and that it would be best to expect anything. Even now. *Especially* now."

"Sound thinking, Jacob," Bordeaux said, his first words since returning to camp.

I nodded to him, but my thoughts strayed back to Agrippina. I sympathized with her reticence over our newfound peace with Galba, but I felt appeasing her could wait for now. I was too exhausted to think about it anyway. I hadn't had a moment to myself since returning from my time with Merlin, and I was exhausted. I may have been immobile and unconscious for the last month, but that didn't mean I'd spent that time in a restive state. Anything but, it seemed, and as Agrippina finally disappeared behind a row of tents, I found myself about ready to collapse. My head grew light and empty, entering a preparatory state for sleep's swift arrival.

As though accepting this fate, my knees grew weak and my eyes closed on their own, and I knew I'd be asleep well before I hit the ground. In most moments when I felt as I did now, I was often scared or angry, aware that in the instances when consciousness was forcibly taken from me, it was because of some outside and often belligerent source. But not this time. This time I was simply collapsing from sheer exhaustion brought on by the most intense, revealing, and interesting episode of my entire life.

Everything seemed right in that moment, and although I could hear Artie's voice screaming my name as I began my fall to the snow, I knew I'd be okay. I'd probably sleep for a week, awaking somewhere in southern Britain, carried on a liter or pulled in a wagon through the tough terrain that would soon become a mud laden nightmare as spring rolled in.

I was okay with that. Wang would pronounce me all right. Just sleeping. Helena would accept that and she'd grow stronger as she watched me sleep, knowing that when I awoke I would feel rejuvenated and better than ever, and with that shared strength we would experience the birth of our son, and feel all the overwhelming joy that must come with such a moment.

My heart soared at the thought as my body fell, and I smiled, but then my head hit the snow and I was out.

***

I awoke after what seemed like seconds of sleep.

I felt neither rested nor revitalized.

In fact, I think the technical term was: shit.

I felt like shit.

But at least I was warm and dry, although it was also dark and noisy. I struggled to open my eyes, and when I finally did, I discovered that I was alone in a tent and bundled up in a blanket like I was encased in a sleeping bag. With a slight struggle, I worked myself free and pushed myself up into a sitting position. Pain shot through my forehead at the movement, and the true shittiness of how I felt started sinking in.

I tried to force away the pain but it seemed an impossible task, so I squinted through glassy eyes and tried to ascertain what was going on. But no details emerged from my inspection. I was in an empty, dark space – not unlike the anteroom in Merlin's realm of existence, the black bit of limbo that had existed just behind his front door, and my immediate assumption was that he had somehow brought me back to his cottage for some reason.

"Merlin?" I called out, hoping to see him again.

But my words met nothing but silence.

I grew concerned in that moment, and forced myself to swing my legs over the side of the bed and look toward what I assumed was the tent's exit, becoming more and more aware of the sounds and noises around me.

There was a commotion outside. Something was going on.

I hopped to the floor and stumbled my way toward the exit. It was quite an exertion just to do that, and I found myself panting from a lack of breath at the completion of even such a simple task.

I paused to take in a few breaths of air, settled myself, and pushed through the tent and into the outside world.

When I emerged I saw a camp full of individuals preparing for war.

They ran to and fro, gathering equipment, weaponry, and armor. Superiors barked orders and underlings did as they were bidden.

Except the individuals before me weren't people.

They were puppets.

I dropped my hands to my knees and squeezed my eyes shut, jerking my head left and then right. I opened my eyes and the world went back to normal. The puppets were gone, replaced by their true human forms. I let out a deep sigh of relief, no longer having any desire to return to Merlin's House of Oddities, Horrors, and Fuck You's.

"Jacob!" The voice came from my left, and I looked to see Vincent running toward me wearing his full combat kit.

"What happened?" I called out as he approached.

"You collapsed. Wang said you seemed fine, just sleeping, so we…"

"No Vincent," I said with a shake of my head, lifting a hand and gesturing out toward the camp. "What's going on? How long was I out? Did we miss Galba's deadline or something?"

Vincent stared at me with wide, sleepy eyes of his own. "No, Jacob. We put you in that tent forty minutes ago and this has nothing to do with Galba. *He's* under attack by a local army. A big one."

"Well that's just great," I muttered. Just when I felt about as horrible as I could possibly feel, it was time to suit up again and get my hands dirty. I turned back to Vincent. "What are our people doing?"

"Galba already rode up to our gates under a flag of truce," Vincent explained. "The army out there is *vast* and he requires our help. I didn't think he was willing to change the terms of our agreement if we helped him, but I also didn't think it would matter if we were all dead, so I agreed to help. Stryker, Brewster, Santino, and Bordeaux are already in the trenches with Galba's army. Cuyler and a few Praetorians are scrambling to erect a higher shooting platform for him."

I nodded my head approvingly. "Good thinking. Any show of good faith we can achieve with Galba will go a long way." I paused and thought for a second. "Where's Archer?"

"I don't know," Vincent replied. "He left after you collapsed and no one's seen him since.

"What about Wang?"

Vincent hesitated. "He's... with Helena."

I took an instinctual step forward. "Is she..."

"I believe she is fine," Vincent soothed, "but until the wounded come in, Wang thought it best if he stay with her. She's been through a lot."

"She definitely has," I agreed. "And Artie?"

"Safe in her tent," Vincent said quickly, finding it easier, as it always was, to give good news rather than bad.

"Good," I said as I started moving off. "Where's my gear?"

"Do you think that's such a good idea?" Vincent asked as he jogged to catch up. "You've been through a lot. I know the orb is out of range, but you're exhausted and weak. You wouldn't be doing Helena any good by getting yourself killed now."

I stopped mid step. The man made a good point.

"All right, fine," I said as I pushed into motion again. "I'll stay out of the fighting, but I still need my rifle and a few mags."

"Jacob, your..."

I winced and stopped moving again, but then forced myself to keep going. I'd forgotten about Penelope, and the memory still cut deeply. It was just the first in what I knew would be a series of memories that would surface and haunt me one day.

Vincent and I ducked into the small tent we used as our armory. I found my MOLLE vest and my Sig P220, and strapped everything together and secured pistol magazines to my vest, feeling slightly better with every motion. When I was finished, I gave myself one last pat down to ensure everything was secure before Vincent and I stepped out of the tent and took off.

We passed through the *porta praetoria*, and were once again confronted with a vast open space between us and Galba's engulfing trench system. We couldn't see anything of our attackers yet, but we could hear the sounds of engagements all along the lines, accompanied occasionally by the sharp staccato sound of rifle fire. It was a chaotic mess as legionnaires and

Praetorians scattered haphazardly, with what seemed like little thought to their overall battle strategy.

Vincent and I found Bordeaux and Brewster minutes later holed up in a small foxhole carved out of the side of the trench. Legionnaires ran back and forth and many scrambled up and out of the trench to join others beyond the defensive system. It was then that I noticed the engaged enemy, and how close they already seemed. I had no idea how they'd pushed through the legions' lines so quickly, especially with leaders like Galba and Fabius in charge.

The edge of the trench was just steps away, growing closer with every long stride I took. When I was a few steps out, I dropped onto my legs and slid into the trench like a base runner trying to steal second. I dropped a few feet and landed ungracefully in a crouch but when I tried to rise, my skull felt like it was made of concrete and I struggled to stand. I reached up and held my head in both hands, forcing myself to straighten slowly with my eyes closed.

I felt a hand on my shoulder and heard Vincent's voice from beside me. "Are you all right?"

"Fine," I said, batting it away and opening my eyes. My vision swirled in a swarm of colors but eventually it settled and everything seemed back to normal. "I'm fine. Let's go."

Bordeaux and Brewster weren't far, but they hadn't yet noticed our arrival. The two were a humorous mismatched pair with Bordeaux tall and massive and Brewster easily the smallest person in our group, but she blazed away with her rifle like any good operator would, sending wave after wave of deadly lead down range and toward targets of opportunity.

"Jeanne!" I yelled with my hands cupped around my mouth, hoping to catch his attention around the blare of their rifles and all the other noises associated with war. He looked up and around as though he were searching for an annoying insect buzzing around his head, but then he caught sight of us and waved us over.

Vincent and I arrived seconds later and leaned up against the earthworks, and I risked a peek over the wall to get a view of the battle, barely aware of the falling spears and arrows that dropped like fat rain drops all around me. No more than thirty meters away was a thin line of legionnaires doing everything they could to keep the enemy back while the rest of Galba's troops prepared their defenses. I could see angry Britons a plenty between the gaps in their lines, stretching from as far left as I could see to as far right, and I had no idea if we were surrounded or not.

"What happened?" Vincent asked. "Why didn't Galba have time to form up his lines outside the trench?"

"No idea!" Brewster yelled as she popped up to fire again.

Bordeaux was slightly more insightful. "We really don't. When we arrived the Britons were already attacking, which was only when the Romans were finally able to push them out of the trenches and work on creating some kind of strategy."

I flicked my eyebrows up, impressed. It was rare to see an army of individuals from such a backward part of the world organize such a conducive fighting force, let alone one that seemed focused on attacking and killing and not simply showboating and taunting. Most barbarian hordes enjoyed the pregame part of battle too much to be particularly efficient.

"So what's the plan?" I asked.

"No idea!" Brewster yelled again as she ducked under an incoming spear that landed a foot away and imbedded itself in the soft dirt behind her. Vincent plucked it from the earth and tossed it over the rim of the wall casually. Brewster stared at him with wide eyes, aware just how close she'd just come to biting it.

"We need to regroup with Stryker and Santino," Vincent suggested. "The six of us could lead a counter attack to punch a hole in their lines. It would be a good way to get legionnaires out of the trench and hitting the enemy's flanks.

"Do it!" Another voice called from beside us. I turned my body against the earthwork and saw Galba had snuck up behind me.

I gave him a look of concern. "You had a pretty good chance to get rid of at least one of your problems right there"

Galba frowned. "The last thing I want to do is kill you, Hunter. If you die, I'm still stuck with the rest of them."

"Good point," I conceded, taking some comfort, deciding not to tell him about Artie for the time being.

"Enact your plan," Galba ordered. "I'll detach a maniple to cover your flanks and send three cohorts to follow. This enemy is tenacious, a most unexpected encounter so far from the heart of it all. They were on us in seconds, with nary a word from my scouts, and with our attention focused on Agrippina's camp, we were left unprepared. Find the Funny One and his friend, and do what you do best."

"You're going to miss us, Galba," I said with a smirk. "Just admit it."

"By the gods, go!" Galba shouted with an upraised arm. "I said I didn't want you dead but I'd have no problem taking a leg from you!"

"Let's go, Jacob," Vincent ordered, gripping my arm with his hand.

Galba's eyes never left mine as Vincent pulled me away, but when he was beyond the range of my peripheral vision, I finally turned my head and focused on finding Santino and Stryker. We ran through the trench, dodging legionnaires, auxilia, Praetorians, and the occasional Briton who'd managed to penetrate the lines. After we'd traversed maybe a fourth of the trench's circumference we finally came face to face with Santino and Stryker, who were running through the trench in our direction. It only took seconds before we came face to face.

"It's a good thing you guys weren't running the other way!" I exclaimed, out of breath and sweating profusely. I leaned over and gripped my knees to catch my breath while Vincent placed his hand on my back.

"Jacob, you shouldn't be here."

"I'm fine, I'm..."

"You've got to go, Hunter!" Santino yelled, reaching out and grabbing my shoulders. He pulled me up and I groaned at the quick movement, feeling it in sore joints as well as my cloudy head this time.

"Go where?" I asked.

"To Helena!" He yelled, his face awash in concern, an odd expression I rarely saw from him.

My mind sharpened at the name. "What happened?"

"Don't know! Wang radioed. Told us to find you. Just go!"

I hesitated but felt my legs already carrying me toward the trench's inner wall. My head was a storm of confusion as I listed toward it, trying to grope for the lip of the wall to pull myself up, but my hands slipped on the snowy bank and I stumbled to the ground. Not a second later, a pair of strong hands gripped me under my armpits and lifted me as easily as one would pick up a kitten. The hands deposited me on the ground above the trench and I turned and saw Bordeaux standing there, his eyes just as concerned as Santino's.

"Go to her, Jacob," He said. "We'll take care of this. I promise."

I struggled to my feet, stumbled, fell, but kept on trying. Finally, I found a rhythm and got to my feet, nodding vigorously as I started to run. My eyes only left Bordeaux's when I was so far gone that I could barely even see him, and it was only then that he ducked away and ran to catch up with the others. I turned forward and quickened my pace, each step a struggle and a source of pain, but I pushed and pushed, step after step, knowing that I would sprint into Death's cold embrace to reach Helena if I had to.

***

I burst into Helena's hospital room an unbearably long ten minutes later, pushing the flaps that barred outsiders so forcefully that I was surprised the whole tent didn't collapsed. But I wished it had, because it would have saved me from the sight before me, a sight that I encapsulated in one single look.

A sight that told me I was already too late.

Helena lay motionless on her table, her head lolled to the right and away from me. At first glance she seemed dead, but then her chest rose just slightly and fell, and I breathed a deep sigh of relief. But then her chest didn't rise again, and my heart sank, but then it finally did only to fall far later than it had the first time. It was then that I realized that while she was alive, her breathing was not normal.

My eyes were torn from her body when I noticed a slight movement beside her. A dark shape in the form of a man stood there, and as it rotated, I realized that it was Wang. He looked up at me in surprise, and went still. As he turned, I noticed his right arm moving in a circular pattern, but now it too stopped. I glanced down and saw a scalpel in one hand and a bloody sanitation cloth in the other.

We stood there, eyes locked for nearly a minute, when I finally found the will to fall to Helena's side, my mind unable to register and understand all the clues within the room to deduce what had happened. I reached out and placed a hand on her forehead, which was slick with perspiration, and carefully moved my other hand over her stomach and slowly lowered it, but I hesitated in confusion when it didn't immediately meet resistance. I twisted my head to look at my hovering hand, noticing that there was still a half dozen inches between it and Helena's stomach. Confused, I finally lowered it all the way, taking note that her stomach, while larger than before she was pregnant, didn't seem nearly as large as it had been just hours ago.

I knelt there, my weak and fractured mind too tired or stupid to come to grips with the situation. I didn't know what to do or how to react, but then I felt a hand fall on my shoulder. I craned my head up and saw Wang looking down at me with a frown on his face. He looked just as speechless as I was, just as hurt, just as pained, just as saddened.

"What... what happened?" I asked, surprised when I realized that I'd asked for no other reason than to help make him feel better.

Wang jerked his hand away and raised it to cover his mouth. "I..." he said, muffled through his hand. He must have realized his fault and lowered it. "I... I'm so sorry, Jacob, but Helena's vitals spiked. She was experiencing intense abdominal pain and there was... blood..." he trailed off, but despite my lack of clarity, I didn't need him to elaborate. "I... I had to perform an emergency C-section. It was all I could do."

"But," I said, my jaw quivering. "It's too early. He's still pre..."

Wang nodded and slowly reached out his hands to help me stand. I let him, allowing him to turn me around, and saw a small bundle of cloth, alone and miniscule atop a table large enough to feast a dozen men. I took a step forward, reaching out a hand toward it, and slowly placed it atop the bundle.

"I'm so sorry, Jacob."

I closed my eyes and dipped my head, surprised that although I now knew what had happened, there were no tears and I felt no overt sadness. I barely felt anything. Just a deep and bottomless nothing. All I felt was empty inside.

"It's not your fault, James," I said, my eyes still closed, knowing such words were just as empty as my soul. Wang wouldn't accept them either, but I'd felt the need to say them just so I could hang on to the last visage of my humanity.

To his credit, he didn't answer. Upset and distraught at having failed his patient and friend, saddened that he'd just lost a nephew of his own, he still knew this was my time to grieve, not his. I would have turned around and hugged him were I able to raise my hand off the bundle that contained my son, but it wouldn't move. It was glued there, fastened there for all eternity by an unknown force I couldn't control... even if I wanted it to.

"Jacob..."

My name hadn't been spoken by Wang this time, but by Helena. I twisted my head around and saw that she'd brought herself to face the interior of the tent now instead of the wall. Wang rushed over to her and checked her, using his few remaining machines to detect what they could and asked her a few questions in a low voice.

I knew I should go to her so that I could offer her comfort, but I couldn't pull away from my son. I looked back down at him again, half tempted to open the rags and look at him, but I couldn't bring myself to do that either. I couldn't bring myself to do anything.

"Jacob..."

This time my name was spoken by Wang, but still I didn't move. I remained, my eyes locked on my boy, still too empty to allow tears to form, let alone fall. I felt a presence behind me and the weight of the same hand as earlier fall on my shoulder.

"Jacob," Wang whispered again. "She needs you."

I nodded slowly and he let go. I sensed him move away, but it wasn't until I heard the slight rustle of the tent that I knew that he had left. Even with him gone, I still couldn't move.

I ground my teeth and let out a growl, willing the emptiness inside me to fill up again. To force myself to feel something. And that's when I let the anger in, anger at Galba and Agrippina and Wang and Merlin – *him* most of all for keeping me in his lair so long that it had weakened Helena. My outstretched hand started shaking and I had to force it into a fist to keep it from tearing free from my arm. I lifted it to my forehead despite its relentless trembling, but a deathly cough from behind me completely snapped me from my indecision, and I whirled around and finally moved to Helena's side.

She looked at me, paler than ever, her eyes barely open.

"Is..." she started weakly, "...is he okay?"

My eyes widened. She didn't know? How could Wang not have told her?

Because she's been unconscious until just now, Hunter. You know that.

She didn't know.

"I..." Should I lie? "I... I think so, Helena. Just rest and get better, that's what's important now."

"I don't think I can, Jacob," she said, her voice soft and distant, her eyes closed. "It feels... worse this time."

"Don't say that, Helena. Everything will be fine. Just like..."

She collapsed, and seemed out cold.

"Wang!" I yelled, and he rushed back in without hesitation. I stepped aside and he checked her, something I knew I could have done, but wasn't sure I could have *actually* done because... because it was *her*.

After a second, he looked back up at me. "She's unconscious. Damn, she's a fighter."

"Will she be all right?"

Wang stood, reaching out to grip my arm. "I won't lie to you, Hunter. I don't know. It's possible, but I'm low on supplies and equipment, and I have to get out there and help the wounded. She..."

He was cut off when Helena started convulsing behind him, perhaps one last pain attack that would send her crashing through the gates of Hades. He swore and turned to help her, but I stood in shock and terror at what I saw, flashbacks running through my mind of images seen five years ago. Wang leaned over her and held her head in his hands, trying to keep her from shaking herself to death.

He twisted his head around and stared at me. "Help me, Jacob!"

But instead of stepping forward, I stepped backward.

Help me, Wang had demanded, but there was nothing I could do.

I wasn't a nurse. I wasn't a medic. I wasn't a doctor. I was just a warrior. I wasn't a shaman or a cleric or a druid. I was an operator. I wasn't a magician. I was a killer. I wasn't a wizard. I was…

I wasn't a wizard.

But I knew a wizard!

I turned and sprinted from the tent, Wang yelling after me. Adrenaline surged through me, pulsating its rejuvenating elixir through my veins so steadily but forcibly that Bordeaux couldn't have stopped me right now. I leapt through the tent and looked around frantically, finding exactly what I was looking for almost immediately.

A pair of legionnaires that looked familiar were running past me to enter the battle.

"Hold!" I shouted, and the pair stopped to look at me, confused.

"Legate?"

They remembered me.

I pointed at one, thoughts that I could barely understand wheeling through my mind at an uncontrollable pace. "Find Minicius and bring him here. Tell him to wait until I return." I pointed at the other. "Take me to my horse."

"Legate?" They both asked again in unison.

"*Now!*" I shouted, and they finally reacted.

They split up as they ran and I stumbled after one toward our stables. It was a short run and I picked Felix out of a crowd of maybe fifty instantaneously. I ran to his side and he bucked and reared back on his legs at the sight of me, as though he knew what had befallen Helena and that he was the only one who could help.

"It's good to see you too, my friend," I said, as he immediately calmed down and seemed to lower himself so that I could more easily mount him. I patted his mane quickly, finally almost ready to cry as the situation unraveled around me, but I placed a foot against the wooden railing that kept the horses penned, and pushed off it awkwardly to land atop Felix.

I didn't even need to kick his sides before he took off running, leaping the high railing and straight toward the nearest exit. The gates parted as we approached and Felix took off, not a care in the world or a thought toward the encasing trench system or the attackers beyond it. Felix seemed to know exactly where I wanted him to go, and I clung to him, somehow knowing he would stop at nothing to get me there.

***

Twenty minutes later, Felix galloped right into the clearing where Merlin's cottage once resided. Only an empty field now, the lingering mist from before was still evident even in the early morning darkness. I pulled back on Felix's reins and he planted his forelegs into the ground and skidded to a stop. I leapt from his back and ran to the very center of the clearing where nothing existed besides snow, the mist, and a log.

I spun in circles, searching, trying to bring myself back to Merlin and wherever he had taken me before.

"Where are you, Merlin??" I shouted with my arms wide. "I know you can hear me! I know you know what's happened! So show yourself!"

I continued to twirl, feeling myself grow dizzy, the adrenaline threatening to overload my body. It was surging so frantically within me that I knew I was running the risk of a stroke or a heart attack or something, but I didn't care.

I needed Merlin and I needed him now.

"Help me, Merlin! You told me all of this is your fault, not mine! You caused all of this, not me! You knew how long you were keeping me from her, and you know you're responsible for the death of my son!! You said we could be happy! That we could have children! Well you were fucking wrong, Merlin! And now it's time to starting owning up to some of that responsibility!"

I pleaded into the wind and trees around me, hearing nothing in return but their near silent wheeze and rustle. No answer came. No apparition revealed itself. No help arrived.

I threw my fists in the air.

"Fuck you, Merlin! Why help me at all if you won't help me now?? Do you think I'll do right by you when I find the orbs now?? Do you??"

But again no answer came.

"Why won't you help me??" I shouted, clearing my lungs of all the oxygen they contained. The adrenaline was leaving my system now, along with the oxygen, and I couldn't stop my body from dropping to the ground. I landed on my knees and sat on the heels of my feet, with my arms resting atop my legs, palms up. It was a position ready to accept an execution by sword thrust to the back of the neck like the ones I'd read about it in my history books a lifetime ago.

And I was ready to accept it now.

Happily.

"If you won't help her," I whispered, my eyes closing, "then help me at least. Just end it. End it all. I don't want any of it anymore"

But still Merlin didn't come, nor did the death I so eagerly desired. I was alone, ready to freeze to death or die of dehydration here in the snow, whichever came first. I was ready, sitting on my knees, a fitting memorial to how empty this world was and how little compassion and hope resided on this paltry plane of existence. It would be a fitting tribute to the worthlessness of life, and how it truly was not worth living.

That's when I felt something touch the back of my neck. It wasn't sharp, however, so not a sword, nor was it warm like the soothing embrace of someone's hand. No, it was cold and wet, sticky almost. I opened my eyes and grew aware of the world again, realizing that Felix was nudging the back of my neck with his nose.

"Stop it," I said, trying to bat him away.

I failed, and he nudged me again.

"I said stop it," I said, more emphatically this time.

But he didn't, choosing instead to push me so hard that I fell into the snow, my head barely managing to avoid bashing itself against the log.

If only he'd hit me a little harder.

With a sigh of defeat, I lifted my head from the snow and opened my eyes. Using my arms to push myself up again, I stopped when something caught my attention. Sitting atop the log was a small object, something that hadn't been there a second ago. I looked at it curiously, noting that it was a small, glass vial filled with liquid. I cocked my head to the side in further curiosity when it I also noticed that the vial looked much like a bottle of sink or bathtub unclogger, the kind that was split in half so that two separate fluids existed side by side but unmixed until it was time to pour them down the drain. The only difference being that this glass container was clear, and that I could see the liquids within: one half bright blue, the other a vibrant red.

I didn't know how, but the adrenaline returned, and I snatched it with a hand, jumped atop Felix, and again had no need to say anything as he carried me back to Helena.

***

I was barely conscious as Felix burst through the lines of Britons, legionnaires, and Praetorians alike. He stormed through small clumps of engaged soldiers, knocking them over with his mass and speed, leapt Galba's trench in a single bound, and didn't even hesitate as he galloped at full bore toward the camp, knowing, apparently that its gates would open magically before him.

And they did.

It was a miraculous sight, one almost as unbelievable as the appearance of the red and blue vial still clutched in my hand. Britons, legionnaires, and Praetorians gaped as he passed them, pausing in whatever they were doing momentarily to point or stare in wonder as he carried me from the edge of the battle all the way to the interior of our camp without breaking a single stride.

I, too, with whatever consciousness I had left, was impressed, and considered giving him a new name like Pegasus or Silver, something more appropriate to the godlike manner in which he performed.

But that would have to wait as he pulled up hard in front of Wang's aid station. He bucked and reared back on his hind legs again, tossing me hard to the ground. I would have been upset, except for the fact that I'd needed the bump. I'd been nearly unconscious before I fell, but was snapped awake at the impact.

I struggled to my feet, but a hand helped me stand. I looked up to discover Minicius had arrived, just as I'd ordered.

"Legate? Are you well?" He asked, his voice rife with concern.

"Fine, Minicius," I said, but had to reach out and grab both of his arms to steady myself. I looked at him, knowing what I was going to say, but still unsure why. Somewhere, deep inside where my fatigue couldn't touch me, something stirred, something that understood what I suddenly had to do. I was certain it wasn't the right choice, but it was the only one my broken mind could think of. "Bring me the orb, Minicius."

"But, Legate…"

"Do it, Minicius! That's an order."

He nodded hesitantly, but seemed compliant. He ran off, and I watched him go for the briefest of moments before I stumbled into the tent, knowing exactly what I'd asked him to do, but still struggling with why. I entered to see Wang standing beside Helena where she lay unmoving, his face filled with anger and directed at me.

"Hunter! Where the fuck did you…"

"Is she alive?"

"Barely!" He exclaimed, stalking forward, seemingly intent on causing me harm. "How could you leave her like that? What kind of callous, heartless, son of a…"

"Shut up, Wang," I yelled, using the last of my strength to push past him and fall against the table holding Helena. I nearly banged my head into it but Wang rushed to my side and helped me up like any friend would, and I heard him questioning me in the background as I raised the vial to eye level and looked at it intently. I half expected some kind of malicious omen to present itself in that moment, some kind of warning that if I gave it to Helena, I would be doing little more than raising a zombie version of her from the dead or turning her into an evil counterpart of herself.

But nothing like that happened.

The vial instead seemed inviting, like it was encouraging me to hurry the fuck up because time was running out. Like the Little Engine That Could, it seemed to call out to me, pleading with me to give it the chance it deserved to do what it needed to do.

To fulfill its destiny.

And who was I to argue with something like that?

I leaned forward and tilted Helena's head back so that she could more easily drink from the vial. She seemed lifeless as I held her head up, but I could still see her chest rise, fall, rise, and fall again. It was a clear sign that she was still alive, but then it didn't rise again, and I panicked, so I upended the vial and sent every last drop of its liquid into her mouth and down her throat.

Wang leaned in carefully, his eyes locked on the vial.

"What is that, Jacob?"

I gritted my teeth determinedly. "My *deus ex machine.*"

His head snapped around to look at me in confusion, but I ignored him. I simply lowered the vial to rest it against Helena's chest and waited. Waited for her chest to rise again. I waited and waited for eternity, but then, for what seemed like no reason at all, it lifted itself again, fell, rose, fell, and entered a rhythm far steadier than before.

A sharp breath exited Helena's lips, startling both Wang and I. She arched her back in a way that reminded me so much of her old pain attacks, but unlike in those instances, her face wasn't awash in agony. It seemed peaceful instead, normal, and I could tell this to be the case because her original coloring was returning as death's grip on her subsided.

I smiled, knowing that it was working, and Wang breathed in sharply and pushed me away. I let him, too emotional to care, and watched him check Helena's vitals. He only needed a moment before he looked back at me, a grin on his face and tears in his eyes.

"She's normalizing, Jacob! I can't believe it! What did you give her?"

"I have no idea," I admitted.

Wang turned again, his face concerned and confused both, but then he looked up at something behind me. I turned and saw Minicius standing there with the orb between his hands wrapped in a cloth.

"Get that thing out of here," Wang ordered as he strode past me and toward Minicius angrily.

For his part, Minicius looked as confused and concerned as Wang had seconds ago, and he looked at me for guidance. As Wang continued to advance on Minicius, I sighed deeply, knowing that what I was about to do would set into motion a chain of events I'd be unable to control, but knew had to be done. Now that Helena was safe, there was only one way to keep her that way.

I locked eyes with Minicius and made a gesture with my hand. Minicius understood.

He looked at Wang and said, "I apologize."

On a good day, Wang could have taken Minicius in a fight easily, but he was tired and was caught off guard by an attacker he had thought an ally. With no time to react, Wang could do little more than watch as Minicius slammed the orb into his head, knocking him unconscious. I looked at my friend on the ground sadly, hating myself but knowing he would have to understand later.

Minicius looked to me for further orders.

"Wait outside," I ordered.

He nodded and left.

I pivoted on my butt and crawled back to Helena's bed, using every ounce of strength I had left to pull myself up and look at her. Her eyes were open now and fluttering from side to side as though in a trance and absorbing information at an astonishing rate, but when I entered her peripheral vision, her eyes stopped, her head shifted to the left, and she looked at me with her eyes as vibrant as ever.

"What happened?" She asked, her voice strong.

"You survived, Helena, but you need your rest. Try not to think about it right now."

"Okay, Jacob," she said, almost contentedly, something I hadn't expected. I risked a glance at the body of my son encased in rags, and wondered if she had forgotten or if she'd even been told yet. If she had forgotten, even if it was temporary while her body healed, I was happy for her, and I wasn't about to disrupt the process.

She closed her eyes again restfully, smacked her lips a few times with her tongue, and seemed to drift off to sleep again. I did everything I could to bring myself to a standing position and walk away as quietly as I could, turning carefully but not without one last look at my son. I was never going to let what happened to him happen again. Not to anyone. Not to Santino, not to Artie, not to Helena. Not to anyone.

It's why I had to leave.

I took a step away from Helena, but after I took another, I heard her whisper, "I love you, Jacob."

I couldn't find it in myself to answer, convincing myself she couldn't hear me anyway. I risked one last glance at her, and felt my throat fall into my stomach. I dipped my head as I turned to leave, the emptiness in my chest persisting.

I emerged from the tent to find Minicius waiting impatiently, also noticing a stream of legionnaires and Praetorians entering the camp, some wounded, others completely fine, if not physically tired.

"What happened?" I asked.

"The course of battle shifted when your comrades broke through the enemy lines and led a counterattack. I think Galba's troops are simply cleaning up any stragglers left behind."

I looked toward one of the gates. "Any word on casualties?"

"There are many, Legate," Minicius said, spreading a hand to gesture toward a triage center off to his left.

"I meant of my friends."

"Oh," Minicius said. "I do not know, but I believe they are alive."

"Good," I whispered, but then held out my hands skittishly. "Please."

I could feel its power already, had felt it the moment Minicius had brought it into the tent. I'd felt a draw well before then even, but it wasn't until I knew it was in my presence that I felt our rekindled bond grow stronger. I was surprised it hadn't yet taken a hold of me completely, but perhaps our time apart had shielded me from it in some way.

I didn't know, but even when Minicius opened the cloth to reveal the orb, I felt no different. The draw was there, the enticement to take it and use it, but it wasn't nearly as intense as before. At least not yet. The orb's darkness was there as well, lingering in the background, ready to entangle me in its negative energy again.

Everything inside me told me to walk away, to not let it take over again. Logic said to run as far and as fast as I could and never turn back. But something was keeping from doing it. Merlin may have been right that bringing us to Ancient Rome hadn't been my fault. It had been an indirect action on my part, something I couldn't control, but that didn't mean every other decision since arriving here hadn't been. Those were active and direct actions on my part, ones that placed myself and my friends in harm's way. Merlin couldn't take credit for that.

There was only one man who could, and there was only one way to ensure I was no longer responsible for anyone but myself.

I was going to find the red orb and take control of it, thus ending the blue orb's negative influence on me forever, but I was going to do it alone. I wasn't going to risk my friends ever again. It wasn't right. It was my burden and mine alone. Once I had both orbs I'd rejoin them and take everyone home, but not until the danger was gone. Merlin had said my mind was stronger than most, so while it would affect me while I searched for the red orb, it was a risk I was willing to take... but alone.

I wasn't about to let Artie fall under the orb's influence and never again would I place Helena or my friends at risk.

Without another thought, I reached out and picked up the orb.

I nearly blacked out the moment I made contact with it, but not out of fatigue, but from a readjustment to power. Energy and strength surged through me, so much more potent and lasting then adrenaline alone, and I felt my mind sharpen and my muscles strengthen. It was an intoxicating power, and now that it had recharged my weary bones, I was ready.

I turned sharply to Minicius. "Prepare my horse and gather my gear and enough supplies to see me through three weeks of travel. Load another with as much as it can carry and meet me near the stables."

Minicius too seemed somehow focused and bold now, and saluted. "With haste, Legate!"

I nodded and watched him go. I waited a moment, allowing wave after wave of thoughts to coalesce from a disjointed web of errant impulses in my mind into a single cohesive plan that would see me through to the end of this. Like a living computer, I felt my mind work with great speed and clarity, and I wasted no time before enacting step one.

I took a step forward, but paused, a brick in my left foot keeping me from moving. I looked down at it in confusion, but then my eyes drifted back to Wang's aid station. I saw nothing but the tent, although my mind knew what was in there. I had to remember who I was doing this for. I had to remember I was doing this for Helena. I was doing this for the love we shared and the future we deserved. Once I'd taken care of business, I'd allow myself the pleasure of no longer having any responsibilities and being there for her.

My foot lightened immediately, and I jogged forward, directing myself toward Agrippina's *praetorium*. Two of her Praetorians stood as silent sentinels at the entrance, blocking my way.

"The empress in indisposed at the moment, Legate," one said. "Please return later."

"No thanks," I said, and smashed the orb into the man's head. His partner acted swiftly, but wasn't quick enough to stop me from swinging the orb into his face. The strength and speed in which I'd acted only invigorated me, and I was entering the tent before they hit the ground. I strode forward, and it wasn't difficult to understand what the Praetorians had meant.

Agrippina stood in a tub of steaming water, bathing herself. She noticed my arrival immediately, and of course made no move to cover herself. I looked her up and down, something she may not have expected me to do, because she narrowed her eyes at me.

"What are you doing here?"

I took a step forward. "Get dressed. We're going to Rome."

It was then that she noticed the blue orb in my hand, and she grinned at me, her smile almost sinister.

"I knew all you needed was a little… push," she said as she hopped from the tub and began the process of drying herself off. I wasn't sure I understood what she meant, or perhaps my mind purposefully did not allow myself to understand, but it didn't matter.

"Gather enough supplies to at least get us through Britain," I suggested, "but pack light. It'll just be the two of us."

She paused, still nude, and smiled at me. "How romantic."

I smiled, but then smothered it. I wasn't doing this for her. I was doing this for Helena. I had to remember that. Agrippina was simply a means to an end. An unwelcome but needed traveling companion for the task ahead.

Even so, I stood there watching until she worked the first layer of clothing over her head, and only then, turned and left her tent.

***

I cinched a strap over Felix's rump, momentarily forgetting the wound he'd sustained there over a month ago. He flinched as I tightened it, and I realized the area might still be a bit tender.

"Sorry, pal," I said. But then gave the strap another pull to ensure it was tight. Felix bucked again, but settled quickly. I gave him a pat on the neck and surveyed my supplies. Almost everything seemed ready.

"Give me a few minutes and we'll go," I told him.

He didn't respond for once and I frowned. It wasn't like him to not respond to things I told him. I wondered if he was getting sick or maybe I really had hurt him more than I...

I heavy hand fell on my shoulder. "Going somewhere, Hunter?"

I turned and found Archer standing behind me, his face a firestorm of fury. He looked angrier than I'd ever seen him before, but I plucked his hand from my shoulder and pushed past him.

"I'm doing this for your own good, Paul," I said as I walked, heading back to our armory.

Romans were still streaming into the camp, returning wearily from the battle. The whole fight seemed more or less mopped up by now, which was good. It would allow Agrippina and I to slip out of here more easily but also keep people distracted enough not to notice.

"The fuck you are," Archer responded, falling into step behind me. "You've never cared about anyone other than yourself, Hunter, and you know it. You're doing this for yourself!"

I whirled on him and slammed a finger into his chest. "I lost my son!" I yelled in his face, and I watched him flinch. "I'm not going to let that happen to anyone else. Not even you, Archer."

He looked surprised. "I... I didn't know, Hunter. I'm so sorry. If I had..."

"How could you know?" I asked rhetorically, turning again and continuing my journey.

"That shouldn't change anything," Archer said defiantly, catching up again. "I'm sorry he's gone, Jacob, but it wasn't your fault and should only prove you need all the help you can get."

"I don't need your help," I whispered just as I reached the armory. I moved to go inside but then Archer put his hand on my shoulder again, stopping me. I let him, knowing there was nothing he could do if I didn't want him to do it. "Get your fucking hand off of me, Archer. I'm warning you."

Tentatively, the hand fell away, and I stepped into the tent. I found a large rucksack immediately, one as big a beach ball, and with a methodical mind and hand, started loading it with mission essential items. Archer stepped into the tent behind me.

"At least let me come with you, Jacob. You could use my help."

"You're only interested in making sure I don't screw you over and leave you to rot here."

"And you wouldn't be?" He accused.

"Of course I would," I admitted.

I stepped to the right to see what limited supplies we had left and made sure to grab a set of NVGs and a few IR sticks before continuing down the line. I continued picking up random pieces of gear: a few K-rations, a two person tent, sleep rolls, a random flashbang grenade, emergency supplies, my SR-25 sniper rifle, extra ammunition, extra magazines, and the like. I left my computer where it lay, figuring I'd never use it again, but picked up one of the spare M-4s lying there as well.

I managed all of this in under a minute and stood to leave, but Archer blocked my exit. We stood nose to nose, eyes locked, unflinching.

"Get out of my way, Paul. I'm warning you."

He stood his ground defiantly, but eventually stepped aside and let me pass. I left, but he was persistent.

"Don't make me stop you, Jacob. You've been through a lot, I understand that. Just think about what you're doing to Helena."

"I am thinking about Helena."

I heard him run up behind me. "No you're not, you're…"

He never finished.

When he put his hand on my shoulder again, I was done with his interference. I whirled around and brought up a fist without thinking or hesitating. It connected with his face and he tumbled backward, but I wasn't finished. I let fly again and hit him square between the eyes, pulled my fist back again and struck him, and then again, and again, over and over with knuckles as hard as steel.

I'd hit him seven times when he finally collapsed and my eighth punch met nothing but air. He fell in a heap, but to his credit, was still conscious, albeit barely. I stared down at him, my chest heaving, wishing he'd give me a reason to keep going. But he didn't, and just sat there meekly like a frightened pussy cat, instead.

My upper lip pulled back in a snarl, but I was too focused now for another soliloquy or forced monologue. It was time to leave, not time for speeches. I turned and walked back to Felix, seeing him with Agrippina seated atop a horse of her own, three other fully loaded ones at her side. She watched me intently as I approached and I waved to her in greeting, but then the stubborn as fuck Archer put his hand on my shoulder again.

The orb was in my right cargo pocket, but that didn't mean I couldn't feel it is omnipresent power. It was always there, like a trusted sidekick or loyal dog that would always have my back, always ready and able to give me the nudge I needed.

In one fluid motion, I dropped the rucksack from my back and grabbed the large knife from my belt in a reverse grip. I yanked it from its sheath and swung it up over my head as I spun around, forcing it downward hard in a stabbing motion as I completed my turn. The knife point kissed flesh and pushed through like it was popping a balloon. It went easily, even as I felt the knife skip and slide off a bone, but that was all right because it still struck Archer right in his heart, just where I'd intended.

A seething, hate filled growl escaped my lips as I thrust harder, feeling the blade sink to the hilt. Deep in my cargo pocket, the orb burned against my leg, its scalding heat d fueling my rage. As the blade came to a stop, unable to sink in any further, a feeling of sweet release swarmed through me. It was almost erotic how much pleasure I took at the simple action of driving my knife into another man's chest.

As the ecstasy receded, I allowed myself a moment to look up from the hilt of my blade and into Archer's eyes, hoping for additional pleasure when I saw them, but it was then that I realized they weren't Archer's eyes at all. Another person had walked up behind me and placed a hand upon my shoulder in his place. Someone else had been the victim of my knife.

Not Archer.

Recognition set it, and I stumbled backward, tripping over my bag and falling to the ground. I back peddled on my hands and feet away from the bag and away from my friend, and I could do little more than watch as the man fell to his knees, his dark eyes filled with terror and a lack of understanding, same as mine.

He looked down at the knife implanted in his heart, knowing his time had finally run out. After all his years, it had come to this, and he looked up at me with his weathered face, but his eyes landed on the bulge in my pocket first. Understanding set in and his eyes finally rose to meet my own, and his next words were made all the more unbearable because he was the only one in my company who would ever say them.

"Forgive... you, J..."

Vincent never finished as he fell to his side.

I stared in wide eyed horror as the closest thing I'd had to a mentor and a father died before me. There was no hope for a last minute rescue from Wang, who lay unconscious himself, and there were no Roman doctors to stabilize him, no magical vials to repair his wounds, and no more visions to change my interpretation of reality.

Vincent lay there.

Dead.

And I'd killed him.

Hands surrounded my chest, and I curled into a ball on instinct, afraid of repeating what I'd just done, but it was Agrippina who held onto me. She wrapped me in a hug tightly and leaned her head in close.

"The fault is not your own, Jacob," she whispered into my ear. "I was watching. You thought it was Archer. He deserved it, and Vincent should not have snuck up on you. This is Archer's fault, not yours."

Her words were oddly soothing, convincing, powerful, and I found myself nodding and pulling myself together in seconds. She helped me to my feet and wrapped her arms around me and buried her head against my chest. "It'll be all right, Jacob. You have nothing to blame yourself for."

I found myself wrapping my arms around her as well, but before I could tighten them, she pulled out of our embrace and led me to my dropped pack, mere feet from Vincent's body. I didn't want to go, but she pulled me there, picked up my bag, and handed it to me

"I'm so sorry, Jacob," she said, and I knew she meant it. The two of us were in this together now, and I could feel the empathy in her flowing through the orb and into me. She'd once spoken of a connection between us, and I felt it now more than ever.

In an odd way, I felt happy just then.

I nodded solemnly and Agrippina put a hand against my chest and helped me turn around, but we only managed one step before we had to pull up short.

Santino stood there blocking our path.

And he wore a face I'd never seen on him before.

It wasn't sad or angry, frustrated or thoughtful. It wasn't even annoyed or condescending, all faces I'd seen on him before, although the last few only rarely. No, the face he wore was completely different from all of those, and I had to dig deep in my memory to recognize it. When I did, the feeling I felt was one I hadn't experienced in maybe twenty years, because the look Santino wore was the same my mother would show me in those moments when she was completely disappointed in me. Those were the worst looks, and seeing it on Santino's normally joyful face cut me deep.

"Let me go, John," I said quietly with Agrippina on my arm, but his eyes never left mine, not even to investigate the fact that Agrippina was present. He simply drilled into me with that look of disappointment that never wavered. I glanced down at Agrippina, then back at Santino. "Are... are you going to kill me?"

And there was no doubt that he could. At this range, there wasn't an orb in this plane of existence or any other powerful enough to give me a fighting chance against him.

"You're my best friend, Jacob," Santino said evenly, his eyes steady. "I could never kill my best friend." He paused. "But a mindless zombie controlled by an evil orb he knew was dangerous to begin with is the kind of bug I could squash over and over and over again."

The orb worked extra hard to keep the fear from distracting me, and it seemed like it was a battle it would soon lose, but then Santino cried out in pain and fell over. I didn't understand exactly what had happened, but then I saw Agrippina's arm protruding from her body holding a knife. It wasn't large, but it was sharp, and it had Santino's blood on it.

"What have you…" I started to speak, but then my words left me.

With the threat of Santino gone, the fear rescinded and the orb took over again. Even so, I looked at Agrippina in disbelief as Santino writhed on the ground from the intense pain of an abdominal stab wound.

"He would have stopped us, Jacob," Agrippina said steadily. "It doesn't matter if the path before you is a dark one, what matters is the destination. This is the only way to keep Helena safe and get her home. We have to go to Rome, and we couldn't do that with him in our way."

"Of course…" I said, trailing off as Agrippina led us away from Santino's fallen body.

I looked down at him, his body growing limper as he fought the pain, but when he was out of sight, I looked away, wondering what it was I had been so concerned about a moment before.

Agrippina helped me atop Felix and I held out a hand to help her atop her own horse. She smiled at me in thanks, and I returned it, feeling excited at the prospect of a new adventure with a beautiful woman and the idea of returning to the Eternal City of Rome.

Finally, a grand adventure worth writing about.

Agrippina reached a hand out and rubbed my forearm. Her touch distracted me and I looked at her again, noticing that her beautiful smile hadn't left her. It filled my heart with drive and determination, knowing that my partner in crime and I would get the job done in a way I never could before.

The red orb was waiting.

When Agrippina realized I'd pulled myself from my trance, she patted my arm lightly and motioned for me to lead the way. I lifted a hand to my forehead and nodded with my imaginary cowboy hat. "Yes, ma'am."

And with that, I kicked Felix into a trot. Agrippina caught up, and the two of us rode with our three supply horses in train behind us. We rode toward the eastern gate and I was finally able to take notice of the fact that dawn was finally upon us. The sun hadn't yet breached the horizon, but it was close, and there was easily enough light to survey the camp by. I barely took notice of the Romans around me, healthy or wounded, but the sight of a pair of bodies on the ground caught my eye. I couldn't quite make out who they were, but I noticed a few of my friends running toward them while a third figure was already kneeling beside one of the fallen two.

Agrippina and I were far enough away that recognition was difficult, but picking my sister out of a crowd was easy. I tipped my imaginary hat in her direction as we rode further away, but the only look she offered me in return was distraught, one with fear and sadness in those distant eyes. Tears streamed down her cheeks so clearly that I was half tempted to turn back, and it was then that I noticed she held one of the bodies in her lap, his head resting comfortably on one of her legs. I couldn't tell if he was dead or alive, but the sight of it combined with the final look of complete defeat on Artie's face before she disappeared behind rows of tents haunted me.

And then Agrippina spoke. "A beautiful morning, is it not, Jacob."

I looked to the sky, noting its early morning blue enshrined by the deep yellows and oranges given off by the sun's imminent arrival. I could just see it beginning its rise, but there was something about this sunrise that confused me. I'd always taken such joy out of witnessing the daily event, using it as a way to revitalize fatigued muscles or focus a frazzled mind. Witnessing one was a yearly tradition I'd had for decades, but as the sun continued its ascent, I felt none of those effects now. Instead, all it offered was a hollow emptiness, not unlike something I'd felt not all that long ago when... something had happened.

I couldn't remember.

"Looks like we can use the sun as our guide for now," Agrippina continued, her long golden locks as beautiful but empty as the sun we rode toward, swaying alluringly in the breeze as we passed Galba's trench system. I stared at her for a moment, finding strength in her image, but when I turned back to the rising sun ahead of me, I felt nothing again.

I decided to ignore it, realizing it was probably a fault of the sun's and not my own. Instead, I thought of nothing more but the unbridled potential of finding the red orb and pairing it with my blue one. That alone filled me with enough motivation to ride into the very heart of the sun if I had to.

I reached into my cargo pocket and removed my glacier glasses, lowered them over my eyes, and smiled, trying to conjure the appropriate imagery in my mind of Agrippina and I riding into the sunrise, our destinies laid out before us, ours for the taking. All I'd needed was a little bit of a push, just as Agrippina had said, and now I had it. I let out a long sigh, letting years of pent up emotion fall from my shoulders in sheets.

I settled myself atop Felix in preparation for a long journey, and even found myself singing to myself as we rode. *"Round, round, get around, I get around, yeah."* The lyrics came easily, and I found myself smiling at the appropriateness of my chosen song. *"Get around, round, round I get around. I get around..."*

"What is that song, Jacob?" Agrippina asked innocently.

"What *I Get Around*? It's a great song by the Beach Boys. Some guy I knew used to love them."

"Who was he?" She asked.

"I... I can't remember," I answered. "Still, they're a good group. They have plenty of hits."

"Perhaps you can teach me a few," Agrippina suggested with a sweet smile. "We'll have plenty of time together in the coming weeks."

I nodded pleasantly. "Sure, I'd like that."

Her smile tightened and she turned back toward the rising sun. I turned as well and continued to sing, knowing that it was finally time to get around to doing what I should have done from the very beginning:

Fix the universe.

Author's Note

Well, this was a tough one to write.

Very tough.

I first thought the story up for this book years ago, back when I'd just finished *The Last Roman* and was beginning *To Crown a Caesar*. I had an idea about introducing Arthurian legend (in a way) and I knew it was time for all of the things Hunter felt responsible for to finally have some kind of repercussion. His descent into madness, if you will, was preordained for the guy the moment he first made contact with the orb. It'd screwed up just about everybody else, so why not him?

Unfortunately, the pregnancy storyline was also one I'd thought up years ago, and knew just had to be included... little did I know that when I finally picked up this book again to complete earlier this year, that my wife and I would be expecting our first child. It made writing that final chapter almost impossible. When I came up with the idea, I didn't really understand how devastating such a thing could be, but I do now. Boy do I understand, and I almost wanted to rewrite the whole damn book by the time I was finished.

But I couldn't do that.

Whether everyone will agree with the course I took will be up to their own personal opinion, but the story is heading in a very specific direction, and I could think of no more low a moment for Hunter to go through than that. I wasn't trying to be malicious. It's just the way I saw the story going as I setup book four: the final book.

Believe me, I wish I hadn't.

But if you're still with me this far (and if you're reading this book when this book is still considered "new"), I'd like to finish my little note by asking for patience for the last book in the *Praetorian* Series. I intend to take some time off when my son is born this November and focus on my family, however, once my wife's maternity leave is up, primary care is going to fall squarely on my shoulders.

Yep, that means stay at home dad status for the most part, which means my writing is seriously going to slow. I wish that wasn't the case, but my family comes first, so while I will still write when I can, my output will suffer. I managed to publish four books within the last fifteen months, sure, but that's only because I'd already two written, and parts of this one were already written as well.

I no longer have that luxury.

The *Starfarer* sequel, which is actually next on my to-do-list, and the final *Praetorian* book, are all empty Word documents right now (although their stories are in my head). So it's going to take some time, and I just wanted to give everyone a head's up.

But back to Hunter, for a moment.

I don't know exactly where his "story" is going to end.

However, I know <u>exactly</u> how his *"Praetorian"* story is going to end. The *Praetorian* Series will definitely end with four books, which will provide a conclusive finale to the events chronicled in this series, but that doesn't necessarily mean I'm done with the universe. Some of you more observant readers may have already picked up on what I mean by that, or suspect where I'm going with it, but all I really mean is that certain things may live on in future books (and no, that isn't any kind of hint either).

But patience will be required.

I hope you enjoyed the book, high points and low points both. Feel free to send me an email with your thoughts, positive or negative, and please leave a review as well (positive ones more welcomed than negative ones, of course). And if you email, I'll be sure to email back as quickly as I can, baby throw up or not!

Until next time, Faithful Readers.

Ed Crichton
Sept, 2013

Author's Note (Revised)

While nothing in *A Hunter and His Legion* itself has changed between this note and the last, my ideas and plans for future writings have. After having just read the above Author's Note, some of you may be a bit upset that you have to wait so long for Book IV, but you're in luck, because I've recently come to the decision that I will be putting Starfarer on the back burner for now, and will instead continue with the *Praetorian* Series, finishing it at four books. Since I try to treat writing as a 9-5 job, which it more or less is, that doesn't mean I work like an automaton, pumping out work just to churn out content and make bank.

Some authors can do that, but I can't.

I've found that all my inspiration when preparing to continue Starfarer has led me toward finishing the *Praetorian* Series instead. All my thoughts, ideas, and eureka moments are for Hunter & Co. right now, not for Lawson & Co. Maybe it's because even I'm uncomfortable with my most recent ending, as I don't like cliffhangers any more than you people do, but this is a book series, and drama sometimes dictates them (unless you'd really prefer a 600,000 word book, I guess). Believe it or not, but the ending to *A Hunter and His Legion* is a cliffhanger even for *me*, and I'm just as excited to get to the end of the series as you are.

So, don't worry. I won't be leaving you hanging as long as initially planned. I'm already deep into the first chapter of Book IV as I write this note, which already has its own fresh surprises, and I'm dedicated to pushing through to the end. I still have to contend with that soon-to-be kid of mine (almost there!), but at least you won't have to wait for an entire other book to be written before I start the last one in this series.

Patience will still be required.

Just not quite as much as you may have thought.

Ed Crichton
October, 2013

Starfarer: Rendezvous with Destiny
If you haven't yet read Edward Crichton's Sci-Fi epic
Starfarer: Rendezvous with Destiny, *his advice is that*
you really, really should. For a brief look at the first few
chapters, keep on reading...

INCOMING TRANSMISSION . . .

TO: John Paul Sterling, Admiral, Allied Space Navy (ASN)
FROM: Alexander Mosley, First High Admiral, Allied Space
Navy (ASN)
ORIGINAL REPORT: Richard Alderman, Colonel, Office of
Strategic Space Intelligence (OSSI) – Original Report Attached
SECURITY LEVEL: CLASSIFIED

XXXXX - XXXXXXXXXX - XXXXX

SUBJECT: Anomalous ISLAND Activity – Action Required
SENT: 11.13.2595 (11:20:11)
AUTHENTICATION CODE: Echo Echo Bravo Zero Zero Seven
Echo

Admiral John Paul Sterling,

This could be big, J.P., so I'll dispense with the usual pleasantries.
Word has been sent to OSSI that our Chinese friends have
encountered an anomaly along ISLAND Transit Route
AlphaCOL–BetaCOL. The spooks haven't been able to get
anything specific out of the Chinese yet, but it has The Star
Destiny Corporation, at least, very concerned.

They're going to lose contact with the ISLAND Liner Sierra
Madre on the aforementioned course very soon, and while OSSI
isn't saying much, we could be talking about another rumored

contact with alien technology aboard an ISLAND. That or they may have simply experienced their first mishap with WeT Tech.

Consider this your unofficial readiness report. Prepare the 3rd Fleet for immediate redeployment back to Earth and launch the *Alcestis* as soon as possible. I don't think I need to remind you to keep your wits about you, John Paul. There's more at play here than even I'm aware of, and I can't offer you much more advice than that. This won't be some silly sim we mucked about with back at the Academy. Something big is about to happen and something about it stinks.

Regards,

First High Admiral Alexander Mosley, ASN
Admiralty Board, Chair
Washington Aerospace Naval Headquarters, Luna

P.S. Should we get through whatever this thing is, I'll get you a case of that ancient Jameson swill you love so much.

`<<<<< SEE ATTACHED FILE FOR ORIGINAL REPORT >>>>>`

SECTION 1
The ISLAND

High Earth Orbit /
ISLAND Liner *Sierra Madre* – Red Zone /
Power Conduction Shaft – Delta /

11.06.2595
07:35:08 Zulu

That which defines mankind is nothing more than what he leaves behind. In no other way will he be remembered when his presence in this universe becomes little more than dust to aid in the formation of new celestial bodies, and the onset of space travel centuries ago only helped to safeguard this legacy. Later, the ability to travel to other planets cemented it. If every human in existence simply vanished from reality, the ISLAND Liner *Sierra Madre* would remain, drifting through the depths of space for time immemorial.

And whoever finds it will think it little more than a hulking piece of junk.

Senior Chief of Electronics Dhaval Jaheed knew that was unfair assessment of a large portion of the ISLAND, but in the presence of so many undocumented, unbundled, ungrounded, and unfamiliar wires, connectors, cables, circuits, and other forms of electronic mayhem before him, gave him pause to curse the wretched ship. It was a safety inspector's worst nightmare, and the Red Zone was already an extremely dangerous, almost mystical, place, quarantined from entrance by all travelers aboard the ISLAND.

Senior Chiefs never sent technicians into the area, mostly because they never needed to, but the occasion had arisen today, much to the dread of every technician under Dhaval's supervision. His rank of ISLAND Senior Chief of Electronics gave him seniority over every electrician or technician aboard the *Sierra Madre*, and made him the only person he was willing to send into such a hazardous portion of the ship. The rest of them were all back in the Green Zone, the outer layer of the ship that surrounded the Red Zone like an egg encasing its yolk.

Despite knowing it was in his best interest to focus on his work, it was difficult for Dhaval not to wonder exactly what kind of genius would let something as important as an ISLAND Liner fall into such disarray. ISLANDs were the sole means of transportation to Earth's colonies, and the only way to keep humanity's presence amongst the stars connected. The mess he was in now was a disgrace to mechanics, technicians, electricians, and engineers alike, but he supposed that's what happened after hundreds of years of neglect.

"Find the breaker yet, Chief?" Asked an unwelcome voice that infiltrated every recess of his mind. It came so suddenly that Dhaval stumbled from his perch overlooking the exact breaker box he had in fact been searching for. He shot his hand out to seize the nearest stabilizing handle, only to have it break away from the shaft in his grip. His life was spared by a safety cable that secured his belt to a ladder rung – which amazingly held firm. Dhaval dangled there for a few moments, his forehead glistening with sweat as he stared down the conduction shaft, noticing the green safety lights fixed to the wall descend only about ten meters before becoming overwhelmed in darkness. The shaft descended for hundreds of kilometers, all the way to the Core, but few knew what was down there.

Dhaval touched a red button on his exo-suit, and a small object shot out from a mechanism on his back. The magnetic wafer attached itself to the metal wall and reeled him back into a standing position upon his perch. Once upright, he deactivated the magnetic anchor and took a deep breath as it recoiled.

"Chief?" Came the disjointed voice in his head again, somewhat more worried this time.

Dhaval gritted his teeth in frustration and keyed his com. "This is Senior Chief Jaheed. I've found the conduit. Initiating repairs now."

"Copy that, Chief. Be careful down there. Some of that equipment could be a hundred years old."

Dhaval paused for the briefest of seconds in frustration before returning to his work.

As far as he knew, he was the first person to visit this realm of the ISLAND since the last round of ship wide upgrades and renovations that had expanded the *Sierra Madre's* overall size and mass to its current level. There may have been the riff raff and Unwanteds who had inherited the bowls of the ship over the past few centuries, but even they were smart enough to stay out of the conduction shafts and rarely breached the Red Zone.

The only reason he was even down here was because the ISLAND's Senior Systems Officer had identified a small power drain that originated in the very spot Dhaval now occupied, one that threatened the ship's next WeT Jump. Such a problem hadn't arisen in the thirty-five years since Dhaval had been conscripted to work aboard the *Sierra Madre*, but it wasn't Dhaval's position to question how such a problem had arisen. His job was simply to fix the broken conduit and bring the conduction shaft back to peak efficiency. All he cared about was that the one hundred year old power box he was currently manhandling seemed repairable. He pulled a data cable from his chest rig and jacked it into a port that seemed like it would accommodate the plug. Numbers and figures poured across the Lens in front of his left eye, most of which was meaningless gibberish even for someone as experienced as Dhaval, but he comprehended enough to tell him it was at least fixable.

Just as Dhaval thought he had enough information to begin, he heard a loud metallic bang above him that reverberated through the shaft. It was repeated a number of times before ending just as suddenly as it began. It sounded like someone carelessly knocking over machinery as they moved through the area.

"Hello?" Dhaval called into the darkness, knowing he was supposed to be alone. He hadn't been sure what he'd heard, but it sounded distinctly like moving people. "Hello?" He repeated. "Is anyone there?"

Only silence answered him.

Dhaval shrugged and eyed the darkness above him one last time before returning to his work.

You're getting paranoid in your old age, Dhaval.

He shifted in his seat and got comfortable on his perch, locking his exo-suit into a comfortable sitting position for a long repair job. The *Sierra Madre* wasn't due to depart on its two year voyage for another nine hours, and Dhaval had no idea how long this was going to take. The last thing he wanted to do was report a failure to Ship Master Na and risk delaying the ISLAND's departure time. This was the young woman's first voyage as ship master of an ISLAND Liner, and rumor had it that she was as ruthless as she was new to the position. Upsetting her would not bode well for even a veteran like Dhaval Jaheed, for no matter how good he was, he was still an Indian aboard an ISLAND – little more than a slave on a farm.

Earth /

Havana, Cuba /
ISLAND Departure Spaceport /

11.06.2595
08:00:00 Zulu

In a time of great prosperity, the most obvious course of action is towards progress.

Growth.

Modernization.

To build towards the future and create a utopia of high tech splendor.

It's what happened in the days following the end of Earth's population crisis and later economic boom that came with the advent of interstellar trade and colonization only a century ago. Cities across the globe became shining, glimmering metropolises of glass and light, more beautiful than ever, but not Havana. Its spaceport may be the sole means of transportation to the High Earth Orbit ISLAND Docking Facility in the western hemisphere, and a prosperous city because of it, but it appeared little more than a dirty small town on the cusp of social annihilation.

At least that's how it seemed like to Carl Lawson as he sat in a local cantina, waiting for the departure time for his shuttle to arrive. The seedy bar was something out of a Western vid, an entertainment genre made famous once again after centuries in obscurity. It was a setting that belonged in a museum, like the one Lawson had in fact seen at the Cleveland Museum of Ancient American History when he was eight years old. The only difference being the lack of holographic personifications of living, breathing humans performing any number of mundane, yet clichéd tasks like bartending, piano and card playing, wenching, and the like. This bar was authentic, with real live people enjoying the relaxed, stress free setting which Havana still exuded. On any other day, Lawson probably could have died content as he sat among fellow travelers in seek of a cold *cerveza*, but life was never completely stress free, especially not with his folks visiting to see him off.

"This isn't what you want to do," his father, John Lawson, said from across the table. "ISLANDs only come back to Earth every three years."

"About two actually," Carl Lawson replied, not understanding his parents sudden desire to dissuade him from leaving. He ignored his father and turned towards the bartender. "*Señor, otra cerveza, por favor.*" The bartender nodded and tossed him a can of beer and Lawson couldn't help but smile.

Where has this place been all my life?

"But you won't know anybody," his mother, Eileen, chimed in with her ever chipper voice. "All your friends and family are on Earth, not to mention your friends in the military."

Outwardly, his mother was the sweet and caring type you'd find in any homestead across the galaxy, but Carl had known the truth behind it since he was a toddler. Underneath that façade of motherly kindness was the attitude of a woman who simply didn't give a shit, and only kept up her disguise to fit in with societal pressures. The fact that she still treated him like a child, instead of the forty-five year old man that he was, said something about her. She was the kind of person who would shop for yet another needless product to sooth her own fickle desires on her Lens' Inter-Lens Service, while maintaining only the barest semblance of attention during what someone else would consider a very personal conversation.

"Mom," Carl said with a sigh. "Why do you think I'm even doing this? The only friend I still have left is coming with me, so why stay."

The statement wasn't a question, and he didn't expect his mother to answer anyway. Not because she knew it hadn't been a question, but because he knew she didn't actually care.

John Lawson ignored his wife and pressed on. "You realize, son, that if you leave, you'll be doing little more than admitting your own guilt and running away in shame?"

Carl turned away from his mother, who no longer seemed interested, preoccupying her attention instead on the young Cuban bartender whose biceps were at risk of bursting through the sleeves of his tropical style shirt. He fixed his father with a stern gaze and lowered his voice.

"Is that why you're here? To convince me to stay on a world that would rather see me hung by the gallows because the firing squad would be too quick? There's nothing left for me here. At least if I go, I can visit in a few years when things have quieted down. In time… who knows? Maybe I'll be able to return one day."

"No one is saying you should go on the Lens and draw attention to yourself, son, but if you stay and lead a quiet life, at least you can say you kept your honor intact and stood your ground."

"Whose honor exactly am I protecting? Yours or mine? Better be careful, dad. You don't want to be taken off the list of all those holiday parties you're always invited to."

"Don't take that tone with me. I'm past caring about whether what happened was your fault or not, but our reputation has already been blemished by all this as it is, and the only thing you can do to repair it is to stare your accusers in the face and refuse to admit defeat."

"I already did that. Don't you remember when they stripped me of my rank and all my accomplishments and held me up as an example to save face with the Chinese? No, I did my part thank you much. I think I'm well and done with all that bullshit."

John Lawson folded his arms and glared at his son, watching as Carl swallowed that last of his beer.

"Don't do this, Carl. Don't expect a home to come back to if you do."

Carl smirked at his father and picked up his travel bag before getting to his feet and throwing some anachronistic monetary coins down on the table. Physical money may have been extinct on Earth for centuries now, but for those traveling to the outer colonies, it was a necessity, not to mention for those few who knew to stop at this lovely hole-in-the-wall before departure. "Don't worry, father. I haven't been coming back to one since the day you tried to save your *own* face in all this at no one's expense but my own."

With nothing left to say to his father, he reached out and grabbed his mother's arm before passing by her. He leaned down and gave her a kiss on the cheek, knowing he'll miss her despite all her faults. "Say goodbye to Lilly for me, mom."

Eileen flicked her eyes away from her beefcake pretty for just a second. "Oh, your sister will miss you terribly. Won't that help you cha…"

"Goodbye, mom."

"Oh, well, goodbye, dear." She turned back to her lustful desire and said nothing else.

Lawson looked back at his parents, now both ignoring him for completely different reasons. He couldn't believe it had come to this. His own parents had turned their backs on him in a time when he needed them the most. When the entire world was against him, he should have been able to turn to them and expect comfort and reassurance, but no such sentiment existed, and he was on his own.

Carl Lawson versus the universe.

He turned and headed towards the door, stopping only briefly to take in the surreal atmosphere of one of the most unique places he'd ever visited. With a nod of approval he walked out into the dusty streets and turned north towards the only sign of progress and hope as far as the eye could see: the spaceport.

And his future.

High Earth Orbit /
ISLAND Liner *Sierra Madre* – Green Zone /
Command Deck – Bridge /

11.06.2595
08:35:16 Zulu

"Ship's status?"

"All indicators save one show green, ma'am."

"What's the situation in Power Conduction Shaft – Delta? Are we on still on schedule?"

"Senior Chief of Electronics Jaheed is on it, ma'am. His controller indicates he should have the problem locked down well before our time of departure."

"Good," Ship Master Mei-Xing Na replied behind a hard smile, pleased at her new crew's performance.

She abhorred incompetency – a cancer that had to be rooted out of as soon as it was discovered – and would not have been pleased with lackluster personnel. Whether her perfectionism was a byproduct of her Chinese ancestry or her own tenacity for perfection was anyone's guess, but she knew that her own personal level of expectation came from hard work and a selfless dedication to the fruition of her life's goals, and today would mark her first steps towards fulfilling her destiny. Today, she would take her first voyage as the ship master of an ISLAND Liner, and she wasn't about to let incompetency blemish such a step.

"Ship Master," another voice called out from her right. "Docking Control has indicated the first wave of shuttles are on approach. We should expect our first class passengers to arrive within the hour."

Mei-Xing nodded, but a sneer crossed her face at the continued use of the Common language amongst her crew. It was an excessively antiquated speech, an ugly speech, burdened and littered with the drivels of the old English language.

It may have been the language of international trade, commerce, and cooperation centuries ago, but the galaxy is so much bigger now! She thought. *With Chinese as the dominant language on more planets than any other, isn't it time for us to speak our own language, with our own people, on our own ships?*

She frowned. There was little hope to be found in such thoughts. The Americans were still too heavily involved in galactic affairs for Common to just go away, even if all they'd been reduced to was a security guard for planet Earth. There was also the problem that while all ISLANDs were crewed by Chinese, they were still staffed by their subservient Indians, creating yet another language barrier. Mei-Xing sighed to herself. Since Common was taught to every new born baby alongside their own native languages, there was no way to change the status quo now.

No matter how disgusting it felt on Mei-Xing's tongue.

"Ship Master?" The voice spoke again.

"Very good, Mister Chen," She said, glancing at the chronograph in the upper right hand corner of the oval Lens situated in front of her left eye.

08:36:02.

Only a minute late. She supposed that was within even her standard of punctuality, especially considering how complex the last twenty four hours before an ISLAND launch was.

She blinked and sent a slight mental nudge towards her Lens, and a visual feed of the docking bay sprang into view. She saw the deck crew scurrying about with guidance lights in their hands, red carpets sprawled along the deck to help facilitate the boarding of travelers, and concierges, ready at the beck and call of any passenger to set foot aboard the *Sierra Madre*.

Good, good.

With another mental nudge, the Lens feed shifted back to her To-Do-List, which she kept as her default setting. She checked off the numbered event concerning the arrival of passengers and looked at the next thing on the list. She already knew what it was, but the internal comfort of continuously checking her lists gave her piece of mind. Item number five for the day was to rest until 14:00:00 when the next item on her list came about. It was barely nine o'clock in the morning, but she'd already been on the bridge for nine hours performing the ISLAND's pre-flight check lists with her bridge crew. Feeling weariness creeping in, she stood and surveyed the bridge.

The bridge was built like the quarter of a sphere removed from the remainder, with the ship master's at the very center, raised above all other stations by a semicircular platform about a meter above the deck. Arrayed around her from left to right, along the curved interior of the viewport that encased the bridge were her officers' duty stations. Everything from navigation to communication to ship's systems and a half dozen other flight sensitive tasks. Beyond these stations, wrapping around the entirety of the curved section of the bridge, was the transparent viewport that connected the bridge to the emptiness of space. It wrapped above and behind and around Mei-Xing as she stood at the foot of her dais, and all she could see was space. It was something she had enjoyed immensely since her first moment on the bridge of her new command only one week ago.

Immaculate, the bridge was lit with bright lights and streamlined interfaces. It had red carpeting on the floor and wood paneling along the bulkheads, luxury items that simply screamed: civilian. It was nothing like the cold steel and colorless white Mei-Xing had seen aboard the Allied Space Navy's ships of war she had toured during her training.

Interestingly, she had to admit that she approved of the sterility of those ships more.

Finally, directly behind the ship master's chair was the lift, which she promptly started for.

"XO," she said as she stepped off her dais. A small man with a well-greased comb over straightened from his position overlooking the shoulder of the ship's Communication Officer.

"Ma'am?" He asked.

"The bridge is yours."

"Aye, ma'am," he replied with a slight nod. Mei-Xing did not return it but made sure her look lingered just enough to be obviously suggestive. Her executive officer didn't dare make mistakes while she was away, and her subtle look served as a reminder that he'd better not. It wasn't that she was unsure of his abilities, in fact, she couldn't ask for a more competent first officer, but that she never dropped her persona, not even for him.

She didn't want her crew to fear her, but she demanded their respect all the same.

She turned and entered the lift, but instead of indicating her intended destination with a simple thought through her Lens, a door whooshed open in front of her, opposite the one she'd just came through. Stepping through, she entered the atrium of her personal quarters, a space about the size of a small living room despite its sole purpose as a place to receive guests and store her footwear.

Once through the lift doors, which silently closed behind her, she immediately slouched her shoulders and rolled her neck. She wasn't a machine, despite what others may think, and she needed to relax as much as the next person. She slipped off her bulky duty boots and placed them in a small compartment that quickly retreated back into the bulkhead after she'd placed them within, and opened the large, ornate door to enter her new home.

Those who knew anything about space travel, especially those like the Chinese or Americans who dominated the practice, understood that space was always at a premium aboard a spacefaring vessel. The Americans would especially understand this, as their use for space travel revolved almost solely around combat, where every cubic inch of a spaceship was used to fit ammunition, life support, provisions, berths, or any number of mission critical essentials. The Chinese understood this as well, and abided by such a concept with most of their ship designs.

But not for ISLAND Liners.

Inter-System Luxury Aerospace Destination Liners had no need to worry about space constrictions. Each ISLAND was almost five hundred years old, beginning their lives as simple transport shuttles that ferried supplies from Earth to China's first colony on Mars in the late 21st century. But as time progressed, repairs and refits had been necessary, giving designers the unique opportunity to build on top of the existing infrastructure, creating larger and larger ships. Four hundred years later, those original ships had grown to immense sizes, each slightly different from the next. Each ISLAND was literally the size of Europe's largest countries, hundreds of kilometers long, and half as wide and tall. Shaped like an angular, blocky cone, the engine block was the wide base and the bridge its tip. They were space worthy countries capable of supporting millions of passengers.

Designed for comfort and leisure, Mei-Xing, as ship master, was entitled to the most extravagant suite on the ship. Two stories with five rooms, three baths, a solar to view the stars, a central atrium, dining room, and equipped with an emergency escape capsule, it was easily the most opulent accommodation available. Decorated in mainly Chinese motifs, Mei-Xing could almost pretend she was back on Earth in her ancestral home that had provided her with so much.

She looked at the vaulted ceilings, tassels, hangings, bronze sculptures, and gold inlaid furniture and sighed. Here was a place worthy of her accomplishments. It was a place where she could relax and enjoy the fruits of her labors. She glanced at the central fountain that flowed gracefully into its basin and touched the water. It rippled at her gesture, and she continued her way towards her room and up the port side staircase, having already chosen that she would only descend down the starboard side one.

It took her nearly thirty seconds to climb the stairs to the landing separating her quarters from the rest of her suite. Reaching out to grasp the intricate handle before her, she twisted and opened the wide double doors and entered her immaculately furnished room that gleamed in pristine opulence. She started the process of undressing herself as she strode across the room, removing each piece of her uniform carefully, meticulously folding each article of clothing and placing them on her dresser and throwing her undergarments down her hidden laundry chute.

Before stepping into bed, Mei-Xing moved towards her full body mirror she'd brought with her from her childhood home. It was an ovoid with gold designs twirling around the edges, coming together at the top to form two small cherubs blowing small horns at the other. It had been a gift from her grandmother for her eighth birthday and she had always treasured it.

What she really loved about the mirror, however, was how it presented her body. Of course, Mei-Xing knew it reflected her no differently than any other mirror, but something about the gold designs and cherubs framed her in a more perfect way.

She was tall for a Chinese woman, standing at 1.75 meters, with a strong and powerful body most women would be hard pressed to replicate. She wasn't particularly beautiful, but she didn't care about such things. Her face was just as hard as her body or her mind, with small but full red lips and dark eyes that could look as intensely serious as they could sultry. Her skin was smooth and soft, but it was the angle of her cheeks that provided her with the prized sternness she was so proud of.

Assured that her face was clear of any blemishes she may need to take care of, lowered her hand and examined her breasts. They were firm and well sized and Mei-Xing hummed in satisfaction. She then turned to the side to inspect her backside, likewise content at its shape and firmness, but then she frowned. Upon closer inspection, she noticed that her abdominal muscles seemed less defined than normal, showing almost an imperceptible amount of paunch over her otherwise taut stomach.

We'll have to do something about that, won't we, Mei-Xing?

The last week hadn't left her much time for physical exercise, and she could now see the results of her sedentary lifestyle. It did not make her happy, but she knew once her ISLAND was successfully under way, she'd have time to work on it again. With one last look at herself, she nodded at her reflection and quietly padded her way towards her bed. Slipping in beneath her silk sheets, she nudged her Lens to deactivate the lights in the room and set her alarm to wake her in four hours.

She needed to be well rested. ISLAND departures were still a big deal for the citizens of each planet it visited, and even though the ship wouldn't be back for another two years, and in that time any mistakes her crew may make well and forgotten; *she* would not forget them. She would take them to her grave – should such a day ever in fact arrive for Ship Master Mei-Xing Na.